What was waiting for me at Roswell...

The room could have been the interior of the world's largest garage. Piles of components and shards of strange alien materials were scattered everywhere. In the very center was what must have been the fairly intact remains of the spacecraft that had crashed at Roswell. It wasn't entirely dismantled, and I could still see the basic shape. The ship looked to be in excellent condition, considering that it had crash-landed. It wasn't saucer-shaped at all, but looked more like a big, metal boomerang. I took a walk around the ship, not seeing anything particularly over-whelming—except, of course, for the fact that it had come from another world.

As I looked around, I had the same sensation I always felt around snakes, except now I couldn't see or hear it. I just knew it was there somewhere, waiting. Out of the corner of my eye, I swore I saw something move. I spun around and stared at one of the corpses. Had it twitched?

The Pandora Directive™

A Tex Murphy Novel

Aaron Conners

PRIMA PUBLISHING

This book is dedicated to Gail Peterson (for the motivation); Chris Jones (for inspiration); Rob Peterson (for good scotch and smokes); Mike, Jeanette, Bruce, Ivar, and Steve (for miscellaneous banter, etc.); and especially my sweet Krissant for all of the above and more.

Prologue

The world took a bullet in the head and now Old San Francisco floats face down in a red sea sky. No one ever really explained what happened. But now the heavens above are a bloody blanket, and the air we breathe is thick with radiation.

This year we bid adieu to the ozone layer and enact a time reversal. At least we don't have to reset our watches. The banks still open for business at nine, only now it's 9:00 P.M. The Surgeon General decided that sunlight was becoming *almost* as hazardous as cigarette smoking and real butter. It doesn't matter to me. I've never kept regular hours.

My name's Tex Murphy and I'm a PI. Somebody somewhere screwed up and sent me here about a century too late. I should be driving a '38 Packard with a running board and whitewalls. Instead, I fly a '38 Lotus speeder. At least I wear the right uniform— soft felt fedora, silk tie, rumpled overcoat, and wing tips.

It's April 2043, forty-five years since World War III came and went. New San Francisco rose from the ashes, but it was reborn without any of the style or flavor of the Old City. So I hang my hat at the Ritz Hotel, in a particularly run-down section of Old San Francisco. I'm one of the few non-mutants in this part of town, but that doesn't bother me. Some of my best friends are mutants. Besides, the rent is cheap and my apartment is big enough to hold my office.

Nothing much has changed since I moved to the city twenty years ago. All I'll ever need is a good bottle of bourbon, a fresh pack of Luckies, a decent haircut, and one more case.

Chapter
One

Chelsee Bando looked deep into her vodka tonic. "I don't know...maybe Phoenix."

I flicked my thumbnail across the match tip and winced as a kernel of phosphorous lodged under the nail, then burst into flame. "So you want to move to the desert." I lit my cigarette and took a deep drag. "Do you think you're ready to face the danger and excitement of central Arizona?"

Chelsee looked up at me with those frosty blue eyes. As usual, my thighs quivered. She took a slow sip of Stohli and shrugged. "I've got an old college friend down there. We've kept in touch.... She says it's nice."

"I can imagine. Square dancin', ten gallon hats, huntin' armadillos...."

Chelsee cut in, "...macho yokels with names like *Tex*."

I leaned back and grinned. Chelsee smiled back, almost stubbornly. We raised our glasses and toasted, silently.

"OK, so why leave San Francisco? A city so wonderful that I choke up whenever I talk about it."

Chelsee ran her fingertip around the rim of her glass in a way that made me quite jealous. "It's not *here* that's the problem. It's just...I feel like I'm stuck. Except, of course, for slowly *sliding* into another age bracket."

"Listen, Chelsee. Age is nothing. It's all in the attitude. Look at me. You don't see me *moaning* about being twenty-eight, do you?"

She smiled despite herself and turned toward the window. "Oh, please. If you're twenty-eight, I'm a nun."

I leaned forward and crossed my arms on the table. "Well, like I said, it's totally subjective. *I* think you're aging *very* gracefully. You don't look a day over thirty."

Chelsee turned back and gave me one of those looks. "I turn thirty tomorrow."

My collar suddenly felt a bit warmer. "Did I say thirty? I meant twenty-six. I always get those two mixed up."

Chelsee turned back toward the window. I wasn't sure if I'd actually offended her or if she was just trying to make me feel like an idiot. Either way, it made me want to talk fast. "Look, Chelsee, the bottom line is, if you weren't a nun, I'd chase you up to my love nest and..."

"Spare me the details, Tex."

Chelsee glanced from the window directly to her watch. "It's getting late—I'm going home."

She got up out of the booth and slipped on her coat. I tried to get her to look at me. She was even more difficult to read today than usual. As for me, if I'd had a tail, I would have been wagging it.

"Big date, eh?"

Chelsee threw her purse over her shoulder and looked down at me in a distinctly caustic manner. "Oh, yeah. Cary Grant...and a pint of Häagen-Dazs. Hold me down." She picked up her vodka tonic, drained it, then slammed it back to the table. "See ya later."

I watched her walk to the door, hoping she would pause, turn, and throw me a wink.

She didn't.

I turned back to the table and buried the live end of my Lucky in the teeming ashtray.

"What a schmuck!"

I looked over to see Rook Garner swiveled around on his usual bar stool, smugly reclining on his elbows—a wrinkly little bastard in sensible shoes. How could I have missed the psychosomatic scent of vinegar in the air? Suddenly, I felt defensive. "What?!"

Rook shook his head and turned back to his beer mug. "You're the PI. Figure it out for yourself."

Behind the bar, Louie showed off his big, ugly grin and idly polished a shot glass. "How're things goin' with Chelsee, Murph?"

"Why? You thinking of making your move, Louie?"

"Naw. Just wondered how she was holding up—big three-oh and all."

Rook barked at me over his shoulder. "If I were your age, I'd already have a ring on that girl's finger. You would too, if you had any sense."

Louie chuckled and set the shot glass under the counter. "Rook seems to think you don't know how to romance a lady."

A snorting sound came from Rook's general direction. "He doesn't know squat!"

A gravelly voice piped up from the end of the bar. "Maybe she just don't like him like that."

A lavishly powdered hooker was curled around a cracked vinyl seat, looking to trade her soul for spirits, if she could find a taker. She took a drag off a thin, brown cigarette crammed into a cheap, plastic holder. "Love or money. Gotta be the one or the other. Nothin' personal, but he ain't no Adonis." She paused to take a slug of quadruple malt. "Probably too old for her, too."

Too old? I was stunned.

Rook jumped in. "I was thirty-two years older than my second wife. And she was a real beauty."

"Age don't matter...unless you ain't got two dimes to rub together. This fella don't look like he can support himself, not to mention the girl."

The hooker picked up her drink and sashayed away from the bar. I pulled another Lucky out of the crumpled pack. Being insulted by a hooker—or Rook, for that matter—didn't really bother me, but maybe I *was* being stupid, chasing after a kid like Chelsee. I was speeding toward my fortieth birthday like a derailed train, though a dab of Wite-Out on my birth certificate had made that my own little secret.

I tossed back the rest of my bourbon. My bladder suddenly felt like a medicine ball. I slid out of the booth and tipped my hat to Louie and Rook. "If you gentlemen will excuse me, I need to powder my nose. You know how it is for us older guys."

As I left the men's room a few minutes later, I passed a figure sitting motionless in a dark corner of the café. The man's face was obscured, but I could feel his eyes on me as I walked back to my booth. When I sat down, I kept him casually in my peripheral vision. Every few seconds, his arm would lift and a tiny light would flare up, followed by a stream of smoke. Even from across the room, there was no mistaking that smell—Cubanas. Expensive, and hard to get in this part of the world. They were the best smoke a man could have—rich, full-bodied. My mouth watered ever so slightly.

Despite the cigar smoker's evident taste, I don't like people watching me. I turned to the window and looked out into the street. My mind wandered over the past few months, since the incident on the Moon Child. My last case had almost been my *last* case. But that's another story. Someday I'll find a Watson and have him start cataloguing all of my exciting adventures. Of course, it'll be tough to keep him supplied with enough good material, not to mention a salary. Business had picked up for awhile, but now I was between jobs. I'd spent all my money, and I was behind again on my bills. That Cubana certainly smelled good. My nose felt like it was wrapping around my face, like a flower turning toward the sun.

"The gentleman in the corner wants to know what you're drinking." Glenda's pencil was poised over her notepad. She chewed her gum furiously, sounding like someone twisting bubble wrap.

"He wants to buy me a drink?"

She shrugged without looking at me.

A sudden thought. "Uh, he isn't, well, you know…is he?"

"Nah. But he smells like money."

"Hmm. In that case, I'll have bourbon."

"Jim, Jack, rocks, water, soda, or neat?"

"No, yes, no, no, no, yes."

Glenda nodded, made a loud popping sound, and walked off. The stranger in the corner didn't move. I packed another Lucky Strike and fired it up. It tasted nothing like a Cubana.

The waitress returned and slid a partially filled glass in front of me. I picked it up, swirled it around, then raised it toward the dark corner. The man motioned slightly with his hand as a fresh stream of smoke emerged from the shadows. I took a sip—first the smell, then the burning in my throat, finally the warmth in my belly. Drawing deeply on my smoke, I turned back to the window.

It was late. People passed by the bar without glancing in, each one going somewhere important. A leggy redhead strode past, all pouty lips and bouncing hair. I swiveled involuntarily, tweaking my lower back and almost spilling my precious bourbon. A voice brought me back just as quickly.

"How is the bourbon?"

I looked up. The man's face was unfamiliar, but the cigar in his hand was an old friend. He was of indeterminate age—probably a little older than you'd think.

"I'm convinced that God himself invented bourbon, thank you. Care to join me?"

He nodded, placed his coat and hat carefully on the rack by the booth, then lowered himself onto the vinyl seat across from me. "I hope my cigar doesn't bother you. It's a terrible habit."

"I've always wanted to make a terrible habit of smoking Cubanas. Unfortunately, it's an addiction I can't afford."

"Ah...a man who knows his tobacco. My name is Gordon Fitzpatrick. It's a pleasure indeed to meet you, sir." Fitzpatrick reached across the table to shake my hand. His hands were soft and unscarred—hands that had never done anything more strenuous than pick up a cup of tea.

"My name's Murphy. Call me Tex if you like."

I looked down at my glass. It was almost empty. "Do you often buy bourbon for complete strangers?"

"Only occasionally. Since I can't drink, myself, I sometimes enjoy the vicarious experience. Besides, you looked like you could use a drink."

"People have been telling me that for years." I drained my glass.

Fitzpatrick watched, amused, as the last few drops hit my tongue. On cue, Glenda arrived with another glass.

I looked down at the glass, then up at my companion. "If I were a woman, I'd think you were trying to soften me up. What is it you want, Mr. Fitzpatrick?"

With a slight smile, Fitzpatrick ground the Cubana stub into the ashtray until it quit smoking. "I like a plain speaker, Mr. Murphy. Let's be frank with each other. I'm looking for an old acquaintance of mine. A Dr. Thomas Malloy. Until recently, he lived in the Ritz Hotel, not far from here. Do you know of him?"

The Ritz had a pretty high turnover, and I'd never made a point of getting to know the other tenants. It was the kind of place where people came when they didn't want to be found. The name didn't ring a bell, but then I'd never been good with names. "Sorry. Never heard of the guy."

"Ah...that's a shame. It's quite important that I find him." Fitzpatrick rose slowly and reached for his coat and hat. He was either a polished bluffer, or knew when to cut his losses. Either way, he smoked Cubanas. He also seemed to need help and, after sitting across from him for five minutes, I desperately wanted one of his cigars. I decided to offer my services.

"Look, Mr. Fitzpatrick, I'm a licensed private investigator. I also live at the Ritz Hotel. If you're looking for help, maybe I could find this Dr. Malloy for you."

Holding his coat and hat, Fitzpatrick lowered himself back into the booth. His face was lit up like a 100-watt bulb. "A private detective! Delightful! I didn't know that one could make a living as a flatfoot in the twenty-first century."

"Well now, I didn't say I made a living at it. I've just got a license."

"So, you only gumshoe part-time? What else do you do?"

"Well, drinking takes up a lot of my time. Avoiding bill collectors and the IRS also keeps me fairly busy."

Fitzpatrick seemed delighted. "Well, Mr. Murphy, it seems that we could do each other some good. I need assistance and you, apparently, need income. Perhaps we should shake on it—or would you like the details first?"

This seemed too good to be true, so it probably was. But Fitzpatrick seemed more than willing to solve at least some of my money problems. Reaching into my overcoat, I found a dog-eared, coffee-stained business card. I apologetically handed it to my future client.

"I prefer to do business in my office. Why don't we meet there tomorrow morning? Bring anything that might help. We'll wait to discuss payment, but I think you'll find my rates reasonable. In fact, if you bring a few of those Cubanas along, I'll give you the special Friends of Tex discount."

Chapter
Two

"This is wonderful." The old man looked around my digs like a kid at a petting zoo. "I feel as though I were in one of the detective movies I enjoyed as a boy."

I nodded, as conversationally as possible. Fitzpatrick had knocked on my office door during a period of valuable REM sleep, and I wasn't fully conscious. Fortunately, he'd brought along a box of Cubanas and, together with a cup of thick coffee, high-quality nicotine for breakfast was bringing me around. My future client seemed as chipper as a poor poker player holding a royal flush.

"Why, I'd half expected to see the name Samuel Spade printed on the door."

"I've always believed that setting and ambiance are essential to reaching a desirable clientele."

"Without a doubt." He brushed a piece of lint from his hat. He seemed to enjoy my film noir philosophy as much as I was enjoying his cigars. I took another puff.

"I don't know about you, Mr. Fitzpatrick, but I've always felt I belonged in the '30s. *1930s,* that is. Ever since I can remember. When the other kids were logged onto Sesame Street Interactive, I was reading Hammett and Chandler. Real paper books, of course."

"Naturally."

"So...now I'm a private detective."

Fitzpatrick seemed almost envious. "It must be quite exciting."

I took another long draw of the Cubana. "Well, let's just say it's a good thing I enjoy the work; it sure as hell doesn't pay very well."

Fitzpatrick nodded sympathetically and reached delicately inside his coat. "That must be my cue." His hand emerged holding a calfskin checkbook. My heart fluttered. I tried not to breathe heavily.

"I charge 500 dollars a day, plus expenses. Contingent, of course, upon my taking your case." Fitzpatrick didn't hesitate. "That seems perfectly acceptable. I suppose you'll need me to give you some details."

I leaned back in my chair and formed a perfect smoke ring. "Please."

Fitzpatrick's face became more serious, and I noticed for the first time how old he looked. Deep lines etched his forehead and surrounded his eyes and mouth. His skin had a transparent quality, though his complexion was quite ruddy for a man of his age and apparent lifestyle. His eyes were the only feature of his face that didn't seem old. He wore no glasses or corneal inserts, and his eyes seemed uncommonly clear and focused. Sure, maybe he'd had radial keratotomy or TDA surgery, but that didn't explain an indefinable something about his eyes, somehow foreign, yet compelling. I looked away.

"As I told you last evening, I'm searching for a man named Thomas Malloy. Before I retired, I was a research scientist and worked quite closely with Dr. Malloy for a time. Our paths diverged some twenty years ago, and we did not stay in touch. Recently, however, I saw a picture of my old friend in a local newspaper, the *Bay City Mirror*. My friend was in the background of the photograph. It was taken at a nearby university, Berkeley. When I went to look him up, I was told that no one named Malloy worked there. I spoke to several people, even showing them the picture from the newspaper, but no one recognized—or admitted to recognizing—Dr. Malloy.

"I was close to abandoning hope when a young woman approached me, saying she might be able to help. She introduced herself as Sandra and said that she had worked with the man I knew as Malloy. He had been known to her as Tyson Matthews. Sandra did not seem comfortable talking to me at that time, so we agreed to meet later."

Fitzpatrick paused dramatically and leaned toward me. "She did not keep our appointment."

My eyes widened appropriately. "Did you talk to her again?"

"I had every intention of doing so. When I returned to the university, I was told that Sandra had quit her job and withdrawn from her classes. Other attempts to locate her proved fruitless."

The story was starting to interest me. With a delicate cough, Fitzpatrick motioned toward my watercooler. "May I?"

"Certainly."

He filled a paper cup halfway, returned to his seat, and took a sip. "As you can imagine, my discouragement gave way to a sense of imperilment. I feared not only for the well-being of the girl, but also of my friend. Macabre as it may seem, I began searching the obituaries in addition to my other inquiries. After several months, I came to believe that I would not see Dr. Malloy again. Then I found another reference to my friend."

Fitzpatrick paused and took another sip from the paper cup. I'd forgotten the Cubana—it had gone out. I set it in the ashtray.

"I have always had an interest in the paranormal and regularly read several periodicals in the genre. In one of these, the *Cosmic Connection*, I read that an upcoming feature would be an interview with a Dr. Thomas Malloy. I contacted the publishers, but they would give me no information. In fact, the interview failed to appear in the magazine. I never was able to determine what had transpired, but five hundred dollars bought me an address where Malloy could supposedly be reached."

"Here at the Ritz?"

"That's correct."

"Apparently another dead end."

"I suppose we have yet to determine that. It is, however, as far as my story goes."

Of course, I was in. The money alone would have done it, but the old man's story had me hooked like a hungry bass. I had an image to maintain, though. I took a moment to relight the Cubana. "I think I can make time to look into this for you. I'll need a copy of the picture from the newspaper and a number where you can be reached. And if you think of anything else that could help, give me a call. The number's on my card."

Fitzpatrick seemed relieved. He produced a business card from his breast pocket and placed it carefully on the desk. "As per your instructions, I brought with me a copy of the photograph." Pulling a neatly folded piece of paper from yet another pocket, he set it carefully beside the business card. He then opened his checkbook and slowly wrote out a check. To avoid staring, I picked up the photocopy of Malloy's picture and unfolded it. In the background of the photograph I could clearly make out the face of an older man, at least in his mid-seventies. I looked up to see Fitzpatrick finish signing his name. He removed the check methodically, blew on it lightly, and handed it to me. I tried not to look, but a bunch of zeros caught my eye and wouldn't let go.

"The Cubanas were more than enough for a retainer, Mr. Fitzpatrick."

The old man replaced the checkbook in his coat pocket. "Consider the cigars a gift from one patron of a dying art to another."

He rose slowly and smoothed the pleats of his tailored trousers. I stood and leaned across the desk to shake his hand.

"I hope this venture will be to our mutual benefit, Mr. Murphy."

I smiled down at the old man. "Call me Tex."

After Fitzpatrick left, I waited for an appropriate period of time, then grabbed the check and my hat and took the fire escape down to the street. It was only 7:00 P.M. The banks wouldn't open for a couple hours, but there was an ATM close by that would cash my check.

Chelsee's newsstand sits directly across from the Ritz. I decided to say hello. She'd left me hanging the night before. I needed to know if I'd hurt her feelings, how much, and what kind of Band-Aid would make it all better.

"Hey...sorry about last night."

"Really. Why?" Chelsee was oozing antagonism. I remembered it was her birthday.

"Well I...you know, I feel like I swallowed my foot. It left a bad taste in my mouth. Metaphorically speaking, of course. My feet actually smell good."

Chelsee didn't smile like she was supposed to. "Don't worry about it, Tex." Her words were nice enough, but her tone was testy. She crossed her arms and looked down. "I know how I look. It's not like I have guys lined up to ask me out...not like I used to."

She looked back at me, her chin up. "I wouldn't want you to mollycoddle me anyway."

It was bizarre hearing Chelsee talk like this. It was so honest, so sad...so pathetic. I didn't know how to react. "Listen, why don't you let me take you to dinner tonight?"

"A date?" She said the word like she'd rather be dowsed in

kerosene and given a lit cigarette.

"No, no, no—just two friends eating some food from the same table. Maybe some polite conversation."

Chelsee mulled it over, then shrugged. "I guess that'd be OK. I mean...yeah, that'd be all right."

Her shoulders seemed to relax slightly. "Look, Tex. I haven't been feeling myself lately. I didn't think this birthday stuff would be any big deal, but I guess it is." She narrowed her gaze, completely unaware of her shiny eyes and moist lips. "I...appreciate you looking out for me."

My face felt like it was turning a bit pink. "OK, it's *not* a date then. I'll pick you up. How's five? Earlier? Later?"

Chelsee's eyes flashed for the first time. "I've got a better idea. Why don't we just have dinner at my place? It'll be quiet, we can talk...plus it'll be a lot cheaper than going out." She paused. "Besides...I have something I want to talk to you about."

I really felt like telling her that, for once, I had enough money to take her out. On the other hand, she'd never invited me to her place before, and the thought of it was substantially arousing. And what did she need to tell me? The possibilities were testing my antiperspirant.

"You talked me into it, Miss Bando. I'll be there at five o'clock sharp.... I may even iron my shirt."

"I feel so spoiled."

"By the way, which should I bring—red or white?"

Chelsee looked all the way into my eyes. My knees wobbled. "Both."

As I stood at the ATM, waiting to see if my check would get eaten, I filed Chelsee away for later (with some difficulty) and tried to devise a plan of action for locating Dr. Thomas Malloy. With the little Fitzpatrick had given me to go on, I figured the best starting point would be back at the Ritz. Somehow, I'd need to get into Malloy's former room. Unfortunately, getting information would involve talking to Nilo Paglio, the owner/landlord/extortionist, and I wasn't his favorite tenant at the moment. It was the second week of April, and I was a little late on my February rent payment. I'd usually been able to hold Nilo at bay by doing the occasional house-detective job, but he'd run out of things for me to do. The Ritz hadn't had the No Vacancy sign on for awhile, and Nilo was breathing down my neck like a dancing sailor on the last night of leave.

For the first time in weeks, I entered the Ritz through the front door and stepped into the lobby. I had four five-hundred dollar bills in my hand and two in my shoe. As usual, Nilo was behind the front desk, sprawled over a chair in the corner, reading a skin mag. A soggy cigar stub smoldered between clenched jaws and cracked lips. It *wasn't* a Cubana. He looked up, his eyes bulging out, and he almost swallowed his stogie as he struggled to his feet. "Hole it right dere, ya sneakin' piece of snot!" Spittle flew everywhere.

"Calm down, Nilo. I'm not going anywhere."

"Damn straight ya ain't goin' anywheres! Where's my damn money?"

I pulled out the four McKinleys and held them up in front of Nilo's red-scarred eyes. "I've got it right here. I just need to ask you about something before I hand it over."

Nilo quit spitting on me, but his eyes didn't leave the bills. "Wha ya askin'? Maybe I ain't talkin'."

I waved the cash slightly, letting Nilo get a good whiff of it. "Tell me about Thomas Malloy."

"Never heard of him." Nilo's unblinking eyes remained

focused on the money. It looked like he was still counting. Keeping the bills in full view, I pulled out the copy of the newspaper photo Fitzpatrick had given me and pointed to Malloy.

The slug pried his eyes off the cash in my hand and glared at the photograph. "Used ta live here. Gone now."

"Which room was he staying in?"

Nilo hesitated, then, glaring up at me, hissed like a cornered alley cat. "Six."

"Anyone else stayed there since Malloy left?"

"No!" The word was forced out like an abscessed molar. I moved the greenbacks tantalizingly close to the landlord's snout.

"Give me the security code to apartment six, and these'll be all yours."

Nilo didn't answer. I waved the bones around. The effect was Pavlovian. "Awright, damn ya! Four—eight—two—seven! Now gimme dose damn things!"

Apartment six was on the second floor. I punched in the numbers, heard a click, pushed open the door, and stepped into the room. It looked just like the other rooms at the Ritz: ratty bed, lopsided dresser, nightstand, scratched-up desk. The place looked as empty as a politician's campaign promise, but it was all I had to go on. I walked to the desk and grabbed one of the drawer handles. As I pulled the drawer open, I heard a floorboard squeak. It didn't strike me as odd until I heard the whooshing sound. A blinding flash of pain seared through my skull as someone turned out the lights.

Chapter
Three

It felt like I was swimming to the surface of a pool of molasses. My eyes slowly focused on what looked like a massive spider web. As the fog rolled off to sea, I realized I was staring at the cracked plaster ceiling in the Ritz Hotel, apartment six. I rolled over and spent the next five minutes attempting to stand. A brighter shade of red light was seeping through the window. I checked my watch—it was 12:03 P.M. I'd been out for more than sixteen hours.

The room looked the same as it had yesterday, except all the drawers had been opened and emptied. Looked like whoever thumped me had given the place a once-over. Maybe he'd missed something.

I was right. The desk contained an empty book of matches and two paper clips. In the dresser, I found a black sock. An empty beer bottle had been left in the closet. For Holmes, this might have been a bonanza of clues. For me, it was diddly. I got down on the floor and peered under the bed. I detected a faint odor. Pawing around through a pile of dust bunnies, my fingers touched something soft and smooth. It was a silk scarf, bright purple and oozing the cheap scent of department store perfume. Judging by the smell, it hadn't been there long. I pocketed the scarf and stumbled back to my office.

The Colonel, my mentor in the PI biz, had taught me long ago the proper cure for a goose egg: a double bourbon with an ice-pack chaser. As I underwent treatment, I leaned back in my chair and tried to think clearly. Who had jumped me, and why? Whoever it was had done a thorough job. I thought about checking around, but anyone good enough to put me out for sixteen hours wouldn't be sloppy enough to be seen. I pulled the scarf out of my pocket and examined it.

There was no label, no identifying marks of any kind. I assumed that the scarf belonged to a woman, but I'd been wrong before. Either way, I was optimistic that finding its owner would put me on Malloy's trail. The question was how. Nilo would certainly have noticed *any* woman who'd come into the Ritz, though I doubt if he'd remember anything about her from the neck up.

The scent on the scarf was memorable, if nothing else. Unfortunately, it was probably available at every discount department store in the city. I looked the scarf over. The purple shade was shockingly bright. The color would almost certainly have caught someone's attention. Chelsee was always good with details. Maybe she could...

Chelsee! Oh, Lord! I checked my watch for no good reason. She was gonna kill me. She'd never believe that I'd been out cold straight through dinner. I jumped out of the chair and caught the corner of the desk, bruising my thigh and upsetting my already unsteady balance. As I stumbled toward the floor, my forehead hit the rim of the metal wastebasket. I spun away, the back of my head slamming onto the hardwood floor. As I waited for the room to stop spinning, I thought that at least now Chelsee might find it easier to believe that I'd been jumped.

With some effort, I got to my feet and made my way down to the street. I'd forgotten that it was midday. Chandler Avenue looked like a ghost town. This time of year, the radometer was off the scale during daylight hours. Chelsee wouldn't open the newsstand until around 7:00 P.M. She was probably at her apartment, asleep. I looked up and down the street. Even the Brew & Stew was closed. Then my ears caught the faintest strain of bluesy piano coming from the alley that separated the Ritz and the Fuchsia Flamingo Club. The Flamingo had just opened in the old Bijou building. The marquee out front trumpeted: "Tonight! Don't Miss Luscious Lucy Lust!" I walked to the end of the alley. A door was propped open. I stepped inside.

As my eyes adjusted to the cool darkness, I made out a broad back hunched over a baby grand. The playing was sloppy, but sincere. This was my first time in the Flamingo, primarily because of the requisite membership fee. I looked around the dark interior. The design staggered back and forth between eclectic and tasteless. The overall feel was a blend of Mayan myth and Vegas vamp, all set to be lit up in pastel neon. But someone loved this place—there was almost as much heart and soul here as bamboo and Naugahyde.

I approached the broad-backed gent at the Larsen grand. He spoke over his shoulder. "Didn't mean to wake ya, Emily. I'll knock it off if it's bugging ya." A sour-looking mutant with a large mustache, he swung his girth around and looked me up and down with a stunningly blank expression. I was clearly not Emily. He stood up. He was huge. "We're closed." The tone implied something closer to "any last words?"

Immediately, I broke into my special "Howdy! I'm Tex! I'd like to be your friend!" smile. "Yeah, I know. I came through that door over yonder. I heard ya playin' that there piano. Sounds mighty fine!"

I hoped my trusty "saddle pal" drawl would confuse him. It was a gamble, but he didn't strike me as Mensa material. The mutant looked me over carefully and seemed to be doing a lot of sniffing. I remembered the scarf in my pocket and pulled it out. "This here is probably what you're smelling. It's not mine."

My saddle pal looked closely at the scarf. "Where'd you get that?" He looked at me sharply. "And quit using the phony accent."

He was on to me. Maybe I was losing my touch. "Uh, sure...I, uh, I found it next door...over at the Ritz. That's where I live. I was trying to find out whose it is."

The mutant took a menacing step toward me. "And that's why you walk into a closed, private club."

This guy was making me nervous. My left eyelid twitched. "Well, no. I, uh, actually...I heard the piano. That's why I came in. The door was open. I wasn't looking for trouble. Really."

The mutant looked toward the door, then back at me. "Give me the scarf."

I hesitated. "Well...I don't know if I should. I mean, it's not yours...is it?"

The scarf was ripped out of my hands. "I'll make sure it gets to the right person."

There was no room for discussion.

"All right, then. Well, thanks. I'll sleep better knowing that everything's been taken care of. I guess I'll...run along then. Good to meet ya. Real nice place you've got here."

The mutant followed me to the door and slammed it shut as soon as I was outside. I paused to light a Lucky. At least I'd learned a few things. Unless I missed my guess, the big goon had mistaken me for someone named Emily on account of the cheap perfume that still clung to me like cat hair on a sofa. He'd also recognized the scarf. Odds were that it belonged to the same woman. I had to assume that she had been in Malloy's apartment recently. And Emily lived—or at least was staying—in the old Bijou building.

I had a hunch that she knew something about Malloy. Now I needed to find out who she was and get her within range of my hypnotic charm. My conversation with Chuckles, the piano player, made me doubt that he'd be of any assistance. I needed coffee.

The Closed sign didn't intimidate me. I knocked on the window and saw Louie poke his misshapen head out of the kitchen. He waved to me, then disappeared. Seconds later, he came to the door and unlocked it. "You're up early, Murph."

Louie held the door open as I stepped inside. The smell of spicy chili billowed from the kitchen. The empty feeling in my stomach immediately became the only important thing in the world. Louie's cuisine didn't win any awards, but it attracted a substantial clientele from all over, even New San Francisco. There just weren't many places left that offered home-cooked meals, a smoking section, and reasonable prices.

"You hungry? I could whip something up in two shakes." Louie was born to feed.

"You sure you don't mind? Smells like you're working some of your legendary chili alchemy."

"Naw. I just finished this batch. It's a good one, but it's gotta simmer for a few hours."

I slumped onto a bar stool, and Louie slid a menu in front of me.

"Want the Armageddon?" I nodded. Louie's house blend was the only java that ever worked for me. It had almost magical properties. "The pot'll be ready in a minute. Be right back."

Louie bustled back into the kitchen. I didn't bother to look at the menu. Western omelet with feta. Wheat toast. Hash browns. Three cups of coffee. My eyes started to glaze over. I didn't want to hurry Louie, but the ketchup bottle at my elbow looked delicious.

The waiting was gonna kill me. I pulled out my crumpled pack of Luckies.

Louie burst from the kitchen, a steaming pot of joe in one hand and an oversized mug in the other. With the first sip of Armageddon blend coursing through my veins, I recited my breakfast mantra. Louie tromped back to the lab. The guy was a true saint—a disfigured cherub in a greasy apron. Here he was, feeding me before the diner was even open, probably assuming that I was broke as usual.

Quite a bit of sun filtered through the clouds. No one passed by. I took another sip from the mug and stuck a smoke in the corner of my mouth. I checked my pockets, but all the red tips were gone. I reached over the bar and grabbed a pack of matches. It was the same type of matchbook I'd found at Malloy's apartment. I lit my Lucky. Maybe Louie knew something. If Malloy had been in the Brew & Stew, Louie would remember.

For once, the food arrived as I was putting my cigarette *out*. Louie refilled my coffee and poured some for himself. "Geez, Murph, when's the last time ya ate?"

I shrugged, my mouth full of salty feta and crispy hash browns. "Don't know. Couple days." I pointed with my fork until I could talk legibly. "God, Louie. This is exactly what I needed this morning."

"Rough night?"

I nodded as I tore a large section out of the center of a piece of buttery toast. Louie took a long sip of coffee.

"So what's the scoop on that guy who bought you the bourbon the other night? Client?"

"Yeah. He has me looking for someone named Thomas Malloy." I wiped my hands with a napkin and pulled out the photo Fitzpatrick had given me. "This is Malloy. I think he may have come in here not too long ago. Recognize him?"

Louie looked intently at the face for a few moments. "I think so. It's been awhile...couple of weeks anyway. Came in with a younger gal. They had the special and a few cocktails."

"Tell me about the girl."

"Real pretty, a little heavy on the makeup. Smelled nice. I think she sings up at the Flamingo."

Louie grabbed the coffeepot and freshened up our mugs. I speared a chunk of feta.

"You ever gone there? The Flamingo, I mean."

He lifted the coffee to his mouth and talked through the steam. "Naw. Haven't had the time. I've been meaning to."

I mopped up the last of my omelet with a piece of toast. Louie waited for me to finish and took my plate away. I was full, but not uncomfortable. The tobacco crackled as I inhaled. I leaned down and pulled one of the McKinleys out of my shoe. When Louie returned, I handed him the five-hundred dollar bill. "Does this bring us up even?"

Louie seemed a little shell-shocked. Maybe he'd already claimed me as a deduction on his tax return. He turned to the cash register, opened it, then swung around and laid three C-notes in front of me.

"That oughtta cover it."

What a liar. I knew I'd run up *at least* a four hundred dollar tab over the past two months or so. I slid off the bar stool, pocketing one of the bills and my pack of smokes. Louie braced himself on the counter and jerked his head in the direction of the two bills. "Don't even think about leavin' here without those."

I walked to the door. "Thanks, Louie. If there's a God, he's saving a seat for you."

I stepped outside and looked up and down the street. I could hear the air traffic picking up, but no one in the neighborhood was out and about yet. My next stops would have to wait until later. Chelsee first, then the Fuchsia Flamingo. My full tummy and I walked back to the office.

Chapter
Four

"A little late, aren't you?"

She looked tired. Through the partially opened door, I could see the kitchen table. Burned down candles. Slightly wilted flowers. An open container of Häagen-Dazs with a spoon stuck in it. A simple "I'm sorry" wasn't going to cut it.

"I'm sorry. I...I really didn't..."

"Couldn't you at least call? Don't you have any respect for me at all?" Chelsee's eyes glistened. She dried her eyes on the sleeve of her bathrobe. "Leave me alone, Tex. I can't talk right now." She started to close the door.

I reached out and stopped it. "C'mon, Chelsee, it's not like you think. Just...give me a chance to explain."

She looked at me defiantly. The tears were coming back. She turned away.

"Look, I know this is gonna sound ridiculous, but..." I paused, then said it as quickly as possible. "I couldn't come because someone knocked me out."

It sounded like the lamest lie ever told. Chelsee gave me a look that said *what kind of fool do you take me for?*

"Really. I'm serious—feel my head. I was out for, like, sixteen hours."

Chelsee's hard stare was merciless.

I took her hand and placed it carefully on my still-tender goose egg. "See? I swear, I really wanted to be here last night, but I was out cold the whole time. You gotta believe me—I wouldn't stand you up. Ever."

She pulled her hand away. Her gaze seemed to penetrate me, reaching straight into my flawed male soul. After a long moment, she released me. Her voice was softer now. "What happened? Are you OK?"

"Yeah, I'm fine. It's not like I've never taken a shot to the head before."

Chelsee pulled a tissue from the pocket of her robe and smiled as she dabbed at her nose.

I grinned and felt a huge weight lift off my shoulders. "Why don't you get dressed and let me buy you a drink?"

She opened the door and motioned me inside. "Might as well. I wasn't planning on opening the newsstand today anyway." She picked up the Häagen-Dazs, licked off the spoon, and replaced the cover. "Where should we go?"

I knew that we should go somewhere in the new city, a nice, quiet place where we could discuss the pros and cons of romantic love, get a little light-headed, maybe go for a walk and watch the sunset—in short, get away from this Malloy case that had gotten me into trouble in the first place. But if we went to, say, the Fuchsia Flamingo, maybe I could make things up to Chelsee *and* get a little detective work done. It was probably a bad idea.

"How 'bout the Fuchsia Flamingo?"

It turned out that the owner of the Flamingo, a fellow by the name of Gus Leach, had given Chelsee a complimentary membership. As we stepped inside the club, we were greeted by the mustachioed mutant I'd met earlier. "Hello, Miss Bando."

"Hello, Gus. This is a good friend of mine. Tex Murphy—Gus Leach."

Leach sized me up. I hadn't made a good first impression, but being a friend of Chelsee's might compensate. Leach looked back at Chelsee, then extended his hand toward me. "We've met, though we weren't properly introduced."

My knuckles popped as he shook my hand. I wouldn't be shuffling cards for awhile.

"Sit anywhere you like. I'll send the waitress right over."

We opted for a corner table. There were only five other people in the club, and we barely beat the waitress to our seats. Chelsee asked for a Cape Codder. Feeling playful, I ordered scotch. Chelsee excused herself, leaving me to survey the surroundings. The Flamingo's interior was a shrine to bad taste on an epic scale, an unparalleled mishmash of exotic themes, neon, and garage sale oddities. The baby grand and a microphone stand were on a stage at the far end of the room. In the center of the club, a small, unused parquet dance floor sparkled under a giant disco ball. Chelsee and the drinks arrived simultaneously.

"This is quite a place. Interesting decor."

Chelsee smiled and stirred her vodka and cranberry juice. "I like it. But then, I've always been secretly attracted to blatant tackiness." Her eyes locked onto mine as she leaned forward and sipped through the straw in her drink.

"Should I take that personally?"

She shrugged coyly. "Take it any way you want."

My right foot spontaneously started tapping like a machine gun. For over a year, I'd pursued Chelsee shamelessly—without her ever giving me the slightest bit of encouragement. Rejection fit into my image—the lone wolf. Besides, it was one thing I was good at. Now she was turning the tables on me, or so it seemed. The hunter had become the hunted. My mouth suddenly dry, I grabbed my scotch and gulped it. Chelsee raised an eyebrow and leaned forward, resting her chin on the back of her hand. I smiled nervously and turned to find the waitress.

"Do you want to know what I was going to tell you last night?" Chelsee's voice had slipped to a throaty whisper. God, I needed another scotch. I signaled to the waitress, then turned back to Chelsee, trying to sound nonchalant.

"Sure." My voice was cracking slightly. I fumbled with my pack of Lucky Strikes.

"I was gonna tell you that I've been thinking...you know...about me and you."

The match shook slightly as it wandered toward the end of my cigarette.

"I have to admit...I used to think you were just another smug, insensitive bag of hormones, going through a midlife crisis. Now that I know you better, I realize this isn't a midlife crisis at all."

The cigarette was calming me down. "Thanks...I think."

Chelsee smiled down at her drink and slowly stirred it with her forefinger. "I've just decided that, underneath it all, you're really a nice guy. And I've always thought you were quite attractive."

She lifted her finger out of the drink and ran it lightly across her lower lip. Lord, she really knew how to pitch my tent. Moving her drink to the side, she again leaned forward and placed her chin on the back of her hand. It looked like it was my turn to talk. I sent a stream of smoke off to the side; I'd regained control.

"This sudden interest...seeing me in a new light—I mean, I don't want to look a gift horse in the mouth, if you'll pardon the expression, but this isn't connected in any way to, say, someone's recently celebrated birthday?"

"I don't know. Maybe. I think that made me take a look at myself, look at what's important. For a long time now I've been on my own. I've decided that independence is overrated. I want to be with somebody. Have someone need me."

"I was married once, you know."

Chelsee nodded.

"It was miserable. Whenever someone tells me to go to hell, I tell 'em I've already been there."

"Would you ever try it again? With someone else, I mean."

I took a long sip of scotch and thought it over. The implications of our conversation were making my head swim. Suddenly, a voice rang out.

"Ladies and gentlemen. The management of the Fuchsia Flamingo is proud to present this evening's entertainment. Please give a warm welcome to Luscious...Lucy...Lust!"

A pitiful smattering of applause accompanied the opening bars of "I've Got You Under My Skin." A slicked-back middle-aged man in a powder blue tuxedo sat at the baby grand. A woman stepped into the spotlight stage right and undulated to the microphone. Her ruby red sequined dress looked like it had been painted on. It wasn't low cut—it didn't have to be. From forty feet this woman looked perfect. She curled her fingers around the microphone and began to sing. I was spellbound. She didn't just sing a song—she made love to it.

I glanced over at Chelsee. She was looking directly at me, not smiling. "Did you forget the question?"

I had. *I've got you deep in the heart of me.* With some effort, I pulled my attention from the stage and tried to remember where we'd left off. "Let's see. Marriage. I don't know. I guess I could...if it seemed like the thing to do."

I really didn't mean to sound distracted. Chelsee didn't respond. The waitress stopped by and confirmed that we did, indeed, want two more drinks. I lit another smoke and looked back toward the singer. I was willing to bet that if I got within ten feet of the stage, I'd catch the scent of the purple scarf. Luscious

Lucy—alias Emily—and I needed to talk.

"Do you know her?" Chelsee was still watching me watch the singer.

"No. But I think she's tied up in the case I'm working on."

"Really."

"Seriously. I can't give you all the details, but I'm looking for a guy. I think this dame used to see him. I've got to talk to her and find out what she knows."

Chelsee picked up her purse and stood up. "Well, I'll leave you to your *investigative* work. Thanks for the drink."

She turned and headed for the exit. I jumped up and almost body-slammed the waitress who was arriving with our drinks. I quickly pulled out my wallet and threw a fifty onto the table. "Leave the drinks. I'll probably be back in a minute."

I caught up to Chelsee just outside the front door. "Where you goin'?"

"Home. I'm tired."

"Look, Chelsee. Don't get me wrong...I care about you—a lot. I just get a little uncomfortable whenever I hear the 'M' word."

"Tex, you don't need to humor me. I don't know what I was thinking."

She crossed her arms and looked intently at the sidewalk. "I've had an offer to sell the newsstand. I think I'm gonna take it. Like I told you the other night, I think I'll try Phoenix on for size."

For some reason, I felt a twinge of panic. "Are you sure about all this? I mean, moving is kind of a big thing. Nothing you want to rush into."

She looked up. "I've been thinking about it for months. I guess I haven't done anything 'cause I wanted to see if we could give it a try. But I don't think it's gonna happen. You're probably right—I'm just getting panicked 'cause I'm thirty and there's no one in my life. I like you a lot...I should probably leave it at that."

She turned away and spoke over her shoulder. "I'll walk home. I could use the exercise."

I didn't know what to say, but I felt like I should say something. "Chelsee...?"

She stopped and turned. "Yeah?"

I wanted to, but I didn't. "Come see me before you go anywhere."

She nodded. I watched her until she was gone. What a schmuck.

Back inside the Flamingo, I drained both glasses. The beautiful woman was getting friendly with the piano and singing a smoking version of "Love for Sale." The thrill had left with Chelsee. I packed another cigarette and called for a double scotch. Scratch that. Make it bourbon.

The singer's act went on for forty-five minutes. She was too good to be playing this section of town. I wondered what her story was, how she'd ended up in a dead-end lounge like this one. The last note of "Misty" faded into sparse, though enthusiastic, applause. With a graceful curtsy that completely contradicted the slinky gymnastics she'd displayed earlier, the young woman made her exit. Draining my bourbon, I casually made my way across the room. To the left of the stage, a doorway led to the restrooms and an ascending stairway. As I stepped through the doorway, a flash of red caught my eye from the top of the stairs. I darted after the girl.

Reaching the top, I turned to my right and saw the singer standing at a door, searching through a full key chain. I approached slowly, to avoid startling her.

"Excuse me. Can I talk to you for a second?"

The girl jumped. She turned to face me and retreated several steps. She was clearly frightened. "One step closer and I'll scream! I mean it!"

I stayed put. My hands were extended with palms out—the universal sign for "nothin' up my sleeve." "Whoa...no need for that. OK? Just hear me out. I promise...I'm not a pervert. Well, hardly ever. And only with women I know *really* well."

The girl seemed less scared but didn't relax her defensive stance. "What do you want?"

The sound of heavy footsteps came from the stairs behind me. I talked fast. "I'm a friend of Thomas Malloy's—I need to find him."

"What the hell are you doing up here?!" Leach pushed past me and stood between me and the girl. I didn't answer; it was up to Emily—I figured the odds were split. I could get her to talk or I could be beaten to a pulp by the big mutant. Leach took a step toward me, fists clenched.

Emily scrutinized me, obviously trying to determine if I was on the up and up. She turned out to be an excellent judge of character. "It's OK, Gus. He just wants an autographed picture. I'll come down in a minute."

Leach looked back at the girl, then at me, clearly irritated. Reluctantly, he moved toward the stairs, his eyes burning a hole in me. As he walked by, he dipped his shoulder slightly, knocking me off balance. I resisted my instincts and kept quiet until Leach was out of earshot.

"That was exciting."

Emily found the correct key and inserted it into the door lock. "We'll have to hurry. Gus doesn't like me talking to guys."

I followed her into her apartment. A quick look around gave

me the impression of being in a wild teenage girl's room. The smell of cheap perfume mingled with stale tobacco smoke. An open bottle of tequila, half full, sat on the table of a brightly lit vanity. One shelf was lined with stuffed animals.

Emily sat on the edge of her bed and clumsily lit a long, thin cigarette. She was younger than I'd thought she'd be. Under all the makeup, she was probably twenty-two, no older than twenty-four. A hard twenty-four.

"You're Tex Murphy, aren't you?"

I was caught off guard. It never occurred to me that she'd know who I was. "Yeah. Have we met?"

She shook her head. "No. I've just heard about you...that you're a PI, that you can help people."

I knew I had a reputation. I'd always thought it was less than flattering. It made me wonder who she'd been talking to. "People usually hire me to do their dirty work. Most of my clients seem satisfied with my work."

"I need you to help me." Emily looked me straight in the eyes. She sounded desperate.

"What kind of help are you looking for?"

"I think someone is going to murder me."

I could see she was trying hard to stay under control. I found my pack of smokes and drew one out. "Why?"

Emily stood up and began to pace. "It started right after Thomas left. About a week ago...he just disappeared—without a word. A couple nights later...I found a note in my room. After I read it, I was so scared.... I told Gus, and he said not to worry about it.... Then I got another note.... I want to call the cops, but Gus won't let me.... He keeps saying it's nothing, just some freak who gets off on scaring women."

She dropped back onto the bed and took a long, shuddering

breath. I didn't like the idea of someone murdering her. "This is really the sort of thing the police should know about."

She took a jittery drag off her cigarette. "Gus says he'll make sure no one hurts me. He doesn't want anyone else taking care of me. I know he means well, but sometimes I just want to...but he's always been so good to me...I don't know what to do."

I've never really believed in coincidence. The timing of Thomas Malloy's disappearance and the arrival of the notes seemed too close to be unrelated. Emily was a strong kid, but she was almost hysterical with fear. I probably would've helped her anyway. It was an added bonus that her problems might give me a lead to Malloy.

I went over to Emily's bed and sat down next to her. My voice was as gentle as brushed cotton. "I'll do what I can to help.... Gus doesn't need to know."

She turned toward me, hopeful and hesitant at the same time. "I don't have a lot of money...but I'd be so grateful." Her hand brushed my thigh, *almost* accidentally. I stood up and moved away.

"I'll need to look at the notes you got—if you've still got them."

"I do. I saved them to give to the police." She crossed the room to a desk and pulled out two pieces of paper. I looked them over. "When did you receive these?"

Emily sat back down on the bed. "Last week, maybe two nights after Thomas disappeared, and then the night before last. They were slipped under my door."

"Has anything else happened, other than the notes?"

"No, not that I can think of."

I slipped the notes into the pocket of my overcoat. "Incidentally, what is your full name?"

"Emily Sue Patterson."

"Listen, Emily, like I told you, I'm looking for Thomas Malloy. If I can find out who's hassling you and get them to stop, will you tell me everything you know about him?"

She thought about it for a moment. "I guess so. I *think* I can trust you....Why are you looking for him?"

"An old friend of his hired me to find him. He might be in danger."

"I'll do what I can. I didn't know him that well, but he was very good to me. The last time I saw him..."

The door burst open. Leach looked from me to Emily and back to me. He seemed almost disappointed that he hadn't caught us in a compromising position. He pointed a cigar-sized finger at me. "You! Get the hell outta here! Emily, you're on in five minutes!"

I tipped my hat to the young lady and walked out the door. Leach followed me, slamming the door behind him. He whispered menacingly at me as he followed me down the stairs.

"Leave her alone, Murphy. Take her away from me, and I'll kill you. Don't you ever forget that. I'll *kill* you."

Discretion being the better part of valor, I didn't reply. Leach followed me to the bottom of the stairs, grabbed me by the arm, and pushed me toward a side door.

"You go out here. And don't bother coming back. I don't like nosy people hanging around my place."

The door slammed behind me. I was back in the alley between the Flamingo and the Ritz. At least I'd learned a lot since the last time Leach had booted me out of his club.

Chapter
Five

I set the needle down carefully. A few seconds of crackling, then Nat King Cole's voice began to fill the office. I walked around the desk and dropped into my chair. The desktop was covered: a partially filled glass, a bottle of JD behind it, a smoldering ashtray, a fingerprint dusting kit, a magnifying glass, and other investigative paraphernalia. In the center of this mess were the two notes Emily had given me. Three hours' worth of analysis, and I was no better off than when I'd started.

One note read: *I'm watching you. I take pictures. Be afraid.* It was written on a plain 8½-by-11-inch sheet in block letters with a standard No. 2 pencil. At the bottom of the sheet was a symbol shaped like an arrow. It seemed familiar to me, though I couldn't think of where I'd seen it before. The second note was identical, except for the content. It read: *It won't be long now. You and I will be together.*

Whoever had sent the notes was one sick, creepy bastard, but he was also very careful. There were only two sets of prints on the sheets: mine and Emily's. No stains, no marks of any kind. Everything he'd used to create the notes was standard, easy to get, and untraceable. There was just one unique thing about the notes: the arrow symbol. It wasn't much, but it was my only angle.

"Certainly has been a long time, Tex." Patty Baker's full, rosy cheeks glistened under false eyelashes and peroxide-friendly hair.

"Yeah, well, you know how it is for me, Patty. Work, work, work."

It was a slight exaggeration, but Patty required excuses. She and I had gotten chummy a couple of years ago. It had been an unintentional foray into the world of one-night stands, but the resulting gentlemanly obligation that came with it would make me uncomfortable every time I paid a visit to the San Francisco PD Main Precinct. One night had been enough to convince me that she must be someone else's type.

Patty pursed her lips and pouted in a somewhat revolting fashion. "I'll bet you could squeeze me into your busy schedule for an evening or two."

"I'll have to take a rain check, sweetheart. I've got a big case going—could keep me busy for months...years, even. As a matter of fact, that's why I'm here. I need to bend Mac's ear for a bit."

Patty gave me a coy, girlish look and ogled me in a way that was supposed to leave me wanting more. She leaned forward, reaching for the vid-phone control panel. A deep, raspy voice jumped out of a speaker behind the front desk. "What?!"

Patty pressed down a button and looked up at me, seductively. Nothing about her look made me change my mind.

"Mr. Tex Murphy to see you, sir."

"God...all right! Send him back!"

Patty punched the door release, and I stepped through the security scanner.

"Thanks, Patty." As I passed her, a paw cupped my backside. I jumped slightly and quickened my pace to Mac Malden's office. I felt violated.

I only saw Mac when I needed a favor from the police department. It was a friendship of convenience, at least for me. I'd unintentionally helped him solve a couple of cases in the past, including the murder of Marshall Alexander, Mick Flemm's robbery spree, and the mysterious death of Rusty the Clown. Mac was old school and knew when he owed someone, even if he bitched every time I asked for anything.

The crusty cop was sprawled in a high-back swivel chair, a bent smoke sticking out from under his mustache and a police report in his hands. His desk was piled with papers, plastic freezer bags full of various items, at least a dozen Styrofoam cups, and a handful of petrified doughnut chunks. Mac set the police report on the desk, took a deep drag, and leaned back. He always tried to look like he was busy doing important work whenever I came by.

"Make it quick, Murphy. I've got about a million things to do, and wasting time on you isn't one of 'em."

"Geez, Mac. I don't see you that often. I worry about ya.... You don't look too good."

"Yeah?! Well, neither do you! You look like crap!"

"Oh, I'll admit, I'm not twenty-eight anymore, but, you know, I *feel* great. I've got one of those juicers, and it really works! I think *you* could do with a nice cabbage and carrot juice blend."

"What'd you do? Quit the PI business and sign up with Robco? I don't wanna buy a damn juicer—and I don't like wise guys comin' in my office and annoying me! So get out!"

"OK. Calm down, Mac. I'm just kiddin' ya. I actually have a reason for stopping by. I want you to look at something."

I pulled the notes from my coat pocket, unfolded them, and set them in front of Mac. He lit another smoke and looked them over carefully. Then he motioned for me to close his office door.

"Where did you get these?" His tone of voice was startlingly unfamiliar. He was looking directly at me, without a hint of the usual acid gruffness or antagonisms.

"A client gave them to me."

Mac handed the notes back to me, then pulled a sheet of

paper and pen out of a desk drawer. Mac scribbled on the paper as he spoke. "They're meaningless. I wouldn't worry about it." He held the sheet of paper in front of me. *I can't talk. Someone might be listening.*

I mouthed "who?" then spoke aloud as Mac wrote some more. "Yeah, that's what I figured, but I thought I'd check it out."

Mac held up the paper. *NSA.* Hot damn. The National Security Agency only got involved in big stuff. Apparently, I'd stumbled into something a hell of a lot bigger than I'd bargained for. I took the paper from Mac and picked up a pencil from the desk. *What do you know about these notes?*

Mac took the sheet of paper. "Did you see the Giants game last night?" He scribbled.

I took my time answering. "Naw. I went out. I haven't seen the paper yet today. Who won?"

"Dodgers, five to four. Got three in the ninth. Manousakis hit one into the third deck." He passed me the paper. *Black Arrow Killer—murdered 7 or 8 in AZ and NV over past 2 years. Arrow symbol referred to in case notes. Another girl murdered here few weeks ago—similar note found. Investigation shut down by Feds.*

I wanted to ask Mac more, but he had that get-out-of-my-office light in his eyes.

"Well, it was good to see ya, Mac. We'll have to go catch a game at Candlestick sometime." I got up to leave.

Mac opened a desk drawer and searched through it. "Oh, Tex, on your way out, could you drop this letter off for me? I'd sure appreciate it." I took a business card from him and stuck it in my pocket.

"No problem, Mac. I'll see ya around."

Patty was on the vid-phone and let me leave without the usual double entendres and hollow hints at future trysts. I was eager to look at the card Mac had given me but decided to wait until I reached the relative privacy of my office.

The business card was ragged and cheaply made. It read: *Lucas Pernell—Investigative Reporter*. The printed number had been crossed out and a new number written in pencil. It didn't look promising, but Mac hadn't given it to me for no reason. I punched in the number on my vid-phone.

"*Bay City Mirror*. Circulation. How may I help you?"

"Lucas Pernell, please."

The video relay was off, and I assumed that the voice had been computer-generated. Amazingly, it wasn't. "Who?"

"Pernell. Lucas Pernell."

"Do you know the extension of the party?"

"No, I don't. I was just given this number."

"Please hold."

Elevator Muzak piped through my vid-phone speakers. An orchestral version of "Scream at the Sky" from Soundgarden's final album. An oldie, but a goodie. A voice finally cut in. "Who are you holding for?"

"Lucas Pernell."

"One moment, please."

A minute or so later, the phone beeped and yet another voice popped out of my speakers. "This is Pernell."

"Mr. Pernell, my name is Tex Murphy. I'm a PI and a friend of Mac Malden. He gave me this number."

"Is this some kind of joke? I don't know any Mac Malden."

Either this was a big mistake, or maybe Pernell was testing me. "Hmm...maybe I got the name wrong. Anyway, I have some notes that might interest you."

There was a short silence. "These notes...are they *sharp*, to the *point*?"

"I guess you could say that."

"You're right. I'm interested. We should meet. I'll let you know when and where."

Click.

I spent several hours scanning the Internet for references to the Black Arrow Killer, but I couldn't find anything. I turned off the computer and poured myself a bourbon. My eyes were dry, and my back ached. A nap sounded good. My fax machine beeped and spewed out a single sheet. I tore it off and read the words *Twilight. 1:00 A.M.*

I'd never experienced the Garden of Earthly Delights that is the Twilight Lounge. It was on the outskirts of New San Francisco. Not quite reputable—not particularly scary. Like a hundred other watering holes, it followed the Lounge Code: dark, not too friendly, and always open. I stepped inside and looked around. I had a pretty good idea what a Lucas Pernell would look like. Glasses, tousled hair, herringbone jacket, khaki trousers, a cheap tie that's always loosened and slightly off center. There were at least four Lucas Pernells in the bar. Fortunately, I must've been the only Tex Murphy.

"You Murphy?"

"Pernell?"

"I'm over here."

I followed the guy to a table in the far reaches of the lounge—past the pool tables, past the dartboards. Even past the life-size cutout of the golden beach vixen and her sweaty beer bottle.

"What do you drink?"

"Bourbon."

"Well, that's a good start."

Pernell caught a waitress's eye, held up two fingers, and pointed at the table. I pulled out my pack of Lucky Strikes, shook one to the top, and pulled it out between my teeth. "Can I bum one of those?"

"Sure." I shook up another smoke and pointed the pack toward Pernell.

We lit up as the waitress set up my first drink and Pernell's second. My fellow bourbon drinker paid the waitress and waited for her to sway back to the bar.

"Let's see the business card."

I pulled out the card Mac had given me. Pernell turned it over and examined it closely. Apparently satisfied, he lit a match and held it up to the card. Fractions of a second short of burning his fingers, he dropped the smoking cinder into the ashtray.

"You said you had notes."

I produced the two sheets of paper. Pernell first looked at them skeptically, with the air of someone whose patience is being tested. Quickly, though, his grip tightened, and his eyes began to move over the paper. After a moment he looked up at me, sharply. "How did you get these?"

"They were given to me by a client."

"How did your client get them?"

"From a stalker, apparently. What do you think?"

Pernell smiled. He carefully removed his glasses and polished them with his tie. "Look, sorry if I wasn't too friendly just now. Most of the people I deal with fall into two groups: idiots and imbeciles. I've got a waiting list a mile long of crackpots desperate to waste my time. Unfortunately, it's a necessary waste of time, sifting the grain from the chaff." He replaced his glasses and picked up the notes. "You, my friend, are one big chunk of grain."

I buried the smoking end of my cigarette into the black

remains of Pernell's business card. "Why don't we pretend—for just a second—that I have no idea how important these notes are. You tell me what you know, then I help my client. Sound like a plan?"

"So you don't know anything about the Black Arrow Killer?"

"Only what Mac Malden told me. Killed a few people in the Southwest a few years ago. Seems to have moved into the Bay Area and apparently murdered a girl around here a few weeks ago. That's all."

Pernell handed the notes back to me. I folded them and put them back in my pocket. "Well, Malden might know more than that, and he might not. Even if he did, I doubt he'd tell you. He'd be stupid to."

"Why?"

"It's a long story."

"Humor me."

Pernell took a swig of bourbon. He looked at me closely, like he was sizing me up, then went on. "When the first bodies turned up in Arizona in the summer of '41, the local police tried to keep it off the wires. Didn't want the bad publicity. So it wasn't until March of '42, when three other victims were found, that the story broke big. Turned out that the killer in all five cases had the same MO. He always sent notes to his victims before murdering them. I went down to cover the story and actually got a chance to see one of the notes. It was like these that you gave me. Exactly like these."

"With the arrow symbol on it."

"Right. And the block lettering—everything. Now, the police weren't too keen on releasing the details, since this type of crime can spawn copycat murders. The black arrow symbol was referred to in reports, giving the murderer the appellation of the Black Arrow Killer, but the actual symbol was never published.

This way, the police would know when the actual killer was involved by this specific arrow symbol."

"Makes sense."

"So, anyway, the killer moved on and racked up two more victims in Nevada before the police could catch up. Finally, a girl contacted the police after receiving one of the notes. The cops moved in and made an arrest. Sources tell me that, at that point, the NSA stepped in and completely took over the investigation. Media coverage evaporated. The guy they arrested was named LeRoy Kettler, though his name was never officially released."

"But they got the wrong guy, right? I mean, the killer is still on the loose."

"Maybe. The court held him over without bail. Before they could get a hearing, the guy hung himself in his cell. Or that was the official story. Everyone seemed satisfied that they'd gotten their man. No one bothered to ask how Kettler had gotten shoelaces into the cell. The case was closed."

"Sounds like you don't buy it."

"I don't. I had some connections at the jail. After things blew over a bit, I got in and discreetly interviewed a few people, including the inmate of the adjoining cell. He believed that Kettler hadn't committed suicide—he'd been murdered. He said that two men in suits had come to Kettler's cell the night before he was found dead. From his description and other details, I think it's possible, even likely, that the men were NSA agents."

"But why would the Feds want to kill Kettler?"

"Maybe Kettler was a fall guy. I could just be a sucker for a conspiracy story, or the real killer could have been a policeman, or someone in the government. Maybe the government had a reason for getting rid of the victims. I've been following that angle, seeing if there was any connection between the victims. On the other hand, maybe Kettler *was* the killer, but for some reason the Feds didn't want the case resolved. I don't know. Regardless, there was a cover-up."

"Mac Malden said that another victim turned up around here. How does that fit into the picture?"

"It doesn't. The girl was a grad student at Berkeley. According to her family, she didn't receive any of the notes associated with the other murders. Her mother is sure that she would have said something. The night she was killed, she wasn't acting nervous or cautious. The next morning, she was found dead in her bedroom, strangled. A note was found in a desk drawer in the bedroom. As soon as the SFPD found the note, the Feds showed up and took over."

As Pernell described the events surrounding the most recent murder, a tingling went down my spine. Unless my intuition was way off, the case was beginning to resemble a spider web. Threads, seemingly unrelated, were coming together toward an as-yet-unknown axis. Fitzpatrick had told me about a girl from a nearby university. A girl who had disappeared. My disbelief in coincidence had never been stronger.

"The girl...was her name Sandra?"

Pernell drained the rest of his bourbon. "Yeah. Collins. Sandra Collins."

He got up from the table and excused himself. My mind was racing. What was the common denominator between Fitzpatrick, Malloy, Kettler, and this young woman, Sandra Collins? There were too few details, too many implications. I lit a cigarette. It helped, though it didn't seem to have instant answers.

"Are you Mr. Murphy?"

"Yes?"

The waitress picked up the bourbon glasses and wiped down

the table. "Phone call for you. On the pay phone...over there."

Another noncoincidence. Someone was calling me on a pay phone in a bar I'd never been in before.

"Murphy here."

The voice was being fed through a modulator. The video relay was off, of course. "Listen carefully, Mr. Murphy. You're on a very dangerous path. I want to see you reach the end of it, but there are many who will do anything to stop you. Even now, your name is reaching the ears of powerful people, people capable of removing all traces of your existence. If you fail, it will be as if you never lived a day on this earth. But there are more important things at stake than your life. Do you understand?"

I really didn't, but I was just going along for the ride, and this guy was driving. "I'm pretty sure I do."

"Good. In one hour and four minutes, you will be at 771 Santa Cena. There is a stairwell on the east side of the building. Go down two flights and wait by the red door. At exactly 2:45, you will hear a click. Open the door, enter, and close the door immediately. Move quickly to the third door on the left. Wait for another click, then enter the office. Check your watch. You will have exactly five minutes to search the office. There will be another click, and you will leave the office. The same thing will happen at the door where you entered. Do you understand?"

I finished jotting down the information. "Yes. But what will happen if I don't..."

Dial tone. I switched off the vid-phone receiver. My PI instincts were napping on this one. Was it legitimate, or was I being set up? The mystery caller had known I was here and probably could have killed me, if he'd felt like it—but he hadn't. That was encouraging...sort of. As much as I hated to, it seemed like the mystery caller would have to fall, provisionally, into the

"Friends of Tex" category. I slipped my notebook back into my coat pocket and returned to Pernell. He'd ordered another round of bourbons, pulled out a notebook and pencil, and seemed ready to give me the third degree.

"I don't suppose you'd tell me the name of your client."

"Sorry. Confidential."

"At least tell me the details of how you got the notes."

"Wish I could. Unfortunately, it would violate my solemn PI oath."

"How 'bout letting me have the notes?"

I considered it. They probably weren't going to help my investigation, but they were evidence. I wasn't sure I should give them up. "What do you want 'em for?"

"Visual aids, man. This story has Pulitzer written all over it."

"Tell you what. I'll give you one of the notes in exchange for any other information you come up with."

"Deal." Pernell pulled a business card from his jacket and handed it to me. "That number's current. I know how to reach you."

I took the card and handed over one of the notes. "I've gotta get going. Is there anything else you think I should know?"

Pernell rubbed his chin thoughtfully. "Your client is certainly in danger. She should have someone with her at all times."

Either this guy wasn't as bright as I'd thought, or I was a lot brighter than he thought. Like smart enough to tie my own shoes.

"OK. Is there anything *you* know that I *don't* know and *should* know?"

"One more thing. When I was following the story in Nevada, I met a guy like you. PI. He asked a lot of questions. A week later, he had a tag on his toe. Suicide, I think."

I threw a fifty on the table. "Thanks for the tip."

Chapter
Six

The building complex at 771 Santa Cena was no different than a dozen others within a ten-block radius. Nicely landscaped, on the plain side. Functional, not flashy. The sign on the front said AUTOTECH. I found the stairwell on the east side and slipped quickly down the stairs. Outside the red door, I checked my watch. I was early...and nervous. Time for a Lucky.

I heard a parental voice in the back of my mind: *Do you do everything your friends tell you to? What if they were all jumping off a cliff?* I dropped the cigarette butt and crushed it under my shoe. The door clicked—I opened it and stepped inside. The interior was as sterile as a tongue depressor. Gray carpet, gray walls, gray fluorescent lights. No decorative touches in sight. I pulled the door closed behind me and hurried toward the third door on the left. I was several paces away when I heard a faint clicking sound. They certainly weren't leaving me any margin of error. I grabbed the door handle and pulled.

It was an office. I was a bit disappointed. I'd figured on something a little more, well, startling. I checked my watch. 2:46. Five minutes to search an entire office. Luck and speed. I was hoping for luck.

A computer sat on a desk; I flipped it on and began searching the desk as it booted. I tore open the drawers, rifling as fast as humanly possible. Probably hundreds of important documents, but nothing struck me as relevant to my search. I turned to the first of two tall filing cabinets, quickly checking the time. It was

2:47. I opened the top drawer and leafed through a batch of manila folders. Photographs, autopsies, receipts. It all looked interesting, but again, nothing useful. I turned to the second filing cabinet. All the drawers were locked. 2:48. The wall was bare, except for a certificate bearing an unfamiliar insignia, and several photographs. I didn't bother to inspect the certificate, but pulled the frame from the wall and checked the back. Nothing.

One of the photographs showed a middle-aged man shaking hands with former President Linderman. I checked it and the other picture and came up empty. 2:49—less than two minutes left. A wastebasket, bookshelf, and Rolodex turned up nothing obvious. The computer was asking for a password. There wasn't enough time. 2:50. I swung my head around, scanning the office for something—anything. A laser disc player sat on a table in the corner. A stack of recordable laser discs was piled underneath. I inadvertently brushed against the small tower of discs, toppling them. Instinctively, I glanced over my shoulder to see if the clatter had attracted any attention. When I looked back at the disheveled pile of discs, I spotted a tiny metal key lying on the floor.

I picked it up and rushed to the locked filing cabinet. Twenty seconds left. I started at the top. No...no...no. I jammed the key into the bottom keyhole and turned it. Tumblers fell, and the lock surrendered. I grabbed the drawer handle and pulled. The interior of the drawer was empty except for a small, antique tin with the Camel logo on the cover. I picked it up. Across the room, the door clicked.

Bolting to my feet, I lunged for the door. Cradling the tin, I hit the door with my shoulder; it opened. Like a halfback breaking through the line and heading for six, I spun to my right and raced down the hall. The door clicked a nanosecond before I hit it. I was on the stairs, running like a madman. Despite the adrenaline rushing through my system, I was sucking air hard by the time I reached my speeder. God, I was out of shape.

The speeder lifted off, and I was screaming back toward the old city. I checked the radar display and decided that I wasn't being followed. My breathing slowly returned to normal. The Camel tin lay innocuously in the passenger seat. Panic gripped me for a moment. What if I'd screwed up? Maybe the tin contained nothing but matchbooks.

I sat at my desk, the Camel tin in front of me. My office was dark, except for the lamplight. The LCD flashed a "3" on my voice messaging unit. They would have to wait. I pushed my thumbs against the front edge of the tin lid. I felt like Charlie opening his Wonka bar. I lifted the lid. The tin was full of photographs.

I sorted through the pictures, holding one at a time under the lamp. Several of the photos on top of the pile clearly showed Emily Sue Patterson in various stages of nudity, but most of the others showed nothing more than close-ups of Emily's apartment's interior. At the bottom of the tin were three photographs of a different young woman. Obviously taken without the subject's knowledge, two of these pictures showed the girl in front of a large building, apparently on a college campus. The other photo showed her in what appeared to be her bedroom. Sandra Collins?

I examined the photographs of Emily closely. She certainly was a piece of work. God had probably taken the rest of the day off after making her. Good thing it was my job to inspect the pictures thoroughly. I scanned every square inch, then moved onto the *other* things in the pictures. Except for Emily, there was nothing unusual in the photographs. The shots of the empty apartment were definitely the room above the Fuchsia Flamingo. Where had these pictures been taken from? Finding the source seemed to be the next step.

I lit a smoke and stood at the window, looking down at Chandler Avenue. The pictures of Emily had been taken from a vantage point directly opposite the Flamingo. Rusty's Fun House. I stared down at the vacant novelty shop. All the windows were dark, though the evil-leering harlequins that adorned the store's facade were lit up by a streetlight. An ancient water tower sat atop the building like a dunce cap. I followed the line starting at the Flamingo and passing through the water tower. The closest building behind Rusty's was a good quarter mile distant. Technically, the shots could have been taken from the far building, but I doubted it. I needed to find a way up to the roof above Rusty's.

Chelsee's newsstand was closed. It occurred to me that she might have left one of the messages on the answering machine back in my office. I'd forgotten to check them. The door to Rusty's was locked, and a sign was posted: *SFPD Crime Scene! Authorized Personnel Only!*

It was just after 4:00 A.M. and the street was still dark. I could hear Emily singing "Misty" inside the Fuchsia Flamingo, but there was no one out and about on the street. I stepped back and kicked the door, just under the lock. A white flash of excruciating pain shot up my leg—I'd caught my toe on the knob. I hopped around for a minute, running through a list of creative expletives that would've made my grandpa proud. When the searing pain finally subsided to a dull ache, I tried again. This time shoulder first. The door gave way, and I burst inside.

I'd had the foresight to bring a flashlight. I turned it on and flashed it around the shop. Everything looked the same as the last time I'd been there, except for a strip of yellow barrier tape placed across the doorway into Rusty's back room. A few months ago, I'd tipped Mac Malden off about the location of Rusty's remains, which I'd discovered over the course of my last big case. A two-bit crook named Mick Flemm had dumped Rusty, big shoes and all, into a barrel of toxic acid stashed in Rusty's darkroom. Naturally, Mac took all the credit for wrapping up the previously unsolved murder and parlayed it into a promotion. I didn't care; my contact in the police force was higher up the ladder, and I was privy to better information.

Nothing had changed in the back room either, except that the barrel of acid had been removed. I started a systematic search. There had to be a way up to the roof somewhere. Half an hour later, I found the entrance, on the wall opposite the front door, under a shelf full of rubber masks. The door was small, like an access panel to a crawl space. I pulled the panel off the wall and flashed a light into the hole. The room behind was pitch black. I set the flashlight on the other side, then squeezed through the opening.

I stood up slowly, moving the beam of light steadily around the interior. The room had odd dimensions, maybe eight feet wide and fifteen feet long. The space above me rose to the level of the roof, at least twenty feet. A few boxes lay strewn about the floor, empty or full of worthless-looking novelty items. At the far end of the chamber, a metal ladder was bolted to the wall.

The ladder led to a trap door in the ceiling...rusty, naturally. I pushed it open and crawled out onto the roof. The lights of New San Francisco sparkled in the distance. The water tower stood exactly between me and the Fuchsia Flamingo. The tower was old and corroded. A rickety ladder led to a small door, high up on the side. A new-looking, sturdy chain and large padlock were attached to the door handle. I suspected I'd found the stalker's lair.

It didn't look like he was home, unless he was some sort of Houdini wannabe.

The padlock wasn't coming off without a key, and I was fresh out of padlock keys. I decided to look for another way in. The reservoir of the water tower was suspended above the roof on four rusted support legs. It looked like a decrepit, metal-shop version of an early lunar landing craft. I walked under the belly of the reservoir and scanned the surface. In the center, I found what appeared to be an eroded panel. A small handle on the panel was just wide enough to wedge four fingers in. I hung on the handle, pulling myself up and down. A sudden cracking sound made me hesitate. Either the panel was coming loose, or the handle was going to rip off. Putting all my weight back on the handle, I expected to drop painfully onto my knees at any moment. A few seconds later, the panel ripped open violently, showering me with rust confetti and decades-old dust.

With no small effort, I pulled myself up into the water tower. I made a mental note to ease up on the Coffee-Mate and get back on my Bullworker program. I laid flat on my back on the reservoir floor, catching my breath and hoping I wouldn't be too sore the next day. After a short rest, I pulled the flashlight from my trench coat and checked out my surroundings. The floor was composed of wooden planks, warped and stained and loaded with splinters. The sides of the tank were copper, rusted to blue-green. The flashlight beam circled the innards of the tank until it crossed the legs of a tripod. I moved the light up the legs until the beam rested on the point where the three supports met.

A camera.

It was an expensive piece of equipment. The lens pointed toward a small hole that had been cut in the wall. I leaned over and put my eye to the viewfinder. Couldn't see a thing. I removed the lens cap and checked the viewfinder again. Still dark, though not lens-cap dark. Pushing a small button popped open a door, revealing a number of switches and knobs. Looking again through the viewfinder, I began to flip switches randomly. The third or fourth switch did the trick. My vision suddenly turned green, giving me a blurry view of Emily's unlit apartment. Careful to leave the last switch in place, I played with the other switches and knobs until the picture became clear. With a few minutes of experimentation, I was able to get unbelievable detail. I could read the title of a magazine from a distance of at least thirty meters.

I pulled the view back far enough so I could get a good look through all three windows in Emily's apartment. A slight movement caught my eye. Trying not to blink, I concentrated on the spot where I'd seen the movement. Minutes passed. Suddenly, a figure emerged from Emily's bedroom. It appeared to be a man, dressed in black and masked. He was carrying an object under his arm. The mysterious figure walked toward the door that led out of the apartment, but didn't open it. Instead, he moved to his right and disappeared behind a dresser. I watched for several minutes, but the masked man didn't show himself again.

I straightened up from the camera. The man was waiting for Emily. I needed to move quickly! I lowered myself to the roof and hurried toward the trap door. The faint sound of applause and whistling came from the direction of the Flamingo. Emily had finished her set. The man was going to kill her. I stumbled down the ladder and ran to the hole in the wall. Dropping onto my belly, I wriggled through the opening, struggled to my feet, and ran for the door. Bursting through Rusty's front door, I sprinted across the street. I wasn't going to get there in time. The bouncer had no time to react as I raced past him. Heads turned as I sped toward the stairs. Out of the corner of my eye, I caught sight of

Gus Leach moving to intercept me. He was a step behind—I vaulted up the stairs. Gus was swearing a blue streak, his pounding footsteps at my heels.

I reached the door to Emily's apartment. My hand had just curled over the doorknob when I was spun around and hit by a large rock. As I crumpled, Leach grabbed me by the lapels of my overcoat and slammed me into the door.

"I told you not to come back here."

"There's someone in Emily's apartment. He's gonna kill her!"

Leach raised his fist.

"I swear to God, Leach! Someone's in there!"

The mutant hesitated, then pushed me aside. His hand went to the doorknob. It didn't move. Leach glanced down at me, then back at the door. Taking a step backward, he lowered his shoulder and smashed through the door. A gunshot. Still dizzy from Leach's right hook, I braced myself and started to stand up. A figure in black burst through the doorway and hurdled me. I staggered to my feet and followed the man down the stairs. At the base of the stairs, the emergency exit door slammed shut. I reached the door and flung it open. Ducking my head out and back, I caught sight of the man racing out of the alley, an object cradled in the crook of his left arm.

I followed the fleeing man onto Chandler Avenue, then back into the alley where the fire escape leads to my office. He ran to the end of the alley and turned left. I followed and looked down the long passage that runs behind the Electronics Shop and the Brew & Stew. He was increasing his lead. Instead of following him, I doubled back and ran out to the street. I headed straight for the newsstand and dove for cover. Peering over the counter I saw nothing. I waited a minute, maybe two, then decided to move. As I straightened up I saw the killer come out from behind the Brew

& Stew and dash across the street, toward the fence between the pawnshop and the Slice O' Heaven. Without much effort, he scaled the fence and dropped into the alley beyond.

I moved as quietly as possible toward the fence. The sound of clanging footsteps was barely audible. He was climbing the ladder to the roof over Rook's Pawnshop. This guy obviously had done his homework on getting around the neighborhood. I couldn't understand why he wanted to be on the roof, but it was my neighborhood, and I *did* know a way to cut him off.

I followed the hidden trail through Rusty's and climbed the ladder to the roof. I opened the trap door slowly, fully expecting a bullet in the face. With a level of stealth that surprised even myself, I slipped out of the trap door and closed it behind me. Hunkering down behind a large swamp cooler, I listened for the sound of footsteps. I heard nothing, except the distant city sounds and excited voices drifting up from the direction of the Flamingo.

Until I heard the speeder. It had to be a Black Avatar. It sounded nothing like my little Lotus model. The engine had a deep throb of staggering power. Only the government and drug lords owned speeders like that. I searched the night sky. It took several moments to locate the speeder—it was flying with the lights off. The Black Avatar was no more than a hundred meters away, moving slowly, headed straight toward me.

Suddenly, I saw my quarry jump up and wave his arms, his back toward me, facing the oncoming speeder. He was on the sunken section of roof between Rusty's and the pawnshop, maybe ten meters from me. The speeder was closing in. I got to my feet and ran toward the man. As I leaped toward him, he saw or heard me, but had no time to dodge or fire his gun. I hit him square, and we fell in a stunned heap. He was the first to recover and planted a fist into the side of my head. As I reeled back, I saw the speeder hovering a short distance away. I managed to unleash a kick into the man's ribs, which left him gasping for breath. Then I got to my feet and lunged, but he avoided me neatly and jammed an elbow into the space between my shoulder blades. I dropped to my hands and knees. A boot slammed into my ribs, rolling me onto my side.

The man moved away from me, toward the edge of the roof overlooking the street. His gun had been thrown clear, three or four meters from where he'd left me. I grabbed a handful of loose gravel. As he bent to pick up his gun, I gathered the last of my strength and jumped to my feet. Everything shifted into slow motion. I started to run toward the man. He looked up, saw me, raised his gun. I threw the gravel. He flinched and threw his left arm up to cover his face. The gun went off. I lowered my shoulder, felt it hit his chest. Another gunshot. He staggered backwards, hit the barrier at the edge of the roof, and toppled over the side. The gun went off again. A scream, the fall, the horrible sound of crushing bones.

The Black Avatar shifted down and sped off into the night.

Chapter
Seven

"Coffee, wheat toast, eggs over easy."

Mac Malden leaned way back in his chair and pulled a Merit out from under his mustache.

"What do I look like, Murphy? A damn waiter?"

"OK, then, a cup of coffee and a doughnut."

"There's nothin' here to eat."

He reached around his gut and stuffed the cigarette butt into the hollow center of a ceramic dog. Slumping back in his chair, he folded his hands atop the lumpy dome that ran from his sternum to well past his belt. No shame, no attempt at camouflage. Oh, they warned him about high cholesterol, the heart attack risk. He even cut back on a few things, like pastrami, egg rolls. But Mac loved his gut and was damn proud of it. Never in a million years would he turn his back on his gut.

"No doughnuts?"

Mac shook his head and reached for another cigarette.

"You've gotta be yanking me. A *huge* building, *full* of cops...*no* doughnuts?"

"You know, Murphy, I get so damn tired of those half-ass doughnut gags, I could puke. I'm not serving breakfast here. All I wanna do is ask you a few questions, listen to some of your stupid jokes, maybe get a couple coherent statements out of you, and kick your butt out of my office. Then you can buy your *own* breakfast."

He stared at me, looking for all the world like a basset hound, exhausted from a trip to the slippers. "What d'ya say? Are you gonna play along?"

It was late, at least 10:30 A.M. It had been five or six hours since Emily's would-be murderer hit Chandler Avenue. I was still on the roof in mid-Lucky when the cops showed up. They called me down, and I got a look at the face of the Black Arrow Killer. It was the same mug I'd seen in the photo at 771 Santa Cena, shaking hands with President Linderman.

The cops took my statement, then asked me if I'd like to come with them and try the new coffee blend down at the station. I happened to know that their coffee tasted like camel spit—they were just being civil. At the SFPD complex, I was politely asked to take a seat and enjoy one of the many fine magazines available. Some of them were no more than two years old.

There was no smoking allowed in the waiting room. Instead, they had a TV. It was a crappy trade-off. I made one attempt to step outside for a breath of unfiltered refreshment, but the sergeant assigned to keep an eye on me didn't like the idea much. Damn nonsmokers.

After what seemed like an eternity in cold turkey/network TV purgatory, I was escorted to Mac Malden's office. By the time the sergeant closed the door behind me, I had my Lucky Strike in hand, already half-smoked. Two other men were in the room, nice suits, standing in the corners. Being outnumbered always brings out the antagonist in me.

It turned out that Mac had been investigating a homicide all morning and it was now almost 11:00 A.M.—way past his bedtime. He always did the questioning whenever I got hauled in. Threatening me with jail time always seemed to cheer him up, but now he was too sleepy to enjoy it.

Mac planted his elbows on the desk and leaned forward. "OK.

Let's forget about breakfast and get this over with. Take it from the top. And for God's sakes, not too many details. I should be in bed, dreaming of egg rolls."

I recounted my story completely, leaving out only minor details, like Fitzpatrick, Malloy, the mysterious vid-phone call, and the jaunt through 771 Santa Cena. After I finished, Mac didn't seem to be satisfied with my version of things. The two suits didn't move.

"So that's the whole story."

"Yup."

"You're sure."

"Absolutely."

Mac burned another Merit. I glanced down and saw that he'd left another one half-smoked in the ceramic dog. Poor sap. Obviously a helpless slave to nicotine.

"Did you know the victim?"

"Who, Emily?"

"No, the one you threw off the roof. The girl's gonna be fine."

"Good to hear. What about Leach?"

"The big mutant? I guess a slug nicked him, nothing serious. Now answer the damn question—did you know the guy you threw off the roof?"

"I didn't throw anyone off the roof. Like I told you, we were Rollerblading...things got out of hand. He jammed his front wheel, and...well, you know the rest."

"Knock it off, Murphy. You seem to forget I'm a cop. A tired, hungry, pissed-off cop. If you don't get off my nerves, I'll toss you in the drunk tank, and we'll try again tomorrow."

Lord, he was a grouch at this hour of the morning, and the well-tailored statues in the corners didn't seem to be helping his disposition. To ease the tension, I proceeded to tell him what had actually happened on the roof. Mac glanced through a sheaf of papers, then waved his hand toward the door.

"OK, get outta here. Your story matches up."

I got out of my chair. "Matches up? With what?"

Mac looked up at me wearily. "We have a witness. You're clear...get lost. Hey, Robinson!"

The door opened, and the young cop who'd kept me from losing at least another seven minutes off my life poked his head into the office. "Yes, sir?"

"Escort Mr. Murphy out of my office. He's free to go."

The young cop nodded. "Oh, and while you're at it, find Ms. Madsen and tell her she can go, too."

I started after Officer Robinson.

"By the way, Murphy! Don't go on any sudden trips for a few days. We may want to ask you some more questions."

"Why would I take a trip, Mac? Around here, every day's a vacation."

Mac waved me out. I stopped by a vending machine and spent $2.50 on a cup of hot camel spit. As I passed the waiting room, Officer Robinson was speaking to an extraordinarily attractive woman. The young cop tipped his hat and walked away, leaving her to gather her coat and purse. According to Mac, this woman had been my star witness. It was fate. I moved in. Destiny had a smell; it was warm and musky. I doffed my fedora.

"Good morning."

"Hello."

My future partner in eternal bliss seemed to be uninformed of, or at least oblivious to, the aura of destiny that surrounded us. Laying her coat gracefully across her arm, she prepared to walk off with my heart crammed into her handbag.

"I hope you won't think I'm being forward."

She glanced up at me with clear eyes. "I won't. Excuse me, please."

She glided past me. I moved quickly to intercept her before she could reach the automatic doors. "Listen. My name's Tex Murphy, and I understand that you just did me a real big favor. I'd like to, you know, repay the debt."

"Thank you, but I'm really not interested."

She was cool. Very cool. Charm was exuding from my every pore. Yet somehow she resisted. It was only a matter of time.

"You want to have dinner tonight?"

"I was planning on having dinner, just not with you."

Ouch. Deep in my psyche, Commander Hormone called for a retreat. I moved aside. The beautiful woman swept through the sliding doors, down the steps, out of my life, and into the shuttle entrance.

Breakfast or sleep? Food generally takes a backseat to almost everything. I took a taxi back to my office and caught a quick power nap. When I woke up, it was late afternoon, and my initial hunger had passed. It was just as well; I always think more clearly on an empty stomach. After firing up a pot of java and a breakfast Cubana, I sat down at my desk and ran through a mental list of things to get done.

I needed to find out the identity of the man I'd run into last night. For now, I'd call him...Bob. Between the clandestine caller at the Twilight and the photographs of Sandra Collins, I had to conclude that Bob was not just a run-of-the-mill pervert. The fact that he appeared to have been searching Emily's apartment implied another agenda besides serial killing. And what about the mysterious Black Avatar speeder? No, Bob was a part of something bigger. Much bigger.

I also needed to make a stop at the Fuchsia Flamingo. I needed more information about Malloy, and it seemed Emily was the only person I knew who could help. And what about the object Bob had been carrying last night? Something told me that it was important. Maybe Emily could give me a lead on it. What kind of shape would she be in after last night's experiences?

My voice-messaging unit beeped. I took a sip of coffee and leaned over to check the display. Five messages. I hit the Play button and settled back into my chair.

The first voice was Chelsee's. "Hi, Tex. Chelsee. Just wanted to see how you're doing. Bye."

The next was a hang-up.

The third was from Fitzpatrick. "Hello, Mr. Murphy. Please call me at your convenience."

Number four was Chelsee again. "Hey, Tex. Just wanted to see if you got my first message. Call me."

The final message was from Lucas Pernell. "Got something for ya. Get a hold of me ASAP."

I hit the reset button and finished my cup of coffee. Three more things to do. I prioritized: clients first, love interests second, informants third. After refilling my coffee mug, I pulled out Fitzpatrick's business card and entered the phone code.

"Hello?"

Fitzpatrick's disconcerting eyes and transparent face flashed onto my view screen.

"Mr. Fitzpatrick. I just got your message. I assume that you called to get an update on the investigation."

"If it's not too much trouble. I certainly hope I'm not inconveniencing you."

"Not at all. Keeping the client informed is part of the deluxe investigative package."

"Wonderful! So tell me, how are your efforts progressing?"

"Very well. I've been able to track down a girl Malloy was seeing recently. I'm about to go see her. I have high hopes that she'll give us some useful information."

"Excellent! Anything else?"

I paused to take another sip of coffee. "I have several other leads, but I won't know how valuable they are until I track them down."

"Well, I won't take any more of your time. If it's not an annoyance, I'd appreciate it if you'd keep me informed as to your progress."

"I'll be happy to."

"Thank you, Mr. Murphy. Good-bye."

The screen went black. Fitzpatrick's obvious impatience was equaled only by his monumental politeness. Though he'd never said anything about a time limit, his tone implied that there was one. My PI instinct said that Fitzpatrick hadn't told me everything. Not by a long shot.

Chelsee either wasn't home or wasn't answering. I left a short message. Concise, yet caring. Romantic, yet noncommittal. I liked Chelsee a lot. Hell, maybe I was even in love with her. Unfortunately, at the moment I was too occupied to decide. Everything had been so much easier back when she'd just blow me off every time I asked her out. This new phase in our romantic development was throwing me for a loop. Maybe she *should* move to Phoenix for awhile. Give us time to sort things through. Besides, I couldn't stop thinking about that knockout at the police station—even though she hadn't seemed too knocked out by me.

I'd think it over later. For now, I was working. I found Pernell's card and punched up the phone code. Two chimes, and the journalist's haggard mug appeared on the screen.

"Just got your message. What's up?"

"Big doin's, Murphy. You got some time?"

I glanced at my watch. It was still pretty early. "Sure. Where?"

"I'll let you know," he growled. "I hate talking on these damn vid-phones. Too easy to wire."

"OK, but make it soon. I've got a full dance card today."

"No problem."

I filled and downed my third cup of joe, satisfying my USDA-recommended caffeine requirement. I was wide awake and rearing to go. The fax machine beeped and belched. I tore off the sheet. *Liverpool Club. 15 minutes.*

The Liverpool Club was a hidden gem in an urban slag heap. It was more of a social club than a bar, though I didn't hold that against it. Solid oak billiard tables, boar-bristle dartboards, tin-paneled ceilings. A nice place. If I hung out with Pernell for any length of time, I might get to know every watering hole in the city. Not an unpleasant thought.

Pernell was lurking in a dark nook. He seemed to have an aversion to bright lights. A lot of my business associates had photophobia. Two bourbons were already busy breathing on the table. It was a little early for the hard stuff, but I decided to call it lunch and move on to more important things.

"What've you got?"

Pernell's voice hissed out of the corner of his mouth. "Remember the story I told you about Kettler?"

My mouth was full of bourbon. I nodded.

"I've still got a contact down in Nevada. He found a cop that knew enough to be useful and was willing to talk. It's huge."

"Unbelievable. An unethical cop. In Nevada, of all places."

"Well, it cost us a bit, but he came through. I've got a copy of his sworn statement locked away in a safe-deposit box. I'd let you see it, but I enjoy being alive. If certain people caught me with the goods, I'd be pushing up daisies by the weekend." Pernell took a hearty slug off his bourbon. His hands were shaking. I couldn't tell whether it was fear or excitement. Probably both.

"Our cop was in on Kettler's arrest. He also sat in on the initial questioning, before the Feds showed up. Kettler confessed to everything. The local boys made up a deposition, and Kettler signed it. The problem is, after the Feds took over, the deposition disappeared, never to be found."

I tried to sort out what Pernell was saying. The Feds knew that Kettler was guilty but didn't want that information to get out. It didn't make sense. It did seem to connect to the curious fact that the Black Arrow Killer, who was dead, had supposedly gone back into business, this time in the Bay Area.

I gave Pernell a rundown of what had happened the night before, hoping that bouncing it off him would give me a fresh perspective, a new lead or two. He listened avidly through another round of Jack Daniels. When I finished, Pernell leaned back and stared up at the ceiling. "Can I bum another cig off ya?"

I handed one over and lit it for him. He smoked like he'd just had sex with Marilyn Monroe. And Jayne Mansfield. At the same time.

"You know who uses Black Avatars? The military." He blew out a long stream of smoke and rejoined the ranks of the carnally deprived. "Tell me again about what this guy, Bob, was doing in the girl's apartment."

"Like I said, he came out of her bedroom, holding an object of some kind. Then he hid by the door and waited for her."

"And this object...it wasn't a jewelry case or something similar—something of value?"

"Didn't look like it. A plain metal box. Like a box you keep recipes in."

"But the girl had valuables in the apartment?"

I tried to recall. "I think so. I seem to remember some jewelry, a couple things worth stealing."

Pernell leaned toward me. I could hear the wheels turning. "So the bottom line is, his primary reason for being in the apartment wasn't to murder the girl. It wasn't even to rob the place. It was to find this object."

It seemed logical. Then a thought occurred to me. "Well, if that's the case, why didn't he just leave? He had what he came for. Why would he try to kill Emily?"

Pernell thought it over and shrugged. "She knew about the box. Maybe the guy wanted to kill her to keep anyone else from finding out about it."

The implications were huge. If what Pernell had told me was reliable and Kettler *had* been the serial killer, some group was mimicking the crimes in order to cover the murders they committed in the course of doing their business. And it was possible that some branch of the government was that group. And I'd become a fly in their ointment. I looked around. I already knew that someone had been watching me. I wondered just how many eyes were on me now.

"I've gotta check in with Emily. Thanks for the drinks."

Pernell was scribbling furiously on a steno pad. He didn't seem to hear me.

Chapter
Eight

The Fuchsia Flamingo hadn't opened yet, and the doors were locked. I pounded a few times and waited. A minute later, the door swung open, revealing Gus Leach's massive frame. He looked beat.

"C'mon in." I'd never imagined the mutant could sound so friendly.

The room was dark, except for a soft white light emanating from behind the bar on the far side. I followed Leach to the light and pulled up beside him on a sparkling purple bar stool. The drink in front of him was at least a triple. He raised the glass to his mouth and reduced it to a shot. He shivered slightly and turned to face me.

"I'm glad you came by. I hope you didn't have any problems with the police."

"Nothing serious."

Leach nodded and got up from his seat. He walked wearily around to the back of the bar. "Want a drink?"

"Sure."

"Bourbon, right?"

"How'd you guess?"

"Physiognomy. It's a hobby of mine."

He filled a glass, neat. Just the way I like it. "You can tell almost anything about a person from their facial features."

"Really? So I have a bourbon face?"

"Something like that." Leach poured himself a quadruple

Bacardi, straight. I tried not to stare. "I really want to thank you for what you did last night. You saved Emily's life."

"How's she doing?"

"It shook her up pretty good, but she isn't hurt. If you'd shown up any later..." He shook his head. "She's upstairs, trying to get some rest."

I took a deep drink. Leach had given me the good stuff. I swirled it around and took a delicate sip. I raised my glass, but he was looking away. Then I turned to see Emily coming down the stairway. Leach set his drink down and walked over to meet her.

"I'm fine, Gus. I just couldn't sleep anymore." She walked toward me and settled onto a bar stool. She was wearing a green, crushed velvet robe. Despite the dark circles under her eyes, she was still stunning.

"Gus told me what you did. I don't know how to thank you."

I could think of a few ways, but it probably wasn't the right time to go into detail. "It was a close shave. I'm just glad you're OK."

Leach was behind the bar, mixing a Bloody Mary. He tossed a celery stalk into the concoction and placed it in front of Emily.

"Thanks." She took a sip. She didn't look like she was in the mood to answer questions, but I didn't have the luxury of delaying my investigation.

"Listen, Emily. I need to ask you about a few things, if you don't mind."

Leach leaned onto the bar. "C'mon, Murphy. She's been through enough. The cops already grilled her last night. Give it a rest for awhile."

"It's OK, Gus. I owe him. Answering a few questions isn't any big deal."

She turned to me and took a deep breath. "Go ahead."

"The man who attacked you took something from your apartment. A box of some kind. What was it?"

"I don't know. I mean, I don't know what was in it. It was a weird box...it didn't open. At least I couldn't figure out how to open it."

"Where did it come from? Do you have any idea why someone would want to steal it?"

Emily glanced up at Gus.

"You don't need to tell him anything. It's none of his business."

Emily looked pensively into the tomato juice and stirred it with the celery stalk. After a long pause, she turned and looked straight into my eyes. "The box was sent to me by Thomas. Thomas Malloy. My husband."

I picked up my bourbon and took a long drink. This was a fine how-do-you-do. Everything I'd seen and heard over the past few days had suddenly shifted around ninety degrees.

"Pardon me for being stupid, but let me get this straight. You're Thomas Malloy's wife?"

"We were married about a year ago. I used to work at another club here in the city. Gus was the manager. That's where I met Thomas. He used to come in and watch me sing. He was so sweet and lonely."

"So, where is your husband?"

"I don't know," she said quietly.

"But he sent the box to you."

"That's right. It came yesterday."

"And there was no indication of where he'd sent it from?"

Emily shook her head. "The box was wrapped in plain brown paper. There was no return address, no letter or anything inside. Just the box."

"How do you know it was from your husband?"

"I recognized his writing on the outside."

I wanted to take a look at the paper the box had been wrapped in. Even without a return address, something about the wrapping might help me track down Malloy. "What did you do with the paper?"

Emily shrugged. "I threw it out, I guess. I don't know where it is."

I'd look for it later. For now, I needed to keep Emily talking.

"Why did Malloy leave? Did he give you any reason for not telling you where he'd be?" The muscles around Emily's mouth tensed, and Leach half-rose from his chair. Immediately, I knew I'd crossed into sensitive territory. I quickly rephrased the question.

"Do you think your husband left because he was in danger?"

Emily didn't respond, but the look on her face said enough.

Everything fell into place. I turned to Leach. "You're a friend of Malloy's, right? He left Emily here and asked you to take care of her until he came back."

Leach glanced nervously at Emily. When he looked back at me, he nodded. Suddenly, I was the only one talking. "Listen, all I want to do is find Malloy. I'm not one of the bad guys."

Both of them were still looking at me.

"OK. One more question, and I'll get out of here. Do either of you know why Malloy's on the run?"

Emily cleared her throat and took a sip of her drink. "Thomas never talked about his work. He said it was better that way, safer for me. I honestly don't know why he left," she said wistfully.

A dumpster sat in the alley by the side door to the Flamingo.

With any luck, the wrapping paper would be inside. Dumpster searching hadn't been a part of my PI training curriculum. The movies that inspired me to become a detective never showed that part of the job. Oh, well. I rolled up my sleeves and dug in.

It was stinking, rotten work. Damp tissues, gum, coffee grounds, little hairy slabs of food. It reminded me of the buffet restaurant my fat Uncle Monty always took me to. I was glad I hadn't eaten anything.

Eventually it paid off. I'd gotten lucky. The brown paper wrapper had been stuffed into a garbage bag with a stack of newspapers and was stain (and smell) free.

I stepped inside my office. Laying the wrapper on the desk, I went to my file cabinet to retrieve my investigative props. Kneeling down, I opened the bottom drawer.

They'd been moved.

I looked through the other drawers in the cabinet and the desk. Nothing seemed to be missing, but someone had certainly searched my office. I inspected the locks on the door to the fire escape, as well as the windows. There was no sign of forced entry. Whoever had broken in had either gotten hold of my access code, or was a consummate professional. Neither possibility was very appealing.

I sat down and lit a Lucky Strike, trying to relax and come up with a rational explanation. Maybe Nilo had gotten bored and decided to snoop around some of the rooms. Unlikely. Nilo would've stolen something. Maybe I'd forgotten to lock the door...no, I was certain I'd locked it.

I didn't want to accept the fact that a professional had gone through my place. Unfortunately, there was no other reasonable explanation. I speculated on why nothing had been taken. Then a thought hit me. The box. Whoever had been in cahoots with the phony Black Arrow Killer knew about the box and hadn't located it. Logically, they'd figure that the police or I had ended up with it.

The vid-phone chimed.

"Hello."

"Murphy? This is Malden."

I flipped on my video relay. Mac looked worried and rushed. "We've gotta meet. Right now."

"Uh..."

"No questions. Meet me at the usual place as soon as you can get there. Bring that woman and your cigarettes. And make sure no one follows you." He switched off the feed.

I had no idea what Mac was talking about. He and I had never met anywhere outside of a crime scene or the precinct. Who was the woman he referred to? Ms. Madsen? He couldn't possibly think that I'd know how to find her. I couldn't come up with any other woman that Mac would have in mind. And why the reference to my cigarettes? I thought it over. Maybe Mac knew that someone was listening in and couldn't actually name the place where he wanted to meet. The woman and the cigarettes must be clues.

I punched up the city directory on my computer. First, I checked for any place called the Lucky Strike. There wasn't one. But there were several places with the word "Lucky" in the name. As I scrolled through the list, a name jumped out at me. The Lucky Lady Café. My cigarettes, a woman. I jotted down the address and hurried out to my speeder.

Ten minutes later, I walked into a greasy spoon on the other end of town. Remembering what Mac had said, I'd been careful not to be followed. Mac was sitting in a booth away from the windows, eating a frosted cake doughnut and sipping coffee.

"I hope this is important. Perry Mason was on, and I'd just

made some espresso."

Mac's face was as serious as a face can be with sprinkles and frosting on it. "The NSA is probably at your office right now. They were coming to get you."

It took a moment to sink in. "What does the NSA want with me?"

Mac washed down the last bite of doughnut with a slug of foul-smelling coffee. "Remember the guy you tossed off the roof?"

"I didn't toss him off the roof," I said indignantly.

"Whatever. Turns out he was an agent. An NSA special agent."

Oh, God.

Mac took a bite out of another doughnut. Glazed.

"His name was Dag Horton. The information came about half an hour ago. Five minutes later, word came through the office that they were gonna nail you. That's when I called."

"So here we are."

Mac nodded, his mouth packed. I leaned against the backrest and pulled out my pack of smokes. What was I going to do? I didn't have a lot of options. They'd catch me eventually, and...then what? Kill me? I'd obviously gotten in the way of something, as well as contributed to the death of an agent. Sure, this Horton guy was as crooked as Lombard Street, but was he murdering women for his own sport, or on behalf of the agency? Maybe they just wanted to question me. A voice in my head said *don't bet on it*. I needed leverage...a bargaining chip. The box.

Mac was watching me, mouthing half a doughnut like a cow chewing its cud. I drew in on my cigarette, then slowly exhaled the smoke in one long breath. "The cops who picked me up last night, did they bring in a box from the crime scene?"

"What do you mean?"

"You know, a box. A metal box that holds 3-by-5 cards. Like

the kind your mom kept recipes in."

An anguished look passed over Mac's puffy face. "My mother didn't keep recipes. When I was eight, she took me and my brothers and sisters to the circus. A couple of days later, she disappeared. She ran off with one of the circus clowns. Beppo. Left my dad to raise all nine of us on his own. I've hated clowns ever since."

It was a sad story, but we all had sad stories. I even had my own reason for hating clowns, but that was a long time ago and I tried not to think about it anymore. "Sorry to bring it up. But you know what I'm talking about, right?"

Mac picked up a sticky bun. The prospect of a third pastry seemed to ease him out of his bitter memories. "Sure. There was no box. Our boys didn't bring in anything except the gun and what was on the body. Took everything to the coroner."

I thought back to the events leading up to Horton taking his last dive. In my mind's eye, I could see him running across the street and scrambling over the fence into the alley. Suddenly, I realized—*he wasn't carrying the box!* His hands were free when he climbed the fence. Horton must have dumped the box somewhere behind the Electronics Shop and the Brew & Stew. And since someone had searched my office earlier today, it was clear that the box hadn't been found. If I could find it first and put it somewhere safe, it might give me just the leverage I needed to keep breathing.

I got up to leave.

"Where you goin'?"

I was feeling a lot better now that I had a plan. "I've gotta go find something. Something the agency wants even more than me."

Mac pulled out a cigarette. "I wouldn't go back to your office for awhile. Knowing the agency, they'll have lookouts crawling all around your place."

"I appreciate the warnings, Mac. I guess I owe you on this one."

Mac waved his Merit at me. "Let's just say we're all squared up. And, by the way, we didn't have this little talk."

Chapter
Nine

I flew my speeder in low over Chandler Avenue, hoping, or rather not hoping, to see something that would confirm what Mac had told me. There were three people loitering near the Ritz—a clearly marked "no loitering" area. Even though the rule was never enforced, the Ritz just wasn't the kind of place people hung around. I had to assume that the loiterers were the Feds Malden had warned about.

I nosed up and headed aimlessly toward the new city. I needed time to think. My first priority was to find the box Horton had ditched last night. Secondly, I had to get back into my office and recover the wrapping paper I'd dug out of the dumpster. Last, and least, I was eventually going to need a place to sleep and maybe take a shower, though I had a first-rate deodorant and tried to sweat as little as possible.

I spent the afternoon in a booth at a twenty-four-hour pool hall. A barmaid with six new stitches in her forehead had been very attentive and only charged me for half my drinks. She said her name was Candy, a nickname her boyfriend had given her for good reason. I couldn't help but speculate that she was looking for a man to tide her over until her true love got paroled. It didn't look like she was going to let me go until I finally told her that *my* boyfriend called me Dumpling.

Outside, it was just getting dark. I felt a little more comfortable looking for the box under the cover of night. Home-field advantage was my only edge on the G-men, and

I intended to use it. On second thought, there was one more thing in my favor. The men waiting for me at the Ritz had no reason to think that I knew about them. Mac hadn't just saved my skin, he'd also given me a head start.

I landed my speeder in the parking lot to the left of the Brew & Stew, in the dead end of the Chandler cul-de-sac. A few people were up and about, starting the business day. I waited in my speeder until it appeared that no one would see me move. Removing a flashlight from the glove compartment, I slipped out and hurried to the alley that ran behind the Brew & Stew.

The alley was empty. At least a hundred meters separated me from the back of the Ritz. I was standing where Horton had been last night when I'd doubled back to the newsstand. The box had to be somewhere close. I paused and tried to put myself into Horton's shoes. The best thing would be to retrace his steps. I walked toward the Ritz, just until I passed the back of the Electronics Shop. Turning around, I began to examine everything in the alley.

OK. I'm Horton. I'm being chased, and it looks like I might get caught. I've gotta dump the box. Someplace where it won't be found accidentally, but where I can come back and find it easily. To my right, there was a concrete wall, eight or nine feet high. Horton could have lobbed the box over the wall, but I doubted it, for two reasons: one, it would be difficult to pinpoint exactly where the box had gone over, and two, the box might be damaged. No, Horton would have found a clever hiding place somewhere in the alley.

I looked around. Several garbage cans and a dumpster stood in and around the alley. I doubted that Horton would have put the box in any of them. Why would he take a chance on them getting emptied before he could return? Of course, maybe he was panicked and not thinking clearly, so I gave them a quick once-over. No box.

Apparently, logic wasn't going to save me any time. I started a methodical search, picking up scraps of garbage and scanning underneath with my flashlight. For almost an hour, I made my way slowly down the alley, searching every inch. Nothing. I was almost at the end when I moved an empty cardboard box and saw the manhole cover. The metal lid was heavy, but I managed to pry it up and slide it to the side. A ladder descended into the darkness. I stepped down.

Holding my flashlight, I scanned around. To my left, two large pipes intersected. The beam from my flashlight reflected off the box, sitting on the cross-section of the pipes! I grabbed it and climbed to the surface. I suddenly felt like getting the hell out of there. Cradling the box, I ran to my speeder, jumped in, and lifted off.

Now I had my leverage. I felt like I'd taken a hostage.

I put the speeder on autopilot and flipped on the interior light. The box was made of metal—lightweight and very strong. It was small, about eight inches by four inches by six inches. One side appeared to be the lid, judging by the almost imperceptible cracks around the edges. Someone had apparently tried to pry the lid open, leaving several barely visible scratches. I turned it over, looking for a keyhole or a disguised latch. Emily had been right—there seemed to be no way to open it. Looking closely, I could see three very thin lines running horizontally across the front of the box. I experimented, trying to get a section of the box to move, but with no luck. Admitting defeat, I set the box on the passenger seat and took the speeder off auto.

Now what? The box was my only bargaining chip, and I wasn't about to be caught carrying it around. I could put it in a safe-deposit box, but then I'd have to carry around a key that could be traced. Besides, a mere safe-deposit box wouldn't slow down the Feds. I could hide the box somewhere, but then if I were caught, I wouldn't have access to it. After some thought, I decided that I needed to put it in the care of someone I could trust. Then I could leave instructions for my ally that would help keep me alive if I were nabbed.

At times like this, I regretted my self-imposed title of Social Leper. I went through the short list of people I counted as friends and realized for the first time how short it was. Louie was a good guy and a true friend, but I'd already asked him for a few hundred too many favors. This one would be too much. Rook was probably my friend, but it was hard to tell. Mac Malden fell into the same category as Rook, plus he'd already done me a huge service.

It came down to Chelsee. I knew I could trust her, but would she be willing to help me? It seemed like half the time I talked to her, I was asking for favors. It didn't matter. I had to see if she was willing. If she wasn't, I'd make other plans, though I had no idea what those plans would be.

"Want coffee?" Chelsee asked.

"What kind you got?"

"Let me think...I've got Parisian Potpourri, Hawaiian Macadamia...I might have a little of the Hungarian Mint."

God, those weren't coffee—they were horribly mutated forms of hot cocoa. They should have names like Chernobyl Chocolate and Three Mile Island Delight. "You don't have any plain old black stuff?"

"Sorry. I do have some plain old Earl Grey."

Tea? Who did she think I was? "Uh...no tea, thanks. Any kind of coffee will be just fine. You decide."

Chelsee walked away, into the kitchen. She called out through the open door. "I'm glad you came by. Sorry I missed your call. I was...out. It's been a busy couple of days."

"Tell me about it." I was willing to bet that my last couple of days had been a little more eventful than hers, though I'd probably done less shopping and watched fewer controversial talk shows. I wondered how much I should tell her about what had happened after she'd left me at the Flamingo. Some explanation was going to be required for Chelsee to do me the big favor I needed.

"Do you like ginger?"

"Sure. But I always preferred Mary Ann."

Chelsee stuck her head into the doorway. "Not the girl, the spice...you dope."

"Oh...I'm not sure. I don't eat a lot of Chinese food."

She walked out with two steaming cups. "Have a sip of this. And try to keep an open mind. It's really good."

I took the mug and held it under my nose. It smelled like the parlor in an old lady's house. I took a drink; it was terrible. "Mmmm...this *is* good." I'd just swallowed more sugar than my body usually had in a month. I was certain that another sip would induce a seizure. I set the cup on the end table.

"So what's in the box?" The metal box had been resting in my lap for the past few minutes. Chelsee had eyed it curiously when she invited me in. I was impressed that she had kept from asking about it until now.

"A piece of a jigsaw puzzle."

"Must be a big puzzle."

I lifted the box and looked it over. "It's tied into the case I'm working on."

Chelsee lifted her cup toward her mouth and spoke through

the sugary mist. "The same case that got you the bump on the head?"

"Yeah."

Chelsee took a luxurious sip of instant ambrosia. "So why did you bring it here? I have a feeling you're about to ask me to do something for you."

Damn women's intuition. They were always one step ahead of me. I set the box down and nervously adjusted my tie. "Well, now that you mention it..."

I told Chelsee I'd been tailing a guy who'd stolen the box. I said he'd panicked and dropped it, but that he'd be back looking for it. Soon.

"So what's the big deal? He stole it. Tell him he can't have it."

"It's not that simple. This guy was, er...has, a lot of big friends. They'll do nasty things to me if I don't give it back to them."

"So you want to leave it *here*?"

Suddenly I realized I was asking too much. I was getting Chelsee involved in something so big that even I was a little nervous. "No...forget it. I shouldn't have even considered it. I'll...find someplace else to hide it."

Chelsee looked at me the way my mom used to. No other woman had ever looked at me like that. It made me feel warm and stupid all at the same time. "Tex, I'll be happy to help. I know you wouldn't come to me in a jam unless you had to. You're a stubborn, egotistical bastard, but you also hate to lean on anyone." She moved to the arm of the overstuffed chair I was seated in and lifted the box from my lap. "I'll keep this safe until you come back for it, OK?"

She set it on the end table. "And I don't need to know anything else about it."

I was relieved, but I felt like I should tell her more, let her know what she was getting herself into. "Listen, Chelsee. These guys are resourceful. I know they didn't follow me here, but it's possible they could track you down. I've got a lot to do, and I don't feel real good about leaving you to fend for yourself."

Some women would have taken offense at my concern. Chelsee didn't; she seemed flattered. She leaned down and held my stubbled face in her smooth, cool hands. "Tex, I can take care of myself. Not that I wouldn't enjoy having you take care of me." Her lips pressed against mine, soft and moist. I kissed her back.

I left Chelsee's apartment, still uncomfortable about leaving the box with her. She had assured me that she would put it in a safe place, and make sure no one ever saw it or knew about it. I had to trust her, but I didn't have to feel good about it.

The first part of my plan was finished. I'd made my bet and was ready to show my hand. I guided my speeder onto Chandler Avenue and landed at the curb in front of the Ritz. Two of the Feds' thugs were on the corner, huddled together over a single flame, lighting both of their cigarettes. I stepped out of the speeder and walked straight toward them. "Evening, gentlemen."

They looked up from their smokes and stared at me like I was a fanatic passing out religious pamphlets.

"It's me! Murphy! The guy you been waiting for!"

The two goons seemed stunned for a moment, then moved simultaneously, each one grabbing an arm.

"Oh...you caught me. All right, I give up." I was half carried, half dragged to a speeder on the far side of the street.

The two thugs shoved me into the backseat, and one of them followed me in. The other jumped into the driver's seat and fired it up. I turned to the stone-faced Fed on my left and gave him a big smile. "So...where we goin'?!"

Chapter
Ten

"Please, Mr. Murphy, make yourself comfortable. Do you smoke?" I nodded. "Would you like a Nat Sherman?"

Ah, Nat Sherman. Tobacconist to the World. "I'd love a Nat Sherman, thank you."

I leaned forward and extracted a cigarette from the case the NSA man held out to me. He was seated casually with one leg up on the front of a desk. His face was hard, his hair cut short and severe. He produced a lighter and lit my Nat Sherman. I leaned back and looked him over. Dark blue suit, neatly pressed. Dark red tie over a starched white shirt. As he leaned back, I caught a glimpse of burgundy suspenders, which matched his brilliantly shined wing tips. I didn't like the look of him.

"Do you know where you are?"

I drew in on my Nat Sherman and savored the quality tobacco taste. "In your office?"

His smile said *I'm going to enjoy killing you.* "That's correct. Do you know who I work for?"

"Can I have three guesses?"

The man stood up. As he walked around to the chair behind the desk, I noticed the name Jackson Cross displayed on a brass nameplate. He sat down in the chair like he belonged there and looked up at the two thugs standing behind me. "This guy's a joker, isn't he?"

Cross shifted his gaze back to me. "Don't dick with me, Murphy. If you don't give me straight answers, I'm going to pull out my gun and shoot you in the face. And I'd really rather not have to bring someone in tonight to clean my office."

His voice was calm. My left eyelid started to twitch.

"I'd guess that you work for the NSA."

Cross leaned back in his chair. "Give that man a cigar. Now for the big question. Do you know why you're here?"

"No idea whatsoever."

"Well, let me refresh your memory. Do you remember the other night? Up on the roof? The man you threw off the roof was one of our agents."

"I didn't throw him off the roof."

"Your actions contributed to the death of an NSA agent. There's also the small matter of interfering in an NSA investigation. Either charge wins you an all-expenses-paid, lifetime trip to Pelican Bay."

Pelican Bay was the new and improved Alcatraz, a place I'd never cared to visit. "All I did was try to save a girl from being murdered. How was I to know that an NSA *investigation* was going on?"

"Tell me how and why you were involved."

If this had been a police interrogation, I would've told him to stick it. This, however, was not the police. Everyone knew these guys were above the law and could kill people whenever they felt like it. I decided to play along, as far as they knew. "The girl at the Fuchsia Flamingo hired me to find out who had left her a couple of twisted notes. I kept an eye on her place and saw your man in her apartment. When I got to the apartment, your agent hightailed it. I followed him to the roof, and he tried to shoot me. We struggled; he went over the side."

Cross picked up a pencil and tapped it on the desk. After a few moments, he looked up at me. "The agent was staking out the

Fuchsia Flamingo. We've known for some time that high-level drug dealings have gone on in the club. A delivery of euphoria was brought there on the night in question. Our agent was in the girl's apartment waiting to make a bust. The girl's life was never in danger...at least not on our account."

The NSA man was lying through his teeth. He sounded convincing, but his eyes and body said something else altogether. "Well, maybe what you say is true. All I know is that it didn't appear like that, and I stand by my actions."

Cross stared at me for what seemed like five minutes. "Tell me what you know about Thomas Malloy."

"Who?"

"You heard me."

"I don't know anyone named Thomas Malloy." Well, that was true. I'd never met him.

He continued to stare me down. I'd never lied so well in my entire life. I hoped it was well enough.

"The euphoria our agent was attempting to confiscate was in a small metal container. It hasn't turned up. I think you've got it. Where is it?"

"I've never seen anything remotely like that."

Cross clapped his hands together and smiled. "Well, I guess that'll be all, then." He motioned to the two men behind me. "You can take him now. Make it clean. Get back here as soon as you're finished."

I felt four large hands on me. They were actually going to kill me. "Hold on! I've got the box!"

Cross waved the goons off. He folded his hands on the desk and looked at me serenely, his eyebrows raised expectantly. "So you do have it. You should have said that in the first place. Why don't you tell us where it is."

"Will you cut me a deal?"

"What do you have in mind? I have to warn you, I usually frown on compromises."

I had to be careful. These guys wouldn't hesitate to kill me. I had a decent hand; now it was time to raise the stakes. "Look, I didn't ask to get mixed up in this business. I'm a small-time PI, living from case to case. It may not be much of a life, but I'm not ready for the Big Finish yet. All I want to do is get out of your hair and keep doing the things people do when they're alive."

"So you'll trade me the box if I promise to let you go, no strings attached?"

"Yeah, that's basically it."

Cross was quiet for a minute. I personally didn't think I was asking for a whole lot. Finally, he nodded. "I'll cut you loose in exchange for the box. Where is it?"

I didn't want to push my luck, but I wasn't going to go soft either. "I'd prefer to deliver it on my own."

"Why should I trust you?"

"Why should *I* trust *you*?"

"Look, you bastard, I could shoot you right where you sit," he said, more calmly than the words implied.

"Yeah, but then you wouldn't have the box. And I guarantee you'd never find it."

Cross sat back and assessed the situation. Apparently, getting this box was his first priority. I wondered what was in it. It sure as hell wasn't euphoria. "How and when will you deliver it?"

I wanted to buy some time. Obviously, I could get it in less than an hour, but I didn't want to rush into anything. "It'll take a little time. Give me thirty-six hours."

"That's too long."

"Look, do you want it or not? I'm willing to hand it over;

you've just gotta give me enough time."

Cross didn't like the idea, but I could see he was going to play along. "OK, Murphy. In thirty-six hours, that box better be sitting on the desk in your office. If you're there, too, I'll have you shot. Once we've got the box, I'll try to forget we ever spoke."

He seemed to be talking straight. It was as good an offer as I was going to get. Cross got up and walked around to where I was sitting. He leaned down until his face was no more than two inches from mine. His steely eyes burned into mine. "Listen to me, Murphy. This is the only time you'll hear me say this. After I get that box, I don't want to see your face again. If I do, I'll put a slug into your eyeball. I'm going to have people keeping tabs on you for awhile, to make sure that you stay out of our way. If you even hear mention of the NSA, I'd advise you to turn around and run. Is that clear?"

I nodded. Something told me that I was getting the deal of a lifetime. Cross motioned to the two Feds behind me.

"Get this pisshead out of my office."

The NSA thugs were courteous enough to drop me off back at the Ritz. Unfortunately, they had *literally* dropped me off while their speeder had been going about forty kilometers an hour. I limped into the lobby and up to my office. I opened the door and flipped on the lights. It was good to be home, but God, it was a mess. The NSA boys had been impressively destructive. The office looked like the scene of an oversized game of fifty-two-card pickup. I hung up my coat and hat. I'd clean the place up later.

After poking around for a few minutes, I was relieved to find that the wrapping paper from Malloy's package hadn't been confiscated. They'd probably ignored it, since Malloy's name wasn't written on it. Lucky for me, or else my little white lie wouldn't have worked on Agent Cross.

Lord, I was beat. Turning down the lights made my eyes feel better. I cranked up my old phonograph, and suddenly Nat King Cole was playing piano in the back of my office. I fell into the chair behind my desk and turned on my banker's lamp. After fishing out a Lucky Strike and pouring myself a tall glass of bourbon, I turned my attention to the brown paper wrapper. Someone knocked at the door.

I'd just gotten comfortable and hated to get up. Briefly, I considered pretending that no one was here but Nat. I rubbed my eyes. It was probably somebody important. Limping across the paper-littered room, I reached the door and opened it.

It was the woman, Ms. Madsen, from the police station.

"Well, hello."

"Good evening." She nodded and waited. "May I come in?"

I was a bit shocked and reacted a little slowly. I stepped aside and motioned for her to enter. She moved toward my desk, leaving a hint of dark fragrance in her wake. I closed the door without taking my eyes from her. She was exquisite. Above average height, auburn hair that just touched her shoulders. Slender waist, curvy through the hips, perfectly shaped ankles. She walked through the paper trail and sat down in one of my newly reupholstered guest chairs.

"Nice place. Decorate it yourself?"

"Sorry about the mess. The housekeeper just started taking Prozac."

I slid into my chair and picked my still-burning cigarette from the ashtray. I motioned toward my smoke. "I hope you don't mind."

"Not at all."

"Can I offer you one?"

"No. Thank you."

I took a drag off the Lucky Strike and looked at her face. Her skin was flawless and very fair. Full, soft lips. Her large eyes were an unusual shade of hazel, close to a golden brown. There was a lot to be read in those eyes. This woman was strong, focused, determined. I decided to take an aggressive approach. "I suppose you came by to apologize for walking out on me at the police station."

Her lips curved into a smile, revealing perfect, white teeth. She cocked her head slightly. It was very appealing. "Why should I? Don't most women treat you that way when they first meet you?"

"Well, yeah. Usually. When they do show any interest, I'm generally too stunned to do anything about it."

She gave me a skeptical, sideways glance. "I seriously doubt that."

"It's true."

Ms. Madsen appraised my glass. "Is that bourbon?"

"It most certainly is. Would you like some?"

"I would."

Finding a clean glass turned out to be more difficult than I'd figured. For a moment, I was afraid I'd have to resort to washing one. When I returned, Ms. Madsen had taken off her coat and laid it across the other chair. Her sleeveless gray dress exposed slender, toned arms. I returned to my chair, poured a small glass of bourbon, and handed it to her. She swirled it around and lifted it in my direction.

"Cheers."

She drank half the bourbon and didn't blink. I was impressed.

"So tell me, Ms. Madsen, what brings you to my little den of iniquity?"

A look of seductive coyness flashed across the young woman's face, replaced almost instantaneously by a more pleasant, polite expression. The signals coming from her were almost contradictory, as if her instinctive nature was assertive and sensual, but her conscious nature struggled to act with cool detachment.

"Please call me Regan."

"OK. But then you have to call me Tex."

She gave me the sideways look. "That's not your real name. What is it?"

"You wouldn't believe me if I told you."

"Try me."

"Sorry. I have to get to know someone pretty thoroughly before I come clean on that one."

"Well, then, maybe you should get to know me pretty thoroughly." There was that sensual thing again. She took another sip of bourbon.

"Maybe I'll have one of those Lucky Strikes after all." I dug one out and handed it over. Instead of taking it from me the way people normally do, she put her hand over mine and bent down to take the cigarette between her lips. Her hand lingered momentarily on my unsteady fingers. I lit a match and reached across the desk. Regan drew in, the end of the cigarette blazing. I focused on her long, slender fingers holding the cigarette as I leaned back and lit a smoke of my own. Regan leaned forward, folding her arms over her crossed legs. "Do you have the box?"

The question may have been the last one I was expecting. I looked her over and decided she was bluffing. "What box would that be?"

"You know what I'm talking about."

"Do not."

Regan leaned back and smoked her cigarette the way only a woman can. Her clear eyes locked onto mine and wouldn't let go.

Eventually, she blinked first. It made me happy. She uncrossed her legs and slid toward the front of her seat. The lower half of her face moved into the lamplight. Her lips were perfect.

"I like to play games, Tex. It makes things more interesting. I think you do, too." Her gaze drifted down to my mouth. "What's your angle, Tex? I'm willing to bargain."

She was good at this. She'd obviously bargained before. Unless I missed my guess, she was probably accustomed to getting what she wanted. Every damn time. Maybe I'd be the first man who'd ever said no to her. Maybe.

"I don't have an angle, Ms. Madsen. My business is my own. I don't have a partner, and I don't like small talk. You're a beautiful woman, but that doesn't change anything as far as I'm concerned."

She moved back, out of the light. It was a tactical retreat. The first assault had failed—time to fall back and regroup. I reached for another Lucky and lit it up. It tasted especially good.

The second assault began. "I have a proposition."

There was no harm in hearing her out. She was making my eyes feel better, and she smelled good. I could sit here all night, listen to classic jazz, polish off the bourbon, and enjoy the company of a stunning woman.

"I saw you get dumped out front. Looked like an NSA speeder. I'm guessing that they're looking for the same box I am, and that's why they invited you in for a chat."

Either she was a very good guesser, or she had me at a disadvantage. I decided not to respond.

"Since I'm talking to you, I would assume that either you gave them the box, or told them you could get it."

I was suddenly uncomfortable. She was too close to the truth to be bluffing. Maybe she and I needed to reach an understanding. "How do you know about the box?"

Regan smiled and wagged her finger. "I'd have to get to know someone pretty thoroughly before I'd come clean on that one."

I smiled back. "Well, then, maybe you should get to know me pretty thoroughly."

Regan bit her bottom lip gently. "Unfortunately, I don't think we have enough time."

"So what's your proposition?"

Her face turned serious. "I'm not sure how much you know. What do you know about Malloy?"

I wasn't sure whether I should answer. Maybe this woman was NSA. Maybe this whole conversation was just a more pleasant repeat of the one I'd had in Jackson Cross's office. "Malloy? Sounds vaguely familiar, but I've never been good with names."

"Well, I'll just assume that you know a little about him. He recently sent out a number of packages like the one I think you've got. The NSA was closing in on him, and he panicked. He split up a lot of information and sent a portion in each of the boxes. I don't think anyone knows exactly how many boxes there are, but whoever finds them all stands to make an ungodly amount of money."

"Where does that leave Malloy?"

"He's a dead man. If the NSA hasn't got him yet, someone else will. Right now, it's a race to see who can get all the data he dispersed and reassemble it."

"You still haven't made your proposition."

Regan leaned toward me, excitedly. "I already have one of the boxes. Give me the one you've got, and I'll cut you in on the deal. If you can help me locate the others, we'll have more money than you've ever imagined. That's my proposition, plain and simple."

There was no such thing as more money than I could imagine. But my instincts told me that the whole thing sounded cockeyed—not to mention illegal. More importantly, I had absolutely no reason to believe that I could trust this woman. Despite my reservations, I was intrigued.

Regan reached for her coat and stood up. "You'll probably want some time to think this over." She fished out a card and jotted something down on it.

"Call me at this number when you're ready to talk. Like I told you, I already have one of the boxes. If it'll help, I'll show you mine first. You can show me yours later." She turned and walked to the door. As she opened it, she turned back. "Don't lose the number, Tex. I think we'd make a perfect fit."

Then she was gone. I needed a cold shower before I could think about anything constructive.

Chapter
Eleven

The brown paper wrapper was nondescript. It could have come from any of a thousand supply stores in the Bay Area. I examined the lettering on the package. Malloy had used a black felt-tip marker. There was nothing unusual or useful in the writing. I went over the wrapper with a magnifying glass, but found nothing distinctive. The only thing left to check was the postmark. It had been lasered on with a meter gun. The mailing cost was $14.90. The date displayed in the center of the postmark circle was April 12, 2043. Three days ago. Around the inside of the circle, it read *City of San Francisco*. I'd hoped that the package would've been sent from a more localized source.

I flipped on my computer and ran a check on post offices in the city. There were 59 of them. I wasn't going to get anywhere at this rate. The postmark had a code under the eagle symbol: PB METER 38874121. Tracing the meter number to the correct post office would at least give me a starting point. Unfortunately, with 59 locations to check, I didn't have enough time to investigate every one.

I lit a smoke and tried to come up with a clever solution. Nothing occurred to me until I looked toward the floor and saw an envelope lying face up in the mess. I dropped to my knees, the cigarette dangling from the corner of my mouth. Crawling slowly across the floor, I examined every postmarked envelope I could find, searching for one with a PB METER code of 38874121.

Most of the envelopes were junk mail, tattooed with a

bulk-mail bar code. At last, I found a letter with the correct meter code. It was from a former client. As luck would have it, he hadn't put his return address on the envelope—it was no help. I kept searching. I'd almost reached the end of the room when I finally found another letter with a matching postmark. It was a bill from a storage unit I'd rented a few years back, in the Mission District.

A hundred years ago, in Sam Spade's San Francisco, the Mission District was a rough part of town. Fifty years ago, god-fearing folk stayed out of the area unless they were armed to the teeth. Now, the Mission District had become a no-man's-land, a place where even the police had stopped visiting. I landed my speeder at the TLC Storage warehouse. A teenage punk was working the counter, in the loosest sense of the word. I reintroduced myself to Ahmad, the gold-toothed proprietor, who was in an office behind the counter area. After politely inquiring as to the price of various storage units, I casually asked where I would find the nearest post office. Eager to please a prospective renter, Ahmad gave me directions, as well as a price list, a calendar, and a hearty handshake.

The post office was in the buffer zone that surrounded the neighborhood. Hookers, pimps, and pushers were going about their business, but less colorful types were also out and about. The area around the USPS building was primarily residential, though there was a neighborhood market and a couple of flesh shops.

I noticed an apparently paraplegic black man seated by the front door to the post office. "Evening."

"You got that right. Can you spare a fin?"

I ignored the request momentarily and pulled out my pack of cigarettes. The man's eyes drifted toward the smokes.

"You want one of these?"

The man nodded and held out his hand. I handed him one,

took one for myself, then did the honors. He held the baby Lucky as if it were the stem of a crystal wine glass. Then he inhaled deeply. I waited for the smoke to come back out; it didn't. I squatted down beside him.

"You spend a lot of time here?"

"Why? You want this spot?"

I didn't think I looked *that* bad. Hell, I had a tie on. "No, I was just wondering if you've been here most of the time during the past three days."

The man took another one-way drag off his cigarette. "Well, lemme think. I get so busy, I lose track of the days...yeah, I've been here for at least three days."

I pulled a twenty out of my pocket and fondled it discreetly. "I'm looking for a friend of mine. Came here three or four days ago and mailed some packages. You think you'd remember his face?"

The man looked at the bill I was holding. "For twenty bucks, I can remember anything you want."

"Look, I'll give you the cash even if you don't recognize my friend's face. I just need to know if he came by here." I showed him the picture of Malloy. His face brightened up.

"Sure, I seen this guy. Old man. Moved real slow. Left me a ten-spot."

"Do you remember, did he come on the bus, or in a speeder?"

"No, I remember him 'cause I know most everyone in the vicinity. He caught my eye on account that I hadn't seen him before. He was walking."

"Which way did he come from?"

The man pointed. "He came from there, and that's the way he went when he left."

"Great. One last question. You know of any boardinghouses in the area?"

"What kind you lookin' for?"

"Oh...something half decent, but not too pricey. A fairly safe place, where I could lie low for awhile. Preferably in the direction my friend came from."

The man considered for a minute. "Go up Valencia Street. They got three or four places like that up around there. Maybe a quarter mile, half mile from here."

I thanked him and left him another smoke for later, along with the double sawbuck. He seemed much obliged.

My gut told me that Malloy was close. It was a great area for anyone who didn't want to be found. I parked my speeder on the corner of Valencia and 20th streets and proceeded to canvass the dark street on foot. A quarter mile made a huge difference. Most of the houses along Rose Street were old but cared for. There were no blatantly visible signs of illegal activity. Everyone I saw seemed concerned only with coming or going as quickly as possible.

The street was full of boardinghouses. I realized I had no plan of action. A one-man stakeout would be practically impossible, since I didn't know which boardinghouse Malloy was in and wasn't even sure I was on the right block. The only way I was going to find my man was through old-fashioned pavement pounding.

The typical boardinghouse has a sitting room, where typical boarders gather to read, watch TV, and get to know their surrogate family members. It's one of the two characteristics that elevate boardinghouses a notch above residential hotels. The other, of course, is good home-cooked meals. Damn, I was hungry again.

It was a slow and exhausting process. At each boardinghouse, I entered the sitting room with an air of confidence and nonchalance that none but the most skeptical would question. The sitting rooms were generally located on the ground floor, near the front door. There were, however, exceptions, and I occasionally found myself walking into the odd bedroom or broom closet.

By and large, though, my canvassing went smoothly. In nearly every sitting room, I was able to identify a talker, a lonely looking man or woman, usually older, who was eager to chat. I would start the conversational ball rolling with a comment on the weather, then sit back and listen politely. Once I'd opened the floodgates, I'd casually bring up the subject of the boardinghouse and ask about the current tenants. If I wasn't careful, I'd unleash a torrent of gossip, guesses as to a certain boarder's seamy past, and a detailed description of the floozy Mr. So and So had in his room the other night.

After a few minutes, I'd casually produce the photo of Malloy and ask if the talker had seen him or knew if he was staying at the house. The talker would stare intently at the picture, hem and haw, then say no, I don't think so, but he certainly reminds me of my Uncle Somebody or Other, who blah, blah, blah, blah, blah. The most difficult part of the process was politely extracting myself.

I visited at least a dozen boardinghouses over a three-hour period. My next stop was a place called the Garden House. Opening the door released the smell of baking chocolate-chip cookies. The light inside was warm and friendly. It reminded me of Grandma's house. Inside, a small, round woman was walking down the hallway, her huge serving tray piled high with large, chewy-looking cookies, straight from the oven.

"Hello, there. What can I do for you?"

The warm smell of fresh cookies was killing me. I removed my fedora and smiled down at the plump little lady. "This is a wonderful place. Do you run it?"

"Yes, I do, thank you. Are you looking for a room?"

My eyes were glued to the cookies. "Maybe. Are cookies included in the rent?"

The little woman smiled. "Please, help yourself."

I picked a fat one from the pile. It was a gooey, chocolaty piece of heaven. As I took a bite, my eyes rolled back into my head, and I was forced to steady myself. The sugar rush was overwhelming.

The plump lady nodded her head, as though this was the usual reaction to her cookies. "Excuse me for a moment. I need to take these to the guests. I'll be right back."

I finished the cookie and licked my fingers like a dog.

The woman returned quickly. "So, what can I help you with?"

I tried to look deeply concerned. "It's my Uncle Thomas. We lost him last week."

The woman's face crinkled. "I'm so sorry."

"No, I mean we *lost* him...as in...we can't find him."

The plump landlady seemed relieved.

"He's getting on in years, and he's not all there, if you know what I mean. He lives alone and, every now and again, he just takes off. Sometimes he gets away for weeks before we find him and bring him home."

I pulled out the photograph of Malloy and handed it to her. "This is Uncle Thomas. A friend of mine saw him around this neighborhood, so I'm checking out all the boardinghouses in the area."

The woman looked up at me, then back at the photo. She seemed uncertain. "You say this is your Uncle Thomas?"

I nodded. "We're all worried sick about him."

"Well, I'm pretty sure this is the man who moved in last week, but he said his name was Todd. Todd Mallory."

I smiled reassuringly. "Like I said, he's only got the one oar left to row with. It's his...Murphy-Barr Syndrome."

"My goodness...he seemed so lucid, so friendly."

I nodded sympathetically. "Yes, it's a strange illness. He usually appears normal. The only symptoms are an uncontrollable urge to relocate and, of course, compulsive lying. When Uncle Thomas has a relapse, it's like pulling teeth to get a straight answer out of him."

The landlady handed the photo back to me and shook her head sadly. "It must be quite a trial for you."

"Well, I know that respecting and caring for your elders is old-fashioned, but it's a responsibility I take very seriously."

The woman took my hand and patted it gently, tears in her eyes. "I wish you were my nephew."

"I wish you were my aunt. My real aunt buys her cookies at the grocery store."

She released my hand and turned, motioning for me to follow her up the stairs. I now had absolutely no doubt that I would eventually burn in hell. We climbed the stairs and walked to the end of the hallway. Reaching the last door on the right, the landlady turned and knocked. She waited a few moments and knocked again, but Malloy/Mallory didn't appear to be in.

"He must have gone out. If you like, I can let you in the room to wait for him. Or you can come downstairs and wait there. I made plenty of cookies."

The thought of more cookies made me hesitate, but I had work to do. "I'll wait up here. That way I can surprise him when he gets back."

The woman unlocked the door and opened it for me. "If you need anything, you just let me know, OK?"

"I will. Thanks for your help. Everyone will be so relieved

when Uncle Thomas is back home, safe and sound."

She closed the door behind me. The room was cozy, with only a small, but comfortable-looking bed, a rolltop desk, and a dresser. I decided to pass the time by searching the room. The rolltop desk was unlocked and chock-full of papers. I searched everything but found only one thing of interest: a notebook full of strange symbols. It didn't look useful, so I left it where I found it. Then I turned to the dresser. I immediately discovered something that was either very significant or completely meaningless: all of Malloy's socks were black. Other than that, I found nothing interesting.

I glanced around. There didn't seem to be anything left to search. The bed covers were thrown up over the bed. I pulled them back to reveal a pair of rumpled trousers. Just for fun, I looked through the pockets. From the front left pocket, I removed a folded piece of pink paper. Opening it up, I saw that it was a receipt from a local realty firm for a one-month lease of storage property. An address was written at the top of the page: 54 Front Street. Down by the docks—mostly old, condemned buildings. I knew where Malloy was.

Chapter
Twelve

The waterfront area had once been a teeming center of commerce. Now its buildings sat decrepit and forgotten, like dust-covered blocks in an attic. I'd heard that most of the properties had been bought up by underworld types, who used them to store things like hot merchandise, drug shipments, and the occasional dismembered body. Some of the buildings could still pass inspection with a small donation and were rented out as practice space for aspiring rock bands and experimental dance companies.

The massive structure at 54 Front Street had no pulse. It looked like it had died about the same time as black-and-white movies (may they rest in peace). From the front, no lights were visible inside. After scaling an eight-foot chain-link fence, I walked around to the left side of the building. I glanced up at the windows pockmarking the wall and saw no sign of activity, no indication that anyone was home. From the rear, I caught sight of a faint, thin, halogen glow seeping out around a window on the sixth floor.

There were three doors at ground level: one in the front, one in the back, one on the west side. Of course, they all felt solidly dead-bolted. I returned to the rear of the building and fired up a Lucky Strike. Smoking is good for a lot of things, one of which is helping me to think. It's also great after sex, baths, and meals and goes with just about anything except milk.

I looked up at the sixth-story window, then scanned my way down the building, looking for any possible way I could climb up.

When I was nine, I'd had an authentic Spiderman uniform. Whenever I wore it, I could scale anything. A twinge of nostalgia ran through me. Of course, even if I could find the uniform, it probably wouldn't fit. No, I'd become a mere mortal and would have to resort to mere mortal methods.

A rusted metal ladder was bolted to the brick face of the building on the far left side and ran all the way up to the roof. Apparently, the bottom section had rusted and fallen off or been broken off, leaving a jagged end about fifteen feet above the ground. If I could only reach the ladder, I could easily climb to the sixth floor. I searched the area around the back of the building. Plenty of junk scattered around, but nothing useful. Then I was struck by a possibility: it might be a tricky fit, but I could probably land my speeder close enough to use it to stand on.

Five minutes later, I was standing atop my speeder, pulling my ever-increasing body weight up onto the first rungs of the ladder with my ever-decreasing muscular capacity. Despite some unpleasant burning sensations and several mysterious popping noises, I finally got my feet onto the bottom rung. I rested a few moments, then began the ascent of Mount Malloy. As I reached the fourth story, the kid in me was saying to look down. The adult, of course, was saying not to. I listened to my inner child and felt the world begin to spin wildly off its axis. It took several minutes before I was ready to climb again.

When I got to the sixth story, I realized that the window I was trying to reach was much farther away from the ladder than it had appeared when I was safely on the ground. It was at least eight feet away, with no apparent way to bridge the gap. If it had been possible to get a cigarette, light it, and smoke it without using my hands, I would've done it. As it was, both hands were locked in rigor mortis on the ladder, and I was hoping desperately that I'd live to smoke again.

It didn't take me long to realize that I wasn't going to get to the window from where I was clinging to the ladder. I began to climb again. Despite sweating palms and slight dizziness, I reached the roof quickly. Thirty feet away I saw a roof-access door. I hurried over, but it was locked. A search of the rooftop turned up no trap doors or other means of entrance. I walked toward the retainer wall at the edge of the roof, directly two floors above the sixth-story window. As I approached, I stumbled over something in the dark. It turned out to be a coil of steel cable.

An idea came into my head that was simultaneously ingenious and ridiculous. I looked around and spotted a metal vent pipe protruding from the rooftop surface. Kneeling down and examining it, I determined that it was sturdy enough. I unrolled the steel cable and fed it down over the side until the end of the cable reached the bottom of the sixth-story window. Making note of the length, I pulled the cable up, then attached the other end to the vent pipe. I wrapped the cable around my hands several times. With a deep breath, I took several steps toward the edge of the roof and hurtled over the side.

I fell for what seemed an eternity, then jerked violently as the slack in the cable was taken up. My eyes, which had closed involuntarily, opened to see the window rushing straight at me. I shut my eyes again and felt the strange sensation of bursting through solid matter. With a loud crash, the window shattered into a thousand pieces. Still not opening my eyes, I let go of the cable and dropped. My feet hit the floor, and my knees buckled.

I looked up and saw a man across the room. He was half-turned toward me and appeared to be in shock. I stood up slowly and made a quick check to verify that everything was still intact. Brushing glass shards from my overcoat, I walked toward him.

"Thomas Malloy, I presume."

The old man seemed paralyzed. I looked him over. He obviously resembled his image in the photograph Fitzpatrick had given me, but in person he had the look of a biblical prophet. He seemed ancient, though his gnarly, hoary look was probably as much a result of cigarettes and booze as the labors of a long and fruitful life. He still didn't answer, so I decided to break the ice. "You know, Dr. Malloy, you're a hard man to track down. I'm pretty good at what I do, but you sure gave me a run for my money."

"You're NSA, aren't you? You're here to kill me."

I gave Malloy my warmest smile. "No. I'm just a simple PI. A friend of yours, Gordon Fitzpatrick, hired me to find you."

The old man relaxed a bit, but was still on guard. "So what are you going to do now?"

I considered for a moment. "Well, first I'll have a smoke."

I pulled out my pack of cigarettes and offered one to Malloy. He took it slowly and sniffed it, then turned and packed it on a countertop. He was obviously no stranger to unfiltered smokes. I pulled out a matchbook and held a lit match up in front of him. He lit the Lucky Strike and inhaled deeply, eyes closed and a faint trembling in his hand. After several seconds, he exhaled and opened his eyes. It looked like he'd caught a buzz.

"This is my first cigarette in four months." His eyes were bright. He took another drag, savoring it. "My daughter made me quit. I think she was just trying to make my last few years as miserable as possible."

Malloy sat down and motioned me toward a nearby chair. We sat and smoked without talking for several minutes. Malloy took a final drag and dropped the cigarette to the floor, crushing it under the tip of his shoe. "Thanks for the smoke."

"My pleasure."

He ran a hand through his unruly thatch of white hair. "So Fitz put you on my trail. Did he tell you why he wanted to find me?"

I shook my head. "He didn't give me any details...he just said that he thought you might be in danger."

Malloy chuckled, then coughed several times. "You don't know much about me, do you, Mr.—"

"Murphy. Tex Murphy. I've found out a little. I know you recently married a young woman named Emily Sue Patterson. I know that you used to work at Berkeley with Sandra Collins, and that you once worked as a research scientist with Fitzpatrick."

"Is that it?"

"Pretty much."

Malloy nodded and scratched his white-stubbled chin. "My life's been in danger for some time now. You probably know I'm wanted by the NSA. Well, a few other little groups would like to get their paws on me as well, some in the government, some in other governments, some in private organizations. Hell, sometimes it feels like I'm running from everyone but the Girl Scouts."

He coughed violently into a closed fist. He didn't look very healthy. I didn't ask if he was all right.

"I knew about the NSA. I had a little run-in with them a couple of days ago. They mentioned your name, but I played dumb. It's something I'm really good at. But I'm pretty sure they believed me."

The old man glanced up at me sharply. "You didn't let them follow you here, did you?"

I thought back to what I'd done over the past six or seven hours. I was fairly certain that I hadn't been trailed. I shook my head. The old man didn't seem one hundred percent convinced. "If they followed you here, our acquaintance is going to be a short one. Better give me another one of those cigarettes."

I pulled out the pack. There was only one smoke left. I handed it over and lit it for Malloy. He leaned back in his chair and inhaled, French-style. "Do you want to hear a story?"

"Sure." I tried to be casual, but I had a feeling that this guy had a lot to say. I wanted to know everything.

"You positive? What I'm gonna tell you could put you in the same danger I'm in."

"Just knowing you has been dangerous enough. Besides, danger's like Jell-O—there's always room for a little more."

Malloy grinned, coughed three or four times, then wiped his eyes on his shirt sleeve. "You ever heard of Project Blue Book?"

It sounded familiar, but I couldn't place it. "Wasn't it some kind of scandal in the testing department at the Naval Academy?"

The old man shook his head, smiling, then coughed again. "No. It was a government-appointed study started in 1952 to determine whether or not aliens had ever made contact with Earth."

I remembered now. I'd always been somewhat interested in the idea of aliens but had never really gotten into the whole UFO scene.

"It was the first time the government publicly addressed the possible existence of UFOs. Of course, their findings were negative, and all reported sightings were determined to be fraudulent or misinterpreted. Most UFOlogists consider Project Blue Book to be the first step in a massive government cover-up."

Malloy coughed again and turned to the desk behind him. He grabbed a can of Crown Cola and took a drink. The desk was littered with books and papers, some of which were covered with symbols like those I'd seen back at the boardinghouse.

"Anyway, the government made an official announcement that Project Blue Book had been closed."

He paused poignantly.

"It wasn't. The truth is, the military had found something at Roswell—I'm assuming you've heard about Roswell—and it wasn't a goddamn weather balloon. It was a spacecraft, and it sure wasn't Soviet. The Roswell Incident was the greatest disinformation campaign of all time. Sure, there were allegations and investigations, books written and witnesses interviewed, but not a shred of tangible evidence was ever released to the public."

I'd heard this kind of talk before, mostly from UFO crackpots. I believed Malloy more than I would believe most people on this topic, but he hadn't told me anything that wasn't already in print.

"So what does this have to do with Project Blue Book?"

Malloy grinned. "Project Blue Book turned into Project Blueprint. I seriously doubt you've heard of it, seeing as how you're still alive. The military made it their top priority and never allowed a leak."

"What is Project Blueprint?"

"The wreckage in Roswell was taken to a nearby underground base. A handful of top researchers with the highest security clearance were essentially given lifetime assignments to the Roswell complex. The spacecraft was not large, but it was chock-full of goodies to analyze. Of course, their first thought was of finding weapons, or technology to help build a better bomb. Remember, we were still in the middle of the Cold War and looking for any advantage possible."

"Seems to me the military hasn't changed a whole lot."

Malloy smiled grimly and nodded.

"You got that right. Anyway, Project Blueprint was the operation concerned with gleaning new information and/or technology from the wreckage. The research continued well into the 1980s. Small advances were made, but it took time for our analyzing technology to catch up with the alien data. Eventually we got there."

"You said 'We.'"

Malloy leaned back and took another sip of cola.

"So I did. I joined Project Blueprint in 1984. As a promising graduate student in linguistics and symbology, I was recruited by the military and given the assignment at age 21. In retrospect, that particular year was an interesting time to join, seeing how Big Brother was firmly in place, and the Peacekeeper was the most powerful weapon on the planet. It now strikes me as being very Orwellian. Anyway, I went to work at the Roswell Complex. My job was to carry on the work of deciphering the hieroglyphics found in the spacecraft. Very little—or I should say, no—progress had been made over the previous thirty-two years. In the years since the Roswell Incident, the military had found no other spacecraft, though plenty of sightings were reported."

The old man was besieged by coughing spasms, which took him a minute to recover from.

"Excuse my hacking. It's become a problem lately."

I waited, impatient to hear the rest of the story. Eventually, Malloy caught his breath and went on. "I'd been working in Project Blueprint for about fourteen years when word came through the complex that there'd been a breakthrough. I never got all the details, but apparently someone had discovered that one of the alien instruments would generate minute quantities of antimatter. Of course, this was technology we were capable of—in theory—in 1998, but the operation was impractical, not to mention potentially devastating. The alien technology worked much more efficiently.

"Naturally, the military was ecstatic about the breakthrough and set about using the antimatter generator to build a new and improved bomb. If you'll remember, the Desert Standoff was in effect by then, and we were looking for a technology edge on the Middle East Bloc. Well, the military had what they needed and started the war. Unfortunately, as you know, things went wrong."

"That's the understatement of the century."

"Yeah, well, the military didn't think it had time to do any testing. Instead, they started a political incident and let it boil until they could plead probable cause. Then they flew a squadron out and dropped a few bombs. I don't know all the details, but apparently the bombs hit someplace they weren't supposed to and started a chain reaction. It ended up being like Chernobyl back in the early '80s, only on a scale a hundred times bigger. As the war raged on, radiation clouds drifted across every continent, seeding the atmosphere to the point of saturation. The military had screwed up big, and even they realized it. They stopped producing the bombs and destroyed the generator, but it was too late. The war ended, but irreparable damage had been done."

Malloy paused for a moment, pondering the sad, stupid, tragic story.

After a short time, the old man leaned forward and spoke, his voice low. "During all this, as I said, I'd been working on the hieroglyphics found in the Roswell spacecraft. We had quite a bit of raw material to work with, but of course, we had no key. The collective set of symbols was an interstellar Rosetta stone, a cryptic code just waiting to be broken. I spent the first sixteen years obsessed with the hieroglyphics. At least a dozen times, I felt like I was on the verge of discovery when, suddenly, everything would fall apart.

"Immediately after the war ended, Project Blueprint was disbanded. The military was embarrassed and decided to terminate the whole operation. I ended up being reassigned to China, where I translated Chinese documentation. Fortunately, I had managed to smuggle out all my notes, records, and physical reproductions from Roswell. In China, I secretly continued my research, always certain that I would eventually make sense of the cryptic symbols...and I did."

If Malloy was telling the truth, if he wasn't just a crackpot driven mad by a lifelong obsession, I could become one of the first people to hear the words of an alien race. According to some people's beliefs, I could essentially be hearing the word of God. I waited breathlessly.

The words never came. With a terrific crash, the door on the far side of the room was kicked open. A masked figure, dressed completely in black, burst through the doorway. Cradled in his arms was an assault rifle. Almost majestically, Malloy stood up and turned toward the figure. Through the open door, I could hear the sound of pounding footsteps. There were a lot more of them coming. Malloy turned back toward me and motioned toward another door.

"Get out of here! Save yourself!"

I hesitated instinctively. I couldn't just leave Malloy. The gunman was leveling his rifle at the old man—he was as good as dead. As I bolted from my seat, I caught sight of Malloy rushing in the direction of the masked figure and heard the rifle go off. Malloy screamed as I tore open the door and plunged into the darkness. As I ran like a madman down a dark corridor, bullets sprayed the door I had just passed through. A dimly glowing Exit sign appeared, and I hit the door at full speed. Rounds of ammunition came flying down the passageway, sinking into the walls around me. I was through the door and into a cement stairwell. I leaped down the stairs, oblivious to any pain or lack of oxygen. Above me, I could hear footsteps in pursuit, and they sounded faster than mine.

Finally I reached ground level and burst through the door. I was on the side of the building. I ran to my left, around the corner to my waiting speeder. No one was waiting for me; whoever they were, they must've never considered that I would make it back this far. I jumped into the speeder and lifted off. Several bullets struck the back of the speeder, but too late. The sound of rounds being fired died out slowly as I sped off into the early red sky.

Chapter Thirteen

Malloy was dead. A guilty voice in the back of my mind said that the NSA had followed me to the warehouse. As I guided my speeder over the city, I tried to think clearly. During our conversation, I'd learned something about the man and felt like I owed it to him to finish whatever it was he'd started. Unfortunately, I had no idea what it was.

I landed at a convenience store and went in to buy a couple packs of cigarettes. Malloy had just been gunned down, and I'd barely escaped, but life went on, and I was out of smokes. I slid back into the driver's seat and decided that my next move should be back to the Garden House. That would be the last place anyone would expect to find me, even if I'd been followed from there in the first place. I wanted to get Malloy's things. Maybe I'd find a clue as to why someone wanted him dead. My only concern was that maybe the bad guys had gotten there first.

I parked the speeder and walked to the front door of the boardinghouse. My knock was answered by the sweet little lady I'd met earlier.

"Back again?"

"Yes...we found Uncle Thomas. I came back to pick up his stuff."

The plump woman stepped aside and let me in. "How is he? Is everything OK?"

She must have sensed that something was wrong. I tried to sound positive. "Sure. Everything's fine."

I didn't think it would be appropriate to tell her that Malloy had been blasted into hamburger. I followed the woman up the stairs to the bedroom. She let me in and left. I looked around the room, realizing that its contents might be the last earthly possessions of Thomas Malloy. An old watch lay on the nightstand. I picked it up and read an inscription on the back. It said: *I love you Daddy.*

I'd faced death before and had several people close to me die. It was never easy. I tried to be optimistic. Maybe Malloy had gone out the way he'd wanted to. He'd taken death like a man. His actions may have even saved my life. I thought of Shakespeare's observation that a man dies once, but a coward dies a thousand times. Was I a coward for escaping? Shakespeare had also said that discretion is the better part of valor. It wouldn't have done either of us any good if I'd been killed, too. Besides, I personally had never fancied the thought of going down on the wrong end of an automatic rifle. I'd always envisioned my death involving being smothered by a Jayne Mansfield twin, but that was just another of my twisted little secrets.

I opened the nightstand drawer and saw a pair of reading glasses, a copy of *Reader's Digest*, and a wad of cash. The bills added up to about two thousand dollars—not a lot, but not chump change, either. I stuffed the bills into my pocket. I'd pay Malloy's board and take the rest to Emily, along with any of Malloy's stuff I couldn't use. She'd probably appreciate the money, but it wouldn't be much of a trade-off. I wasn't looking forward to telling her what had happened.

I found a suitcase under the bed and began throwing everything into it. One of the desk drawers contained two old, stained notebooks. I wanted to look them over but had to keep reminding myself that there would be time for that later.

Ten minutes later, I shut the door behind me and went down the stairs. Everything in the room had fit into the suitcase. The plump landlady came out to meet me.

"Did you get everything?"

"I think so. It certainly will be good to get this whole situation straightened up."

"I'm sure." The little woman smiled pleasantly.

"By the way, how much did Uncle Thomas owe you?"

"Oh...nothing. He paid ahead through the end of the week." She reached into her apron pocket and pulled out a hundred-dollar bill. "This is how much he overpaid."

I patted her on the shoulder. "Please. I know Uncle Thomas would want you to keep it."

She hesitated, then folded the bill back into her pocket. She reached out and took my free hand warmly. "Tell him thank you, and that he'll always be welcome here. He's such a very nice man."

I nodded and turned to leave, then turned back. "Do you remember anyone else coming by here looking for Uncle Thomas?"

The woman thought for a moment, then shook her head. "Not that I know of."

My speeder lifted off Valencia and hovered for a few moments. I wasn't sure where I should go. My office sounded like a bad idea. If the guys in masks had been NSA agents, they could have recognized me, and word might be getting back to Jackson Cross. Even if the hit squad hadn't been NSA, I could be tracked down by the license plate on my speeder. I was also carrying a recently murdered man's belongings and didn't want to be apprehended by anyone, including the police. I had to get someplace safe, and fast. Almost automatically, I set course for Chelsee's apartment.

Fifteen minutes later, I was standing outside the door to Chelsee's digs. A note was taped to the door, my name written on the envelope. I pulled the envelope off the door and examined it. The flap was not stuck down, but tucked inside. It looked as though the envelope may have been sealed, then reopened. I pulled out a note from inside and read:

Dear Tex,

By the time you read this, I'll probably be on my way to Phoenix. I'm sorry for the way I've been over the last few days. As I'm sure you've guessed, I'm having a hard time deciding what I want right now. Sometimes I think I'm in love with you, and the next time I see you, we're pals. Other times, I get upset and never want to see you again. I've decided to take a break for awhile, think things through, try to figure out what's best. I hope you aren't hurt by my decision, but I wanted to leave while things were going well. I'll give you a call soon and let you know how things are going.

Love, Chelsee

P.S. You left a couple things at my place. I dropped them off at Louie's.

I slipped the note in my pocket and left. Now I had yet another thing to think about. It wasn't fair. My brain was already sore. I needed a bourbon. I decided to risk a trip to the Brew & Stew.

The place was packed. Louie's diner usually got the insomnia crowd. He stayed open until everyone went home and usually did a lot of business even after the sun came up. I was too beat to visit the Fuchsia Flamingo—at least that's what I told myself. I'd leave the dirty work for tomorrow. Besides, I had a suitcase full of things to look through.

I stepped inside the Brew & Stew and breathed in the hearty scent of Louie's famous lamb stew and fresh buttery biscuits. The place was jumping, and Louie was bustling around, face red and eyes bulging. Despite his bulk, he was a miracle of efficiency, filling coffee mugs, juggling plates, and remembering a dozen drink orders, all at the same time.

He also seemed to be moderately clairvoyant. I'd been standing at the door for only a few moments when Louie turned toward me. He looked me over, then pointed toward the kitchen. Firmly grasping the handle to Malloy's suitcase, I stepped through the crowd and behind the bar like I owned the place. Louie held the swinging door open and ushered me into the heart of the Brew & Stew. The place was an olfactory factory. The smell of onions, garlic, cilantro, feta, sharp cheddar, fresh bread, and butter all mingled with the primary aroma of lamb stew and biscuits to create an almost visible culinary palette.

"It's a little crazy out there, Murph. Sorry I don't got a table for ya."

"That's OK, Louie. I really wasn't hungry until I stepped in here."

Louie flashed me his big, toothy grin. "My diner seems to have that effect on people. I think it's my gift in life. Have a seat. You want a drink?"

I nodded gratefully. "Bourbon, if you don't mind."

I sat down on a chair in the back corner. Louie ducked out of the kitchen and returned a minute later with a triple bourbon straight up. I took a deep swig and felt better. "So...you need a place to stay tonight?"

I was caught off guard. How did Louie know?

"Sorry?"

He motioned toward the suitcase in my hand. "I figured they might've kicked you outta your place."

I laughed, a little nervously. "No...everything's settled up at the Ritz."

I thought for a second, then decided to confide. "I'm in kind of a jam right now. I shouldn't go back to my office for awhile."

Louie gave me a big grin. "Geez, Murph. You know you can always crash here."

"You don't mind? It'd only be for tonight...well, maybe two nights."

"No problem. Those stairs go right up to my apartment. There's a couch up there that folds out. The place is kind of a mess, but make yourself at home."

Louie turned to leave. "If you're not ready to call it a night, come out to the bar. Or you can stay in here if you like."

"Thanks, Louie."

The big galoot waved me off and stepped out through the swinging door. Carrying the bourbon and Malloy's suitcase, I walked up the stairs. Louie was one hell of a guy. Anyone else would have asked questions. Not Louie LaMintz. He was, however, a real slob. His apartment looked like the aftermath of a Shriners' convention, or like my office after the NSA had come to play. I cleared out a small area on the floor and sat down. After a long slug of bourbon, I opened Malloy's suitcase and went to work.

After fifteen minutes, I'd turned up nothing more interesting in Malloy's clothes than lint balls. Setting the clothing aside, I picked up one of the notebooks. It was filled with drawings of the strange symbols and incomprehensible chicken-scratch liner notes. I flipped through it for several minutes, but someone would have to decipher it for it to be of any use to me. The other notebook seemed to be a journal, but the entries, like the liner notes in the first notebook, looked as though they'd been written in some kind of unintelligible shorthand. I'd need to find someone who could translate them, though who that would be, I didn't know.

Next up were two old paperback books. The first was called *There Are Messages from Outer Space*, written by J.I. Thelwait. I opened it up, and a slip of paper fell out. Probably a bookmark. Malloy had only gotten to page fifty-seven. I picked up the slip of paper and read *ASE_%_info@ccm.inet.com*. Then I put the slip of paper back into the book and dropped it into my coat pocket.

The second book was titled *Puzzles to Amuse and Challenge*. At a quick glance, it looked like Malloy hadn't done any of the puzzles. I slipped this book into my coat pocket, too. Puzzles were always a good way to kill time, though admittedly I didn't foresee myself enjoying much free time in the immediate future. Malloy had had some other miscellaneous items, like a traveler's alarm clock and a penknife, but none of them looked particularly important.

I emptied the suitcase, then turned to my bourbon and emptied the glass. Except for the unreadable notebooks and maybe the E-mail address, I felt like I'd come up empty. I had to be overlooking something. I turned my attention to the suitcase itself. After poking and prodding the interior for five minutes, I was pleased to discover a false panel. Using Malloy's penknife, I pried it open. Inside, there was a small computer disk. I didn't have a computer handy, so I stuck the disk in my pocket.

In the lining of the false panel, I discovered a small pocket. Reaching inside, I found several photographs. One was an old picture of a youthful-looking Malloy, in uniform. I flipped the photo over and saw the words *Promotion—1988*. A second snapshot was a wedding picture, showing Malloy with a beautiful woman. An inscription on the back read: *Wedding Day—April 5, 2007.*

The next picture showed a newborn baby. There was nothing written on the back. The last picture showed Malloy, his wife, and a teenage girl. The young woman's face looked familiar. I turned the photo over and read the inscription: *Dad, Mom, Regan—2028.*

I sat back, stunned. The girl in the picture was Regan Madsen. It was a fairly old photo, but I was sure of it. She was Thomas Malloy's daughter.

I thought back and ran through my conversation with her. Nothing in what she'd said would indicate her relationship to the dead man. I wondered why. What was her angle? Was she trying to find her father? Was she working with him or against him?

Too many questions and no answers. She and I needed to have a little chat.

I found Ms. Madsen's card, with a number handwritten on the back. A vid-phone sat on a stand by Louie's bed. Sitting on the edge of the bed, I punched in the code.

A bland female voice answered. "Imperial Inn. How may I direct your call?"

"I'm trying to reach Regan Madsen."

"Is she a guest?"

"I suppose so."

"One moment."

I listened to dead air for a few seconds, then an annoying beeping sound. After about thirty seconds the beeping stopped, and the bland voice was back again. "There's no answer. Would you like to leave a message?"

I wasn't sure where I was going to be for the next few days.

"No. I'll try back later."

It was late, and I'd had a full day. As I disconnected the vid-phone, I suddenly couldn't keep my eyes propped open. I laid back on the bed, intending to rest for a few minutes.

Chapter Fourteen

I woke up to see Louie's battered-looking face grinning down at me. "Hey, Murph. I'm makin' breakfast. You want some?"

I rubbed my eyes and tried to get my bearings. At first, I couldn't even remember where I was, let alone why Louie was there. I sat up on the edge of Louie's bed and looked around groggily. The sofa bed was folded out.

"Sorry. I didn't mean to fall asleep on your bed. Looks like I forced you onto the couch."

"Don't worry about it. When I came up, you were out cold. Didn't even take off your overcoat. I figured I'd better let you alone. Besides, the sofa's pretty comfy."

He was lying again. The fold-out bed looked like a torture device.

My mouth felt like a dirty dish towel—I hadn't brushed before bed. Damn. My toothbrush was back at the office. A slug of mouthwash would have to do, though a cup of Louie's Armageddon blend would probably be an effective substitute. I stood up and stretched. Breakfast sounded good. Louie clapped me on the shoulder. "You look hungry. I'll go down and put on some coffee."

He opened the door, then turned around. "Oh…you'll probably want to wash up. The bathroom's through that door."

Washing up sounded almost as good as breakfast. I splashed cold water on my face, then stuck my head under the faucet and soaked it. Slowly, my brain began to function. As I toweled off, I went through the events of the night before, listing the things I needed to get done. First, I needed to contact Regan Madsen and get the scoop on her and her father. Second, I needed to tell Emily. Third, I had to call Fitzpatrick and tell him what had happened. I was sure that he knew more than he'd told me, and now that I was right in the thick of things, maybe he'd clue me in.

My clothes smelled like a barroom floor around closing time, but the rest of me was refreshed. Louie's place might not be pretty, but it was safe and homey. Stepping out of the bedroom, I caught a whiff of French toast, coffee, and bacon. My heart leaped for joy. If I ever decided to get married again, I was going to find someone like Louie, only more attractive. Maybe he had a good-looking sister. Hmmm....unlikely.

Louie was standing at the grill, waving a spatula like a conductor's baton and humming "Hit the Road, Jack" in at least three keys. He caught me out of the corner of his eye and a gave me a sheepish look. "Cup of coffee for ya out on the counter."

"Thanks." I sat down on a bar stool and pulled out my Lucky Strikes. It looked like I'd slept on the pack. I took out a flattened cigarette and lit it up. The Armageddon was piping hot and went down like high-octane fuel. By the time I finished the cigarette and coffee, I'd been transformed from a Vespa scooter into a Harley Hog. My engine was revving when Louie exploded through the kitchen door, loaded with sizzling plates of food and a steaming pot of coffee. "I hope you're hungry, Murph. I went a little crazy."

The plate Louie slid in front of me was piled high with thick, golden slices of French toast, glistening with maple syrup. Strips of crisp bacon were stacked around the edge. Louie set a similarly laden plate and the coffeepot on the counter. Making his way around the bar, he plopped down onto the bar stool beside me and proceeded to fill our coffee mugs. I cut a four-layer pie slice out of the stack, drenched it in the buttery syrup, took a bite, and saw angels. A bite of hot, salty bacon and a slug of joe. A three-way marriage made in heaven.

For some time, we spoke nothing but the language of food: chewing noises, grunts, saying *Mmmmm*, and pointing toward related objects, such as coffeepots and syrup bottles. After a good twenty minutes, my gas gauge hit full, and I set down my fork and knife. The plate still contained enough breakfast for a family of three. I poured my third cup of Armageddon and reached for a post-prandial smoke. Louie was mopping up the last of the syrup on his plate. Even he was slowing down.

"You should be canonized, Louie. The Patron Saint of Greasy Spoons."

He dabbed at the corners of his mouth with a napkin. "I ain't too religious, Murph. Besides, they already got a St. Louie."

We sipped our coffees. Louie's face turned serious. "Chelsee came by the other day."

"Yeah, I know."

Louie gave me a quizzical look. "She left me a note at her place...said she was leaving and that she was gonna drop off some things of mine over here."

Louie nodded. "I got your stuff up in my apartment. Forgot to get it...remind me before you leave."

Another pause. I didn't want to seem too eager, but I was curious. "So, did you talk to her at all before she left?"

The big, ugly grin. "You mean, did she say anything about *you*?"

I blew out a stream of smoke through a conceding smile.

"We talked for a bit. She's having a hard go of it."

"Meaning what? Me? Turning thirty?"

"Yeah. All of it. I told her everyone goes through a phase like this. I haven't yet, but of course I'm still young. I'm fifty-eight, and I still ain't ready to settle down."

Louie took another sip of the Armageddon. "Tell me, Murph, you ever been in true love?"

I crushed out my cigarette. It was a symbolic gesture. "Sure. I was married before, remember?"

Louie snorted. "The only thing easier than fallin' in love is gettin' married. I'm askin' if you ever been really, truly in love."

I thought for a moment. "Well, I've always had this thing for Jayne Mansfield."

"C'mon, Murph. I'm trying to talk here."

I shrugged. "I suppose I've been in love a few times. I don't know about being *truly* in love...whatever that means."

"I tell ya, Murph. It's chemicals. Up in your brain. We got these chemicals going nuts. That's why we fall in love too easy."

"So what's your point?"

"My point is, falling in love don't mean a lot. What's hard is knowing someone well and still likin' 'em. But that ain't even the hardest thing...and the hardest thing is what makes all the difference."

"So what's the hardest thing?"

Louie's voice was soft. "Finding someone you can trust."

My big, lumpy friend took our plates and lumbered into the kitchen. I lit up another smoke. Louie was right. In retrospect, I'd never really trusted anyone. That wasn't why my marriage hit the skids, but it was probably my excuse for not trying again.

Louie emerged from the kitchen and refilled his coffee mug. I flicked an ash off my Lucky. "So what's your advice?"

Louie took a sip of steaming java. "Chelsee's ready for commitment. She'll give you the first shot, but she ain't gonna wait around forever. A lot of guys in this world would give their right arms for one minute of Chelsee's attention."

Donor programs being what they are, Louie might or might not have been exaggerating, but I got the point. Once again, I was mired in my ever-repeating pattern of wanting only the things I couldn't have. Chelsee was beautiful, intelligent, strong, and sexy. She represented everything good I'd ever looked for in a woman. I was probably in love with her. Maybe I even trusted her—at least as much as I was capable of. All the requirements were satisfied. Only now I wasn't sure. It was like the old Groucho Marx line: I would never get involved with a woman who'd get involved with someone like me. The indecision was unbearable. Maybe Chelsee was right, and a little break would help to clear things up.

In the meantime, I had other pressing business. I thanked Louie for his advice and French toast, not necessarily in that order, then reminded him about the things Chelsee had left for me. We went up to his apartment. I put Malloy's things back into the suitcase and closed it up. The two paperbacks, the photos, and the computer disk were in my coat. When I finished, Louie handed me a bank card, Lucas Pernell's business card, and a Pez dispenser.

"Thank God. I thought I'd lost this." I held up my Spiderman Pez shooter.

Louie admired it. "Good thing she found it."

I pocketed the items. "Are you sure this is all? I mean, there wasn't a box of any kind, was there?"

Louie shook his head. "No, that's all of it."

"All right. I've got to get a move on. Do you mind if I leave my suitcase here?"

"Of course not, Murph. You can leave your things and stay as long as you like."

"I appreciate it. So long, Louie."

I left through the back door in the kitchen. It was fairly early in the evening, but it was already quite dark. I walked up the alley behind the Brew & Stew to the back of the Ritz. I had to get into my office for several reasons, even if the place was being staked out by the NSA. As long as no one was actually inside my office, I was pretty sure I could get in and out without being seen. I peeked into the alley that ran alongside the Ritz and out to Chandler Avenue. There was no one in sight. I hurried across to the back of the Ritz and climbed a pipe that ran down from the roof. It was familiar and sturdy and ran right by the window at the back of my apartment. I peered through my window. It was pitch black inside. Holding onto the pipe precariously with the one hand, I was able to slide the window open.

Seconds later, despite a likely hernia, I was in my apartment. Closing the window behind me, I limped across the room. Suddenly, a glimmer of light swept under the door to my office. I froze. For at least a full minute I stood like a post, ears straining. Apparently, the intruder hadn't heard me enter. The light flashed again past the door. I moved quietly, until my hand wrapped around the doorknob. Tensing my muscles and ignoring a painful hernial twinge, I threw open the door.

A masked figure whirled around, and immediately the flashlight went out. I lunged in the direction of the trespasser, but moved too slowly. Hitting what must have been one of my chairs, I stumbled and fell to the floor. To my right, the door to the fire escape flew open, and the intruder was gone like a shadow. By the time I limped to the door, no one was in sight.

I closed the door and waited for my eyes to readjust to the darkness. Whoever had been in my office, it probably wasn't the NSA. The Feds had no reason to be secretive. Besides, an NSA agent would have just shot me, not run away. So who was it? This was a rough part of town, but I doubted that it had been a run-of-the-mill break-in. My office just wasn't the kind of place someone would want to rob. Whoever had broken in had to be connected to the Malloy case. The only thing I knew for sure was that, even though the thief probably wasn't NSA, the agency was watching. And they had one eye on me and one on the clock. It was a little after 8:00 P.M.—I had less than fourteen hours left...and counting. I decided to leave the lights off.

The office was already trashed from before. I didn't get a good look at the intruder, but I hadn't seen anything except the flashlight in his hands. Regardless, there was nothing relevant to be found here. The box was either still at Chelsee's apartment, or she'd taken it with her. I was inclined to believe that she'd left it. Otherwise, she probably would have mentioned in her note that she had taken it. Now I'd have to search her place to find the box. Why did I have to do everything the hard way?

My first priority was to look at the disk I'd found in Malloy's suitcase. I crept to my computer and turned it on. When it finished booting, I stuck the disk in and ran it. A message appeared on the screen: CONTENTS ENCRYPTED. PLEASE ENTER AUTHORIZATION CODE. I wasn't surprised, but it certainly was a pain. Without a hope in the world, I began typing possible passwords. THOMAS, MALLOY, REGAN, ROSWELL, FITZPATRICK, BLUEBOOK, BLUEPRINT, PEKING, SPACESHIP, 1984, ORWELL. Everything possible that I could think of. Nothing worked. Frustrated, I popped the disk out and shut down the computer.

As I slid the disk into my coat pocket, I felt the paperback books and remembered the E-mail address. I crossed the room to my modem. To my horror, it was now in three easy-to-carry pieces, undoubtedly courtesy of the NSA thugs. How could they? What had this little gadget ever done to them? Now I was going to have to borrow someone else's modem.

The voice-messaging unit had a short message from Regan Madsen, asking me to call her as soon as possible. The second message was from my broker, telling me he had some bad news about my 401K dividends. The last thing I needed to hear about. The third message was from Chelsee, telling me she had arrived and asking if I'd gotten the note. She left a number, which I jotted down in my notebook.

The final thing I needed to do was purely hygienic. I changed my clothes and grabbed my toothbrush, a bottle of aftershave, and my deodorant. Being manly doesn't mean you have to smell like it. I left the way I came in.

I had one more visit to pay before leaving Chandler Avenue. Not wanting to risk going in the front, I walked to the side door of the Fuchsia Flamingo and knocked. After knocking again, the door opened a crack. A large, ugly bouncer, not Leach, stared down at me.

"This ain't the entrance, pal. Go around front."

I smiled pleasantly. "I don't want to come in. I need to speak to Gus Leach, please."

"Mr. Leach is working up front. Go around and talk to him there."

"I need to talk to him here."

The troll's voice went up a notch. "You tryin' to be stupid? Go around front."

"Look, friend. I don't want to make trouble, but I have something extremely important to tell Gus. It's a private matter, and we need to discuss it here. If you don't mind."

The bouncer opened the door and moved his massive frame

into the just slightly larger door frame. "I say you can't come in. You wanna make trouble?"

I took a step back, still smiling pleasantly. "I'd rather not, but I really have to see Gus. I'd be happy to pay you for your effort."

With startling quickness, the giant troll grabbed the lapel of my overcoat. "OK, that does it."

The bouncer's fist came at me. I jerked my head, causing his punch to glance off. It was like being hit in the face by a baseball instead of a bowling ball. I struggled like a gazelle in the jaws of a lion.

After the third punch, I was about to go limp and play dead when I heard Leach's voice. "Let go of him, Hoss."

The pavement slammed into my head. Through the birds, stars, and other metaphorical light flashes, I made out Leach pulling me to my feet.

"You sure have a way with people, don't you Murphy?"

I was too busy focusing to respond.

"So what are you doing trying to get in the side door?"

Slowly, my speech returned to normal. I recounted to Leach what had happened with Malloy. Leach's reaction was subdued, but I could see that the news of Malloy's death affected him deeply. I wanted to find out more about what their relationship had been, but time was golden. I'd come to deliver the news and the cash I'd found, no more. After a moment of silence, Leach thanked me for letting him know. He took the money from me and said he would tell Emily later. I asked if I could come back at another time and ask a few more questions. Leach nodded and went back into the club.

Still woozy, I bent down and brushed gravel off my trousers and overcoat. There was a neat little tear on the side of my left pant leg. Damn it. I'd just changed.

I walked back down the alley, behind the Ritz, the Electronics Shop, and the Brew & Stew, to my speeder. As I stepped out of the shadows and into the parking lot, my nose caught a familiar scent, and a voice startled me.

"A lovely evening."

Gordon Fitzpatrick was leaning against the brick wall, a Cubana nestled flavorfully between his index and middle fingers.

"It certainly is."

Fitzpatrick took a puff off his cigar. "I believe it's time we had a talk, Mr. Murphy."

Chapter
Fifteen

"It's an unfortunate turn of events."

I sat quietly, smoking and watching Fitzpatrick's furrowed face. He looked off, someplace far away, and played absently with a ring on his right hand. "Extremely unfortunate."

I flicked an ash off my Cubana and surveyed Fitzpatrick's hotel suite. I'd heard that the Savoy was deluxe, but seeing was believing.

Fitzpatrick swung his gaze around to me and mustered a meager smile. "Well, I suppose that brings our partnership to an end. What do I owe you?"

"I think you owe me some details."

The old man kept his eyes on me, but turned his head slightly and threw me a quizzical look. "Details?"

I leaned forward, elbows on my knees. "Look, Mr. Fitzpatrick, Malloy was onto something big. And he was gonna spill the details to me just before someone popped in and turned him into corkboard. Not only am I interested in finding out what Malloy was going to tell me, but I also feel like I owe it to him to find out who killed him and why."

I leaned back in my chair and prepared to take another puff. "I'm going to stay on the case for awhile longer, and, to be honest, I think you can give me some helpful information."

I seemed to have taken Fitzpatrick by surprise. His eyes were fixed on me. "There's no reason for you to get involved. As you saw, just being around Malloy was perilous. Being entangled in his business would undoubtedly prove to be just as treacherous. A word of advice, Mr. Murphy: take the money and walk away."

He was sincere, but it was a wasted effort.

"It's too late. I'm already involved."

"And why is that?"

"Well, counting last night, I've had three little incidents in the past week that could have left me collecting dust on a cold slab." I detected a hint of bitterness in my own voice. Talking about my own death always made me testy. "It may be my quintessential male 'screw it or kill it' mentality, but I have a hard time turning the other cheek."

"If you're looking for revenge, I think it likely that you'll end up on that cold slab after all."

"It's not revenge. It's the...thrill of the hunt."

"You located Malloy. The hunt is over. Let me pay you, then go back to your life."

"I'm not talking about Malloy. I'm talking about the boxes."

Fitzpatrick was taken aback. It wasn't clear whether he was startled or just confused. I wanted to know which one it was. He turned his face away and examined the dark corners of the room. Like someone breaking a New Year's resolution, he reached for his ring and began fiddling with it again. After some time, he moved his eyes back to me, then to the glass sitting on the armrest of my chair. "More bourbon?"

I nodded and handed him the empty glass. Fitzpatrick rose slowly and walked to the table on the far side of the room. He spoke over his shoulder. "If you insist on becoming involved, I must be certain that you can be trusted and relied upon. If my suspicions are confirmed, we will be up against formidable opposition."

Fitzpatrick turned to face me and replaced the stopper in the bourbon decanter. "This is not something you can dabble in. If you want in, I must insist on complete commitment."

"I've never had trouble committing—except, of course, to women. Count me in, one hundred percent."

He returned with a healthy serving of straight bourbon. "I'll warn you at the outset: I don't know more than I've told you about Malloy's recent activities. I knew him quite well many years ago, but as I told you, we didn't stay in touch. I received an anonymous message some time ago, which led me to believe that he might be in danger."

"You don't know who would've sent the message?"

Fitzpatrick shrugged. My bet was that he had a few guesses. "It may have been Malloy himself, though I don't know how he would have located me. But that's beside the point. All I have to go on is a vague theory as to why Malloy's life was in jeopardy, based on what I knew about his work years ago."

"Malloy told me a little about his work on the Blueprint Project."

"Good. That will save some explaining, though you may then already know a lot of what I know."

"Well, go ahead. I'll stop you if I've heard anything before."

He took a sip of tea and cleared his throat. "I met Thomas Malloy in China, during the winter of 2002. He was doing translation work for the government. I happened to be living in Peking at the time. The two of us became friends. After several years, Malloy began to confide in me about some of his confidential interests, especially Project Blueprint. Did he mention his work with the alien symbols?"

I nodded. "I think that some of the stuff I recovered is related to his research with the symbols."

"I'm eager to see what you found." Fitzpatrick's eyes gleamed.

"We'll examine that as soon as possible. At any rate, Malloy showed me some of the work he'd done. He felt confident that he'd deciphered some of the hieroglyphics, but he was still far from a significant breakthrough. What little he believed he had translated, however, was fascinating. His interpretation of one section seemed to refer to another spacecraft. Whether the second ship had come before the one in the Roswell crash, or was to follow, Malloy didn't know."

"Pardon my ignorance, but that doesn't sound like the kind of information that would get someone killed."

Fitzpatrick considered for a moment. "He was at the very beginning of the deciphering process. Who knows what else he might have discovered. Maybe the notebooks will help us follow his trail. Now, I've told you what I know. Tell me what you've learned. You mentioned something about a box."

Starting from the beginning, I explained what happened with Emily Sue Patterson, then my run-in with Jackson Cross. At the mention of the NSA, a concerned look passed over Fitzpatrick's face. I then told him about finding the box. For the time being, I left out Regan Madsen and the fact that she said she had a box like the one I'd recovered. I finished my story and drained the bourbon.

"I assume you don't have the box with you."

"No, I don't have it with me. It's hidden away someplace safe."

"Tell me more about it. What does it look like?" he asked eagerly.

"It's fairly small, about the size of a recipe box, if you know what I mean. The strangest thing is that it doesn't open—at least I can't see how to open it."

Fitzpatrick nodded, as if he expected to hear this.

"Are there any markings on the exterior?"

"Just some scratches by someone trying to get it open."

Fitzpatrick picked up my empty glass and went to the well for the third time. "I think I've seen the box you've described. In China, Malloy had four or five such boxes. They were unique versions of the traditional Chinese puzzle box. Malloy said he'd had them made specially. They were made out of material recovered at Roswell, which he'd made off with after Project Blueprint was disbanded. At the time, the boxes were simply a novelty. Malloy kept spare change and other trifles in them. In fact, I think he actually kept recipes in one of them. He was quite an excellent cook."

"So you know how to open them?"

Fitzpatrick returned with my bourbon. "No. Malloy never told me, and it never occurred to me to ask."

I thought back to my conversation with Jackson Cross. It seemed like it had been a week since I'd been taken to the NSA office, but I realized suddenly that it had been less than two days. I checked my watch—the thirty-six hours Cross had given me were almost up. I knew that I couldn't give up the box, but I was also concerned with my future. I decided to lay out my cards and let Fitzpatrick help me figure out my best hand.

"The NSA gave me an ultimatum to give them the box within thirty-six hours. That was about thirty-three hours ago."

"You're surely not thinking of turning it over?"

I shook my head. "No, but I don't know what I should do. If I run out on the NSA, they're not going to rest until I'm slowly, painfully dead. I'd just as soon avoid that."

Fitzpatrick seemed lost in thought for some time. "How would you feel about giving me the box?"

"I'm not sure. Can I trust you?" The biggest sucker question in the world. Asked a million times, always answered the same way.

"Yes, you can. I have as much money and other luxuries as I could ever want. My motives here center solely on following the trail my old friend pointed me toward. I don't know where it will lead, but I intend to reach the end. If you join me, I believe that will improve my odds of success."

With that little pep talk, he'd convinced me to trust him. I was going to give him the box. Now I just had to find it.

Chapter
Sixteen

The phone rang five times, followed by a pause, a click, and a pleasant, girlish voice. "We're not in at the moment. Please leave a message, and we'll get back to you. Thanks."

I hung up. Under normal circumstances, I'd wait until I could talk to Chelsee before breaking into her apartment. Unfortunately, I was short on time.

The door to Chelsee's apartment was dead bolted. I pulled out my bank card, but it was no use. Without a key, the only possible way to get in was to kick down the door, always a last resort. I searched around the doorway, hoping to get lucky and find a spare key. No dice. I lit a smoke and paced around, waiting for my muse to speak. Where would Chelsee keep a spare?

The newsstand.

I flew back to Chandler Avenue and made my way furtively to the newsstand. The street was pretty quiet, with almost no foot traffic. I ducked in behind the magazine racks and glanced up toward my office. It seemed to be empty. I didn't feel like I was being watched, but I still tried to be as stealthy as possible, just to be on the safe side.

I began my search, flipping through magazines, opening books, moving huge piles of publications. I ran my hands along the sides and bottoms of all the shelves. Ultimately, I reached a point where the only thing left to do was dismantle the entire newsstand. I thought it over. If Chelsee kept a spare key here—

which was appearing less and less likely—she would hide it somewhere easily accessible. Tearing down the shelves wouldn't turn up anything. It looked like I'd have to go back and kick in the apartment door after all.

As I turned to leave, I accidentally bumped a metal frame full of newspapers. Before I could react, it tipped over, spilling papers everywhere and making a loud clatter. I peeked up over the counter. No one was around. Then I reached down and started to pick up the newspapers. There was a brick facade behind where the metal frame had been standing. One of the bricks appeared to be loose. I grabbed it and pulled. It slid out neatly. I leaned down and lit a match near the opening. A house key sparkled in the firelight.

Ten minutes later, I was inside Chelsee's apartment. It was a small place—a piece of cake to search. At least that's what I thought for the first half hour. I looked through every drawer, every cupboard, every closet, under the furniture. The box was nowhere to be found. I sat down at the vid-phone and tried once more the number Chelsee had left me. Still no one home.

It occurred to me that I hadn't checked the appliances. I went to the kitchen and looked through the stove, the microwave, and the dishwasher. Finally, I opened the refrigerator. It was practically empty. I pulled out the crisper tray. Nothing. I opened the freezer compartment. Two ice cube trays and a half gallon of chocolate ice cream. I closed the refrigerator and fired up a cigarette. Where else would it be? I smoked and mulled for five minutes. Maybe I was going to hurry up and wait after all. I crushed out the Lucky Strike. I could use a snack.

I got a bowl from one of the cupboards and a spoon from the silverware drawer. Opening the freezer, I grabbed the ice cream, set the container on the kitchen table, and lifted the lid. There was the box.

I punched in the number for the Imperial Inn. The operator connected me and, a few moments later, Regan Madsen's staggeringly beautiful face appeared on the screen.

"Hello, Tex."

"Hi."

"You ready to get together?"

I certainly was. Stay cool, Murphy. "I think I can squeeze you into my busy schedule."

Regan smiled exquisitely. "I like the sound of that. When?"

"Whenever you're free."

"Oh, I'm never free, but I do have some time. Why don't you come over here? We can meet in my room."

It was an appealing suggestion, but I was bringing the box along and wasn't completely sure I could trust her. "I never go to a woman's hotel room on the first date. It'd be scandalous behavior for a chaste young man like myself."

Regan raised an elegantly curved eyebrow. "I promise, I'll be gentle."

"Well, in that case, it's totally out of the question."

Her smile was flawless. "You know, some men wouldn't be so resistant."

"Yeah, well, some men see a pretty face and turn into a pile of goo. I'm not so superficial."

Regan conceded with a feigned pout. "All right—if we have to—we can meet somewhere that won't offend your integrity or virtue. There's a lounge here at the Imperial. When can you be here?"

"Give me half an hour."

"Make it twenty minutes. I hate to wait."

The Imperial Lounge was a class joint—real leather seats, wooden phone booths, and a sofa in the men's room. Scores of celebrity-autographed photos were hung over shiny silver wallpaper. The bartender wore a tie and didn't seem to hate his job.

"Guest?"

"Meeting one."

"First time in, right?"

I nodded and blew out a stream of Lucky smoke.

"What'll you have?"

"Bourbon, straight up."

The bartender turned and poured two fingers' worth into sparkling crystal. He turned back and placed the glass in front of me with the care of a pediatrician. "I'll comp this one. Think of it as the Imperial Welcome Wagon."

I pulled out a ten-spot and tossed it onto the bar. "Think of this as a tip."

The bartender tapped his forefinger twice on the bar and picked up the bill. I took a sip and slowly scanned the lounge. The bourbon was first-rate—another reason to love the Imperial Lounge. The place was pretty big. There were maybe a dozen people in various stages of intoxication, but they were so scattered, it made the place look practically empty.

I had known it would only take me ten minutes to get here, but I wanted to get in before Regan did and survey the territory. There was no particular reason to think the NSA would be following her, but I wanted to check for myself. The place looked clean. I turned back to the bar and picked up half a Lucky from the large crystal ashtray. A minute later, as I extinguished the smoke, I caught an alluring scent, and Regan slid onto the bar stool to my left. The bartender hurried over.

"Evening, Ms. Madsen. What can I get for you?"

"A glass of Pinot Noir, Douglas. And one more of whatever my friend here is drinking."

"Put it on your room tab?"

"If you would."

Regan looked at me in the mirror across the bar. Her voice was low and magnetic. "We really should start meeting like this."

I took another shot of bourbon. "I don't know. What about your husband? And the kids...how many are there now? Six, seven?"

"Fourteen, actually."

Douglas, the bartender, returned with our drinks. Regan raised her glass. "To impossible standards."

We both drank. It felt like we'd started a ritual. Still holding her wine glass, Regan reached under the bar stool and picked up a shopping bag. "Shall we adjourn to a dark corner?"

I pocketed my smokes, drained my first bourbon, and stood up, grabbing my backpack from the floor. Carrying my second bourbon, I followed Regan across the room. She had a smooth stride and jaunty posture. Her presence was that of something free and untamed—probably impossible to catch, though she seemed to be indicating availability.

We sat at a small table in a corner. Regan chose the seat next to me, but not too close. She leaned down, away from me, and came up with an elegantly styled accessory item, which also happened to contain cigarettes. I lit a match and held it up to the cigarette cushioned softly between her ripe lips. Again, her cool hand wrapped around mine. Regan drew in, removed the cigarette from her mouth, and blew out the match. My stomach flip-flopped like a fish on a boat deck.

"You brought the box?"

I lit a smoke to calm myself down. "Yeah, but we need to discuss something else first."

Regan leaned back, holding her cigarette at a very feminine angle, and crossed her legs gracefully. Her manner implied that she was expecting a completely different subject than the one I had in mind.

"Tell me about your father." My tone was serious, but Regan ignored it.

"This isn't your idea of foreplay, is it?" She wasn't going to volunteer anything. She'd probably never had to in her entire life.

"Tell me about Malloy. Thomas Malloy. Your father."

Regan's smile disappeared like a Kennedy at a car accident. A look of panic crossed her face for just a second before she recovered. She was good, but now I had the upper hand. "How did you find out?"

"That's irrelevant. The fact is, I know who you are. Now I want some straight talk."

Regan's hand trembled slightly as she smoked. She didn't seem accustomed to being out of control. Her agitation just increased my resolve. I had her on the ropes and wasn't about to let her loose.

"Back in my office, you said that Malloy was a dead man. That's not the kind of thing you hear from loving daughters."

"Well, it's true. He's brought it on himself. I tried to warn him, but he wouldn't listen. He's never listened to me."

"Actually, that's not true. He told me you made him quit smoking."

Regan jerked forward. "You talked to him? When? Where is he?"

I lit another smoke. Regan probably deserved to know what had happened to her father. She was off-balance as it was. Maybe telling her now would give me a good indication of their relationship. It was a cold, calculated ploy, but I needed to know.

"I talked to your father last night."

Regan was impatient. "Where is he? I want to see him."

"It's too late."

The beautiful face went pale. "What do you mean? He's dead?"

I nodded and took another slug of bourbon.

Regan looked off, away from me. Her legs were crossed and she was leaning forward, elbow on her knee, right hand covering her mouth.

I smoked in silence for several minutes. When Regan turned her gaze back toward me, two glistening lines ran from the corners of her eyes to each side of her mouth. She moved her wine glass and picked up the napkin from underneath. Her composure was almost unbearable. She dried her eyes and nose, then took a sip of the Pinot Noir. She started to speak, but choked slightly.

I've never known what to do when a woman cries. More than anything, I wanted to hold Regan and tell her that everything would be fine, that I'd take care of her. But I didn't. I couldn't afford to. Sometimes, being a cynic is a pain in the ass. I watched her cry, wanting to comfort her, but knowing full well that more than one sap has fallen for an act just like this one. I followed my head: when in doubt, doubt.

Regan's voice trembled. "Will you excuse me?"

She headed for the ladies' room. I watched her until she reached the door, then turned back to my distilled and roasted friends. Suddenly, I realized she'd left her shopping bag and purse. I peered over, into the bag. There was a box inside, very similar to the one I had. I leaned back and took a drag.

She was on the level. My PI instincts were usually pretty accurate, though they only worked sporadically, like a stereo speaker with a short. My judgment of human nature, on the other hand, was terrible, as my choice of wives and investment brokers clearly showed. But I was sure this time. Regan was so upset, she'd forgotten all about the box. If she'd been putting on an act, she never would have let it out of her sight.

I signaled the bar and ordered another drink for both of us. After several minutes, Regan returned to the table. To the untrained eye, she looked as though nothing had happened. Her strength of character was enviable. I wanted to get to know her thoroughly. My voice was soft. "I'm sorry you had to find out this way."

Regan looked up from her wine and attempted a hollow smile. "Me too."

There was a long pause.

"Do you still want to talk? Or should I come back later?"

She took a deep breath and exhaled slowly. Her shoulders went back and her hollow smile filled out a little. "I'll be fine." She downed the rest of her wine. "All I need are a couple more bottles of wine and a little time to think. I'll have the wine now and do the thinking later."

I watched her, hesitantly. She took out another cigarette and lit it herself.

I went to the bar and brought back a full bottle of the Pinot. Regan seemed to have regained her composure. I filled her glass and sat back. "I suppose you want to know everything," she said.

"Of course."

"OK. I'll tell you what you want to know, but first, tell me...what happened."

I explained briefly. The only part of my conversation with Malloy that I mentioned was what he'd said about quitting smoking. Regan listened intently and even smiled at my description of her father. When I finished, she drained yet another glass of wine and refilled it.

"All right, from the beginning. I was an only child. My father and mother both worked for the government and met while they were assigned to Peking. I spent most of my childhood in China. My mother died when I was eighteen. My father and I were always close and got even closer after she died. Until...well, until about a year ago. He remarried...someone I didn't think was good for him." Regan gestured toward me. "Well, you know her. That's how you ended up with the box."

I acknowledged her without speaking.

"After he married Emily, we couldn't be around each other without arguing. I haven't seen him for months."

"How did you end up with the box?"

"He sent it to me. It arrived about a week ago."

"Do you know why?"

Regan stubbed out her cigarette. "People were trying to get their hands on his work. If he thought they were getting close, he probably divided up the information they were looking for and sent it out to a handful of people he could trust."

"What's in the boxes?"

"I don't know, exactly. My father never told me much about his work. He said that it was better for me not to know about it, but I used to snoop around. I found out a few things."

"Like what?"

"As you probably know, he was a linguist. He had notebooks filled with odd-looking symbols. They looked like they might be Egyptian. I think he was trying to translate them."

"So what makes you think that these symbols could some-how be worth a fortune?"

"I overheard a conversation he had with a stranger a few years ago. The man said that he could handle the transaction, which would be worth an astronomical amount. Those were his exact words. Dad refused. He said that some things shouldn't be bought or sold, regardless of the potential payoff."

What Regan was telling me seemed to jibe with what I knew about Malloy. "Did you ever see the boxes before? Did he have them at the house where you grew up?"

"He had them for a long time. Unfortunately, he only showed me how to open one of them. And it's not the one I have."

Regan reached down, then set the box she'd brought on the table. It looked very much like mine, except that it had a design on it. I got the box out of my backpack and set it beside the other one. Regan looked it over carefully.

"This isn't the one I know how to open, either."

We sat in silence, staring at the boxes for some time. Question after question went through my mind. Two Pandora's boxes. What was inside them? What contents would be important enough to die for?"

Regan's voice broke into my reverie. "So, what do we do now?"

I thought it over for a bit. "Well, I suppose we need to figure out how to open these."

"What if we can't?"

"I guess we should put them someplace safe and figure out where the other ones went. Do you have any idea who else he would have sent a box to?"

Regan was quiet for a few moments, then shook her head. "No."

"We need leads. I want you to see what you can dig up. Even if you don't like her, I think you should talk to Emily and see if she can help. In the meantime, if you don't mind, I'm going to take these boxes and see if I can get inside them."

From the look on her face, Regan didn't seem really comfortable with the idea, but I wasn't giving her any options—we were going to play it my way. I put both boxes into my backpack.

After they were securely stowed away, I leaned toward the beautiful woman and took her hand. "You're going to have to trust me, Regan. Help me find the other boxes. We'll get everything together, then decide what to do. OK?"

She was vulnerable, and clearly hated it. After pulling away and collecting her things, she stood and looked down at me. "I guess I have no choice, do I?"

She started to walk off, then stopped and turned back. "Don't run out on me, Tex. I've already lost my father."

I looked up at her deep, clear eyes. "I won't."

Chapter
Seventeen

I had other things I wanted to discuss with Regan, but I'd grilled her enough for a day with such bad news in it. I sat in the lounge for awhile longer, examining the boxes. What had Fitzpatrick called them? Chinese puzzle boxes? Whatever they were, they had me baffled. Maybe Fitzpatrick could figure them out. My instincts had already decided to trust the old man. Letting him hold onto both boxes was safer than carrying them around, and if he could unlock them, it would be an added bonus. In the meantime, I'd be free to track down the other boxes.

I flew back to Fitzpatrick's hotel. He confirmed that the boxes did indeed appear to be the ones Malloy had owned in Peking. I left him hunched over one of them, examining it closely.

Sitting in the driver's seat of my speeder, I considered my next step. The two boxes were as safe as they could be for the time being. Regan would, I hoped, go out and find a lead for me after she licked her wounds for a while. Chelsee was on the back burner. The deadline Jackson Cross had given me had come and gone, but I was still among the living. I supposed that was a good sign. Maybe I should contact Mac Malden and see if he could give me any estimates on my current life expectancy.

Then there was the matter of getting past the encryption on Malloy's disk and reading whatever information was there. Unfortunately I had no idea what the password was. The only real lead I had was the E-mail address that had fallen out of the paperback book. I racked my brain, trying to think of where I could get onto the I-Net. No one I knew subscribed. Hold on a second. Malloy had a computer at the warehouse. People don't typically carry E-mail addresses without having Internet access. Maybe Malloy had been hooked up where he was working.

I flew over the waterfront area and landed for the second time at 54 Front Street. The outside of the warehouse looked no different. I was willing to bet the inside had changed significantly. The first two doors I checked were locked, but the side door was slightly ajar. I didn't like the look of it. Glancing around, I couldn't see any vehicles parked anywhere close. I stepped inside.

There hadn't seemed to be so many steps when I'd sprinted down them last night. By the time I reached the third floor, I was panting. Here and there, I saw chips in the concrete walls where my pursuers' bullets had struck. Was I dragging myself straight into a date with an armor-piercing slug? With some effort, I resisted the urge to turn back and continued on to the sixth floor.

The door into Malloy's former work area was closed. I paused, my ear to the door. There was no sound coming from within. I turned the knob and pushed the door open slowly.

The room was spotless. I'd expected to see a Pollock-esque display of blood and brains. Instead I saw a perfectly tidy, unused office space. Temporarily stunned, I walked around the area, trying to picture what had changed. The desk Malloy had been working on was still there, but a quick search showed that it had been cleaned out. The file cabinet must have been there before, but it, too, was empty. There was nothing to find. Not a scrap of paper, not a single rubber band or paper clip. And no indication that a man had been gunned down in this very room less than twenty-four hours ago. Whoever the hit men were, they were good.

Malloy's computer was in a corner, on the floor. I picked it up and set it on the desk. It didn't take long to get everything attached and ready. As I expected, the active data storage clip had been removed by whoever had cleaned out the place. All I could hope for was that Malloy had stored his modem access commands in ROM. If he had, I could log on even without a data storage clip.

He had. Within seconds, I was ready to surf. With the familiar whining and screeching noises, I was welcomed into the world of virtual communication. I pulled out the *There Are Messages from Outer Space* paperback, removed the bookmark, and typed in the E-mail address. After a short wait, the Message to Send screen popped up. I typed in *We need to meet* and clicked Send. Several minutes went by with no reply. I dug for my smokes.

The cigarette was smoked almost all the way down when I heard a beep. I clicked Open and read the message displayed. *Is this Malloy?*

The sender's ID was listed as Anonymous. I typed another message. *Malloy is dead.*

I sent the message and waited for a minute. Another beep. *Who are you?*

A friend. I was the last one to see him alive.

A longer interval passed. Whoever was on the other end was probably debating how to deal with me. Beep. *How much do you know about Malloy?*

Mr. Anonymous was testing me. *He died with a secret. I'm trying to find out what it was and keep it away from the bad guys. Can you help me?*

I was coming on pretty strong, but I didn't have time to pussyfoot around. This guy was either going to help me or he wasn't. His message came back. *Do you know about the box?*

He was interested. Luckily, I had a trump card. *I have two boxes.*

It took only fifteen seconds to get a response. *413 Viña del Mar. There are ears everywhere.*

The sloppily painted sign at 413 Viña del Mar identified the place as the Cosmic Connection. The tiny storefront was wedged between a fruit stand and a sex shop in a run-down business section just off the Wharf. The display window was filled with charms, amulets, UFO books, and astrology charts. It didn't look promising.

I opened the front door and stepped into the incense-filled shop. The interior was long and narrow, with old, creaky shelves bulging with boxes and books, reaching to the ceiling on either side. The place felt and smelled like an attic, stuffed with a mix of mysterious treasures and worthless relics.

A man stood behind the counter. His age fell somewhere between twenty and forty, with a face that was boyish, yet spottily bearded. His tiny wire-rimmed spectacles made him appear both scholarly and deranged. A baggy cardigan dwarfed his narrow shoulders and emphasized his hunched posture. From the pallor of his skin, I assumed that he saw as little of the sun as possible.

"Can I help you?"

I glanced around to make sure we were alone and approached the counter. "This is 413 Viña del Mar, right?" The man nodded. I thought back to the final E-mail message I'd received. "There are ears everywhere."

My new acquaintance squinted his eyes at me and pursed his lips solemnly. "Wait here."

He hurried to the front door and locked it. Then he leaned into the display window and flipped over the Open sign. Finally, he pulled down a shade to cover the door, leaving the room very dark. With a businesslike stride, he turned and brushed past me, heading toward a door at the back of the shop. "This way."

I followed him into a back room, eerily lit by an aquarium, a lava lamp, and a half dozen candles. The smell of incense was strong. My New Age guide motioned for me to sit down. I sat on a solid oak chair with a spiderweb design in the backrest. My arm rested on a heavy wooden table covered with dusty tomes, yellowed documents, and splotches of candle wax. Maybe while I was here, I'd try to make contact with my Great-Aunt Rita and see what she'd done with my X-MEN comic books.

"What's your name?"

"Murphy. What's yours?

"Ellis. Archie Ellis. Here's one of my cards. Do you have one?"

I reached into my overcoat and pulled out a wad of business cards. Finally finding one of my own, I handed it over to Mr. Ellis. As he looked it over, I checked out the card he'd tossed in front of me. *Archibald Ellis. UFOlogist...Mystic...Occult Expert...Licensed Tarot Reader...Numerologist.* I looked up, thinking of what Lucas Pernell had said about wheat and chaff. This guy struck me as a loony tune, but Malloy had been in contact with him. And he was still my only lead.

Ellis finished examining my card and looked up. "So, you're a PI."

I extended my hand across the table. "Good to meet you, Mr. Ellis."

His handshake was aggressive. "Call me Archie."

"OK, Archie. Let's talk about Malloy."

"Tell me what you know."

I spent the next fifteen minutes giving Archie a quick overview of what had happened. None of the principal players' names were mentioned (and I referred to the NSA as an unnamed federal agency), but Archie didn't seem to mind. He soaked up everything I said. My story continued up to the point where

I found the E-mail address. Ellis leaned back and pressed his fingertips together.

"Would you like some herbal tea?"

Only if I were in the middle of a desert, dying of dehydration. "No thank you."

Archie pressed his church steeple hands against his lips, lost in thought. I waited patiently. "You said that you have two boxes."

I nodded and pulled out my smokes. Archie's cool facade evaporated in horror as his eyes caught sight of my Lucky Strikes. "I don't allow any smoking in my shop. Sorry."

Looking peevishly at the smoldering trays of incense, I reluctantly replaced the pack. Damn health nuts. I couldn't wait to find out what this bozo knew, then get out of his New Age little shop of horrors.

"I've got two boxes, both of which came from Malloy."

Ellis leaned back in his chair. "Small, right? Made of a strange material...no way to open them?"

I confirmed with a slight nod. "You've seen them."

"I had one."

It was hard to believe that Malloy would've entrusted something important to this crackpot, but he seemed to know what he was talking about. "What do you mean you *had* one?"

"It was stolen, along with a disk I recorded during my interview with Malloy."

Three or four questions came into my mind at once. First, the box. "When did this happen?"

"Six days ago."

"Go on."

Ellis obviously felt stupid admitting that the box had been taken from him. "I'd only gotten the box the day before. Malloy had mentioned boxes during our interview, so I assumed that he was the one who'd sent it. There was no letter with it, no return address. I hid it here in the back room. The next evening, I came in here just after I opened the shop, and someone had broken in. The only things missing were the box and one of the interview disks. I tried to contact Malloy but couldn't get through to him. Since then, I haven't left the shop."

"Tell me about the interview with Malloy."

Ellis seemed relieved to change the subject of the box. "I publish a magazine called the *Cosmic Connection*. Maybe you've heard of it."

I nodded, vaguely remembering that Fitzpatrick had mentioned it. Ellis was pleased. "Well then, you know we have feature articles, investigative reports, and interviews, all concerning the supernatural, particularly all things extraterrestrial. I have contacts throughout the field of UFOlogy, one of whom is a man named Elijah Witt. He's a legend among those of us who study alien encounters."

The name didn't sound familiar.

"Mr. Witt and I have corresponded for some time. Maybe six months ago, he wrote and said that a friend of his, Thomas Malloy, was coming to town and that I should hook up with him. Actually, Malloy contacted me."

"Do you know what he was doing here?"

"Well, Mr. Witt was a professor at Berkeley for decades. He still has honorary status, though he's retired and lives in seclusion in the Northwest. Anyway, he pulled some strings and got Malloy use of a research lab at the university."

"What was Malloy working on?"

Ellis shrugged. "He wouldn't go into a lot of detail, but he did use a strange term: the Pandora Device. I have no idea what it means."

Fitzpatrick had said that he'd tracked Malloy to a nearby university. If Ellis' information was reliable, then I could assume that Malloy was at Berkeley creating, or working on, something called the Pandora Device. I shifted in my seat.

"What else did Malloy tell you?"

"Well, he talked about Roswell, of course. Actually, I still have that part of the interview."

"I thought you said it was stolen."

Ellis got up and walked toward an old wooden cabinet. "It was a long interview. I filled up an entire disk. After I started a second disk, we only talked for another five minutes or so. The first disk was stolen with the box. Luckily, the other disk was still in the video recorder, which I had taken home with me. I was going to publish a transcript of the interview in my magazine, but having the disk stolen ruined that plan."

He looked through the cabinet for a moment, then pulled out a disk in a blank sleeve. "This is it. You want to look at it?"

It didn't sound like there was much to see on the disk, but I wasn't about to jump to conclusions. A laser disk player sat on a nearby shelf. Ellis clicked it on and slid in the disk. A moment later, Malloy's face appeared on the screen. Ellis' recorded voice came from off-camera.

"Sorry for the interruption," Ellis' voice said. "You were saying..."

"As you know," Malloy continued, "the Roswell Complex has been shut down for years. Most people don't know that a tremendous amount of alien equipment and technology was, and still is, stored there."

"What type of equipment and technology?"

"Who knows? The best minds in the military couldn't figure them out. But I'll tell you this: the ship that crashed in Roswell was loaded with equipment. Several of the people on the project that I talked to said that it looked more like a supply ship than an exploratory craft. There were duplicates of almost everything on board. One device looked like it functioned as some sort of power cell, and there was a second one stored on the ship. Some of the analysts speculated that once they knew how to operate everything, the second set of equipment could be used to construct another ship. Of course, this was pure conjecture. As I said, the analysts never did figure anything out. Except, of course, the particle accelerator."

"Hypothetically speaking, do you think, with today's technology, scientists could create their own extraterrestrial craft?"

Malloy shrugged. "It's possible. Of course, all the alien equipment is still stored at the Roswell Research Complex."

"That could be a problem."

Malloy smiled conspiratorially. "More like impossible...if the rumors are true."

Ellis leaned into the picture and shook Malloy's hand. "Thank you for your time."

"My pleasure."

Ellis ejected the disk and returned it to the wooden cabinet. "See? There's not much there."

"What was Malloy referring to...the rumors about Roswell?"

Ellis seemed amused by my ignorance. "You haven't heard? That story's been around for ages. You must know that the Roswell Complex was shut down just before the war ended. The rumor is that one of the final projects turned into a major disaster. Apparently, several mysterious containers were recovered from the alien crash site. Researchers spent decades trying to figure out how to open them. After they'd stumbled onto how the particle accelerator worked, someone hit upon the bright idea of using it on the sealed containers. Well, they got the containers open, and all hell broke loose. Whatever had been stored inside was living matter. No one knows whether it was toxic or viral, but it killed off most of the researchers before anyone knew what was happening. The complex was quarantined and hasn't been opened since."

My tax dollars at work. From everything I'd learned over the past week, it seemed like nothing was foolproof as long as the military was involved.

Ellis broke into my thoughts. "So, what are we going to do now?"

I didn't like the "we" reference. Archie might have been reading too many Batman comics, but I wasn't in the market for a sidekick, especially one who drank herbal tea and preferred incense to good, clean tobacco.

"*I've* got to find out more about this Pandora Device. I'll probably need to contact Elijah Witt, as well."

Ellis' eager expression scrunched into a defensive frown. "I don't think that's a good idea."

"Why?"

"Well, Mr. Witt's a very important, very private person. And he doesn't talk to outsiders."

Archie sounded like he was talking about his pet hamster. I restrained myself from telling him that I really didn't care what he or Mr. Witt thought or did. "Oh, well. I guess that's my hard luck."

Ellis relaxed. "So...is there anything else I can tell you about?"

It was time to smoke. As I got up from my chair, one other question occurred to me. I reached into my pocket and pulled out the *There Are Messages from Outer Space* paperback. "You ever read this?"

Ellis looked at the book closely. "Sure. Mr. Witt wrote it. It's really good. See? The author's name is J. I. Thelwait. That's an anagram for Elijah Witt."

I slipped the book back in my pocket. Ellis kept talking, his tone becoming more anxious. He was like a fisherman about to lose the big one. "You should read *Foucault's Pendulum*, too. It explains everything. The Telluric Currents, the Templar Plan. It's all in there. Umberto Eco was a prophet."

He got up quickly and hurried around the table, placing himself between me and the door. "You should also read *The Fifth Column*. It's great. It proves that there's a giant conspiracy in the government. Aliens have been living among us for generations. It even hints that one of our presidents was alien, or at least half-alien. It's all documented. The crop circles...the alien abductions...the government knows about all of it. Heck, they're in on most of it!"

I moved past Ellis into the main room of the shop. He didn't even pause. "If you want my advice, trust nobody! I can tell that you're on the level, but most of the time, you never know. The aliens are everywhere!"

I stopped at the door and turned back with an exaggerated look of suspicion. "How can I be sure that you're not an alien, Archie?"

It was like I'd slapped him. He didn't recover for a few seconds. "Everyone knows—aliens deny their own existence. I wouldn't talk about them if I was one."

I smiled indulgently. "Ah...of course. Well, now that I know you can be trusted, I'd better be moving along. I'll be sure to keep your advice in mind."

Ellis hurried to the door and unlocked it. "It was good to meet you, Murphy. It's always nice to meet another believer. Keep in touch."

Chapter
Eighteen

I stepped out of the Cosmic Connection and lit up a much-needed smoke. Leaning against my speeder, I inhaled deeply. My mind reeled, trying to sort out all the information I'd acquired over the past few days. It was like trying to stuff a marshmallow into a piggy bank.

I tried to arrange the details chronologically. OK, first an alien spacecraft crashes at Roswell. The military moves in, confiscates the wreckage, and convinces the media that it was all a misunderstanding. Everything is taken to a secret complex near Roswell, where it's analyzed unsuccessfully for years. Malloy joins Project Blueprint and works on deciphering the alien symbols. Eventually, technology catches up, making it possible for the military to figure out some of the alien equipment, in particular an advanced particle accelerator. Our boys in the Pentagon figure out how to use it to build a better bomb, only it turns out to be a very bad bomb. We win the war, but lose the ozone. Project Blueprint is shut down; Malloy is transferred to Peking, where he spends the remainder of his career translating manuals and continuing his research on the alien symbols in his spare time.

So far, so good. Now it gets a little murkier. Malloy eventually has a breakthrough. He is now, apparently, the first and only Earth creature to read an extraterrestrial communication. So what does he do? He retires, comes back to the States, goes to Berkeley, and starts building something called the Pandora Device. He then disappears, surfacing only to give an interview to a crackpot. A short time later, he sends out at least three, maybe more boxes, which no one seems to know how to open. Then he's gunned down, seemingly by the NSA.

This thread got me from Point A to Point B. Unfortunately, it didn't really account for most of the peripherals. What was Malloy's association with Fitzpatrick? How did Elijah Witt figure into things? How was the murder of Sandra Collins linked to Malloy?

Then, of course, there were the highest priority questions. What was the message in the alien symbols? What was in the boxes? How many boxes were sent, and where were they?

My head felt like a vid-phone booth crammed full of fraternity pledges. I needed a stiff drink and a soft mattress.

I got back to the Brew & Stew just as Louie was closing up shop. "Hi, honey. I'm home."

"Hiya, Murph. You got in just under the wire. I'm gonna have a nightcap. Want a brandy?"

I slipped off my overcoat and tossed my fedora onto the counter. "I only drink brandy when I play bridge. That is to say, never."

Louie laughed. "OK, sue me for trying to introduce some culture into your life."

He reached under the counter and presented me with a full bottle of bourbon and a fancy crystal sipping glass. I grabbed the top of the bottle and twisted, hearing the faint popping sound and the sigh of virgin whiskey ready to fulfill its destiny. A full glass of bourbon and a well-packed Lucky Strike. Throw in a good night's sleep and a decent haircut, and I'd be in bliss.

Louie reached over and lit my cigarette. "Looks like you had a long day."

I carefully blew a long stream of smoke away from his big,

lumpy face. "How can you tell? Don't I usually look like this?"

"Pretty much. Your eyes are just real bloodshot."

"*You* think they look bad. You should see 'em from this side." It must've been all the damn incense. And Ellis didn't want me smoking in his place.

Louie and I sat drinking in silence for a few minutes. I was dog tired. When we finished our drinks, Louie turned out the lights, and we headed up to hit the hay. This time, I got to sleep in the torture device.

After a surprisingly decent sleep and a double Armageddon, I went to work on Louie's vid-phone. Checking in with Fitzpatrick, I learned that he hadn't had any luck opening either of the boxes. I then called Regan and arranged to meet her at the Imperial Lounge. She seemed to have recovered from our previous conversation and was back to her former self. I wasn't sure if that was good or bad.

I returned to my seat at the counter and picked up the first edition of the *Bay City Mirror*. It was still pretty early, and I really wasn't in a hurry, so I decided to do the crossword. I took a sip of Armageddon and found the puzzle. After twenty minutes, three cigarettes, and a refill on the joe, I'd filled in a grand total of five answers. I don't know why I like puzzles. All they ever do is make me feel like an idiot.

My eyes wandered over the page. Below the crossword was an anagram puzzle. I never did those—they were too much work. Suddenly, I remembered what Ellis had said about Elijah Witt, how he always used an anagram as a pen name. I pulled out the paperbacks from my overcoat pocket. Sure enough, the author of *There Are Messages from Outer Space* was J. I. Thelwait. The letters could be rearranged to make Elijah Witt.

Immediately I was curious. I picked up the second book, *Puzzles to Amuse and Challenge*, and looked in the table of contents. Finding a section devoted entirely to anagrams, I saw that Malloy had solved all of them. I flipped through the rest of the book; he'd skipped everything else.

I had a hunch. According to Ellis, Witt and Malloy were in touch with each other. Both were interested in anagrams. I opened the cover of Witt's book. The inside title page had been torn out. I ran my finger over the first page and felt some markings. After getting a pencil from Louie, I lightly traced over the first page. Letters began to appear, some in words, others in apparently random order. When I finished, there was no complete answer, but it was obvious that Malloy had been attempting to make an anagram out of the title *There Are Messages from Outer Space*.

With reckless optimism, I tried my hand for awhile, but I realized within minutes that I was accomplishing nothing. I put the paperbacks away and turned back to the newspaper. Lucas Pernell's byline caught my attention. The piece dealt with the history of local government corruption. An idea hit me like a blind-side haymaker. The *Bay City Mirror* produced its own puzzles. I was willing to bet that they were generated by some kind of computer program. I also had a gut feeling that Malloy's anagram of *There Are Messages from Outer Space* was going to end up being important. And I just happened to know someone who worked at the *Bay City Mirror*.

I fished out Lucas Pernell's card and punched in the number. After several minutes, I got Pernell on the line. "Just read your article in today's *Mirror*. Good stuff."

He sounded equally annoyed and flattered. What's up, Murphy? I'm pretty busy."

"Can we talk? I mean now, over the phone?"

Pernell gave me a scrutinizing look. "Important?"

"I'd like to think so."

He checked his watch. "You know where. The first place. Half an hour."

I beat Pernell to the Twilight Lounge by five minutes. On the flight over, I'd thought of something else I needed to ask about. I didn't know how often he spoke to Mac Malden, but I needed to contact Mac as discreetly as possible and find out what he knew about the NSA—specifically, what they were doing about me.

Pernell threw his hat and coat into the booth and slid in. "Got an extra bad boy?"

I pushed my pack of Lucky Strikes across the table. Pernell pulled one out and leaned over as I lit my ex-cigarette. He slumped against the back of his seat and exhaled through his nose. "What's up?"

I packed a smoke of my own. "You want a bourbon?"

Pernell flashed a hint of a cynical smile. "Oh, this must be good."

I caught the waitress's eye and signaled for two bourbons. It was still pretty early, but I figured it was happy hour somewhere.

"So...spill it."

I smoked my cigarette and waited for our drinks to arrive. "You still working on the Black Arrow Killer story?"

Pernell nodded in mid-gulp. "Why? You got something?"

"I do. Maybe enough to help you wrap up the details."

The reporter reached into his frayed sports jacket and pulled out a pen and notepad. He opened the pad, licked the tip of the pen, and looked up at me expectantly. "Let's have it."

I buried my cigarette stub into the ashtray. "Hold on. I need two favors. I'll trade."

Pernell was leery. "How good is your information?"

I smiled. "Remember the best sex you ever had? This is better."

The reporter grinned fiercely and drained his bourbon. "What do you want me to do?"

I pulled out *There Are Messages from Outer Space*. "Ever heard of this?"

"Sure. It's like a bible for UFO nuts."

Everyone except me knew about this book. "I have reason to believe that someone made an anagram out of the title. I need to find a computer program that will check for all the possible anagrams."

Pernell shrugged. "That's easy enough. I know the guy who does the anagrams. I'm sure he can take care of things for you. I'll give you a call when he's had a chance to check it out. So what's the other thing?"

"I need to contact Mac Malden."

Pernell gave me a dopey look. "Go ahead. Don't let me stop you."

I leaned forward, lowering my voice. "Look, I'm in a little trouble with a certain powerful government agency. As far as I know, they're staking out my office, and Mac seems to think his transmissions are being monitored. I haven't slept in my apartment for two days. I have to contact Mac and see if he's heard anything new."

Pernell considered for a few moments. "That second thing, I'm not too excited about that. Tell you what—you give me some of the dope, and I'll decide whether I want to shake on it."

It seemed reasonable, and I didn't really have much choice. I told Pernell about tracking down the Black Arrow Killer, up to the point where I followed him to the roof. I left out Emily's name and the part about the box. When I finished, Pernell looked up at me like I was a ten-thousand-dollar hooker who'd just said "time's up."

"So then what happened? Did you find out who it was?"

I lit up a smoke. "Shall we give Malden a call?"

Clearly frustrated, Pernell reached into his jacket and pulled out a cellular vid-phone. He pressed a rapid-dial button.

After a few seconds, I heard Mac's familiar rasp. "What?"

Pernell covered the mouthpiece. "What do you want me to ask him?"

"Ask if he's heard anything recently about his old friend, who brought the woman and the cigarettes the last time they talked."

Pernell repeated my message.

Mac had apparently forgotten. It took him a minute to catch the wave. "Oh, yeah, that useless bastard. I haven't seen him for awhile, but if you run into him, let him know that the bill collectors have backed off. They were pretty damn upset at first, but it looks like someone paid his bills for him. Don't ask me why. All I know is that, for now, everything looks OK."

Pernell answered. "All right, Malden. I'll let him know if I see him."

Why would the NSA have backed off? If the Feds were giving me some slack, they were probably just waiting until I wove enough rope to hang myself with. Having the NSA watching and waiting would be like having a bum ticker. Everything would be fine until the minute I dropped dead. But at least it gave me some breathing room.

Pernell pocketed his vid-phone. "Is that what you wanted to hear?"

I took a drag off my smoke. "Yes and no. But I appreciate your help."

He hunched over his notepad. "I'd send my grandmother up the river for a hot story."

I gave him all the details: the struggle on the roof, the Black Avatar, Dag Horton's name. For good measure, I even described my little trip to the NSA office, and meeting the delightful Jackson Cross.

"I knew it!" Pernell was lit up like the resident floozy at an office Christmas party. "I was sure the NSA had their dirty paws all over this thing. With my connections, I'll have this story on the front page in a week."

Under normal circumstances, I'd have been nervous about Pernell publishing the story. The NSA could easily put two and two together and come up with who the "anonymous source" of all the information was. But, for better or worse, I'd already offended the agency. Stepping on their metaphorical toes one more time shouldn't make much difference.

I was about to get up when I remembered another detail Pernell could help me with. He was bent over his notebook, scribbling. I waited for him to finish. "You got a few more minutes to burn?"

"It'll make me thirsty."

I caught the barmaid's eye and motioned for another bourbon. "You remember Sandra Collins?"

Pernell nodded impatiently. "Yeah. Berkeley."

"Look...I won't bother you with the details, but she figures into this whole mess. Do you know what she was doing at the university before she was murdered?"

A flicker of interest crossed Pernell's face. He played with his empty glass, thoughtfully. "It's been awhile...she was hired to work as an assistant on some research project."

He paused and looked up at the barmaid who'd arrived with

his bourbon. He took a sip as I paid for the drink. The waitress walked away, and Pernell spoke softly, the glass halfway to his lips. "She was working with a guy named...it began with an M...Mann, Mathers, Matlin..."

He paused and took a drink.

"Malloy?"

Pernell shook his head with a mouth full of bourbon. I tried to think back. Fitzpatrick had said that Malloy was using an alias. What was it? Pernell looked apologetic. "It's been a long time."

I remembered. "Matthews? Tyson Matthews?"

Pernell snapped his fingers and pointed at me. "That's it! Matthews. Anyway, Sandra Collins turned out to be at the top of her class in optical science. Holographic projectors, virtual reality simulators, that sort of thing. That's apparently how she got onto the project. It was just her and Matthews working together."

"Did you ever talk to this Matthews guy?"

"No. He disappeared from the university a little bit before the murder. I didn't really try to track him down."

"Did any of the authorities find out if he was involved? Or if what Sandra was working on figured into the murder motive?"

Pernell finished off his drink. "Not that I know of. For all the police knew, it was the Black Arrow Killer, open and shut. Apparently, the Feds treated it the same way."

"Do you think there's anyone at the university who would know what Sandra and Matthews were working on?"

"No. I asked around. It was an airtight project, sanctioned by someone way up on the food chain."

Pernell flashed a sneaky grin. "You got something interesting you want to tell me?"

I got up from the table. "Not today. Maybe sometime when I'm really broke and really thirsty."

Chapter
Nineteen

"You smoke too much."

I looked up from my matchbook, a Lucky dangling from my lips. "Yeah, so?"

Regan smiled serenely as I lit up. "I have a theory about people who smoke too much."

I exhaled a tremendous amount of smoke. "Please, enlighten me."

"Smokers are lonely. Cigarettes are their one good friend. No matter what, they can always reach into their pocket and find their little friend, Mr. Smoke."

"I'm not a lonely guy."

Regan leaned forward, chin resting in her hand. "Sure you are."

I inspected my tie and flicked off a lint ball "I've just found myself to be the only consistently reasonable person I know."

Regan sat back as our waitress arrived. "The two of you must be very happy."

A glass of wine for Regan and a cup of black coffee for me. I'd already had a bourbon with Pernell. Catching a buzz around lunchtime wasn't on my list of things to do. I looked around. The Imperial Lounge was busier than it had been yesterday. It made me a little nervous, but crowded rooms always did. I looked back at Regan as she finished leaving a soft, red impression of her lower lip on the outer rim of the wine glass.

"You certainly didn't pull any punches yesterday." Her tone

was as cool as a mint julep. I stared into the ashtray as the butt of my cigarette gave up the ghost.

"Was I too hard on you?" I looked up and met Regan's eyes. She was smiling in a way that made me curious.

"Don't flatter yourself, shamus. I'll let you know when you're too hard."

She certainly had a way with a phrase. "There you go again, twisting my words. How do you expect us to get anything accomplished with you talking like that?"

Regan tossed me a mocking pout like it was a bone. "I'll be good...if you insist. But you're brushing off an *extremely* sincere effort. You should be ashamed of yourself."

"I am." I reached down for my backpack and pulled out the notebooks I'd taken from Malloy's room. Setting them on the table, I took a sip of coffee. It tasted like dishwater. Louie could teach these people a thing or two about brewing a pot of joe. Regan leaned over the table to get a look at the notebooks.

"What're those?"

"Notebooks."

Regan looked up sarcastically. "Really? How do they work?"

"They're full of paper. People write in them. These particular notebooks belonged to your father."

The caustic look evaporated. "My father? Where'd you get them?"

"That's not important. What is important is finding out what's written in them. Your father used some kind of shorthand. I can't make out a thing. I was hoping you could."

Regan pulled one of them across the table and opened it. She flipped through the pages quickly, pausing only to moisten her fingers. After some time, she looked up and took a sip of wine. She seemed to enjoy making me wait.

"What do you think?"

She set down her glass and looked back at the notebook. "He never liked to write on the computer. Most everything he wrote was in notebooks like this."

"Can you read it?"

She flipped pages idly. "Some. It'll take awhile to get through it all."

I was relieved. "How long do you think it'll take you to figure them out?"

Regan closed the notebook and reached for her Pinot. "I'll let you know when I'm done."

I was impatient, but her tone said that I'd just have to wait and like it, damn it. She drank the rest of her wine, subtly making love to the glass. On cue, the waitress arrived and asked if we'd like another round. Regan said yes, leaving no room for discussion. When the waitress left, Regan reached across the table and took one of my smokes.

"I hope you don't mind."

I motioned nonchalantly. She lit the cigarette with her eyes locked on mine, like she was kissing another man. Her wine arrived, and the waitress sloshed a stream of so-called coffee in the general vicinity of my cup. Regan smiled as I mopped up with a cocktail napkin. "Tell me something...something interesting about yourself."

"What do you want to know?"

"Anything. I feel like you know a lot more about me than I do about you. It's not very fair."

I retreated to my pack of Lucky Strikes. "I was married once. How's that?"

"Only once? That's not very interesting. Everyone's been married once."

"I never said I was interesting."

Regan poised her cigarette over the ashtray and flicked delicately. "So, what was she like?"

"Beautiful, intelligent, sexy...and rotten to the core."

Regan smiled indulgently. "So why did you marry her?"

"I lost a bet." I took a drag and wished I hadn't brought up the subject.

"Do you hate all women now?"

I shook my head and reached for my cup of dishwater. "They're like tequila, the greatest thing in the world until the one night you overdo it. After that, the slightest whiff of it makes you want to vomit. For a long time, you can't even think about it without getting nauseous. After awhile, you take a little sip, and you're surprised to find that you can keep it down. Eventually, you go back to drinking it, but you never, ever forget that first miserable night." I took another sip of dishwater. It tasted a bit like Cuervo.

"Nice metaphor."

"Glad you enjoyed it." I propped my elbows on the table. "So, tell me, what's your philosophy of love?"

Regan stared into her Pinot Noir and bit her lower lip. "I...dance with love—until it tries to lead." She looked up seductively. "And I love to dance."

"What a coincidence. I used to give lessons. Dance lessons."

Regan cocked an eyebrow. "Really?"

"Yeah. Old family tradition. I know 'em all—tango, samba, watusi, Charleston—"

"How about the Forbidden Dance of Love?"

"I know it, but I quit doing it. Kept throwing my back out."

Regan smiled and sipped her wine. I thought of something I'd been meaning to ask. "So...where did the name Madsen come from?"

Her smile became less sincere. "I was married."

Turnabout was fair play. "What was he like?"

"Oh, you know...handsome, intelligent, sexy...and rotten to the core."

"What a coincidence."

Regan cradled the Pinot in her hands. "He was my tequila. Now I drink wine." She took a sip. "I won't make that mistake again."

"What do you mean?"

Regan set the glass down and leaned back. "I let myself be controlled by someone. I didn't like it. Now I'm in it for myself." She looked back at me, defiantly.

I raised my mug. "Here's to looking out for number one, and sticking our necks out for nobody."

Regan relaxed and smiled, then lifted her glass to my coffee cup. "To us."

She was a piece of work. I was tempted to spend a few more hours looking into that flawless face, but I'd fallen enough for one day. My attraction to Regan wasn't the warm, comfortable kind that I felt toward Chelsee. Instead, it was a fierce, primal craving that ached in my gut. She was a backdraft of desire, dancing, writhing, a mass of exploding embers that could easily blind anyone foolish enough to stare too long.

I excused myself and placed a call to Fitzpatrick at the Savoy. He was still working on the boxes, but no luck. I hung around the vid-phone for a few minutes, going over the game plan. Pernell was handling the anagram problem, but it was way too soon to find out what he'd learned. Regan was going to go through Malloy's notebooks. Hopefully she'd turn something up. It seemed like all I could do was hurry up and wait. I decided to fly back to my office.

I couldn't see any nefarious loiterers on Chandler Avenue, so I parked and entered the Ritz brazenly. No surprises. It was good to be home. I flipped on the light, hoping that a cooperative brownie had come in and cleaned up, but the place was as trashed as I'd left it. Whoever had broken in the other night must've felt shortchanged. Half the fun of breaking into a place is getting to ransack it.

I went straight to the shower, then shaved. After changing my clothes, I went to my desk and checked my voice-messaging unit. There were two messages. I pressed the playback button and dropped into my chair.

"Hi, Tex. Lavercan Kimbell here. I just wanted to touch base with you on the PI Pension/401K, now that we're past the first quarter. Boy, it's been crazy." My investment advisor laughed nervously. "Well, anyway, I just thought I'd let you know that not all the news is bad. I mean, we *did* lose quite a bit, but that's really the best thing that could've happened. Now we can buy more shares, and when we hit an upward swing, we'll make up for the past four or five years. Well, that's about all. Call me if you've got any questions."

Lavercan was a sincere man, with no apparent talent for investment strategy. At this rate, I'd soon own more worthless stock than anyone in the world. Luckily, I still had my Franklin Mint Civil War chess set—my true nest egg. The thing had to be worth a fortune. Hell, all the pieces were made of fine pewter.

The second message came up in hushed tones. "There are ears everywhere. I've got something to show you. Stop by as soon as you can."

Ellis. I wondered what he had to show me. Probably a touched-up still from *Plan Nine from Outer Space*. But, since I didn't have anything better to do, I figured I'd drop by.

"Clearly, Kennedy knew about the alien infiltration of the government. Extraterrestrial contact was made by the Russians all through the '50s. It's well-documented. The way I see it, the aliens had to get rid of Kennedy before he exposed them. LBJ was certainly under their control, if not actually one of them. Vietnam was nothing more than a ruse to divert the attention of the American public."

Ellis took a sip of mineral water and gave me a knowing wink.

"Without question, the Depression of '98 was a veiled attempt by the aliens to throw our political system into chaos. Fortunately, the administrations of Dole, Gingrich, and Linderman recognized the threat and purged most of the aliens from high-ranking positions. Now we're in what I call a "secondary state of checks and balances."

"That's fascinating."

Ellis had started babbling the minute I stepped into his shop. He was like a drum solo—there was nothing to do but wait for it to end. It looked like he'd finished.

"So what was it you had to show me?"

"Oh, yeah. Sorry. I just get a little hyped when I find someone who understands what's really going on. I've got a lot of, well, I think they're brilliant, theories, but it's hard to find people you can trust."

He got up and walked to a file cabinet. As I watched him remove a key from the chain on his belt, I couldn't help but feel a sense of ambivalence. On the one hand, Ellis was obviously lonely, isolated by his intensely conspiratorial beliefs, yet eager for companionship and shared vision. I felt a pang of empathy for this misguided, but sincere, nerd. All he needed to be happy was a crackpot pal, someone to share in his convoluted skein of warped theories. On the other hand, he was too annoying for me to ever be his pal.

"Here it is." Ellis handed me a manila folder labeled *Roswell: Alien Equipment*. Inside were a handful of reproduced drawings, photographs, and faxes. As I leafed through the contents, Ellis spoke with the air of someone watching someone else open a gift.

"After you left, I got to thinking about how you'd seemed pretty interested in what Malloy had said about Roswell. At the time, it didn't occur to me to show you the pictures I've collected of the alien equipment."

He paused excitedly. "What do you think?"

The pictures looked like the kind you could find in the center of any old alien-encounter paperback. The objects depicted resembled everything from salad spinners to art-deco staplers. Out of politeness, I looked through most of the pictures before handing the folder back to Ellis. It looked like I'd made a wasted trip.

"Good stuff. Where'd you find it?"

"Here and there. Most of it came from a safe-deposit box belonging to a certain Major Barrett. He worked on Project Blueprint and catalogued almost all of the alien artifacts. When he died last year, he willed access to the safe-deposit box to Elijah Witt, who personally sent me copies. They arrived yesterday."

"They certainly make a nice addition to your collection." Ellis beamed self-importantly. I glanced down at my watch. "Wow, it's late. Well, thanks for showing me the file. I've got to get back to work."

Ellis' eyes darted around the shop, as though he were looking for something else to show me. I made my way quickly to the door.

"See you later, Archie. I'll let you know if there's anything else you can help me with."

Ellis looked over at me with a hint of desperation. "You sure you have to go? I could make up a nice pot of herbal tea."

"I'll take a rain check."

I was antsy—and out of things to do. I decided to fly back to the office and kill some time cleaning the place up, a last resort if I ever heard one. As I stepped into the lobby of the Ritz, Nilo looked up sourly from his magazine.

"Someone here to see ya." He jerked his head toward the corner. I was surprised to see Fitzpatrick seated primly in one of the ragged lobby chairs, his hands folded over a small cardboard box. As I approached, I could discern a hint of excitement beneath the refined veneer.

"Good evening, Mr. Murphy." I looked down at the box and had a pretty good idea what was in it.

"Come on up to my office."

"Would you mind?"

Fitzpatrick extended the box toward me. He then reached for his hat and slowly rose to his feet. Several minutes later, we were seated amid the wrack and ruin of my office. Fitzpatrick was more animated than I'd ever seen him. "At last, I've met with some success."

Both metal boxes were inside the cardboard one, along with what appeared to be a small lamp. I pulled out the contents and placed them in front of me on the desk. Fitzpatrick was like a proud parent on baby's first Christmas, smiling eagerly and barely containing himself. I examined the boxes—they didn't look any different than before.

"I don't get it. Did you find a way to get these open?"

"One of them. I won't bother you with all the details. Suffice it to say that I tried various methods without success. I finally wondered if Malloy might have used the equivalent of invisible ink on the boxes. When I purchased this ultraviolet scanner and ran it over them, certain markings became visible." He smiled and waved toward one of the boxes. "Please. Try it for yourself."

I switched on the UV scanner and moved it slowly across the box. Two parallel lines appeared, running horizontally across one side of the box, dividing the side into three sections. There were also three circles about the size of nickels, one on each of three sides. I touched the circles and traced my finger over the lines. Nothing happened. I looked up at Fitzpatrick's beaming face. "So what's the secret?"

Fitzpatrick moved closer to the desk. "For one person, it requires a certain amount of manual dexterity. With both of us, it will be considerably simpler."

Fitzpatrick picked up the UV scanner and ran it over the surface, revealing the nickel-sized circles. "Press on two of the circles."

I did. Fitzpatrick positioned the UV scanner so that it was aimed at the side of the box with the two horizontal lines. He then pressed on the third circle. A small arrow symbol appeared in the center of the top section. Fitzpatrick then placed his thumb against the top section and pushed to the right. It slid sideways about half an inch. "You can stop pressing now."

He leaned back in his chair and produced a Cubana from his pocket. I turned the box so that the three-sectioned side was facing me. "Now what?"

The old man held an expensive lighter to the end of his cigar and puffed for several seconds. I could barely wait. "Slide the top section back about halfway, then slide the center section to the right."

"OK."

"Now slide the center section all the way to the left. Then slide the lower section to the right about one quarter inch."

"Done."

"Slide the top section to the right."

When I followed the final instruction, I could hear a small spring release. The top of the box popped open. I glanced up at Fitzpatrick, whose smile was visible through a cloud of Cubana smoke.

"I must apologize for making you go through this little ritual. I'm afraid I have a theatrical streak."

"No need to apologize. Foreplay is healthy. Not that you should take that personally." I looked down at the box and flipped the lid open. I expected to find some kind of bizarre alien object or maybe a chunk of kryptonite. At the very least, there should have been a mechanical gadget, a piece of the Pandora Device. Not even close. The contents consisted of a long, thin metal pin and a photographic slide. With more than a little disappointment, I looked up at Fitzpatrick.

"Is this it?"

Fitzpatrick nodded, still smiling. I reached into the box and pulled out the slide. Holding it up to the light, I saw a drawing of a not-very-interesting-looking object, tube-shaped, with metal caps on either end, and what appeared to be a light source in the center. It looked familiar, but I couldn't place it. The metal pin was about the length of a pencil with a smaller diameter. There were several notches in the stem and a large head on one end. Fitzpatrick reached for the slide and examined it.

"What do you make of this drawing?"

"Looks like a space-age Coleman lantern to me."

Fitzpatrick looked out at me from behind the slide. "You sound as though you consider it meaningless."

I shrugged. Fitzpatrick set the slide down. "To quote Shakespeare, Mr. Murphy, all that glisters is not gold. Malloy would not have included this slide if it were meaningless."

Fitzpatrick was right. I sat back in my chair and thought it over. I'd seen the object somewhere before. Suddenly, I remembered. It had been in the file Ellis had showed me. "If Malloy put the slide in the box, he must've meant for someone to locate this object."

Fitzpatrick flicked a large ash off his cigar. "That is a reasonable assumption."

"I think I might have a lead on where to find it."

"Excellent."

I picked up the UV scanner and ran it over each side of the second box. The only markings that appeared were two squares, about the size of stamps, on opposite sides of the box. "You couldn't get this one open?"

Fitzpatrick shook his head.

"Possibly the metal pin from the first box is needed to open a box we have not yet located. I would imagine that whatever is to be used on those squares will also be found in another box."

"I wish I knew how many boxes we were looking for."

Fitzpatrick ground the stub of his cigar into an ashtray, then slowly lifted himself out of his seat. "I'll leave you to your investigations. Shall I leave the boxes with you?"

I returned everything but the slide to the cardboard box. "You'd better hold onto them for awhile. I've had too many uninvited guests in my office lately. If you don't mind, I'll keep this slide."

Fitzpatrick nodded and picked up the box. "You'll let me know about any new developments."

"Sure thing."

Fitzpatrick had taken a taxi to my office. I gave him a lift back to the Savoy, then flew to Ellis' shop. It was getting late, and the sun was peeking out behind the skyline of New San Francisco as I landed in front of the Cosmic Connection. The Closed sign was out, but I knocked on the door anyway. After a few moments, Ellis came out from the back and opened the door for me. "Change your mind about the herbal tea? It's great for insomnia."

"No, thanks. I'm sorry to come by so late, but I needed to check something really quick." I handed the slide to Ellis.

He walked to the counter and flipped on a lamp. Turning the light toward his face, he held up the slide. "Where'd you get this?"

"That's not important. You recognize it?"

"Of course. It's one of the objects Major Barrett catalogued." Ellis turned off the light. "You want to check the file again?"

I nodded. We walked into the back room. Seconds later, Ellis was flipping through the contents of the manila folder. He quickly found what he was looking for and passed it to me. I looked it over. The drawing was identical to the one on the slide, but with a number written at the bottom of the page. I looked up at Ellis, who was hovering excitedly. "What can you tell about this thing?"

Ellis responded like a game-show contestant. "Item number 186. Barrett described it as "the power cell." According to the major, three of them were found in the spacecraft recovered at Roswell. One was attached to a console; the other two were in a storage compartment. The one in the console was irreparably damaged, but the other two were intact. The research scientists decided that they were some kind of alien battery and tried to disassemble one of them. The other was catalogued and stowed away. As far as Major Barrett knew, they never could figure out how it worked or even what it was for sure."

"So at least one of these is probably still intact and stored at the Roswell Complex."

Ellis looked at me incredulously. "You're not thinking about going to the complex?"

I handed the sheet back to Ellis. "Maybe."

"You're insane, Murphy! You can't get in there!"

"Why not?"

"You think you're the first person who ever thought about getting in there? Hell, every UFOlogist in the world would like to take a look around the complex."

"So why don't they?"

Ellis leaned forward earnestly. "Look, first of all, the site is secured. The military doesn't want anyone getting in. It's only accessible with top-level security clearance."

"What if I had clearance?"

Ellis shook his head. "Listen, I personally know of four different attempts to get in. Only one person lived to tell about it. He was in the last group to try it. They planned the expedition for a year. They had all the equipment, the security clearance, everything. The guy who survived said they were able to get past the security barriers. He stayed topside while the others went down into the complex. They were only supposed to be inside for four hours. This guy waited for thirty hours. The rest of the group never came back up."

It sounded like a ghost story to me. The trail Malloy had left for us led straight through Roswell. Ellis was unwilling or unable to help me get in, but he had told me what I needed to know. Now I just needed to find a way in.

When I got back to my office, I decided to get in touch with Fitzpatrick. When he'd hired me, he'd said that he and Malloy had worked together years ago in China. The more I thought about it, the more I began to think that Fitzpatrick had met Malloy earlier, probably at Roswell. Maybe I didn't have anything more than a gut feeling, and I couldn't think of a reason why Fitzpatrick wouldn't want me to know about it, but I was almost sure of the fact. And now that Malloy was dead, Fitzpatrick was the only person I knew that might've been there. Maybe he would know what I was in for and even help me get there. It was late, but I called anyway.

After seven or eight beeps, Fitzpatrick's weary face appeared on my video screen. I must have woken him up. "Sorry to disturb you, Mr. Fitzpatrick. I got that lead on the object we saw on the slide."

"Wonderful! And you should feel free to contact me at any time." Always the polite one. "What have you found out?"

"Apparently, the object is stored somewhere in the Roswell Complex. Malloy referred to it in his notebooks as item number 186."

"You intend to go to the Roswell Complex?" Fitzpatrick asked anxiously.

"Looks that way. You did work there at one time, didn't you?"

Fitzpatrick looked down momentarily, then turned his gaze back toward the screen. "Yes, I did. That's where I met Thomas Malloy."

"Why didn't you tell me before?"

"Roswell is a subject I do not care to discuss. I had hoped that our search would not require going into my past. Nevertheless, it appears that we have no choice. Are you certain that a trip to the Roswell Complex is absolutely necessary?"

"That's why I called. I need to find a way in."

"I don't know if I can help you. My security clearance is a thing of the past."

"Any suggestions?"

"I'm afraid you'll have to rely on your own judgment and resourcefulness."

"Well, I thought I'd run it by you. If I don't contact you within three days, you'll have to assume that I've shuffled off this proverbial mortal coil."

Fitzpatrick's face registered a surprising degree of concern. "Are you sure there are no other options?"

"I can't see any. Listen, if I'm not back in three days, I need you to get in touch with a Ms. Madsen at the Imperial. She's working on an angle that could turn up some information on the other boxes. She doesn't know most of what's going on, so I'd prefer that you not contact her unless something happens to me."

"I understand. I can tell you one thing you should know before you go to Roswell."

"What's that?"

"I left the service before the base was shut down, but I've heard talk. Have you learned that the complex was quarantined?"

"I heard something to that effect."

"The complex has been sealed off and powered down. Since there never was any news of an outbreak, the military may have been able to contain whatever it was that inspired the quarantine. If you gain entrance, be aware that there may be something in there, dormant, waiting to be unleashed. Don't take any unnecessary risks."

"I try to make that a policy."

"Very well. Good luck, Mr. Murphy."

Chapter
Twenty

The security alarm blared as I sprinted through the dark corridors, wildly searching for an exit. With a violent lurch, I sat up in my bed. The vid-phone was beeping. I reached over through a groggy fog and hit the receiver. "Yeah," I growled.

"Listen carefully—" It was the same modulated voice I'd heard on the vid-phone at the Twilight, the first time I'd spoken to Lucas Pernell. I struggled to reach full consciousness. This guy made every word count. "Your next step will require security clearance. Follow these instructions immediately. Any delay on your part could be disastrous. Do you understand?"

"Who is this?"

"I said, do you understand?"

"Yeah."

"Your questions will be answered later. All you need to know is that there are two forces at work in this situation. You have only two certain allies, myself and the keeper. Beyond that, you can trust no one. If the people who oppose us win, the effects will almost certainly be catastrophic. For reasons which must remain unexplained for now, you are in the middle of the struggle. There is no time to spare. You must trust me and do what I tell you."

I'd done what this guy had told me to do at Autotech and lived through it. Whoever he was, he obviously wanted to keep me alive, which was more than I could say for some of the other parties involved.

"OK, what do you need me to do?"

"Go to the place where I first made contact with you. Go to the cigarette machine and pay for a pack of cigarettes, but press the blank button on the far right. You will get what you need. Is that clear?"

"Sure."

The call was terminated. I laid back down and stared at the ceiling, now completely awake. Apparently, I was on my way to Roswell.

After getting dressed, I decided to make one more call. A not very subtle voice was telling me that I might be making a permanent stop in New Mexico. I figured I'd better call Regan before I left, in case I didn't make it back. I woke her up, just like I'd done to Fitzpatrick the night before. Regan was much prettier. She also seemed to wake up friendly.

"I dreamed about you. Want details?"

Seeing Regan's face on the vid-phone screen was making me feel highly irresponsible and less than enthusiastic about going to Roswell. "You're a siren, you know that?"

"Well, correct me if I'm wrong, but I seem to remember that the sirens' song was lethal. My intentions are a lot less dangerous and a lot more pleasurable."

"Yeah...maybe."

"You don't believe me? C'mon over, and I'll prove it to you."

"I'm sure that's exactly what the sirens said." With a great deal of effort, I pulled my eyes away from her pouting lips and swung the conversation around to the original subject.

"Listen, Regan, I could stare at you all day, but I actually had a reason for calling."

She opened her eyes wide in exaggerated anticipation. "Do tell."

"I've got to leave town for a day or two. I just wanted to let you know."

"I'll go with you. It'll only take me a minute to get ready."

I shook my head. "Sorry. After this is all over, we'll go somewhere together, if you want to."

"Promise?"

"I swear on my sacred PI oath."

Regan threw me a skeptical look. "OK. You'd better call me as soon as you get back."

"I will."

"Well, I'll let you go then," she said, pouting attractively.

"Listen, Regan, there's one more thing."

She smiled at me. "If, by some freak chance, anything should happen to me, an acquaintance of mine will contact you. His name is Fitzpatrick. You can trust him."

Regan looked worried. "Where are you going?"

"Don't worry about it. I'll be fine. I just want to cover all the possibilities."

"If you get yourself killed, I'll never, ever forgive you."

"OK, that's too big a threat. I won't. Hey, I've got to get going. I'll let you know when I'm back." I punched the button, and Regan's concerned face faded to black.

I quickly jotted down a list of things to take with me. A few tools would probably come in handy. Wire cutters, screwdrivers, a laser blade, bolt cutters, a flashlight, a lock-pick set, maybe a rebreather. It would probably be a good idea to have a firearm. Ever since I'd lost my gun in a fit of seven-card stud optimism, I hadn't enjoyed the same sense of security. I hoped Rook could set me up with something at the pawnshop.

I went into the kitchen to see if I had any food to take with me. Ideally, I wouldn't be gone more than a day or so, but I had to make allowance for delays. A search of the cupboards turned up a can of tuna fish, an essentially empty jar of peanut butter, and half a box of saltines. I grabbed the crackers.

All the tools I'd listed were stored away in a closet. I was even fortunate enough to find an unused package of batteries for the flashlight and the laser blade. I threw the tools and crackers into my backpack and left the office.

At the pawnshop, I talked Rook into loaning me a .38. He wanted collateral, but I managed to talk him out of it. I didn't bother to tell him that there was a decent chance I wouldn't be back, or he'd never have fronted me the gun.

Feeling moderately prepared, I got into my speeder and headed toward the Twilight Lounge. Ten minutes later, I set it down in the parking lot. The place was practically deserted. I sauntered casually over to the cigarette machine and inserted a ten-dollar bill. After four attempts, the machine ate my bill and flashed Make a Selection. I pressed the blank button on the far right and heard a light thump as something dropped into the dispenser tray. Bending down, I picked up a hard pack of Dardos de Pulmones. Without making eye contact with anyone, I ducked back out of the bar.

I hurried to my speeder and slipped into the driver's seat. The pack certainly looked real. I peeled off the plastic wrapper and opened the top. Inside were three access cards—one blue, one green, one red—each with a military insignia and a bar code. There was also a black-and-white ID badge with my picture and a bar code. My designation was Colonel T. Murphy, Special Agent, NSA. Damn.

The last item in the pack was a sheet of paper, folded. I spread it out and read a brief, typed message at the top of the page. It read: *The access cards are color-coded. Use them on the panels of the same color. Security should be automated and can be shut down with the green card. If stopped, use NSA ID. If successful, do not carry object any longer than necessary.* Below the message was a set of coordinates. I programmed the coordinates into the speeder's guidance system and lifted off.

The trip took about four and a half hours. Without the actual coordinates of the base, I could have pulled a Moses and wandered in the desert for years. The complex was camouflaged from the air and built into the side of a rock outcropping. For miles around, there was nothing but red-yellow dirt and the occasional gnarled, bony plant clinging to life for no apparent reason. I couldn't help but think of Rook.

Roswell had been built long before the advent of speeders and had no apparent doming security. I set the speeder down in the center of the compound, between two massive buildings that looked like aircraft hangers. The open compound area was approximately one hundred yards square, bordered by a fifteen-foot-high chain-link fence. A garnish of barbed wire adorned the top of the fence, and large power cables ran along the ground on the perimeter. Touching the fence would probably pump enough juice through me to run every espresso machine in Los Angeles for a week.

A smaller building, probably a guardhouse, sat at one end of the compound, where a dirt road intersected the chain-link fence. Behind the two huge structures, I could see a good-sized steel door built into the side of the rock ledge.

I opened the speeder and stepped out onto the floor of the compound. It was asphalt but had acquired a layer of sand over the years, allowing it to blend in seamlessly with the ground all around the complex. As far as I could see, no one had been anywhere near where I was standing for days, months, maybe years. In fact, there were no footprints at all.

There were, however, footsteps. I turned around to see two men. One, vaguely uniformed, was emerging from the guardhouse at a leisurely pace. The other, in full, shiny MP attire, was sprinting toward me and fumbling for the holster on his hip. I turned toward my pursuer and waited patiently for the ten seconds or so it took him to reach me.

"Freeze!"

I was already frozen.

"Get your hands up where I can see them!"

He was young, maybe twenty-four. His face was flushed, and the gun wavered slightly in his white-knuckled hands. I dug into my coat for my pack of smokes.

"Don't be reaching for anything! Get your hands up!"

I pulled out the cigarette pack and displayed it calmly. "Keep your pants on, Deputy Fife."

Junior was obviously incensed, but unsure of what to do. He'd probably never pulled a gun on anyone in his life, though I was willing to bet he'd wasted untold hours fantasizing about it. In his wildest dreams, he couldn't have imagined that whoever he lost his gun-waving virginity to would be so apathetic.

I pulled out a Lucky. "Got a light?"

"Drop the cigarette and get your hands up!"

"It's not loaded."

"Drop it!"

The second man trudged up from behind. "Put a lid on it, Todd." He was older, probably in his late fifties. His MP shirt was open, revealing a dingy white T-shirt. His pants were baggy khaki trousers, and he was wearing sandals. He walked past Todd, the security guard, and pulled a lighter from his shirt pocket as he approached me. "Float me one?"

I held out the pack of Lucky Strikes, and the older guard drew one out. He lit my cigarette, then his own. "I ran out of smokes three days ago. Pure hell. Can you imagine being in a place like this with no smokes?"

I smiled compassionately. I'd run out of cigarettes before, and it hadn't been pretty. Behind the older guard, Todd lowered his gun, looking like a kid whose baseball had just gotten stuck on the neighbor's roof. His polished-to-a-fault, military-issue footwear was coated with dust. I felt a little bit sorry for him. The Roswell Complex didn't look like it got much action.

Up close, my smoking partner didn't appear to be as old as I'd pegged him, but he had the wrinkly brown face of a surfer-cum-alcoholic. He took a long drag and looked up at me.

"Sorry about the welcome. Todd here is new on the job. I think you startled him."

"I have that effect on strangers. It must be my hat."

The older guard nodded. Todd stepped up. "It's against regulations for a civilian to be on the grounds. We have to arrest this guy."

I looked from Todd to Cigarette Guy. He looked back at me and shrugged. "If there's one thing Todd knows, it's regulations, though we may have extenuating circumstances here. You don't happen to have an extra pack of Luckies, do you?"

"Sorry."

"Well, I'm afraid Todd may be right. Looks like we'll have to arrest you."

Todd perked up noticeably. "I'll go get the handcuffs!"

"Don't bother. Here's my identification."

I reached into my coat for the NSA ID and handed it to the older guard. He looked it over thoroughly, with Todd peering eagerly over his shoulder. After a few anxious moments, he handed it back to me. "NSA, huh? Haven't had one of you boys down here for years."

"Sounds like you've been here awhile."

"Hell, what is it now? Twenty-three years. Six months... a couple weeks." He glanced at his watch. "And about five and a half hours. I love this job. I don't know who I pissed off, but they got me back real good."

He turned and looked at Todd. "Todd doesn't know what he did either, but he's here to replace me. I'm training him to take over all my important duties. Tomorrow we're gonna go over how to make a decent quiche in the microwave." He looked back at me. "So, Colonel Murphy, what brings the NSA to our little corner of nowhere?"

"I've got to get into the underground part of the complex. By the way, I didn't catch your name."

Todd's eyes got as big as Oreos. The older guard raised an eyebrow. "Willis. So you're going down? Hasn't been anyone down there since the war. At least not since I've been here. Don't suppose you can tell me why."

I shook my head. "Top secret. A matter of national security. Course, that's what we do, you know."

Todd caught his breath long enough to squeak in Willis' direction. "How do we know he's who he says he is? No one's supposed to go into the underground section. That's the one thing they kept telling me."

"Shut up, Todd." Willis glanced sideways at the younger guard as though he were the tenth person to tell him that he had a rip in the seat of his trousers.

"I know what they say. It doesn't apply to the NSA. They can commandeer a bathtub while you're in it taking a shower if they want to. They're not accountable to anyone, not even the military. If you give Colonel Murphy any crap, he might just decide to blow your head off."

I straightened my tie. "Well, I'm glad we understand each other. As for you, Todd, I suggest you check your regulations. The NSA is the exception to every rule. Now, if you aren't too busy, I could use a little help with directions."

Willis was as cooperative as a man who'd been saved from nicotine withdrawal, and Todd was too cowed to raise any more objections. We walked to the guardhouse, and they disarmed a half dozen alarm systems. It was obvious that Willis had never done this in his twenty-three years of service. At one point, he pulled a lever to restore power to the underground complex. As he did it, he gave me a look that said, "Are you sure you know what you're doing?"

Forty-five minutes after I'd landed, I was escorted to the large steel door in the side of the rock ledge. Willis stuck a key into a keyhole on a panel door. The panel opened, and the old guard punched in some kind of code. With a dusty groan, the steel door swung open.

I stepped inside and looked around. The room was small and empty, except for an open elevator on the opposite side. The walls and floor had been carved out of the stone, and the dim, fluorescent lighting gave the interior a harsh, cold feel. The two guards were waiting outside like a couple of kindergartners on the first day of school.

"Before I go down, tell me something. I've heard rumors about why the military shut this place down and sealed it off. What do you know about it?"

Todd looked at Willis, terrified. Willis cleared his throat. "The higher-ups don't like to talk about it, but I've heard a few things.

Bad things."

"Such as—?"

"Well, when I first got assigned here, they told me never to turn on the power to the underground area, no matter what. I asked 'em why. They just said never, ever do it, under any circumstances. Some people say there's aliens down there. They say they're photo-somethin'…I don't remember the word. Something about being attracted to the light or heat. They say that's why the military shut the place down, quarantined it. They say the aliens killed almost everyone down there and almost escaped. I guess you're gonna find out for yourself."

Chapter
Twenty-One

I stepped into the elevator and surveyed my options. There were buttons for Levels One, Two, and Three, all of which were underground. Since I had no idea where to look, I decided to start at the top and work my way down. I pressed the button for Level One, but nothing happened. To the side of the button panel, I noticed a blue card slot. Pulling out the blue card I'd been given with the NSA ID, I stuck it in the slot. The buttons lit up, and the elevator doors slid shut. I pressed the button for Level One again. This time the elevator shuddered, then began to descend. After five or six seconds, the elevator came to a jarring stop, and the doors slid open.

A large, black number one was painted on the wall opposite the elevator. I stepped out into a hallway and looked left, then right. The low, white fluorescent light gave the hallway the look of a morgue. There was nothing to see immediately, so I turned to my left and walked down the hallway. My shoes left faint imprints in the thick layer of dust on the tile floor. My footfalls echoed all around the hallway. The moldy smelling air felt dense, like breathing through a dust rag.

I reached the end of the hallway, where a second hallway ran perpendicular. A sign informed me that the dormitories were somewhere to my left, the mess hall and recreation center to my right. I decided to look around the living quarters first.

The walls on this level were painted light purple and were completely unadorned. About thirty feet from the spot where the hallways intersected, I saw the first of a series of doors with numbers painted on them. I tested the knob on the first one, but the door was locked. I moved on to the second one, which was unlocked.

I opened the door and stepped into a long, fairly narrow room. Twelve single neatly made beds stood in two parallel rows. Each one had a corresponding locker. Except for the thin layer of dust on everything, the dorm looked immaculate. I walked to the nearest locker and opened it. Inside were several changes of clothing, shoes, and toiletries. After checking several other lockers, I decided that there wasn't much to see.

As I was about to leave, I spotted a piece of paper on one of the beds near the rear of the room. It turned out to be an unopened letter, addressed to Corporal Bryce Ellsworth. The return address was the Ellsworths of Ames, Iowa. I checked the postmark and saw that the letter had been posted on November 11, 1996. Turning the letter over in my hand, I debated whether or not to open it. I seriously doubted that anyone was going to claim it. Besides, the statute of limitations had to have expired.

I tore open the yellowed envelope and pulled out several lined pages, a photograph, and a few newspaper clippings. The content of the letter was typical newsy, mushy, howdy-from-home stuff. I tossed it onto the bed. The photograph showed an older couple posing alongside a young couple with a baby. Fifty years had passed since this picture was taken. The older folks were undoubtedly deceased, their places taken by the young man and his wife. What had happened to the man these people had sent the letter to? Did he die here in the complex? Or did he escape and make it back to his family?

I turned my attention to the newspaper clippings, which were very well-preserved. The headline on the first trumpeted: *Desert*

Standoff Enters Fourth Month. The story detailed how United States forces were massing on the Iraqi border. The second article's headline read: *President Dole: We're Prepared for War*. The third clipping was taken from a publication of ill repute and blared: *Military Ready to Unleash Alien Weapon!* In retrospect, this article seemed to be surprisingly accurate. It referred to the Roswell crash and the recovery of a mysterious object, which the military had cleverly incorporated into a Doomsday Device.

After I finished reading Corporal Ellsworth's mail, I decided that the dormitory had nothing more to offer. I returned to the hallway and walked to a door at the end. It was labeled Restricted Access, unlike those leading to the dormitories. I tried to open it, then looked for a slot where I could use one of the cards in my pocket, but no such luck. Turning back, I went on to the mess hall.

Like the dormitories, the eating area was neat, austere, and of absolutely no interest. I found the door to the kitchen and took a look around. Cupboards, cabinets, and shelves contained tons of canned goods, herds of bagged, powdered milk, an ocean of bottled mineral water, and acres of cracked wheat in barrels. At least I wouldn't have to go hungry. Out of curiosity, I checked several freezers and a refrigerator, finding nothing more intriguing than some potentially award-winning science projects.

My next stop, the recreation area, was a gigantic hybrid, half gymnasium, half airport lounge. The amenities included three full-size pool tables, dartboards, a boxing ring, free weights, a half-court basketball floor, a handful of conversation pits, a dozen couches, and two large-screen televisions. It looked like a decent place to kill time, but I wasn't in the market for leisure. After a short scan, I continued to search elsewhere. The hallway outside the mess hall and the recreation area led to a door identical to the one I'd seen by the dormitories. Apparently, I was sealed off from the rest of Level One, at least on this side.

I walked back to the elevator, then continued on. The part of Level One I had access to was shaped like an H, with the left side containing the locations I'd searched. The right side contained a series of storage areas, with everything from gas masks to basic tools. I didn't find anything that would help me locate the power cell.

I went back to the elevator and pressed the button for Level Two. Seconds later, the elevator doors opened. The facing wall was identical to the one on the upper level, except a number two was stenciled on it. I stepped out into the hall and looked around. Something different was immediately noticeable. Part of it was the even thicker quality of the air and the blast holes pockmarking several spots in the floor and walls. My eyes were immediately drawn to the corpses.

Seven bodies were strewn on the floor of the hallway, the nearest one only several paces away. As I got closer, I saw the horrible, staring face of what had probably been a young man, his eyes fixed and unseeing. I bent down and took a closer look. His eyeballs were shrunken and seemed to have the texture of old rubber. His skin was chalky and wrinkled. If I didn't know better, I would've thought his body had been mummified. The mouth was open, as if he was screaming at the moment he died.

The other corpses were all in the same condition. Two of the dead men were wearing lab coats; the others were wearing old Air Force uniforms. The sensation of being in a morgue was overwhelming. I'd never been particularly comfortable around death, but this place was far worse than a run-of-the-mill mortuary. A sense of foreboding began to seep into my bones like a humid chill.

I stepped over and around the bodies on my way down the hall. At the end, I encountered another sign. The Biology Laboratory was somewhere to the right, the Metallurgy Laboratory to my left. I looked in either direction, and then something grabbed my attention. At the end of the hallway to my left, the Restricted Access door was ajar.

There were no corpses in this section of the hall. The dead men had probably been trying to reach the elevator when they met their maker. I reached the Restricted Access door and pushed it open. The color of the walls in this section were tan, obviously a superior shade to the light purple of the less important areas. I was in a long tunnel, with three doors on the left side and four on the right. About seventy or eighty feet away, I saw another Restricted Access door.

The first three doors on the right had nameplates affixed to them with the descriptions Security, Communications, and Records. The last door on that side had no nameplate. On the left were the Administration Office and the Data Storage room. The last door seemed to be the entrance for a large room, which sported the ominous moniker of War Room. Halfway up and to the right of each door was a scanning device. It seemed like I'd need an identification badge of some sort to get into these rooms. After checking all the doors in the area and verifying that none of them would be easy to get into, I returned to the light purple area.

I had a hunch that the room I needed to get into was the Records Room. It seemed a likely place to find some kind of cataloguing system, which might give me the specific location of the power cell. I was also intrigued by the War Room, but being in the complex was starting to make the hair on the back of my neck stand up. All I wanted to do was find the power cell and get the hell out of Dodge.

I needed to find an identification badge that would get me into the Records Room. My first thought was to see if any of the dead men were wearing identification badges. None of them were. There probably weren't many people who worked in the complex who had high-level security clearances, but there had to be one somewhere. I spent the next hour searching every nook of Level Two.

There were four work areas in all: the Biology Laboratory, the Metallurgy Laboratory, a Computer Science Lab, and a Linguistics Research Office. Identification badges were in short supply, but I did stumble across several things of interest. In the Metallurgy Lab, I found samples of a strange material resembling aluminum foil. Maybe fifty pieces of varying size were lying around the work area. I picked up one of them. It felt cold to the touch and had an odd cloth-like feel to it. I folded it and set it back on the counter. Within seconds, it unfolded into its original position with no visible crease.

On one part of the counter, a Bunsen burner was surrounded by swatches of the material. I pulled the book of matches from my pocket and held a flame up to one of the pieces. It had no effect whatsoever.

In another part of the lab, I found a box full of objects that looked like miniature I beams, about a quarter-inch thick and ranging in length from half an inch to more than four feet. I couldn't tell what they were made of, but I guessed it was some kind of plastic. I picked up one of the longer pieces. It was absolutely weightless. Closing my eyes, I couldn't even tell that there was something in my hand. I figured material that light must be extremely fragile, so I tried to snap it in half. I couldn't bend it even a millimeter.

In the Biology Lab, I found yet another strange material. It was black, shiny, and almost as thin as tin foil. Since it could have been a cousin to Bakelite, the material wouldn't have appeared to be anything out of the ordinary, if it hadn't had an unusual density and been staggeringly strong. I also recognized additional samples of the miniature I beams floating in various solutions. In every case, the objects hadn't decomposed in any way.

Looking around the Linguistics Research Office, I recalled my conversation with Malloy. I was probably standing in the very place where he did his work on the cryptic alien symbols. After some searching, I found several boxes of the I-beam structures. These, however, had symbols on them. The symbols were very small, less than a fingernail wide, and a shiny purple color. There were many different characters, primarily consisting of geometric shapes, leaf-like figures, and variations on circles. Other characters could have been Chinese in origin, to my highly untrained eye. The writing was beautiful and mesmerizing. I suddenly understood Malloy's lifelong obsession with finding the meanings behind the symbols.

Throughout my search, I felt increasingly that I was not alone. It wasn't so much that someone was watching me as that there was another presence close by. I heard nothing, saw nothing, and couldn't pin down any apparent reason for the feeling. I hadn't seen any other corpses, though I tightened up every time I opened a door or turned a corner.

Only one accessible area was left to comb on Level Two: the Computer Science Lab. My first impression of the area was that it looked like a typical customer-service office, with dozens of cubicles, each containing a standard-looking, if old-fashioned, work station. Further exploration confirmed that no identification badges were lying around.

Toward the back of the room, I saw a door cracked open a couple of inches. I walked over and tried to push it open farther, but it wouldn't budge. Putting my eye to the opening, I was shocked by what I saw. It looked as if a battle had erupted on the other side of the door. The door connected the Computer Science Lab with a much larger area that had blast holes everywhere. It looked as though a fire had broken out, charring sections of the walls. I couldn't get an accurate count of the dead bodies, but there were at least two dozen. Seeing all the devastation, I decided that something must have been dislodged in the battle that prevented the door from swinging open. I put my shoulder into the door, but it didn't budge. Then I put my eye back to the crack and, to my excitement, caught sight of an identification badge.

A corpse lay about five feet beyond the door, his back turned toward me, a plastic-encased badge clipped to the belt of his trousers. All I had to do was reach out and grab it. Of course, the body was out of reach, and the door wouldn't open enough for me to get my arm in anyway. I leaned against the door, focused on the badge and, for several minutes, tried to figure out a solution. I considered giving up on it, but I'd already gone through the entire level and come up empty. Jury-rigging was in order.

I went to the elevator and returned to Level One. In the recreation area, I picked up a pool cue and removed a dart from the dartboard. Now that I had the two pieces of my salvaging device, I just needed to find something to hold them together. I remembered seeing the familiar silver sheen of a roll of duct tape in one of the storage rooms. God, I loved duct tape. Very few problems couldn't be solved with duct tape and/or a coat hanger.

With the duct tape, I attached the dart firmly to the end of the pool cue. Returning to the door at the back of the Computer Science Lab, I soon pulled the identification badge through the narrow opening. Flushed with my success, I hurried back to the Restricted Area and waved the badge in front of the sensor by the door to the Records Room. With a barely audible click, the door opened.

I stepped into the room, and my expectations fell. It was much larger than I'd hoped it would be. Rows and rows of file cabinets stared back at me dauntingly. Time to smoke. I'd been hunting feverishly for several hours and suddenly realized that I needed a rest. A chair sat by a desk near the door. I collapsed into it and lit my cigarette.

After my second smoke, I decided to start looking. For three and a half hours, I went through drawers, files, and boxes, hoping to randomly stumble across a reference to the power cell and where I could find it. Then I caught a lucky break. In one drawer of a file cabinet, I caught sight of a label marked simply *#186*. Inside the file were several photographs of the power cell. The slide I'd seen was a drawing, so I'd had no reference to determine how large it was. For all I knew, it could have been as big as a punching bag or as small as a fuse. In the photograph, several objects were visible in the background. The power cell looked to be no more than eighteen inches in height and as big around as a coffee mug. The file also held a number of papers, including a description submitted by whoever had originally catalogued the object. Several addenda were seemingly contributed by various researchers who had performed tests on the power cell. The last document was a receipt, indicating that the item had been placed into storage. Area G, Level Three.

Leaving behind everything but the receipt, I hurried to the elevator. I inserted the blue card one more time and pressed the button for Level Three. A warning light appeared on the LED: Access Denied. Oh, great. The red and green cards brought the same result. It still wouldn't let me go down. I stuck the cards back into my pocket and considered what options I had, if any. My search of Level Two hadn't turned up any alternate routes. It was the elevator or nothing.

I thought it over. Whatever had killed the people here had either originated on Level Three or in the room behind the Computer Science Lab. I was more inclined to think that it had come from below. Malloy had said that almost everyone had been killed before the military sealed off the area. So far, I'd only seen twenty-five or thirty corpses. The base must have had several hundred people working here at the time. Where were the other bodies? They had to be on Level Three.

That had to be the reason why the elevator was denying me access. The first step in containment would have been to seal off the source. The security office! That's where they would put a lock on access to Level Three.

I exited the elevator and hurried back to the door for the security office. I waved the identification badge over the sensor outside the security-office door. With a click, the door opened, and I walked in. The place was disorganized, as though a pack of four-year-olds had gone through it. There were no signs of laser blasts or anything similar, but the floor was littered with notebooks, computer disks, and overturned chairs. Around the perimeter were surveillance camera displays, showing literally hundreds of locations within the complex. One set was labeled Level Three. In most of the shots, I saw extensive laser damage...and bodies. Hundreds of bodies. Whatever they'd let loose here, it had definitely originated on the lower level. Right where I needed to go.

I explored the room until I found the console that regulated the elevator. A button was labeled Level Three Access. I pressed it.

A message appeared on the console screen: *Please enter confirmation code.* Damn it. I got down on my hands and knees and started sorting through the notebooks, papers, and handbooks scattered around on the floor. After several minutes, I found a manual titled *Security Protocol.* I flipped it open to the table of contents. One of the chapters was titled Codes. I read through it, but no specific codes were given. The basic principle outlined in the chapter was that security should change the confirmation codes on a daily basis. As I was about to toss the handbook back onto the pile on the floor, a 3-by-5 card fell out. On it were seven or eight numbers, all but one of which were crossed out. It was worth a try.

I pushed the button, and the message appeared again on the console screen. There was a ten-key pad on the console. I punched in the numbers from the 3-by-5 card. The message disappeared, and the button lit up.

I ran back to the elevator and stuck the blue card into the blue access slot. This time, pressing the Level Three button presented no problem. With a shudder, the elevator came to life and began to descend. I was seriously doubting whether I was up to this. Maybe the creature, or whatever it was, was dead now, but I wasn't going to bank on it. After a wait twice as long as between Levels One and Two, the elevator came to a thumping halt. The doors separated, and I stepped out into pitch darkness. My flashlight was on, but I had an overwhelming need to turn on the lights. I ran the beam over the wall to the right of the elevator doors until I found a switch. As I flipped the switch, a hiccup of light flared like lightening, and then a network of dim flourescent bulbs awoke.

I was standing on the edge of a slaughter. Dead bodies were everywhere. Seeing them on the monitors in the security office had prepared me somewhat, but I'd never been at the scene of a massacre before. The air in the room was unbearably thick. I opened my backpack, pulled out my rebreather, and strapped it on. Now I was breathing normally, though the sight of at least forty corpses had my heart racing. I checked the bodies nearest me. They were in the same condition as those I'd seen on Level Two: looking mummified, with rubbery eyes and mouths open.

The room could have been the interior of the world's largest garage. Piles of components and shards of strange alien materials were scattered everywhere. In the very center was what must have been the fairly intact remains of the spacecraft that had crashed at Roswell. It wasn't entirely dismantled, and I could still see the basic shape. The ship looked to be in excellent condition, considering that it had crash-landed. It wasn't saucer-shaped at all, but looked more like a big, metal boomerang. I took a walk around the ship, not seeing anything particularly overwhelming—except, of course, for the fact that it had come from another world.

As I looked around, I had the same sensation I always felt around snakes, except now I couldn't see or hear it. I just knew it was there somewhere, waiting. Out of the corner of my eye, I swore I saw something move. I spun around and stared at one of the corpses. Had it twitched? I must have imagined it. God, I had the creeps.

With just a hint of panic, I picked up speed. Referring to the receipt, I quickly located the storage area where the power cell was supposedly kept. But the door to it was padlocked, and even a good-sized laser blast in the door hadn't penetrated into the area beyond. I opened my backpack and pulled out my bolt cutter. Without much effort, I snipped through the padlock bars, pulled the padlock off, and opened the door.

Inside the room, two walls looked like big, metal library-card catalog cabinets, each numbered individually. On a third wall was what looked like a display case—the kind you see at museums. There were several shelves behind the Plexiglas. The objects stored there ranged from bizarre to banal, but I had no inclination to examine them. I turned to the metal cabinets and followed the numbers around the room until I reached number 186. I pulled the drawer open, expecting to find nothing inside. I was wrong. There was the power cell.

Then, I heard the noise.

I extracted the power cell and walked quietly back to the storage-area door. Barely opening it, I took a peek outside. I waited for several moments before deciding I'd just been hearing things, and went through the door. I looked around, but didn't see anything dangerous or threatening. Then I caught a movement out of the corner of my eye. I turned and focused.

One of the corpses was moving.

My first thought, as happens quite often in extreme situations, was completely irrational. I wondered how someone could have been injured and stayed here in the complex all these years without medical attention. I reconsidered and suddenly realized that I had no sane explanation for the movement of the corpse. I had the power cell and that was all that really mattered. I moved toward the elevator, not caring about anything except getting above ground and going home. Suddenly, another corpse moved.

I froze. Sounds of rustling and scraping echoed softly through the dead air. I spun around. Behind me, other bodies were moving. My breathing became shallow. All around me it appeared as if an army of dead men was coming to life. Some of the bodies twitched uncontrollably. Others convulsed violently. I was in a house of horrors. I turned and ran.

Just as I reached the elevator doors a loud, low groan filled the chamber. Without thinking, I turned to see what had caused the sound. Maybe fifteen meters away, one of the corpses shook with a tremendous spasm. Transfixed, I watched as a greenish-gray mist seeped from the mouth of the dead man. I'd never seen anything like it. The mist was transparent and moved fluidly, but seemed to have too much mass to be floating in the air.

The mist rose slowly toward the fluorescent lights high above the floor. The light surrounding me slowly assumed a green tint. Most of the corpses were now groaning and convulsing and emitting more greenish-gray mist from their mouths. A chorus of groans grew louder and louder. The walls were now glowing green. Clouds of the green mist continued drifting toward the fluorescent lights. Despite the terror surging through me, I couldn't take my eyes away from the scene.

With a strong effort, I turned away and pressed the button for the elevator. As I waited for the doors to open, I looked back. The mass ascension was slowing. Then, to my horror, the clouds began to drift toward me. The doors to the elevator opened and I quickly stepped inside. The doors slowly closed behind me.

Still holding the power cell with one hand, I fumbled through my pockets for the blue passcard. The first passcard I found was the red one. I dropped it and continued searching. Green light glowed through the cracks around the elevator doors. I found the blue passcard and inserted it, then pushed the button for Level One. The elevator shuddered and started to rise.

I leaned against the wall and closed my eyes. My heart was racing uncontrollably. The elevator vibrated comfortingly as it carried me closer to the surface. I took a deep breath, then opened my eyes. Mist was seeping in through the cracks under the elevator doors. I dropped the power cell and slid into the corner.

I was trapped. The mist was more transparent than it had been before, as if it had stretched in order to slide under the cracks. It sparkled as it slowly rose from the floor.

I looked around the interior of the elevator wildly, desperately. I felt a tingling sensation on my face and hands, as if the muscles there were going to sleep. The elevator continued its slow, grinding ascent. My eyes began to sting. On one of the walls I spotted a small panel with the words "Emergency Only" on it. This qualified. My hands tingled painfully as I ripped the panel door off. The inside of my mouth now felt as if it were coated with sand. Inside the emergency panel was an old-fashioned telephone and a small, red fire-extinguisher. I grabbed the extinguisher, pulled the pin, and pointed it at the mist, which had now filled almost the entire interior of the elevator. Foam spewed from the extinguisher nozzle. The light emanating from the mist dulled to gray. I continued spraying in every direction. The tingling on my face and hands began to fade. The extinguisher began to cough. It was almost empty.

The elevator lurched to a stop. The mist had vanished. The elevator doors opened as I dropped the extinguisher and grabbed the power cell from the floor. I ran out through the vault door into the compound and raced toward the guardhouse. The two guards started violently as I burst inside.

"Turn off the power to the underground complex!"

Todd looked like his bladder had just said sayonara. Willis looked at me stupidly.

"Now! Turn off the power!"

Grasping my message, Willis hurried off. I followed and made sure that he didn't make any detours. Thirty seconds later, the power had been shut down. Grabbing a full-size fire extinguisher from the wall and still clutching the power cell, I ran back through the vault door to the elevator. I waited anxiously to see if the alien mist was going to escape. After some time, I began to relax. I waited a while longer, then returned to the guardhouse. The guards looked too frightened to even ask what had happened. I was still too frightened to tell them.

There was one thing I needed to say, however. "I want you to go lock that vault door, destroy the key, and then put the complex into a deep freeze. And if anyone ever comes here again, I don't care who it is, I don't care if it's the damn president, and they want to go underground, you have orders direct from the NSA to blow their stupid brains out. Got it?"

Chapter
Twenty-Two

I wondered whether my hands would ever quit shaking. It wasn't just the thought of how close I'd come to ending up like the mummified corpses in the Roswell Complex, it was the fact that I'd almost let loose a plague worthy of Moses into the outside world. I'd come half a blond hair from becoming the conductor on the Train to Oblivion. I'd screwed up plenty of times in my life, but this would have been the end-all. Probably literally.

I opened the window of my speeder and lit a much-needed cigarette. Sure, I'd gotten lucky, but there are worse things than luck. Besides, what was luck but preparation meeting opportunity? Most importantly, I'd found the power cell. Rationalization in hindsight has always been one of my strengths.

Having the power cell in the speeder with me was eerie, like carrying an urn full of someone's ashes. It looked innocuous enough, not particularly strange or alien. But it had been constructed somewhere far away, by the hands of extraterrestrials. I looked down at it and wondered what its purpose was. Was it a weapon, or nothing more than an alien flashlight? What would a hand grenade look like to a visitor from another galaxy?

Now that I was clear of the Roswell Complex and headed home, I felt a sudden urge to not have the alien device in my immediate vicinity. Besides, the anonymous caller had said that I shouldn't carry it any longer than absolutely necessary. I decided to get to the nearest sign of civilization. I checked my flight path and saw that I'd be passing close by Albuquerque within several minutes. My heart had finally dropped out of my throat, and I realized I was famished. Maybe some spicy Southwestern food would clear my head and give me an idea of what to do with the power cell.

Regretfully, I'd never been to Albuquerque. Prior to the war it had been a thriving city, populated by New Age cowboys, misanthropic artists, and sun-baked granola eaters. Now, it was a dusty, ramshackle oasis amid miles of desolation. Nearly all the city lights ran in two parallel lines down either side of Lomas Boulevard—Las Vegas without any of the excitement.

I landed my speeder in front of a dilapidated but warmly lit eatery called the Last Chance Diner. It wasn't much of a name, but neither was the Brew & Stew. A sign in front read Best Food for Miles. Some local wit had spray-painted a line through Best and written Only above it.

Over chicken-fried steak and gravy, I formulated a plan for temporarily getting the power cell out of circulation. I didn't want to keep it with me any longer than I had to, and I couldn't think of an utterly secure place to keep it. After due consideration and four cups of coffee-colored water, I finally decided to put my faith in United Parcel Express. Sure, UPEX was known for making deliveries in pieces, but if the power cell had survived an interstellar crash, it would probably survive a rugged delivery.

After I finished the cholesterol plate, I asked for directions to the nearest UPEX office. I boxed the power cell and addressed it to the Savoy Hotel, care of G. Fitzpatrick. For the first time in my life, I paid the extra thirty bucks to have the package certified; I wasn't about to let them misplace an extraterrestrial device. The man at the counter told me that the package would get to the Savoy in two days. I accidentally left a fifty on the counter to help remind him. With any luck, it would arrive when we were ready for it. And, hopefully, I'd find out exactly what I was supposed to do with it during the next few days.

Feeling significantly less burdened, I got back in my speeder and pointed it toward home. As I pulled out of Albuquerque, I caught sight of a sign: Phoenix 332 Miles. I checked my geo-grid. Phoenix wasn't that far out of my way; I could be there in less than two hours. Maybe I should pay Chelsee a surprise visit. After Roswell, I needed to see a friendly face.

Then I reconsidered. I didn't have an address and I hadn't brought the phone number, and Phoenix wasn't a small place. Besides, even if I knew where to find Chelsee, maybe she wasn't ready to see me. And what would I say to her? Now that I thought about it, I missed her, but Lord knows, I wasn't ready to put a ring on her finger at this point, not with Regan moving into the picture. Oh, the confusion.

Four hours later, I unlocked the door to my office, an exhausted, gurgling mass of undigested steak batter and grease. I stumbled into the bedroom and hit the bed face-first. It must have been post-traumatic stress. I couldn't remember ever being so utterly spent. After what seemed like a minute and a half, a pounding sound roused me from a puddle of drool. Blinking stupidly, I lifted my flat, creased face and pushed my aching body up from the bed. The annoying thumping was coming from the door. I staggered through my office and turned the knob.

"What?"

I was too tired to keep my eyelids up. Something smelled good. If only I could get my eyes open.

"Where have you been all my life, handsome?" It was Regan.

I stepped aside, discarding all vestiges of vanity and self-respect, and opened the door wide. She stepped past me and walked toward one of the chairs at my desk. Involuntarily, my left eye opened halfway. She looked devastating. Dropping into the seat and crossing her legs elegantly, she turned her gaze back toward me.

"Did I wake you?" She was a paragon of intuition. I grunted and wandered over to the mirror. God, I was a mess. My face looked like a balled-up pair of khakis. It desperately needed to be steam-cleaned and pressed. I excused myself and crawled into the shower. Between the hot water and the potent deodorant soap, my synaptic functions reluctantly emerged from hibernation. I toweled off and slipped on a bathrobe. Grabbing the pack of smokes from my overcoat, I walked into my office. Regan was just returning to her seat. Apparently, she'd been doing a little snooping.

"Find anything interesting?" I walked past where Regan was primly seated and dropped into my desk chair. She looked at me openly, the very epitome of innocence.

"What do you mean?"

"Searching a PI's office would be like me going through your purse."

Regan smiled disarmingly. "You can look in my purse. I don't mind."

"That's not the point." I lit a cigarette and blew a stream of smoke toward the ceiling. Out of the corner of my eye, I could see Regan still smiling at me.

"Are you always this friendly when you get up?" She was incorrigible. It didn't seem to matter that I was annoyed. The more I got to know Regan, the more I realized that I'd have to take her on her own terms. Being upset by her uncontrolled curiosity was like resenting a carrot for being orange. She was the way she was, and if that wasn't good enough, then too bad. Unfortunately, even in a state of pique, I was overwhelmingly attracted to her. What I really wanted to do was leap over my desk and show her all the steps of the Forbidden Dance of Love. But caving in to carnal desire at this point would only condone her attitude. I had an image to uphold.

I turned back to her, a pillar of strength in terry cloth. "So, did you find anything useful in the notebooks?"

"Maybe. What's it worth to you?"

"Do you take checks?"

"Sorry. I require full payment...up front." Her tone allowed for very little interpretation. Be strong, Murphy.

"I'm a little insolvent right now, though I'd be happy to write you an IOU."

"There'll be interest charges—you'll have to make regular payments."

"That's OK. As soon as I get my finances organized, I'll completely satisfy the debt...with interest."

Regan made a nice sound. "I'm looking forward to it." She reached down and pulled the notebooks from her purse. Opening one of them, she took out several loose sheets of paper and handed them to me. "This is a summary of what I was able to figure out. Ninety percent of the contents are the alien symbols and notes on translating. As far as I could tell, there isn't much of anything useful until the end of the second notebook. It's all pretty vague."

Regan's notes had frequent references to OE and EW. The context implied that these were people. EW was almost certainly Elijah Witt. As for OE, I had no idea who it could be. Other information included references to PD and the Roswell Complex. The number 186 was noted, which just happened to be the item number of the power cell I'd recently liberated from Roswell.

"What do you think this means?" Regan had come around

the desk and was now standing behind me, pointing at the PD reference. "Do you think he was working with the police?"

I shook my head. "I'm pretty sure it stands for Pandora Device."

Regan sat down on the corner of my desk. "Excuse me?"

"The Pandora Device. Apparently, your father was working on it not long before he died."

Regan folded her arms. "How do you know about it?"

"It's a long story. The important thing is, I'm pretty sure that it's tied up with the boxes we're looking for."

Regan leaned forward excitedly. "So what does this Pandora Device do?"

"I don't know. But it's obviously something big. Seems like everyone and their grandmother is trying to get their hands on it."

Regan jumped up and walked away. "I knew it! I wasn't sure exactly what he was working on, but I knew it'd be worth a fortune." She whipped around to face me.

"We're close, Tex! We've just got to find the other boxes. And then...we take Manhattan!"

I didn't really want to put a damper on her enthusiasm, but there were other considerations. "Don't you think we should find out what the Pandora Device is first? Maybe it's something we don't want to let into circulation."

Regan pulled up, a blank expression on her face. "What are you talking about? That's why we're in this. For the money."

I considered telling her about Fitzpatrick and the warnings he'd given me. Regan only saw the financial possibilities. She needed to be aware of the other ramifications, but I decided to keep Fitzpatrick out of the mix for the time being. "Whatever your father was working on, he wanted to keep it away from the NSA. That tells me that it's the kind of thing that could be bad if it fell into the wrong hands."

"Then we'll only sell it to the right people."

"And what if it's not that simple? What if it's something that would be better locked up forever than let loose?"

"That's not an option. Whoever we sell it to, I don't care what they do with it, whatever it is. It was my father's work, so by rights, it's now mine to do with what I will. I don't necessarily want the NSA to end up with it, but it's my birthright, so to speak, and I'm going to cash in on it. And I can work with you or I can do it alone." She suddenly looked around the office. "Where are the boxes?"

"Not here."

"Well, where are they? I want to keep them myself."

"They're hidden away, someplace safe."

Regan's face turned a shade redder. "You don't have the right to keep them from me. They're mine!"

"No, they're not."

She turned on her heel and began pacing around the room. I waited patiently. After several minutes, an abrupt change came over her, like the sun slipping out from behind a cloud. She walked toward me and knelt down on the floor beside my chair. Placing her hands over mine on the armrest, she peered up into my eyes. "You're right, Tex. I'm being foolish...and irresponsible. We'll wait and see what the Pandora Device is. If there's nothing terrible about it, we'll make a lot of money and live happily ever after."

Maybe she was on the level, maybe she was baiting a hook with me. Either way, I reached down and ran my hands through her hair.

"You'll take care of me, won't you Tex?"

There were very few things I wouldn't have done for her at that moment. She kissed my hand, then stood up and returned to her chair. "So, what do we do now?"

Like a sign from God, the vid-phone beeped. I leaned forward and hit the Receive button. Lucas Pernell's face appeared on the screen. "Hey, Murphy."

"What's up?"

"I've got the stuff you wanted. You want to meet?"

"Yeah."

"Same place?"

"Sure. Give me an hour."

I flipped the vid-phone off and turned back to Regan. She wanted to ask who Pernell was, but she was trying desperately to be a good girl. That made me happy. I didn't offer any explanations. Instead, I thought of an errand she could run that would give her something to do while I met with Pernell. If she got lucky, she might even get some useful information.

"I have to go hook up with this friend of mine. In the meantime, there's something you can do for me." I pulled a notepad from one of the desk drawers and wrote down Archie Ellis's name and address. Regan took the address and looked it over.

"I want you to go talk to this guy. Runs a UFO shop called the Cosmic Connection. Remember the EW your father referred to in his notebooks? I think it stands for Elijah Witt."

Regan picked up a pen from my desktop and jotted the name down. "Who's he?"

"He was, apparently, a friend of your father. He's also a bigwig in the UFO community. Wrote a book called *There Are Messages from Outer Space*. He almost certainly knows something about the Pandora Device and whatever else your father was working on."

Regan looked up from writing. "What am I supposed to do?"

"This Ellis guy has been in touch with Witt. He knows where

to find him but won't tell me where. I want you to see what you can find out. Ellis is a lonely guy. He'll say almost anything to keep a conversation going. With someone like you, he'll probably trip over his tongue, telling you anything you want to hear."

"And what if he doesn't cooperate?"

"I'm sure you'll think of something. You strike me as being a capable bluffer."

"I don't know if I appreciate that. Anything else?"

"Yeah. Ellis received one of the boxes from your father. When I spoke to him, he said it'd been stolen from his shop just after he received it. There was no reason for him to lie about it, so I think he was being straight up. I have a hunch that the box is now with the NSA, but you should see if you can find out who could've ended up with it. We might need it to find this Pandora Device."

"I'll see what I can do. Is that all?"

"Don't tell him that you know me. Keep it casual. He gets suspicious real easily."

"What do you want me to do after I get the information?" she asked, looking at me suggestively.

"Meet me back here. I shouldn't be gone too long. Plan on a couple hours."

Regan nodded and got up from the chair. We walked to the door, and I opened it for her.

She stopped and looked me squarely in the eyes. "I'm sorry for the way I acted. I know I can trust you to take care of things...to take care of me. It won't happen again." She reached up and gently slid her cool hand onto the back of my neck. Our lips met softly, then deeply. As she pulled away, she gently bit my lower lip. A previously unused nerve flared into existence, lighting up my entire left side, all the way to my instep. Without another word, Regan ducked out the door and left.

Chapter
Twenty-Three

"Here's the printout." Pernell opened a medium-sized valise and pulled out about ten pounds of computer paper. He dropped it in front of me with a resounding thud.

I handed him a smoke. "Is this it? I was expecting something substantial."

Pernell smiled and turned his head slightly as he exhaled. "Hey, you wanted all the possible anagrams. *There Are Messages from Outer Space* has thirty characters. The guy who does the anagrams down at the *Mirror* told me that there would be ten million trillion possible combinations."

He waved his hand toward the computer printout. "Those are only the combinations that contain at least four English words with four or more letters."

I glanced over the first page, then flipped through the rest. The sheer quantity was mind-boggling. Pernell was smiling at me. "Shouldn't take you more than a couple weeks to get through that stuff."

"Maybe I'll get lucky."

"I'd start at the back and work forward. I always find what I'm looking for at the very end." Pernell snuffed his smoke and closed up the valise. "By the way, I followed up on the information you gave me. Everything checks out. It's gonna be one hell of a story."

"I'm sure the NSA's gonna love it."

Pernell grinned viciously. "Yeah. I know."

He was playing the journalistic kamikaze, pointing his nose straight toward the NSA and damning the torpedoes. I wondered if he knew what he was getting into. To the agency, we were two little bugs. At any time, a huge NSA shoe could descend from the sky and crush us. The difference between me and Pernell was that he wasn't scared. Apparently he'd never had the pleasure of Jackson Cross's company.

"You're in the middle of something big, aren't you?"

I nodded.

He narrowed his gaze and leaned forward. "How 'bout letting me in on it?"

"Can't do it."

Pernell looked at me thoughtfully. "What's your price?"

"Don't have one. Sorry."

Pernell grimaced. "In my line of work, I have to coerce information out of people all the time. A lot of times, I get it for free. My first offer is usually cash. If that doesn't work... sex, drugs, whatever. I've gotten pretty good at it, but I can't get an angle on you. It bugs me. What's your weak spot?"

"Uh...math."

"C'mon, you know what I'm talking about. Most weak spots are above the neck and below the waist. But the biggest weak spot is thinking that you don't have one."

"We hardly know each other, Pernell. I usually make people buy me dinner and take me out dancing before I confess my fatal flaw."

Pernell raised his hands in a gesture of resignation. "Fine. Just remember, whether you know it or not, there's a weak spot in there somewhere. Maybe I can't see it...maybe you can't either, but it's there. And someone will find it eventually."

"Someone already has. It's just above my knee. Drives me crazy."

He stood up and cradled the valise under his arm. "I like you, Murphy. It's been good knowing you."

I watched Pernell walk to the door and exit the lounge. The pile of computer paper sat in front of me like the last pie in a pie-eating contest. It looked too big to tackle, but I needed to find that one magical anagram hiding like a needle in the proverbial haystack. This was going to require a distilled beverage. Bourbon, please. No, make that a double. I reached into the inner pocket of my overcoat and pulled out a pen. A drag on a Lucky Strike and a deep gulp of bourbon, and I turned my attention to the anagrams.

I'd always hated English classes. After two hours of poring over the computer printout, I finally figured out why: I hated the actual letters. My fourth bourbon was a distant memory, and I was out of smokes. I walked across the bar to the cigarette machine with a handful of quarters. Psychedelic patterns consisting of unnatural combinations of vowels and consonants blurred my vision. A harshly attractive woman cast a dog-eared smile in my direction. Sorry, honey. No time for romance. I've got anagrams on my mind.

I dropped quarters into the machine slot for several minutes, then collected my cigarette pack and returned to my table. Squinting through the smoke, I started round two. The process was like playing a slot machine. Each new combination was a potential winner, but they kept coming up lemon/orange/bell. Occasionally, I'd run across a near miss, such as FEAR SCHEMERS REMOTE OUTER PASSAGE. I once dated a New Age poetess who would undoubtedly have found deep significance in this type of random combination, but I was fairly certain it wasn't what I was looking for.

Hours passed. Except for the occasional trip to the porcelain bank, I was glued to the printout. Eventually, even the barflies had to admit defeat and head for home. I was about to order from waitress number three when I saw the line I'd been searching for: MERGE THE FOUR RARE CASES TO SEE MAPS.

It had to be the right one. It seemed as likely as anything that the puzzle boxes contained a map of some kind. To what, I couldn't know for sure. Maybe the Pandora Device.

Suddenly, I thought of the disk I'd found in Malloy's room. Would this anagram help me break the encryption on the disk I'd found in Malloy's room? There was only one way to find out.

Back at my office, I slipped Malloy's disk into the drive of my computer. Once again, I got the message CONTENTS ENCRYPTED. PLEASE ENTER AUTHORIZATION CODE. This time, I typed in MERGE THE FOUR RARE CASES TO SEE MAPS. INVALID PASSWORD—TOO MANY PARAMETERS. Damn. I typed it in again, changing the "FOUR" to a "4". No luck. I tried it again, changing the "TO" to a "2". Still no good. I sat back and thought it over. Maybe I was being a chump. Maybe the password had nothing to do with the anagrams. Worse, maybe the anagram I needed wasn't the one I'd found. The thought of going through the rest of the anagrams made me want to vomit.

I leaned back over the keyboard. For the hell of it, I typed FOUR RARE CASES. The screen blinked. I was in.

Hello, Elijah. I see you figured out my little puzzle. And since you're reading this, I'll assume that something has happened to me. You always said I was looking for trouble. Well, I think I've found it.

You should already have received a package from me. I've sent similar packages to four others. The five of you are the people I trust most in this back-stabbing, self-destructive world. Collectively, you are the Council which now holds the key to a locked door, beyond which lies the knowledge of ancient and distant intelligence.

As you know, visitors from other worlds have come to our little corner of the galaxy. You've always believed, but now you have a chance to see evidence with your own eyes. Unfortunately, there are others who want what I've discovered, and not for the altruistic motives we share.

For that reason, I have created something I have taken to calling the Pandora Device. The contents of the package I sent you must be used with those contained in the packages sent to the others. Together, you will learn what I've discovered. Together, I hope that your combined power, influence, and wisdom will determine what should be done.

You know I have a tendency to belabor the point, but let me end by saying this: what awaits you is something the world may not be ready for. If this is your conclusion as well, keep in mind that it's better to destroy something than allow it to destroy.

Sincerely,

Thomas

I paged down to a schematic drawing of an odd-looking contraption. It vaguely resembled a camera with all the attachments hooked on. Under the drawing was the caption *The Pandora Device.* Paging down again, I saw that the contraption was comprised of three interlocking pieces. It appeared to have a small control panel.

So this was the Pandora Device. It seemed utterly innocuous. I looked at the diagrams closely, trying to fathom what message, what power, could be contained inside. Malloy had given no further clues.

I read the message to Witt several times, then leaned back away from the computer. Unless Malloy was a terrible exaggerator, the implications were even more serious than Fitzpatrick had led me to believe. For the first time, I wondered whether it was my place to be in the middle of this. Regardless, I *was* in the middle, with no way out. And Fitzpatrick was counting on me. I needed to find the other boxes.

Fitzpatrick already had two of the boxes: Regan's and Emily's. Archie Ellis had received one, but it'd been stolen. I didn't have high hopes of finding that one, but I'd have to try. Another box, obviously, was in Witt's possession. That left one box unaccounted for. Maybe it had been sent to OE. Unfortunately, I had no clue who that was, though his or her identity would probably turn up if I kept looking.

For the time being, I decided that the trail of my investigation led through the Cosmic Connection. Ellis was my only link to locating Elijah Witt. I wasn't optimistic that Ellis could help with finding out who'd stolen his box, but maybe Regan had gotten some information regarding Witt. I picked up the phone and called her hotel. She wasn't in. Feeling impatient, I decided to pay Ellis a visit and beat Witt's address out of him if I had to.

The door to the Cosmic Connection was locked, and the Closed sign was out. I peered into the darkness, trying to see if Ellis was around. The place appeared to be deserted. I knocked on the door several times, but there was no answer. I checked the lock, but it was a dead bolt, shut tighter than Rook's wallet.

A narrow alley ran down the right side of the shop. I followed it to the end. There was no back door on this side of the building. I started back toward the front when I noticed a small piece of rain-stained plywood crate on the ground, set against the side of the building. Just on the off chance, I knelt down and pushed it aside. A small, cracked window looked big enough for me to squeeze through, though I'd have to take off my fedora. It was a big price to pay, but this was a big job.

After a few minutes of trying to pry the window open, I resorted to brute force and kicked it in unceremoniously. Managing to climb through without tearing my overcoat, I found myself in the bowels of the Cosmic Connection. With nothing more than five second intervals of match light and my innate sense of direction, I stumbled around the dark basement until I found a light switch. Shadows sprang up around me, and I found myself amid a jungle of cardboard boxes, piles of books, and a plethora of indescribably odd objects. To my right was a rickety set of stairs leading up to the main floor. I reached the top and, throwing open the basement door, stepped into Ellis's shop.

The smell of incense was much less noxious than it had been before. Ellis wasn't here, and my guess was that he hadn't been for awhile. But I was wrong.

As I looked around, I caught sight of something behind the counter. As I approached, I saw the bottoms of a pair of old sneakers. Leaning over the counter, I looked straight into the glazed, unseeing eyes of Archie Ellis. The hole in his head was new. A pool of congealed blood had gelled around him. He looked like an overgrown kindergartner taking a nap on a giant raspberry fruit roll-up.

Life was getting cheaper by the minute, and I felt like the Grim Reaper's calling card. I lit a smoke. Poor bastard. I checked around. Whoever had killed him, it hadn't been a burglar. Who was I kidding? He'd gotten waxed on my account. He wasn't worth killing for any other reason. Malloy, I could understand, but not Ellis. Things were coming to a head. Someone was going around, tying up loose ends, maybe trying to find the box Ellis no longer had. Whatever was going to happen was going to happen soon. I needed to find Witt.

I made a systematic search of the Cosmic Connection. I don't know how long Ellis had run his shop, but he'd collected a few lifetimes' worth of paraphernalia. One entire section of the store was piled high with newspaper articles, magazine clippings, and news-wire photographs. Several file cabinets were stuffed full of correspondence. There were racks of home videos, undoubtedly of UFO sightings, and an impressive library of laser disks, dealing with all forms of paranormal subject matter. Ellis had apparently stashed things in one spot until there was no room left, then moved to another section of the building.

After some time, I found the most recent dumping ground. Rooting through the stacks of paper, I found what I was looking for: a scrap of paper with the name J.I. Thelwait, Witt's alias, written on it. There was also an incomplete mailing address: PO Box 24, Richfield. The state and zip code had fought a battle with a coffee stain and lost. They were smeared to the point of illegibility. But at least I had an address. Now I just needed to find out where it was.

I seemed to remember Ellis saying something about Witt retiring to a place in the Northwest. He could have been trying to throw me off, but it was a good place to start. There was a vid-phone on the counter, sitting on top of a vid-phone directory. I opened the directory and found the page with the area-code listings. Starting with one of Washington state's four codes, I dialed 1-509-555-1212. The operator's voice came on and asked for a city. I said Richfield and asked for the number of J.I. Thelwait. The operator told me that Richfield was in area code 206. The 206 operator informed me that there was no one by that name listed. I asked him to check Elijah Witt. No luck.

In Oregon, there was no city named Richfield. California had a Richfield, but no Elijah Witt or J.I. Thelwait. I resorted to checking the other western states. The Richfields in Nevada, Utah, and Idaho didn't pan out. Montana, New Mexico, Texas, and Arizona had no Richfields. I wasn't too keen on trying every state in the country. Could Ellis have meant western Canada? Maybe Witt was across the border. I dialed the number for Canadian information. There was, indeed, an Elijah Witt in Richfield, British Columbia, but his number and address were unlisted. I didn't care. Just like the Mounties, I had enough to get my man.

Chapter
Twenty-Four

I called the police from the vid-phone at the Cosmic Connection, leaving an anonymous message about Ellis's body. His murder was weighing heavily on me, and there was nothing I wanted to do more than find out who'd blasted him. I wondered if Regan had gotten to him before the bullet. An unsettling thought occurred to me. No, I couldn't believe that. Ellis wasn't the first person to die in this chain of events and probably wouldn't be the last.

I flew back to my office. It was late, and I figured I'd be better off with some sleep and a fresh start. I picked up some Chinese food on the way. When I got home, there was a message on my answering machine. I pushed the playback button and slumped into my chair with a box of pan-fried noodles. Chelsee's face appeared on the screen.

"Hey, handsome. How come you're never there when I call? You're not actually working, are you? Well, I just wanted to tell you that Phoenix is fun, but I miss home. I've been doing a lot of thinking, and I'll be back soon. I'll buy you a drink, and we'll compare scars. So, I guess that's it. Bye!"

A slight twinge appeared in my stomach. For the first time in my adult life, this sensation had to do with romance, and not with fear, booze, or indigestion. With some irritation, I realized that I missed her. I'd been so busy the past couple days, I hadn't had time to think about anything so trivial as women, but now that I thought about it, I was a little lonely. I took a hot shower and missed Chelsee even more.

As I lay in bed, floating into the Freudian abyss, I saw Regan and Chelsee, standing like sentinels in a vast desert landscape. Regan's auburn hair nestled around her flawless face, her eyes deep and dark, her slender arms extending toward me. Chelsee was like the sun, golden and smiling, her hands resting on her narrow hips. Then, like wraiths emerging from the mist, faces appeared behind Regan. First Fitzpatrick, then Malloy, then Ellis. With a feeling of regret welling up inside me, I turned back to Chelsee, and she was alone. Her warmth reached out to me, and I closed my eyes.

When I opened them, I was lying on a beach. My grandmother was blocking the sun, lecturing me on drinking straight out of the milk jug. I'd lost my dog, and Paul McCartney appeared, wearing a sombrero over a sequined gown with lavender pumps, trying to sell me life insurance. The pan-fried noodles had taken over.

The flight to British Columbia the next day was nothing if not scenic. The great Northwest was still one of the least developed areas in the country. I set the speeder on autopilot and tried to think of a brilliant plan that would get me into Elijah Witt's stronghold. Everything I'd heard about the man indicated that he was a recluse of titanic proportions. I also had an inkling that he was probably on the upside of well-to-do. My experience in the PI business had taught me that money plus reclusiveness generally resulted in expensive alarm systems and nearly impenetrable security.

Not that I didn't enjoy a challenge. But something told me that I'd have to meet Witt head-on. Now I just had to come up with an utterly convincing, possibly endearing lie. By the time I reached Richfield, I had a few mediocre ideas, but nothing I felt particularly comfortable with.

A sign at the city limits proudly welcomed me into the warm and industrious arms of 18,611 plaid-wearing lumberjacks. The hamlet of Richfield was a three-dimensional postcard, complete with a pint-sized Main Street and quaint shops with names like Mossy Oak.

Witt's address was a post-office box, which wasn't going to do me any good. His house was somewhere in the vicinity, but I wasn't about to canvass the entire town. Maybe if I knew which neighborhood he lived in, I could fall back on my old missionary disguise. Unfortunately, I'd left my pamphlets and glassy-eyed look back at the office. I'd have to locate Witt's place some other way.

I'd never lived in a small town, but I'd watched enough reruns of *The Andy Griffith Show* to wing it. And, as any experienced watcher of the show knows, anything worth hearing passes through the town barbershop. I glanced into my rearview mirror and decided I needed a trim anyway. As I flew in slowly over Main Street, a revolving red-and-white-striped barber pole stood out like a lighthouse beacon in front of a tiny building on the far end of the street. A sign above the door said it all: Fred's.

I parked my speeder and climbed out. A group of children stood at a safe distance, their faces looking as though they'd just seen Godzilla tromping over a nearby hill. At first, I thought they might be awestruck by my fedora, seeing as how it was a hat with no earflaps. On further consideration, however, I realized that there were no other speeders on the street. All the vehicles were the old-fashioned earth-bound types. As far as the kids knew, I was some terrible alien, come to have my hair cut before destroying the town and abducting them to take back to my home planet.

A bell tinkled as I opened the door. Entering Fred's Barbershop was like entering a Norman Rockwell hologram. A fiftyish, bespectacled gentleman, whom I took to be Fred, was meticulously trimming the borders of an elderly man's bald spot. Fred was sporting a standard-issue white jacket over a white shirt and a tie with a knot the size of an eight ball. His hair was lacquered back with a hearty helping of Brylcreem, and his pencil-thin mustache was trimmed to a fault.

Besides Fred and the gent in the chair, two ancient checker players were plying their trade in the corner, and a cigar-smoking fat man was reading *Hunters' Weekly*. A younger man sat with a nervous-looking little boy, who was probably being initiated into the Fellowship of the Barbershop Lodge.

I took a seat in the corner, removing my hat and smiling in a neighborly fashion at the thirteen eyes watching my every move. One of the checker players wore an eye patch. Fred was the first to lose interest and returned to his client. The only sounds in the place were the snipping of scissors and the plunking of checkers. My smile hadn't lost any of its luster, but it didn't seem to be working. I decided to make the first move. "This sure is a beautiful town."

The silence in the barbershop was as thick as the goo in Fred's hair. After what seemed to me to be an awkward silence, Fred spoke without looking up. "New around here, aren't ya?"

"Yeah. This is my first time in Richfield. I'm from San Francisco."

"Come all the way up here for a trim?"

I laughed, probably a little too loudly. "No. Just came up to visit a friend of mine."

"Really? Who's that?"

"Elijah Witt."

Fred stopped snipping. Everyone in the room was looking at each other, like they were trying to figure who'd just made that awful smell. Apparently, I'd tripped a local land mine. Fred was a cool customer. After a slight hesitation, he resumed snipping. "So, how do you know Mr. Witt?"

This seemed like a good time to test my first falsehood. "I was one of his students at Berkeley. Thought I'd pay him a visit, since I was in the area. Unfortunately, I've never been here before. I'm not sure how to find him."

The fat cigar-smoker gave me a suspicious leer. "Seems kinda dumb to come for a visit when you ain't got the address. How'd that happen?"

My brain was clicking like lobster claws. "Well, I wanted to surprise him. We haven't seen each other for at least fifteen years."

The fat man turned to Fred. "I don't know about this guy. Somethin' don't seem right about him."

"Don't be unneighborly, Stan. He's just not from around here, that's all." Fred looked up at me. "Ain't that right, Mr.—"

"Murphy. Jake Murphy. Yeah, I'm afraid I stick out like a bone spur around here."

"Got that right." The words were mumbled from the direction of the checker game. I seemed to have worn out my unwelcome. I decided to leave before these hicks started playing "Dueling Banjos" and making pig sounds.

"Well, I'll come back later when you're not so busy." There was no response. My standard Murphy charm had apparently deserted me. I needed a stiff drink and time to compose myself. Fred's Barbershop was nothing like the one Andy Taylor went to.

There was a bar across the street called the Juniper Saloon. I lit a cigarette and crossed the street, being careful not to get hit by one of the four-wheeled relics passing by. I walked in and took a seat at the bar. The place must have gotten more through-traffic than the barbershop. The bartender was the first person in Richfield who didn't look at me as though my face were covered with festering boils. I ordered bourbon straight up. The bartender confirmed my order appreciatively, as though he'd expected me to ask for a beer.

I drained the JD and ordered another. I'd tipped the bartender just enough to leave me alone and yet not so much that he'd feel obligated to make cardboard conversation. I was just finishing my third helping when someone slid onto the bar stool beside me. The young man from the barbershop gave me a nod and waved off the bartender. He'd come in to see me, not to have a drink. With some trepidation, he turned and spoke. "Sorry about what happened back there. Not everyone around here is so narrow."

I shook the last drops out of my glass. "I was beginning to wonder."

The young man smiled.

"My wife and son and I moved here not too long ago. I work at the paper mill. It took awhile for us to fit in. This isn't a tourist town, and the locals are always suspicious of anything new."

"Tell me something. What was that reaction I got when I mentioned Elijah Witt? I felt like I'd mentioned the evil dragon that descends on the town and eats everyone who isn't bolted into their house."

The young man shook his head. "He's a queer one, Mr. Witt. He lives outside of town in a huge mansion. Only a few people have ever seen him. You should hear all the rumors flying around about him. Some say he has aliens living there with him. Others swear they've seen strange lights in the sky up around his place. Still others say he's a communist."

"My god. A commie?"

The young man shrugged his shoulders. "I don't believe any of the wild stuff. I guess he's written some books about UFOs that have got everyone spooked."

"I guess it doesn't take much around here."

He shook his head in agreement. "Ignorance breeds fear. But I just wanted to talk to you before you left Richfield thinking that everyone here's unfriendly."

"I appreciate it. Want a drink?"

"No. My son's waiting out in the truck. I gotta get home for dinner."

He got up to leave. I decided to join him. We stepped outside. "By the way, could you point me in the direction of Mr. Witt's place?"

"Sure. Take Main Street down to Elm and take a right—"

"No, I just need the actual direction. I've got a speeder."

He craned his neck to check out my vehicle. After admiring it for a minute, he turned back and pointed. "Due west."

Chapter
Twenty-Five

I was still unsure of how I would get in to see Elijah Witt. As I navigated my speeder out of town and over the densely forested terrain, a sprawling mansion came into view, nestled into the side of a pine-covered hill. It had to be the place I was looking for. I landed on a spacious cul-de-sac at the front of the mansion. Half expecting to be overtaken by a pack of salivating guard dogs, I got out and walked to the door. The only sound in the air was the rustling of the trees and the chirping of birds.

I rang the doorbell and waited for several minutes. Just after I'd rung a second time, the door was opened by a decrepit-looking old man, wearing a herringbone jacket and a bow tie.

"Mr. Witt?"

The old man gave me a look as dry as day-old meatloaf. "Hardly."

He spoke with the clipped English accent and stiff-upper-lipped manner of a man still bitter about losing the American Revolution. With my mongrel American facial features and homespun Midwestern accent, I probably represented everything this guy hated about the Colonies. I resisted the urge to slip into my Southwestern drawl and really irritate him. "Is Mr. Witt in? I've come a long way to see him."

The old man made no attempt to be subtle as he looked me over like a suspect in a police lineup. After a long silence, he looked up at me disdainfully. "Whatever it is you're selling, sir, Mr. Witt is not interested. Good day." He started to close the door, but I'd come too far to give up this easily.

I stuck my foot in the door, causing the old man to look at me as though I'd slapped him lightly across the face with a pair of white calfskin gloves. Maybe some humor would lighten the situation. "Are you sure I can't interest you in a few magazine subscriptions? If I sell three more, I win a free trip to Knott's Berry Farm."

With unspeakable contempt, the old man looked at me, then at my foot, then back at me. He was apparently in no mood to be cajoled. "That was just a joke."

"Yes, I know."

"Look, I don't mean to be impertinent, but it's very important that I at least get a message to Mr. Witt. I'll be happy to wait outside if you'll at least take it to him."

The limey looked down at my foot again, then seemed to decide that I wasn't going to go away unless he at least made a pretense of helpfulness. "Very well, sir. What is your message?"

I rooted through the pockets of my overcoat and found a nearly empty book of matches. Taking a pen from my inner pocket, I jotted down the words *Merge the Four Rare Cases to See Maps*, then handed the matchbook to the old man. "This is very important."

"Of course it is."

He folded the matchbook and waited for me to remove my foot before closing the door. I turned away from the door and dug for my smokes. There was no guarantee that the old Brit would even bother to speak with Witt, but I was planning on camping out at the front door until I got an audience with him. I was just crushing out my Lucky Strike on the flagstone walkway when the door opened behind me. "Mr. Witt will see you."

"Great. Listen, I sure appreciate your help. Love your accent."

The old man groaned audibly.

I was ushered into a foyer with a ceiling high enough to practice punting in. On the far side of the room, by a fireplace big enough to throw a bookcase into, was a heavyset figure sporting a pipe. As I crossed the room, the figure turned toward me, and for the first time I laid eyes upon the intimidating countenance of Elijah Witt. I strode forward, hand extended and face lit up like a No Vacancy sign.

"Mr. Witt! Pleasure to see you again!"

The ornately carved pipe protruded from Witt's full, ruddy face like a pump handle. Dark brown eyes surveyed me intently from beneath bushy white eyebrows. The eyes didn't leave me as he took a match from the book I'd given his lackey and set it to the nest of tobacco in the bowl of his pipe. Witt nursed his Captain Black to a full boil, then wagged out the match and tossed it casually, along with the matchbook, into the roaring hearth. "What's the meaning of that message?"

My gaze automatically went to the fireplace as I quickly thought up something clever. "Well, it's kind of a long story."

"It may not seem like it to you, but I'm a busy man."

"I know that, sir. I won't take much of your time."

"Where did you get the message?"

I felt like I was on the witness stand. Witt's piercing presence was akin to that of the erudite Perry Mason, whose very demeanor caused the most callous criminal to break down in the trial scene at the end of every episode. I considered coming clean and telling Witt what was happening, but I had a pretty good idea that he'd just as soon spend an evening bowling and eating chili dogs as hand over the box Malloy had sent him. Besides, even if Malloy trusted Witt, I had no reason to.

Nonetheless, the box would be safer with me or Fitzpatrick.

It was just a matter of time before the NSA tracked down Witt and pried the box from his rigor-mortised hand. Rationalization is a way of life.

"Ever since I took your class at the university, I've been a big fan. I read somewhere that you do anagrams, so I was playing around with the title to your latest book which, by the by, I really enjoyed. I thought that sending you an anagram message might interest you enough to see me."

Witt looked at me like the liar I was. I'd gone from merely nervous to downright panicky when he finally spoke. "What's your name?"

"Murphy. Jake Murphy."

"Do you believe in coincidence, Mr. Murphy?"

The question caught me off guard. "Uh...sure. As a matter of fact, one time I'd just come out of the supermarket with a gallon of sherbet—"

"I don't."

"What do you mean?"

"You say you were a student of mine?"

"Yes sir."

"When?"

"Let me see...it would have been fall quarter, 2027."

"You know, Mr. Murphy, I never forget a face, and I don't remember yours."

My heart started pounding, causing my eyes to bulge and my face to slowly turn red. "Well, I'm embarrassed to admit it, but I cut class quite a bit back then."

Witt took a step toward me, a stream of pipe smoke trailing over his right shoulder. "I don't believe you, Mr. Murphy—or whatever your real name is." He moved another step closer. I tried to stand my ground and keep up my increasingly shoddy pretense, but his unrelenting stare was becoming painful. "Who are you really? Come clean with me, boy."

"I, uh...well, I—"

"Let me guess. Journalist, right? Sent up here to do a story on that odd fellow Elijah Witt. Is that it? My god, you people won't take no for an answer."

I hung my head in feigned resignation as a sudden wave of relief swept over me. Witt had had me on the ropes, but now he'd dropped his left. All I had to do was throw a subtle right cross. I lifted my head and gave Witt my best "caught-with-my-hand-in-the-cookie-jar" expression.

"I didn't want to come, Mr. Witt, I swear it. It's just that I'm the new kid down at the paper, and they always stick me with the rotten assignments. Three months ago they sent me off to Oakland to do a story on the gang wars. I didn't get out of Intensive Care for three weeks."

For the first time, Witt smiled around his pipe stem. If there was one thing I was good at, it was sounding pathetic. "What's your name, son?"

"It's Murphy, actually."

"Who sent you up here?"

"Pernell. Lucas Pernell. The rotten bastard."

Witt's expression shifted from amused to thoughtful. "Pernell, eh? You work for the *Bay City Mirror*?"

"Yes sir."

"Pernell's good. He's one of the primary reasons I get the paper sent up here. Done some damn fine investigative reporting. If he'd come up himself, I might even give him an interview."

"Actually, he didn't ask me to get an interview."

Witt ignored my comment as he clenched his teeth onto the stem of his pipe and reflected for a moment. "Tell you what, why don't you get him on the phone, and we'll set up a time when I can meet with Mr. Pernell."

"Well, I don't know if—"

"The phone's over there, son." He pointed to a nearby desk. I hesitated. My good fortune was making a sharp U-turn. If I called Pernell, my whole charade might be exposed.

"See, the thing is, Pernell wants me to do a story on UFO sightings, and he said that you had the best collection of source material on the subject."

Witt was adamant. "You can help yourself to what I've got, but first let's get Pernell on the horn. Go on." He waved me toward the phone, his air that of a man accustomed to rapid and thorough obedience. I dug through my pockets to find Pernell's number.

"What's the problem? Can't remember the number?"

"Like I said, I'm the new guy at the *Mirror*. Plus my short-term memory is shot. I can't remember what I had for breakfast." I turned back. "This is a long-distance call, you know."

"Good God, son, you want me to help you make the call?"

I found Pernell's business card and punched in the code. After several beeps, Pernell's face materialized on the screen. I could hear Witt walking up behind me. "What's going on, Murphy? Got something new for me?"

"Listen, Pernell, I'm here with Elijah Witt. Just like you told me. Except he wants you to do the interview." I could have been speaking Swahili as far as Pernell was concerned. His face looked like a nun had just sworn at him.

"What the hell are you talking about?"

Witt was now looking over my shoulder. My armpits were passing from the clamminess stage straight into outright dampness. "Remember? You sent me up here to see if Witt would let me look through his library for source material on the UFO story I'm writing down at the *Mirror*."

Pernell gave me a blindingly vacant stare. My left eye was winking like a strobe light. After a lengthy pause, the journalist finally caught up. "Oh, yeah. Sorry. Slipped my mind. I've been real busy with the NSA story. You do have that additional information for me, don't you? You know, the stuff we discussed at the Twilight?"

The bastard had me over a barrel, and he wasn't about to do me a favor gratis. But I wasn't in a position to barter. "Yeah, I've got it. I'll send a copy to you as soon as I can get free."

Pernell smiled and leaned back in his seat. "So what's the situation?"

Witt pushed me aside and stepped up to the vid-phone. "Good to meet you, Mr. Pernell."

"Likewise."

"I understand you'd like to set up an interview with me."

"Well, I know you're a busy man."

"I'll make time to meet with you. I've been an admirer of your work for some time."

Pernell's smile widened. "Well, that's just fine. When's a good time for you?"

"Anytime between now and the end of the month."

Pernell flipped through a date book on his desk. "Tell you what, why don't you let me check through my schedule, and I'll get back to you. In the meantime, I'd take it as a great personal favor if you'd do what you can to take care of my assistant."

"Certainly. Pleasure to finally meet you, Mr. Pernell."

"The pleasure's all mine. See you soon, Murphy."

My shirt was a little damp, but somehow I'd survived unscathed. Witt led me from the foyer down a long hallway and through a massive set of oaken doors. The library was a vast, octagonally shaped room with a high, domed ceiling and bookshelves stretching up as far as the eye could see. Some of the sliding ladders were so tall, I was surprised that Witt didn't ask me to sign a no-fault waiver in the event of a back-breaking fall. There had to be ten thousand volumes in the room, none of which I had the slightest interest in browsing through. I don't know what had made me think of asking for access to source materials, but it had seemed brilliant at the time. I wasn't sure what I was going to do now.

"So, what kind of information are you looking for?"

The image of Malloy came into my head, and I thought back to our conversation. "Roswell. I'm researching the UFO crash at Roswell and the government's disinformation campaign."

Witt puffed on his pipe, his eyes twinkling. "Interesting subject, but what do you plan on writing about? Everything's come out already, as far as everyone knows."

"That's what everybody's telling me, but I think there's more to it. It's always been an obsession of mine."

"Well, we have something in common, Mr. Murphy." He gestured grandly around the room. Feel free to look through whatever you can find. In the meantime, I've got some correspondence to take care of. If you don't mind, I'll leave you to your own devices."

It was more than I could've hoped for. "I think I can manage."

"The books you're looking for are up there, under the heading Roswell. If you need anything, ring the buzzer over on the desk. My valet will help you with anything you might need. I'll check in on you a bit later." Witt tramped out of the library, leaving me alone. The kid was in the candy store.

Chapter
Twenty-Six

I had no doubt that Witt had received one of the boxes from Malloy and ensconced it somewhere in his sprawling mansion. My PI instincts could sense it, like a good poker player smells a bluff. But the old recluse wasn't naive enough to put me in the same room with it, without knowing he could trust me. Which, of course, he couldn't. At least I'd gotten my foot in the door. Now I needed to be quick, careful, and lucky, three adjectives rarely used in the same sentence.

I looked around, trying to find a logical starting place. The library was a boundless, teeming smorgasbord of possibilities. My eyes drifted to the vid-phone, then to the desk under it. I'd always found desks to be personal microcosms, wooden and metal monuments to their owners' lives, crammed full of correspondence, receipts, and forgotten reminders jotted down on scraps of paper. It was as good a place as any to begin my search.

With almost two decades of hands-on experience, I rifled Witt's desk with the precision of an assembly-line worker. It took no more than fifteen minutes to determine that there was nothing of importance to be found. I wasn't surprised; anyone with Witt's mentality would undoubtedly keep anything of value locked away from prying eyes.

I finished with the drawers and turned my attention to the desktop. Bills sat in a pile under an Easter Island paperweight. Checking out Witt's utility records wouldn't help me locate the box, but I wasn't about to leave any stone unturned. I flipped through the envelopes, all of which had been opened. At the bottom was a phone bill. Maybe a look at Witt's long-distance calls would turn up some information.

The list of long-distance charges took up two and a half pages. Witt certainly seemed to spend a lot of time on the horn. I ran my finger down the first page. He called all over the world, three to four times a day. The second page contained nothing to attract my attention. On the third page, I noted that the last calls recorded for the billing period had been made three days earlier, about the time he would have received the box from Malloy. That afternoon, there was an extremely short call to San Francisco. Witt had probably tried to contact Malloy as soon as he got the box. Witt had followed the first call with another to a different location, again in San Francisco. This second call was almost fifteen minutes long, implying that he'd gotten whoever he was trying to reach at that number.

After that, there was the first of three calls to the same place in Los Angeles. The first two calls were only seconds long, but the third was forty-eight minutes. Between the first and second calls to Los Angeles, a call had been placed to Tucson, Arizona, also very brief. I guessed that the short calls had reached answering machines or disconnected service messages. Perhaps receiving the box had set Witt into action, possibly trying to contact others who had ties to Malloy.

I jotted down the phone numbers in Los Angeles, San Francisco, and Tucson, then returned the bills to their resting place. Now what? I glanced around the room, hoping the trail to the box would pop out at me. Maybe Witt had installed some kind of hidden entrance in the library. Sure, it was a long shot, but I'd seen it in enough movies to consider it a valid option. I made my way slowly around the perimeter of the library, scrutinizing the bookshelves for any spot that might conceal a latch or trigger. At one point, I found a curious-looking knot in the wood. With a sense of excited expectation directly attributable to having read the entire Hardy Boys series, I pressed the knot. Nothing happened.

I continued to make my way around the room. On one wall, between two sections of bookshelves, I found an odd-looking light switch. I couldn't put my finger on what made it seem strange. Attempting to be thorough, I flipped the switch. As far as I could tell, it had no effect. I tried it again several times without results, then moved on to yet another enormous fireplace, similar to the one I'd seen in the foyer. A careful inspection turned up nothing.

I came full circle without finding a secret entrance. It appeared that the library was a dead end. The idea of venturing out into the rest of the mansion wasn't particularly appealing. If Witt or his limey lackey saw me, I had no doubt I'd be shown the door in quick fashion. Of course, I could always say I was in desperate need of the facilities. They'd buy that. One just doesn't say no to a full bladder.

I started to cross the room to the door. My wing tips made a solid clunking sound on the hardwood, then changed to a muffled thump as I trod across a handsome Oriental rug. Toward the center of the rug, I came to a dead stop. My last footstep had sounded different. I turned and tried the spot again. There was no question about it. There was a hollow spot in the floor. I began stomping all around the area, like I'd stumbled into a herd of cockroaches. Only the one spot, about four feet square, sounded hollow. Throwing a hasty glance over my shoulder, I hurried to one side of the rug and began to roll it up. A few moments later, the outline of a trap door was exposed. Dropping to my hands and knees, I inspected the cracks in the floor. There was no apparent means of lifting the door, and the cracks were so small, I had no way of getting my fingers in to pry it open.

My eyes searched the library anew, looking for something, anything, that I could use as a lever. On the far side of the room, close by the fireplace, I spotted a sharp-tipped poker. Seconds later, I'd jammed the end of the poker into one of the cracks and was prying like a madman. After several minutes, I'd gouged the hell out of the floor and determined that the door was not going to be forced open. Either it was locked from below or I'd missed some kind of trip device in my search of the room.

My mind immediately went back to the mysterious light switch I'd seen earlier. I hurried over and looked at it closely. Suddenly I realized what made it look odd: there were no screws or holes in the faceplate. It didn't appear to have anything attaching it to the wall. I pressed my fingertips under the side of the faceplate and applied some pressure. It was held firmly to the wall. I tried the other side. The face plate popped open like a tiny door. In the opening behind, I saw a knob. I grabbed hold and twisted. From behind me, I heard a spring-loaded *ka-chunk*.

I turned to see one side of the trap door jutting up from the plane of the floor.

I grabbed the exposed end of the trap door and lifted. It came up with almost no effort. Underneath, I saw a set of stairs, beyond which there was no light source. I stepped down and descended into the pitch darkness. The air was cooler than upstairs and smelled slightly musty. The mansion didn't appear to have been built more than maybe ten years ago, but the cellar felt ancient.

The light from the library above provided only about six feet of visibility in any direction. To my left, I made out a square shape on the wall. Running my hands over the surface, I realized that it was a fuse box. I found the flip latch and opened it. Now was not the time to make a mistake. Nothing would attract attention like cutting off all the power in the house. I gently touched the rows of switches. All were set to the right side except two, one at the top and one near the bottom. Maybe flipping one of them would get me some light, but which one? There was only one way to decide. *Eeny, meeny, miney, moe...* I flipped the top switch. The cellar flared to life, bathed in the yellow-orange glow of firelight.

I turned away from the fuse box and found myself staring down a long passage. The walls and floor were made of stone, and the light created eerie patterns across their rough texture. Small metal lamps protruded from the wall along the right side, each emitting a flickering flame. I was curious to see how the lamps had been lit by flipping the switch in the fuse box, but my lifelong interest in lamping techniques would just have to wait.

I was close to the box now. Just the atmosphere of the cellar and the clandestine entrance would have been enough to tell me that, but my instincts could smell it as clearly as a neighborhood barbecue. I walked down the passage and saw several doors on either side. The first door was to my right. I pushed it open and saw racks of dusty wine bottles, aging expensively in the darkness. I was thirsty, but I'd forgotten to bring along a corkscrew. And I was willing to bet that all the bottles had those annoying corks in them.

I closed the door and moved on to the next room. I pushed the door open and peered in. The light from behind threw a flickering swath onto a massive, ornately carved wooden table and a high-back, velvet-lined chair. A five-pronged candelabra sat on the table. I searched through my pockets and found a book of matches. As I lit the candles, the room became visible around me, but my eyes were focused on an object lying on the table.

It was the box.

Several tools were scattered around it, as though Witt had been trying unsuccessfully to open it. I picked up the box and looked it over. It was identical to the others I'd seen. I tucked it under my arm and put out the candles. Suddenly, a voice spoke. I froze in my tracks, startled. The voice was coming from above me and to my right. After several moments, the voice spoke again. I could barely make out the words. I moved closer. The voice had a slight echo, as if it were coming through a pipe. I decided it must be traveling through an air duct, or something similar. I strained to listen.

"How many are there?" It was Witt. I couldn't hear whoever he was talking to.

"I've been in touch with Oliver." A new name. I wondered who he was and what he had to do with anything. Maybe he had the last box.

"Day before yesterday." There was a short pause. "He went to Colombia. Business."

The silent partner went on for some time. Witt cleared his throat. "Yeah, he said he received it, but he doesn't have it with him. No, he said we can't get it. We have to wait until he gets back. He said he can get it as soon as he returns."

A long pause. "Tall. Wears a fedora."

In a flash of transcendental awareness, I knew I was being discussed. Whoever was on the other end of the conversation knew who I was. A brighter man would probably have made a break for it at that moment, but I wanted to hear everything Witt had to say. Maybe he'd drop a name, or enough information for me to deduce who he was talking to.

"Yeah, he's here."

My heart crept up into my throat—they were on to me.

"I'll take care of it."

I spun around and tore out of the room. Witt didn't know I'd overheard him. Maybe he wouldn't go straight to the library and leave me enough time to escape the way I came in. I dashed down the passageway and turned to climb the stairs. From above, I heard the library door open. For an instant, I flirted with the idea of confronting Witt. He wouldn't be any match for me—unless, of course, he had a gun. I decided I couldn't chance it. I turned and ran back down the passageway. There had to be another way out.

I reached the end of the passage and turned left, which I guessed was toward the front of the mansion. This section of the passage was not so well lit, but I continued on. Heavy, hurried footsteps echoed behind me. Straight ahead, I saw another flight of stairs. I hit them at a dead run and vaulted toward a door at the top. I threw open the door, expecting to see a gun barrel pointed at me. To my surprise, I was alone, standing in a hallway. Although I had no idea which way to go, I turned to my left and moved quickly down the hall. Up ahead, I saw what I thought was the foyer. As I was about to run for it, I heard the limey's voice. Instinctively, I turned to a door on my right, opened it, and slipped into the room beyond.

I'd picked the wrong door. A young woman, wearing nothing but an oversized bath towel, was staring at me incredulously. Her body was turned in profile toward a large vanity with a well-lit mirror. Behind her, I saw a large, round tub. She had turned her head to look at me, but otherwise hadn't moved. Her hair was short, dark, and still wet from her bath. Her exotic facial features didn't require any makeup.

Under any other circumstances, I would've paid good money to be in this position. As it was, I was feeling a significant level of discomfort. "Sorry for barging in. I just wanted to check to see if you had a towel I could borrow."

The young woman remained amazingly calm. "What's your name?"

"Call me Tex. I'm a friend of Mr. Witt's. You must be his...daughter? Granddaughter?"

"I've never seen you before."

"I've never been here before. It's a beautiful place. Especially in here." The young woman looked me up and down, then took a step toward me, hands on her hips.

"Most of my uncle's visitors are old. I've never found any of them very interesting." She paused, as though expecting a response from me. I wasn't sure where she was going with this. All I knew was that I could hear a faint commotion outside the door.

"So, you're Mr. Witt's niece? What's your name?"

"Vasha."

"Pretty name."

Vasha took another step toward me. "Thanks. So, how long are you going to be visiting?"

"Oh, I'm afraid I've got to be getting along pretty soon."

"What a shame."

There was a brief moment of silence as I weighed and balanced the many implications of that statement. My contemplation was rudely interrupted by a knock on the bathroom door.

"Vasha?" It was Witt. "Vasha?"

More knocking. The young woman looked from me to the door, then back to me. She moved closer and motioned for me to move against the wall. Then she went to the door and opened it a crack.

"Yes?"

"Are you all right?"

Vasha hesitated for what seemed like a week. "Of course. Why?"

"Well, darling, don't be alarmed, but we seem to have a burglar on the grounds."

"A burglar?"

"Now, I don't believe he's dangerous, but, just to be safe, you should lock this door until we catch him. I'll let you know when we've got him."

"I'll stay right here." Vasha shut the door, then put her ear to it, waiting for her uncle to leave. She then turned to me and smiled.

"So, you're a friend of my uncle's? Or a not particularly dangerous burglar?"

"Neither, actually." For the first time since I'd come into the bathroom, I remembered I was carrying the box. Vasha looked down at it, then up at me.

"I suppose you brought this box with you?"

"No...not really."

Vasha seemed to be a lot more comfortable than I was. I wasn't altogether sure why she had covered for me, but it appeared to make her feel like she was in control of the situation—which she was.

"So what happens now?"

Her smile made me even more uncomfortable. I wasn't sure whether she was coming onto me or just wanted to mess with my head. Either way, my antiperspirant was failing me.

"Well, I guess I'll let you get back to your after-bath activities."

"I don't think so. The way I see it, you owe me a favor."

I took a step back. "Uh...I think I know what you're talking about and usually I'd be more than happy to do you a favor. Maybe even two or three. Unfortunately, I really am pressed for time."

Vasha looked repulsed. "I don't know what kind of Adonis you think you are, but, for the record, I don't find you very attractive."

I'd heard this kind of talk before, but it still takes me by surprise. Now I was really confused. "So why didn't you tell your uncle I was in here?"

"I don't tell my uncle much of anything. The only thing I really want to tell him is 'It's been nice knowing you.' That's where you can repay the favor you owe me."

"What do you mean? You want me to take you out of here?"

"You catch on quickly."

I thought it over for about a second and a half. No way. The last thing I needed was a kidnapping charge. If Vasha wanted to get away from her uncle, she was going to have to do it without my help. "Sorry kid. I appreciate your help, but you're asking too much. Now, I'd really like to stick around and chat, but I have to be running along." I moved toward the door.

"Take one step out of this bathroom and I'll scream."

"OK, fine." I grabbed the doorknob and flung the door open as she screamed. I turned to my right and sprinted for the foyer. I reached the front door without being accosted, threw it open, and raced toward my speeder. Out of the corner of my eye, I saw a man I hadn't seen before moving to intercept me. He was younger and larger than either Witt or the limey. I got to my speeder, pulled up, and turned just as he reached me.

"OK, I give up. Here's the box." I thrust it into the man's chest. Momentarily stunned that I wasn't putting up a fight, he instinctively took it. With both hands full, he'd left himself wide open. I decked him full across the chin and dropped him like a bad habit. I bent down, picked up the box, and climbed into my speeder. Within minutes, I was miles away, headed for the border.

Chapter
Twenty-Seven

On the flight back to San Francisco, I replayed in my mind the conversation I'd overheard between Witt and the mystery caller. Who was Witt in cahoots with? NSA? Unlikely. Everything I'd heard about him indicated that he'd always been a poster child for unorthodoxy and nonconformist ideology. A man like that could never be coerced with the threat of death or violence into abetting forces he knew to be against his own beliefs. Malloy had talked about factions in the private sector wanting to obtain his information, probably for purely financial gain. Maybe Witt needed to raise a large amount of capital to finance a pet project. It was a stretch, but people did worse things for less money every day.

There was another thing I'd overheard that was even more suggestive—the name Oliver. I thought back to the OE reference from Malloy's notebook. Oliver E—. I wondered what part he was playing in this whole scheme. From what Witt had said, this Oliver apparently had one of the boxes—with any luck, one of the two boxes still missing. I still had no idea where I was going to find the box that had been stolen from Archie Ellis. My gut told me that it was securely in the possession of the NSA. If that was the case, I could only hope that its contents were not essential to completing our task. My one optimistic angle was that, knowing Ellis, Malloy would have sent him the least important piece of the puzzle. For now, I had to concentrate my efforts on tracking down Oliver E—.

I arrived back at my office and checked my messages. Regan,

Fitzpatrick, Rook, and Pernell had all called. Rook was in a tizzy because I hadn't returned his .38. That blackmailer Pernell was eager to get his compensation for having bailed me out. Unfortunately for him, I hadn't specified exactly when I'd pay him back. Both he and Rook would just have to wait.

Regan, on the other hand, I wanted to get hold of. I had a few questions to put to her. One that I'd hesitated asking myself concerned Archie Ellis. As far as I knew, she could have been the last person to see him alive. I could see no reason why she would want him dead, but I knew that she was determined to claim her father's inheritance and wasn't going to let anyone stand in her way. I had to find out what had happened.

"Hello, Tex. What have you been up to?"

"I tracked down another box. I don't suppose you stumbled onto the one stolen from Ellis."

Regan smiled. "Oh, I'm good, but not as good as you. No, I didn't have any luck with Ellis."

"So you did go see him."

"Of course. You told me to, darling."

"Tell me what happened."

"There's not much to tell. I chatted with him, turned the charm setting up to eleven, batted my eyelashes, the usual. He made you look like a pushover. I'm fairly certain he doesn't like women very much. Maybe you should go talk to him and try a different approach."

"I'm afraid I'd do all the talking."

"I don't know. He strikes me as a rambler." Nothing in her conduct or appearance cast doubt on her story.

"I went to see Ellis after you did. He had a brand-new bullet hole in his forehead."

Regan paused, not knowing what to say. She didn't appear to

be shaken by the news, but then, she'd only met Ellis that one time. After a moment, she shrugged her shoulders. "It's too bad, but I didn't know him. Who do you think did it?"

"I'm guessing the NSA, but I'm not sure why they'd rub him out if they had the box."

"Maybe they don't have the box."

"That's certainly a possibility," I said, although I had no idea who else might have it.

"So what do we do now?"

I thought it over. My PI instincts were a flat line. My head told me that Regan was on the level, but the business with Ellis left a bad taste in my mouth. I felt better about tracking down Oliver E. on my own. "For now, I think you should just sit tight. Unless you've got an idea on how we can follow up on Ellis's missing box."

"Sorry, my dear. I only work miracles in more intimate settings." I had no desire to indulge Regan's invitation for sexy banter. Even if I'd been in the mood, there just wasn't enough time.

"I've got a lead to look into. By the way, do you remember anyone your father knew named Oliver?" Regan thought it over.

"Sounds vaguely familiar, but I can't place it."

"If you remember anything, call me."

"Why don't you come pick me up? Let me help you with this new lead."

I didn't want to put her off, but things were coming to a head, and I always preferred to work alone in crunch time. When it came right down to it, I was the only person I really trusted. "Sorry, Regan. I've got to handle this one on my own. You just stay there where I can reach you, and I'll get in touch later."

"You better mean that literally."

I disconnected the call and lit a smoke. Fitzpatrick should know what had happened. I punched in his number and let it ring. With luck, he would know something about the enigmatic Oliver E. and save me some time. Unfortunately, the Savoy switchboard operator told me he wasn't in. I left a message, then hung up. I was going to have to do my investigating the hard way.

I pulled my notebook from my pocket and opened it to the page where I had written down the numbers from Witt's phone bill. I started with the number in Los Angeles. After two beeps, a young man's face appeared on the video screen.

"Mulder Memorial Museum. How can I help you?"

"Is Oliver in today?"

"I'm sorry. Mr. Edsen won't be in for several days. Can I do something for you?"

Oliver Edsen. By the way the young man referred to him, he was probably the museum director or had some other important position. I asked the young man for the address and business hours. After I disconnected, I checked my watch. If I topped out my speeder, I might just get to the museum before it closed. Within five minutes, I was headed south.

I flew like a man possessed and reached the museum in record time. As I made my approach, I got a good look at the building. It was impressively designed and appeared to have been recently constructed, three stories of gleaming glass and steel. I jumped out of my speeder and hurried to the front door. I was only seconds late, but the door was locked. Pressing my face to the glass, I peered inside, but there was no one in sight. These people took closing time seriously.

I considered my options. First, I could try to get inside, but it would probably be better to attempt a break-in later, when normal people would be in bed. Second, I could just get a room somewhere and start over tomorrow. After some quick contemplation, I decided I didn't feel like waiting that long. I'd come back in a few hours and practice my burgling skills.

Not far from the museum, I found a reputable-looking café. I hadn't eaten all day and suddenly realized I was famished. Breakfast being the most important meal of the day, I ordered blueberry pancakes with a side of bacon and coffee. After I ate, I spent the next couple hours exploiting the restaurant's free-refill policy and reading the *LA Times*.

Eventually, the traffic slowed down, and I figured it was probably late enough for criminal activity. I flew my speeder to a used-speeder lot, about half a block from the museum, then walked the rest of the way. From the front door, I could see lights on in the back. A cleaning woman emerged and flipped on the lights in the front. I moved quickly away from the door and walked around to the right side of the building, into a narrow alley. A van with the words Carl's Cleaning Service stenciled on the side was parked here. Maybe twenty-five feet down the alley, a short, mustachioed man was leaning against the wall, smoking a cigarette. Just behind him, I saw a door slightly ajar, with a thin beam of light streaming out. Suddenly, a smoky, drinky voice spoke from behind me. I turned to see two working girls giving me the eye.

"Hello, sailor. Lookin' for a date?"

The woman who'd spoken looked at me with bleary eyes under a wig colored in a way God never intended. Her face was made up to the point of disguise. For all I knew, it could have been J. Edgar Hoover under there, and he'd been dead for decades. Her companion looked younger, though, of course, I was just guessing. The younger woman's eyes were still moderately clear, contrasting disturbingly with her painted face.

"How're you girls tonight?"

"We're doing all right. Why don't you let us show you a little piece of heaven?"

"You're not Jehovah's Witnesses, are you?"

The older woman looked to the younger one and smirked. "We can be if you want us to. You wouldn't be the first."

"No thanks. Actually, I'm not looking for any company right now."

The older woman shrugged indifferently. "Your loss."

The working girls turned and started sauntering back the way they came. I peeked around the corner and saw my little swarthy friend was still there. I turned and caught up to the women. "Tell you what. My friend's taking a smoke break just around the corner over there. It's his birthday, and I'd kind of like to give him a surprise. How much do surprises cost in this part of town?"

The older woman didn't blink. "Two hundred. Each."

"I only need one of you."

They looked at each other. The younger woman spoke for the first time. She wasn't as young as I'd thought she was. "What the hell? It's a slow night."

I shelled out the cash and sent them around the corner. After a minute, I peeked around and saw my little friend flanked by the women, heading toward the dark end of the alley. I crept toward the door and slipped inside.

"Carl? Get in here, Carl!"

Off to my left, I could hear the cleaning woman yelling. I ducked to my right and hurried out of sight. Behind me, I could hear the woman stomping toward the side door. I took cover behind a table and looked up as she appeared. She was holding a mop and looked pretty upset. Then she stuck her head out the door and yelled for Carl again. Setting down the mop, she went outside. As she moved through the doorway, I caught a glint of something on a counter by the door. I walked over and saw a ring of keys. Snatching them up, I turned and moved away from the door.

I figured Oliver Edsen would have an office somewhere in the museum, probably on one of the upper floors. I ran up a flight of stairs to the second floor, moving as quickly as possible and keeping my eyes and ears wide open. If there were other cleaning people in the building, I at least wanted to see them before they saw me. Luckily, the second floor seemed to be deserted. It didn't take long to find Edsen's office. According to the nameplate on the door, he was the museum's director. I tried the doorknob, but the office was locked. Pulling out the keys, I began trying each one. On the eighth key, the door unlocked. I threw it open and stepped inside.

I thought for a minute before flipping on the light. Maybe a light would attract attention—but the cleaning people were here, and they were turning lights on and off all over the place. It would probably be OK. Unless, of course, the cleaning people saw the light. Maybe the cleaning woman had found Carl. If she had, I doubted they'd notice much of anything for a few minutes.

Turning on the lights, I went to Edsen's desk. All the drawers were locked. I glanced at the key ring, but Edsen would certainly keep his own desk keys. The one bookcase held nothing much that I could see. A filing cabinet was also locked tight. I looked through the things on Edsen's desk, but he seemed to be annoyingly organized.

Several framed photographs were mounted on the walls. In one, I saw the familiar face of Elijah Witt. Standing next to him was a tall, thin man with a gaunt, clean-shaven face. Since he appeared in several of the other pictures, I figured he had to be Edsen.

As a last resort, I checked out the garbage can. Beneath the Styrofoam coffee cups, newspaper, and cigar butts, I found an envelope. It was empty, but there was a sticky note attached to it. On the note was written: *LAX, Flight #1881, Dep. 4/22, 4:05 P.M., C-16, Arr. 4/26, 11:33 P.M.* It had to be the itinerary for the trip Edsen was on. I thought back to what I'd heard at Witt's when they were talking about Edsen: *He said he received it, but he doesn't have it with him.... We have to wait until he gets back. He said he can get it as soon as he returns.* He'd left the box at the airport! That's where it had to be!

I turned off the lights and left Edsen's office. No voices came from the first floor as I descended the stairs. I set the keys on the counter where I'd found them and peeked out the door. From the end of the alley and around the corner, I could hear the cleaning woman giving Carl an earful. Poor guy. I ran to my speeder and set course for LAX.

Like any other major airport, LAX is a sprawling, bustling, overcrowded Tower of Babel. I parked my speeder and entered the main terminal. After following signs for several miles, I found myself in the vicinity of Gate C-16. I looked around and saw six different banks of storage lockers. If my hunch was correct, Edsen had dumped the box into a locker just before getting on his plane. Provided that the NSA hadn't yet been tailing him, an airport storage locker would be as safe a place as any to keep the box.

Now I had only two small problems to deal with. I had to find out which locker Edsen had used, and then get into it. Such trivialities wouldn't have slowed down the NSA. The NSA. I still had an NSA badge in my wallet. It was certainly worth a try, seeing as how I had no other reasonable plan.

I found my way to the security office and stepped inside like

I owned the place. A burly young man, sporting a crew cut and a bushy mustache, sat at a reception desk reading a comic book. Slowly, he raised his eyes and looked at me. "Yeah?"

He had the look and sound of a high-school dropout who wasn't quite bright enough to make the police force. And was probably still pissed off about it. He wasn't someone I'd want to come to blows with. Hopefully, he'd heard of the NSA.

"Do you have cameras on all the storage locker areas in the airport?"

"That's restricted information."

I pulled out the phony NSA badge and held it up to his face. "Not from me."

The burly guard studied the badge. I couldn't tell whether he was trying to decide what to do, or just having a hard time sounding out all the words. After a few moments, he looked back up at me. Apparently he had heard of the agency.

"What can I do for you, Agent Murphy?"

"A criminal we've been after flew out of this airport two days ago. He left a piece of contraband in one of the storage lockers. I need to find out which one, then get it open."

"What's a contraband?"

"It's kind of like a box. I'll show you when we find it."

The thought of helping a real government agent seemed to brighten up my stupid friend. He made a call and led me deeper into the security area. After several minutes, I was introduced to a supervisor, Ms. Hatch, a woman with biceps bigger than my thighs. "I hate to inconvenience you, Agent Murphy, but I need to take a look at your identification. Security procedures, you understand."

I held up the badge. Ms. Hatch looked it over several times. "If you don't mind, I'd like to call in and check your credentials. Not that I don't trust you, Agent Murphy. It's just not as hard as it used to be to get bogus identification badges."

She was calling my bluff. My pair of threes and I were looking shaky. The only thing I could do now was take a cue from Jackson Cross. I decided to grit my teeth and lie through them. "Look, Ms. Hatch. I haven't got time to dick around with a peon wannabe cop like you. That act may play in Peoria, but not in the big leagues. If you don't give me the information I'm here for, I'll have your ass fired so hard, you'll smell like charcoal for a month."

Ms. Hatch obviously wasn't accustomed to having such a tone taken with her. Her eyes glared for a moment, then she backed off. If I were on the up and up, I could certainly make my threats good. She seemed to decide it wasn't worth the risk.

"Sorry. I know the NSA doesn't have to work through procedures like we do here. I'll clear everything for you. Let me know if I can help."

"Oh, I'll let you know. All I need is access to your videotapes and a technician to assist me."

"Yes sir. Right this way."

Ms. Hatch led me into another room and set me up with an extremely intimidated computer geek. I told him what I needed, and he came back with six video disks, one for each of the storage locker areas around gate C-16. We spent the next hour viewing the disks, checking all the footage between 2:30 and 4:00 P.M. We were onto the fourth disk when I finally saw what I was looking for. The tall, thin figure of Oliver Edsen approached and opened one of the lockers. He pulled a small duffel bag from under a coat draped over his arm. Looking around nervously, he slid the bag into the locker, inserted several coins, then locked the door and removed the key.

I turned to the technician and asked which locker had been used. He checked the disk, then reran the footage. It was locker

16402. In keeping with my NSA persona, I didn't thank him and left. I returned to Ms. Hatch's office and informed her that locker number 16402 was to be opened for me immediately.

Twenty minutes later, I was outside the airport, a small duffel bag in my hand and a big skip in my step.

Chapter
Twenty-Eight

Back at my office, I called Fitzpatrick. "It's good to hear from you, Mr. Murphy. You're a difficult man to pin down. Difficult indeed."

"That's what my girlfriends have always said."

"I'm sure. Incidentally, I received your package. I'm sure you have a tale to tell."

"Frankly, I'd just as soon forget about it. I've had more pleasant experiences."

Fitzpatrick didn't press the matter. "So, what news have you?"

"I've got two of the three remaining boxes. Do you know a man named Oliver Edsen?"

"I know of him. Did he give you one of the boxes?"

"In a manner of speaking. I think we should meet."

"I agree. Thomas seems to have set things up so that all the boxes must be present in order to assemble the complete picture. Nonetheless, perhaps four boxes will be enough." The eagerness in his voice was unmistakable.

"Do you want to meet here at my office?"

"No...I think you should come to the Savoy. Perhaps we should invite all those involved. It seems that Thomas wanted everyone to be present. Can you contact them?"

The thought of confronting Witt again didn't appeal to me, but Fitzpatrick was right. "I'll see what I can do. I know that Oliver Edsen won't be able to come."

"I'd prefer to have Mr. Edsen in attendance, but I'm afraid we haven't the luxury of waiting."

"I'll try to reach the others and get back to you."

Fitzpatrick disconnected. I got out my notebook and found Witt's number. The limey informed me that Mr. Witt was not at home and might not be back for several days. I wondered if he was on my trail. My next call went to Regan.

"How did it go?"

"Fine. I got another box."

"Wonderful! Is that it? Do we have all of them?"

"No. There's still the one stolen from Ellis at the Cosmic Connection. I'm hoping that we can work around it."

"So, now we get the other boxes and open them, right?"

"Yeah, but there's something you need to know first."

Regan's smile faded. "What?"

"Someone else is involved in this."

"Who?"

"An old friend of your father. Gordon Fitzpatrick. He's the one who got me mixed up in all this in the first place."

"I don't intend on splitting this three ways."

"Fitzpatrick isn't in this for the money. He's in it because he was concerned for your father."

"I don't care why he's in this. The Pandora's Box, or whatever it is, is mine. It belonged to my father, and now it's mine. I'm not going to let anyone take it away from me."

"No one's taking it away from you. That's why I called. Fitzpatrick and I are going to meet with all the others who were contacted by your father."

"Why do the others need to be there? Why don't you just get the boxes and meet me?"

"Your father set it up so all the boxes had to be opened together. I think the reason he did it was so that everyone involved would be a witness to whatever it is we're going to see."

Regan obviously didn't like the idea.

"C'mon Regan, no one's going to steal this from you. The only hang-up would come if we find out that your father's work is too dangerous to let out of the bag. And if that's the case, I'm sure you'll agree with everyone else on a course of action."

Regan seemed to relax a little. "You're still on my side, aren't you?"

Her vulnerability felt authentic. I realized once again that she was just a kid, caught up in something way over her head. She didn't want to admit it, but she was nervous and needed to know she wasn't alone in the world. "Of course I am."

Her smile returned. "All right. When are we going to get together?"

"It depends on the others. I'll let you know."

"I'll wait for your call."

As soon as I was off the phone, I grabbed my hat and hoofed it over to the Fuchsia Flamingo. Gus and Emily had just as much stake in this thing as anyone else and deserved to be there at the unveiling. I walked through the front door and scanned the joint for Gus, but he was nowhere to be seen. A young mutant approached me and asked for my membership card. I told him I'd just come by to talk to Gus and/or Emily. The mutant said that they'd gone out of town two days ago, and he didn't know when they'd be back.

Of the eight people mired in this scenario, one was dead, one was out of the country, and three others were unaccounted for. That left me, Regan, and Fitzpatrick. I returned to my office and called to tell Fitzpatrick what had happened. He told me to come over anyway. I then talked to Regan, who said she could be ready by the time I got there.

I picked up Regan at the Imperial Lounge, then flew to the Savoy. We didn't say much on the way. My gut squirmed like a chump wrestler caught in a stranglehold. Regan was tough to read, but her eyes were bright, which usually meant her mind was running in overdrive.

I landed in front, where the valet service was waiting. Regan and I walked into the lobby and took the elevator up to the eighteenth floor. I leaned against the elevator wall and assessed my companion. She was looking anxiously at the LED display. God, she was beautiful. I hadn't been close to her for awhile. I'd forgotten how appealing the view was. Her lips were parted slightly. My mouth was suddenly very lonely. It was either kiss her or talk.

"Nervous?"

Her eyes stayed glued to the changing floor numbers. "There's a better word for it."

"I didn't bring my thesaurus."

Regan didn't respond immediately. My eyes drifted up to the display. When she spoke, her voice was like velvet. "I feel like I'm about to make love to someone I've wanted for a long time."

"We've only known each other for a few days."

The flawless profile smiled. "Not you. Yet."

The number eighteen flashed in unison with a muffled chime, and the door slid open. We turned to the right and walked down the hall. Reaching the door to 1813, I raised my hand to knock. Regan's hand went to my cheek and turned my face toward hers. Suddenly her lips were on mine. It was a deep, wet kiss that felt like a rich appetizer, with the promise of a full dinner to follow shortly. She pulled away and slowly opened her eyes. "For luck." She patted my cheek and stepped back.

I took a moment to compose myself, then knocked. After a few moments, Fitzpatrick opened the door. "Hello, Mr. Murphy."

I doffed my fedora. Fitzpatrick's gaze turned to Regan. "Please come in." We stepped into the hotel room.

Across the room, seated in an overstuffed chair, was Elijah Witt. "We meet again, Murphy." Witt folded his hands over his round stomach and smiled at me like an elementary school principal who'd just caught a truant. I wasn't sure what to say. Fitzpatrick spoke from behind me.

"Mr. Witt tells me that the two of you have already met. I don't believe, however, I've had the pleasure of meeting your lovely friend."

I turned back to Fitzpatrick. "This is Regan Madsen. Thomas Malloy's daughter."

Regan smiled pleasantly and extended her hand. Fitzpatrick looked her over as they shook hands. "The plot thickens." The old man motioned toward Witt. "Ms. Madsen, this is Elijah Witt, a longtime friend of your father's."

Witt made no move. "I didn't know Thomas had a daughter."

Fitzpatrick looked toward Regan, then me, and gestured toward two chairs. We sat down. Fitzpatrick walked toward an end table, and picked up a smoldering Cubana from an ashtray.

"I remember Regan from China. Of course, that was many years ago." He looked toward Regan, appraising her again.

"I must say, you've become a very beautiful woman. Luckily, you took after your mother, though I see some of your father in you. Especially in the eyes."

Witt shifted in his seat. "How do we know she is who she says she is?"

Regan crossed her legs and responded coolly. "Maybe you'd like to see a copy of my birth certificate."

"Documents can be faked."

"Well, then, I guess you'll just have to take my word for it."

I interjected. "She's on the level, Mr. Witt. I can vouch for that."

Witt turned his professorial gaze in my direction. "Is that so? I suppose I should blindly believe you, especially after you came into my home under false pretenses, then proceeded to rob me. I think not."

Fitzpatrick turned toward Witt in a cloud of smoke. "Mr. Murphy and I have been working together in this situation since the beginning. He has demonstrated his commitment repeatedly. If you cannot trust him in these matters, then you cannot trust me."

Witt harrumphed. "I'll defer, if you insist. But I don't like it."

Fitzpatrick ignored the postscript and turned toward me. "Since you brought Ms. Madsen, I'll assume that she has earned your confidence."

I nodded, but inside I was asking myself a few questions. What if, after everything that had happened...? It seemed impossible, but it had happened before. I turned to Regan, who gave me a wink. It didn't help.

Fitzpatrick blew out a puff of smoke. "Well, then, that's settled. We should get on to business. Would either of you care for a drink?" We both declined. "Mr. Witt, why don't you tell our friend Murphy your part in this matter."

Witt glanced at Fitzpatrick impatiently, then turned to me. "I met Malloy years ago. I'd written several books that touched on certain theories which Malloy had experienced firsthand. Some people consider me something of an authority in the field of UFOlogy. Malloy arranged to meet me. After we got to know each other, he showed me the alien hieroglyphs. I provided Malloy with copies of other writings, supposedly of alien origin, hoping that they would help him in the deciphering process. From that time on, we stayed in contact." Folding his arms again over his girth, Witt turned his eyes toward Fitzpatrick.

Fitzpatrick flicked the ash off the end of his Cubana and looked at me. "As you can see, Mr. Witt is on our side. It turns out that there was no reason for you to steal the box from him, though it may have sped up the process. Mr. Witt can be quite stubborn." From the corner, Witt snorted. Fitzpatrick continued. "I believe we've come to the proverbial moment of truth. It seems that what we are about to learn will prove to be of great importance. Thomas went to great lengths to make certain that no one person had all the information. I believe he intended for this reunion to be a council of sorts, attended by the people he considered most trustworthy, including myself, Mr. Witt, Ms. Madsen, and Mr. Murphy, who is representing Emily Sue Patterson, Thomas's widow. It is regrettable that two others, Oliver Edsen and Archie Ellis, cannot be here with us."

After an appropriate moment of silence and a puff on the cigar, Fitzpatrick spoke again. "Thomas feared the intervention of several powerful groups. We have reason to believe that one of these is the NSA. Mr. Murphy, why don't you tell Mr. Witt what has happened."

Witt seemed at least mildly interested. "The first box I found had been delivered to Malloy's wife. After some ugliness, I got the box, and an NSA agent ended up dead. I got hauled into an NSA office and met with a man named Jackson Cross. He wanted the box and seemed to have no compunctions about killing for it. Well, I ended up with the box after all and expected to catch an agency bullet in the brain for it. But for some inexplicable reason, the NSA backed off."

Witt stirred. "Why do you think that is, Mr. Murphy?"

I shrugged. "I don't know. Maybe they decided to let me do all the work, then move in, hoping to catch all of the boxes in one place."

"Like they are right now."

"I was careful."

"I think you have too high an opinion of yourself, Mr. Murphy," Witt sneered.

"Well, did you bring the box Malloy sent you? Oh, I forgot. I have it."

"That's enough!" Fitzpatrick's voice was raised for the first time since I'd met him. "This is not the time for petty squabbling! We're all in this together, and we are obliged to cooperate. Now, Mr. Murphy, let's have the boxes."

I reached into Edsen's duffel bag and pulled out the box I'd stolen from Witt's place and the one I'd recovered from the storage locker at LAX. Fitzpatrick took one from me and walked across the room to a desk. Regan and I followed. On top of the desk, I saw the first box, the one originally sent to Emily, which had already been opened. Beside it lay the long metal pin that had been inside the as-yet-unopened box I'd gotten from Regan, and the power cell. God bless UPEX.

Fitzpatrick sat down and flipped on the ultraviolet lamp. When he held Edsen's box under the light, a small square materialized on one side. Fitzpatrick touched the square, but nothing happened. He pressed on it again and moved the box around. Keeping his finger pressed to the square, he picked the box up. On the underside, a hole had appeared. He picked up the long pin from Emily's box and slid it into the hole. The top of the box opened.

Witt joined us as Fitzpatrick set the newly opened box down

on the desk. Inside was a square piece of metal about the size of a Scrabble tile, and a small component about three inches square. It looked like it could be an attachment used on a professional photographer's camera. There was a short stem protruding from it and two holes which looked like typical receptor slots. Fitzpatrick leaned back and released his breath. "This must be the first piece of the Pandora Device."

Setting the component, metal tile, and box to the side, he moved the box Regan had given me under the lamp. The small squares I'd seen before were revealed. Fitzpatrick picked up the metal tile and placed it on one of the square areas of the box. The tile was magnetic and stuck to the box surface, but nothing happened. He then pried off the tile and placed it on the other square, with the same result.

"May I have the other box, Mr. Murphy?"

I handed Witt's box over, and Fitzpatrick placed it under the lamp. Again, two squares appeared on the box surface, but these were connected by a thin line. Fitzpatrick repeated the process of applying the tile to first one square, then the other, but the box remained sealed. Regan moved closer to the desk.

"How about trying it this way?" She reached down and pressed her finger on the metal tile, which was still fixed to one of the squares. Exerting some pressure, she slid the tile along the line. As soon as it reached the other square, the lid popped open. Fitzpatrick smiled and turned his face up toward Regan.

"Excellent work, young lady. You seem to have inherited your father's ingenuity."

Regan beamed. Fitzpatrick opened the lid of the box, revealing another metal tile and the second piece of the Pandora Device which was similar to the first component. Removing the first metal tile from the top of Witt's box, Fitzpatrick then applied both tiles to the corresponding areas on Regan's box. It opened. Inside was yet another component. The third component looked like the other two, but had several switches and buttons on one side. Fitzpatrick turned to me.

"You've seen the schematic of the Pandora Device, have you not? Do we now have all the sections?"

"The schematic only showed three. But Malloy said he sent out five boxes."

"This device is our only concern at present."

Fitzpatrick and I carried the three components to the end table, so everyone would have a clear view. It took no more than five minutes to assemble the device. When it was finished, all eyes were glued to the strange contraption.

My palms were wet. The excitement in Witt's eyes belied his gruff, passive exterior. Regan's face was flushed, her breathing short. Fitzpatrick seemed the most composed, but his hands trembled slightly as he touched the Pandora Device. He touched several buttons and switches as though he knew what he was doing, and suddenly a light appeared. A holographic image began to materialize, a ghostly figure of Malloy. It spoke.

"Since you're seeing this, I assume that everyone is present. I've brought the five of you together for a very important reason, so I won't waste time with introductions and too much explaining. The fact of the matter is that you are now a council, and it is your responsibility to make a very important decision. What I'm about to reveal may be the greatest discovery in the history of our planet, and may also be the most devastating.

"As you know, I have spent most of my life trying to decipher the alien symbols discovered in the Roswell spacecraft. Well, I have now lived to fulfill my ambition. This is not the time or place to give a full translation, but one detail must be addressed. The alien hieroglyphics say that another spacecraft came before and is still here. And I know where it is.

"The alien craft was an exploration ship, designed to travel many light-years. The translation indicates that it was like the Roswell craft, only much larger. As some of you may know, the Roswell ship carried a lot of equipment, including particle accelerators. What you probably don't know is that it also carried pods of antihydrogen.

"For years, scientists have known that interstellar travel would be nearly impossible without significant quantities of stable, stored antihydrogen. For almost as many years, scientists have met with little to no success in creating and storing it. I believe that first spacecraft has a huge supply of stable, stored antihydrogen.

"If our society were ready for such a discovery, I think it would be the most wonderful ever. It might allow us to finally break the barriers of space travel, explore other galaxies, contact other civilizations. Unfortunately, we're not ready for it. We proved that forty years ago.

"I'm leaving you the decision of what to do. If this information gets into the hands of the wrong people, it could result in total and complete destruction. In my opinion, the craft must be taken off the planet and destroyed. Otherwise, it may destroy us.

"Good luck, my friends. Pandora's box has been opened. It's up to you to close it."

The image faded. I pulled out a cigarette and lit it up. Now I was ready for a bourbon. No one spoke as I walked to the bar and poured myself a drink. Finally, Fitzpatrick spoke. "This is much worse than I ever imagined."

I took a long drink. Witt's voice was strained. "Undoubtedly it must be destroyed. I think we're all in agreement on that."

Regan looked up and spoke. "I'm not sure we are. Maybe my father's experiences with the military have biased him. Just think of the possibilities. And it would certainly be worth a lot of money."

Witt's tone was chastising, a teacher correcting a recalcitrant pupil. "Money is not a factor. What we're talking about is a force thousands, maybe millions of times greater than the atomic bomb. It would be like handing a child an automatic weapon. We would certainly destroy ourselves." He glanced at Fitzpatrick.

Fitzpatrick looked back, uneasily. "There is little to be gained by discussing the ramifications. The fact is, we must act. Our first step is to find out the ship's location." He flipped another switch. The device emitted a green light, and a three-dimensional map appeared. Unless my geography skills had totally abandoned me, the latitude and longitude placed the craft somewhere in northwestern Peru. As we watched intently, the map began to move, and we were taken in over the projected terrain.

When the display faded, Fitzpatrick turned to me. "Mr. Witt and I must contact some of our sources. I suggest that you try to find this place. With luck, you may reach the area and locate the ship without interference from the NSA or any other group. We will send two other search parties via different routes. In the event that any of us are detained, the others may reach the location."

He walked to his desk and pulled an object from one of the drawers. "This is a communication device, not unlike an auto-page. It links up directly with another, just like it, which I will keep with me at all times. Not only can you send a message, but we can also trace you to your immediate location. If you find the spacecraft and it's all clear, the code will be 111. If you locate the ship but are followed, use the code 222. If you don't find the ship right away, send the code 333 to let us know where you are, and that you're still looking. When you're ready to send us a message, press the pound sign, then enter the code, then press Send."

Fitzpatrick handed me the communicator. I slipped it into my pocket.

"Mr. Witt will be occupied with organizing everything necessary for the retrieval and disposal of the ship."

Witt pulled Fitzpatrick into a corner, where they began laying out their plans. Regan walked over to where I was standing, near the bar. She reached past me for a glass and poured herself a bourbon. After a small sip, she turned to me, standing close. "So when do we leave? I'll need to go back to my room and pick some things up."

"*We're* not going. *I'm* going."

Regan raised an eyebrow. "Really? And when was that decided?"

"Oh, about forty years ago. I'm a solo kind of guy."

Regan tossed down her bourbon. "Well, get over it. I don't know what kind of a woman you think I am, but I'm not going to stay home like some delicate little society flower." She slammed her glass onto the bar and spun away. She stormed off, grabbed her coat and purse, and walked to the door. "I'll catch a cab home. Don't leave without me." She slammed the door and was gone as quickly as my bourbon.

I refilled my glass and sat down. I wasn't going to take her, no matter what she said. It was going to be hard work and dangerous. The last thing I needed was someone else to worry about. Witt and Fitzpatrick were talking earnestly. What was I doing in this mess? These guys had taken Malloy's message in stride, almost as if they had expected its contents. Personally, the circuits in my head were blown. All I knew for sure was that I was going to Peru in the morning. Talk about being in over one's head.

I poured a third bourbon. It was helping. Slowly, strangely, my head cleared. Maybe this wasn't your standard detective work, but it was a responsibility on a large scale, the kind you just don't turn your back on. I drained the bourbon. There was a lot to do before I took off, and time was running out fast. I walked to the door. Witt's voice cut me off. "Hold on, Murphy."

I turned around. Witt lumbered toward me. "Take this." He handed me a card. On the back were a name and a number. "This guy'll get you down there safely. I'll let him know you're coming first thing tomorrow. Go home and get some sleep. When you meet this guy tomorrow, bring along enough supplies to last for three days. We'll meet you by that time."

I nodded.

"And don't take the woman. I don't trust her, no matter what you and Fitzpatrick say. We have no margin of error. There can be no distractions, no excuses. Everything depends on what we do now. We have to succeed. No matter what."

Chapter
Twenty-Nine

I picked up my speeder from the valet, half expecting a couple of NSA agents to be waiting in the backseat. I guess it was my lucky day.

As I flew back to my office, I was a jumble of excitement, weariness, and anxiety. Malloy must have known the burden he was dumping on his friends' backs. If only he'd never made the discovery. The spacecraft, if there actually was one, had been here for hundreds, maybe thousands of years without being found. Maybe it could've lain there in peace for another million years. Maybe we could have thrown ourselves into extinction without ever finding it. As it was, the proverbial cat was out of the bag, and it was one gigantic cat. Witt was right. If there was antihydrogen stored on the spacecraft, there was no question that it needed to be destroyed. It was the last thing we needed in circulation.

When I got back to my office, I couldn't remember ever being so tired. Tomorrow I would be flying to Peru to help locate and scrap an alien spacecraft. Definitely something to write home about. Unfortunately, the thought of it was sapping any meager amounts of energy left in my weary, forty-year-old body. I stumbled into my bedroom and pulled up abruptly.

Regan was stretched languidly across my bed, a thin veneer of silk draped over her creamy skin. God, of all the times to tempt me. I wasn't sure if I was strong enough to deal with this now. I leaned against the door frame and lit a cigarette. "I suppose you've already sat in my chair and eaten my porridge."

Regan looked up at me feverishly, her eyes bright. "It took you long enough. I was afraid I'd have to start without you. Hope you don't mind—I thought I'd get comfortable while I waited. I'm feeling *extremely* comfortable."

"You look it."

She moved restlessly and immodestly. "How long does it take you to smoke a cigarette?"

"Why? You in a hurry?"

"That's one way to describe it."

I walked toward the bed and crushed my Lucky Strike into an ashtray on the nightstand. Regan ran her hand across the bedspread, her eyes following my every move. She was putting off more heat than a space shuttle on re-entry. I took a step back and stared down at the most desirable woman in the world. "Tell me, Regan, do you always get what you want?"

"Only if I really want it."

Her shallow breathing was contagious. With no small effort, I turned and crossed the room, removing my hat and overcoat. I looked back at Regan, steadying myself on the dresser. "I've never really understood women that well. Could you explain to me exactly what's happening here?"

"Don't tell me you've never done this before."

"Just once...by myself. It confused me and made me feel dirty."

Regan smiled seductively. "Come over here, little boy."

I walked back across the room and sat down on the corner of the bed. Regan sat up and loosened my tie. "If we're going to be in this together, I need to know that you're in all the way."

"I have to warn you, I failed all my commitment classes in college."

Regan's fingers moved slowly across my ear and into my hair. "I can teach an old dog new tricks."

"I don't doubt it."

Her face was close to mine, her eyes focused on my mouth. "Promise me, Tex. Promise that you'll stay with me and see this to the end."

"I'm not taking you with me, Regan."

"You can have me, and everything else you ever wanted. Just for taking me with you." I only wanted one thing in the world at that moment. I was standing at the edge of the abyss, bits of gravel tumbling into the chasm and falling forever. Suddenly, a face came into my mind. Chelsee's face. I got up from the bed and backed away. Regan looked up at me, her face twisted in confusion. "Don't do this to me, Tex. I've already lost my father. I don't want to lose you." She was changing tactics. I couldn't believe the negligee approach had ever failed before, but she seemed to have other tricks up her sleeve.

"I want you, Regan. And I don't want you to think I don't care for you or what happens to you. I do. The problem is, I think you're trying to force me to choose between you and what I think needs to be done."

Regan turned a shade darker. "So you're on the side of those old men? What the hell is wrong with you? I can give you everything. I can love you like you've never been loved. I don't know much about the antimatter, or whatever it is my father was talking about, but I know that it's worth a fortune. A fortune that can be ours."

"I don't want to argue about this. The way you look is making it difficult enough."

Regan swung her legs over the side of the bed and stood up. Grabbing her clothes from a chair, she stormed past me. I turned to watch her leave. At the door, she whirled around. "You blew it, Tex. You could have had it all." With that parting shot, she threw open the door and disappeared into the night.

Chapter
Thirty

The pilot Witt had hooked me up with was named Smitty. He didn't ask questions. In fact, he only spoke when absolutely necessary, which was fine with me. I hadn't slept well, and I was weary beyond description.

Smitty threw my backpack into the back of his Avatar and curtly told me there was room to sleep in the back if I wanted to. I gladly took him up on the offer. Witt had apparently given him all the information he needed to get me where I needed to go. We took off, and I almost immediately fell asleep. Surprisingly, I slept deeply and thoroughly, the kind of dead sleep where you're too tired to dream. At one point, I woke up disoriented, only to slide back into the tar pit of the subconscious.

When I finally awoke, I had no idea how long I'd been out. I rubbed my eyes and sat up. Smitty was like a statue at the helm. I climbed up to the passenger seat and pulled out my pack of smokes. "You mind?"

Thankfully, Smitty shook his head. I leaned back in my seat and stared out the window, taking a deep drag. We were up high, higher than I'd ever been in a speeder. Of course, the Avatar was no ordinary speeder. We were out over the ocean. "Where are we?"

Smitty glanced down at the console. "Fifty miles off the west coast of Colombia."

"How much longer?"

Smitty shrugged. "Ninety minutes, maybe."

There didn't seem to be much hope of conversation, so I

turned my full attention to the window for the remainder of the flight. After about an hour, we moved in over the coast and headed inland. The terrain below was green and hilly. A few minutes later, we reached the beginnings of a mountain range, covered in tropical vegetation. Smitty began the approach, eventually getting down to an altitude of no more than five hundred feet. He began checking his instrumentation more frequently. We dropped even lower, and Smitty looked out the window, apparently searching for a likely place to set down. Five minutes later, we touched down on a large, exposed piece of rock in the center of some very tall trees.

"This is it. I can't get any closer to the coordinates."

"Which way should I go?"

Smitty pointed, then reached back and grabbed my backpack. He thrust it toward me. "I'll meet you back at this spot in three days, at exactly 10:00 A.M."

"Is that Pacific Daylight Time?"

He didn't smile. I wasn't sure he could. I opened the door and stepped out of the Avatar. Smitty shut the door and lifted off immediately. I didn't bother to wave.

After the speeder disappeared over the trees, I looked around. I'd only been in the jungle once before, during the Martian Memorandum case. Being here confirmed my lifelong status of urban junkie. I was already missing coffee.

I threw the backpack over my shoulder and trudged off in the direction Smitty had pointed me. I climbed steadily for ten minutes. Above me, a canopy of intertwined branches filtered out most of the sunlight. The jungle floor was matted with vines and plants, but was fairly easy to cross.

Suddenly, up ahead, I saw a wall of stone covered with a thick layer of vines. The wall was comprised of square, cut stones, man-made. My pulse began to race.

I hurried to the wall and followed it. After thirty feet or so, I turned a corner and saw the facade of what might have been an ancient Mayan temple, set into the side of a hill. The undergrowth had almost swallowed the surface of the stone, nearly obscuring the structure. Climbing a set of inlaid stone steps, I reached an opening in the facade. Vines hung across it like a beaded curtain in a 1960s dance club. The vines were surprisingly thick and strong, but I managed to pull them aside. I fished a flashlight out of my backpack and stepped into the darkness.

I'd taken only a few steps when a flock of startled birds, or maybe bats, fluttered past my head. I dropped to my knees automatically, shielding my head. Quickly, my sense of fear turned to disgust. The floor was coated with a thick layer of dusty bat guano. I stood up and didn't bother to brush off my trousers.

The passage I was standing in was quite narrow, about six feet across. The ceiling was only about six feet high, causing me to stoop. The walls were surprisingly smooth; if they'd been cut out of stone, they'd been well-polished. The ceiling, as well, was smooth and glassy-looking. The passage led upward at a fairly steep pitch. I climbed for at least five minutes before I reached a junction.

I had no idea where I was going, or even what I should be looking for, but all paths seemed to lead upward. I encountered numerous tunnels, always at right angles to those they intersected. There was no way these passages had formed naturally. In fact, they resembled old air-raid shelters more than cave corridors.

After several twists and turns, I spotted a light emanating from a point ahead of me. Following it led me into a massive, cavernous area. High up in the cavern, regularly placed slits in the rock allowed beams of light to enter. Whoever had designed the layout had been ingenious. The cavern appeared to be empty, except for several figures carved into the walls. These tunnels were obviously ancient.

Around the perimeter of the cavern were seven openings, leading into hallways similar to those I'd been walking through. I took a stroll around, looking for any indication that would tell me which doorway to take.

Then I saw the footprints. They led from one of the doorways into the center of the cavern. After some milling about, the person had made a decision and entered the opening opposite where he'd come in. The prints were from fairly small, well-shod feet and had definitely been left recently. The natives in this area were small-statured and had had access to modern conveniences, such as hiking boots, for decades. Maybe these prints were left by some local adventurer. Or maybe not.

I decided to follow the prints and walked to the third doorway, keeping the beam trained on the trail in front of me. I followed through numerous twists and turns, sometimes retracing my steps, other times crossing our two sets of prints. I began to doubt that whoever I was tracking knew where he was going. It wasn't a comforting thought.

Eventually, the tracks led into a small chamber, approximately twelve feet square. The shoe prints led to the far side of the chamber, then seemed to vanish. I leaned over and followed them to where they ended. Suddenly, I was off-balance. The floor seemed to be dropping out from under me. Before I could tell what was happening, I was sliding down a long ramp, heading straight for a rectangle of light. I'd dropped my flashlight and was now grasping and scraping for something to get hold of. The ramp was smooth, and I continued to gain speed until I entered the opening at the base of the ramp. Abruptly, there was nothing under me. My stomach turned over as I free-fell for what seemed like an eternity. Eternity ended unceremoniously as my locked legs hit a hard surface and buckled.

Lying on my back in a blanket of bat guano, I stared up at the distant ceiling and wondered if I'd ever walk again. I was fairly certain that the adrenaline in my system was temporarily blocking a tremendous amount of agonizing pain, and that it would be merely a matter of minutes before it wore off. Even if I wasn't broken, I seriously doubted that I would ever smell good again.

After several moments, I looked around and took in my new surroundings. I was in another cavern, but this one was perfectly cylindrical and very tall, like the interior of a giant, stone beer can. Near the top of the cavern, probably fifty feet up, I saw a large window, or maybe a small door, with golden light streaming through it. The opening I'd come through was right in front of me, about twenty feet up the cavern wall. A large stone statue sat in the center of the floor.

I began to think that I'd survived my fall intact. There'd certainly be a tremendous amount of bruising involved, but I'd gone that route before. I rolled onto my side and saw a figure sitting off to the side. It was Regan. Her knees were drawn up to her chest, with her hands clasped around her legs. She was staring at me placidly, her expression somewhere between annoyance and amusement.

I got up from the floor and checked for broken bones. Everything seemed to be in place. I dusted off my trousers and gave Regan a nonchalant look. "Fancy meeting someone like you in a place like this."

"I could say the same thing."

"Been waiting long?"

"No, I just got here. Came in the same way you did. You all right?"

"I think so. A little confused." I walked over to where Regan was sitting against the wall and sat down beside her. "So, what are you doing here, if you don't mind me asking?"

She looked at me with more than a little resentment. "Oh, I should be waiting back in my hotel room like a good little girl, right? Well, I'm sorry. It's not in my nature to sit around and let someone else make my decisions for me. As soon as I realized you were bailing on me, I got a charter down here."

I pulled out a Lucky Strike. The pack must've cushioned my fall—the cigarette looked like an albino candy cane. "So how is it you got here first?"

Regan shrugged. "Maybe I had a faster pilot. Or maybe I left before you did."

I took a drag off the Lucky and handed it to Regan. She took it without any intention of giving it back. I pulled out a second cigarette and lit it. "What are you doing here?"

Regan stared straight ahead as she smoked. After a minute, she turned toward me. "I could see that you were gonna go along with those two old doddering idiots. What do they know? Here we are, sitting on the greatest discovery in the history of the world, and they say let's get rid of it. Great idea! Who cares how valuable it is, how much the technology would be worth? NSA would pay billions just for the antihydrogen!" She took a final drag and flicked the cigarette across the chamber. Her frustration was almost tangible.

I looked at her face, trying to understand how she could be so blind to the implications. "There's no question that whatever we find in the ship would be worth a lot of money."

"Exactly! That's why we should—"

"But that's beside the point. Didn't you hear what Witt and Fitzpatrick were saying? We're not ready for it. We would destroy ourselves."

"And maybe we wouldn't. Why can't we give society the benefit of the doubt? Maybe what happened during the war taught everyone a lesson. In the hands of people like my father, the new technology could open doors to possibilities we've only been able to imagine."

"Listen, Regan. The problem is that it wouldn't end up in the hands of people like your father. Things like this never do. They always end up in the wrong hands. We can't take the chance."

Regan stared silently at the ceiling of the chamber. After several minutes, she stood up and brushed herself off. "I suppose we should find a way out of here."

Apparently, our discussion was over. I had no idea if she had decided I was right or not. Not that it really mattered. The only choice had already been made. I got up and began to look for a way to escape from the chamber. The only visible exits or entrances were the chute door and the Rapunzel window. Maybe there was some kind of hidden door or trap, like the one I'd stepped into up above.

The chamber had a diameter of eighty feet, more or less. The statue in the center of the room was at least fifteen feet high. It resembled the drawings and photographs I'd seen of what UFOlogists described as "ancient spacemen." The face was typically childlike and lacking in detail, but the large eyes, halo around the head, and strange garb made the figure look vaguely odd and ominous. On the floor around the statue, a square mosaic pattern was carved into the stone. On the perimeter of the chamber, placed at four equidistant points, I saw what appeared to be perfectly cubical stones. I approached one of them and examined it. Clearing away a layer of guano, I could see that the cube was not sitting on the surface of the floor, but was set into a hole cut in the floor. I tried to lift the stone, but it wouldn't budge. When I stepped up onto the stone, it sank to the point where it was flush with the floor surface. It had to mean something, but I wasn't sure what.

The other three stones all did the same thing.

"Hey, Tex, look at this."

Regan was staring at the mosaic pattern around the base of the statue. She cleared off the dusty droppings to reveal a strange pattern. At each of the four compass points on the mosaic, a figure of a bizarre-looking creature had been carved into the stone. The creatures were slender and long-limbed, with large, black eyes and no mouths or noses. All of them had their arms raised and were looking up. I didn't think it was coincidental that the position of these creatures corresponded exactly to the positions of the square stones. I told Regan that I suspected the pattern was showing us how to get out of the chamber. All of the stones depressed when I put my weight on them. I had Regan stand on one of the stones, with the same results. We tried standing on two of the stones simultaneously, but it had no effect. Maybe all four had to be weighed down for anything to happen. Come to think of it, I wondered what *would* happen.

I needed to find two heavy objects. Regan's backpack contained nothing more substantial than a small pickax. It certainly wasn't heavy enough, but the statue was. Maybe the pickax would be sturdy enough to pry a few big chunks of rock off the statue.

I picked away at the statue for several minutes. Eventually, I got a pile of sizable stone pieces. I piled them onto two of the square stones until they finally sank to the level of the chamber floor. Excitedly, I directed Regan onto one of the remaining stones. Taking a deep breath, I stepped onto the final stone.

Nothing happened for several seconds; then the whole

chamber shook slightly. Suddenly, to my dismay, the walls started sinking. Regan was craning her neck around, trying to take in what was happening. I glanced up and was startled to see the ceiling slowly descending. The whole chamber floor was being raised. We were halfway to the high window. I wasn't sure what would happen if I stepped off the square stone, so I stayed on it and yelled across for Regan to do the same. The ceiling was approaching quickly.

When the distance from the floor to the window reached about six feet, I stepped off the stone. Regan followed, but the floor kept rising. I sincerely hoped that we wouldn't continue on past the window and get smashed between the floor and ceiling. When the floor reached the base of the window, the chamber came to an abrupt stop, throwing both of us to the floor. I got up and helped Regan to her feet. Across the chamber, I looked out the doorway and saw the sky.

Regan reached for my hand and held it tightly. We walked to the doorway and stepped out of the chamber. It took about twenty seconds for my eyes to adjust to the sunlight. When my vision cleared, we were standing on a massive rock ledge. Out over the horizon was the roof of the jungle. I heard Regan gasp and turned to see where she was looking. Fifty feet to our left, under a layer of twisting vines, I saw the spacecraft.

Chapter
Thirty-One

Neither of us moved for a moment.

The ship was quite large, maybe seventy feet long and ten feet high. From where we were standing, it looked triangular, not like the boomerang shape I'd seen on Roswell's lowest level. The surface was metallic and shiny. Several black patches on the exterior could have been windows. There were no openings readily visible.

We walked cautiously toward the craft. For some time, we walked around it, saying nothing. I touched the surface, which felt no different than any other metal. Regan came around the side. "It's beautiful." She continued to stroke the metal, awestruck. "It's like a huge Christmas present, just waiting to be opened."

I pulled out the communication device Fitzpatrick had given me. "I guess I should call Fitzpatrick and let him know that we found it."

Regan turned sharply. "Don't call!" She came closer. "Let's keep this to ourselves. It'll be for just you and me."

"That isn't how it works, Regan."

"But it can be. Just think of the life we can have together. I know some people...all we need to do is tell them how to find the ship. They'll give us all the money we'll ever need, and we don't have to do another thing, except fly away and spend the rest of our lives together. We'll be able to do anything we want, go anywhere we want."

Regan reached out and touched my face. Until this moment,

her words might have tempted me, but now I saw her in a different light. She really didn't care about anything but money and herself.

"It's not right, Regan."

Suddenly, she was angry. "What are you going to do, Tex? What have you got to go back to? Look at your life! A run-down apartment. Barely enough work to pay your bills. It's a dead end, and you know it. You can play it safe, stay with your little mutant girlfriend, go through life struggling and never taking a chance. Or you can have it all, including me. Is there even a choice?"

I stepped back. "Yeah, there's a choice, and I've already made it. My life may not seem like much to you, and my little mutant girlfriend may not be the most glamorous woman in the world, but I happen to feel a certain obligation to do what's right, not just what serves my own interests. Even if I went along, I don't think it would ever work out for you and me. I don't like the way you think."

Without warning, a voice spoke from behind me. "What a lovely speech."

I spun around to see Jackson Cross, a gun in his hand pointed at my chest.

He motioned toward the communication device I was holding. "Hand it over." I hesitated. "If you'd prefer, I can blast a hole through you, then get it."

There was no room for argument. I handed it over. Cross smiled at me. "I thought you'd be more surprised to see me."

"I figured the NSA would be hanging around. I'm just wondering why I didn't smell you before now."

Cross laughed maliciously. "Oh, I'm not here on official business. The agency isn't involved. This is purely personal, just between me and Ms. Madsen, here."

I turned back toward Regan. Her eyes met mine coolly. "Sorry, Tex. It's just business. I offered you a piece of the action. You've got no one but yourself to blame."

I couldn't stop looking at her face. She'd taken me in completely. Her demeanor was calm, but I could detect a hint of regret. She wasn't proud of what she'd done, but that wasn't about to stop her.

Cross laughed behind me. "Disillusioning, isn't it?"

I turned around to face the leering bastard. "So the two of you came down together? How come I only saw one set of footprints?"

"Standard NSA procedure—two-pronged approach. Regan entered on the low side; I flew the Avatar and made a systematic search of the area. I found the spacecraft a few hours ago. In fact, I was waiting up here when I saw you get dropped off down below. I guess Ms. Madsen forgot to tell you that I was here."

Regan had circled around to stand next to Cross. His gun remained pointed at me as he turned and smiled at my Delilah, then back at me. "I learned about Malloy's work through the NSA. It sounded like a good personal opportunity. While I was trying to track him down, I met up with Ms. Madsen here. I figured she could help me, so I offered her a chance to become partners. She was ready to sell out her father in a heartbeat."

"I didn't sell him out." Regan's eyes flashed.

Cross turned serenely, the smile on his face unchanged. His tone dripped acid. "Oh, I'm sorry. I forgot. You just wanted your rightful inheritance."

He turned back to me. "In any event, she and I found out that Malloy had sent the boxes. I had some trusted associates watching for them in different places. We were looking for one at the Ritz when you stumbled into our path. Then, of course, you ended up killing one of my men who was staking out the Fuchsia Flamingo. We watched the Collins girl, but she never got a box. We had a little more luck with Ellis."

Regan broke in. "You didn't have to kill them, by the way. There is such a thing as an innocent bystander."

Cross chuckled and shook his head. "Sweet Regan. Poor, sweet, naive Regan." His voice went deadly. "Don't interrupt me again."

Cross turned his attention and his gun back toward me. "I wanted you out of the way, but Regan convinced me to give you a chance. After I watched you work for awhile, I decided to let you do the work, which turned out to be a good decision, don't you think? Now here we are. All according to plan."

"You're not going to get away with it, Cross."

He laughed again. "Really? I don't see anyone here who can do anything about it."

Regan spoke up. "That device he gave you is his contact with Witt and Fitzpatrick. I know how it works. Let me have it. I'll send the message that we haven't found anything."

Cross watched her until she finished, then smiled at me. "There. That should give us plenty of time. I've alerted our buyer. He should be here with everything we need within a couple hours." He leveled his gun at my forehead.

"As for you, Murphy, I've wanted to blow your head off from the first time I saw you. Not that I don't like you. You seem like a resourceful guy. I just like to kill people. It's unbelievably satisfying."

I caught Regan's eye. "After the way you played me for a sucker, I think you deserve to pull the trigger yourself."

Regan looked away uneasily. "I left before you did, hoping it would save you." She looked back at me. "You're too good for your own good."

"If I ever get out of this situation, I'll try to keep that in mind."

Cross stepped forward and leveled the gun at my chest. "Enough talk! Say good-bye, Murphy."

Suddenly, a sound came from behind us. A hatch swung open from the side of the spacecraft with a vaguely hydraulic hiss. A pair of wing tips under neatly pressed trousers appeared on the steps of the hatch door. Slowly, a man descended. It was Fitzpatrick.

"Don't shoot. If you spare him, I'll show you how to find what you're looking for."

Cross whirled around, the gun now pointed at Fitzpatrick's forehead. "I don't know who you are, but you should know, I generally frown on blackmail."

"You don't know what you're looking for. I do."

Cross hesitated, apparently weighing the old man's offer. Slowly, his arm went down. "OK, old man. I won't kill him...yet."

Fitzpatrick bowed his head slightly. "Follow me."

Cross walked around behind me and placed the tip of his gun barrel into my lower back. When he nudged me, I started up the steps toward the hatch, Cross right behind me.

The area just inside the entrance was quite large, though there wasn't much head room. It appeared to be a control center. There was a soft glow in the room, but no distinct light source, as if the very material the room was constructed from was emitting the light. The area was circular, like the interior of an egg, with three doorways spaced evenly to the left. One doorway was open, and a reddish light was blinking from beyond. The control center had no seats, though what appeared to be consoles lined about a third of the circumference on the right. No switches or buttons were visible, only flat surfaces with markings on them.

Fitzpatrick's voice interrupted my examination. "We are

standing in the midst of history. Those who came with this ship may have been our forefathers. If not the fathers of our race, they at least were guardians and guides to our ancestors. This is a holy place."

He turned his gaze past me, toward Cross. "You would sell this. How can money mean so much to you? If I could, I would preserve this, to show what our civilization might become when we are wiser and more prudent. It is a pity that we are not even close."

Cross laughed cruelly. "You and Murphy are full of pretty words today, aren't you?" He motioned toward the red light. "What's in there?"

Fitzpatrick appeared reluctant to say anything, but answered. "The main power cell."

Cross pushed the gun painfully into my spinal column. "Let's go take a look, shall we?"

As we entered the chamber, I saw that the source of the light was mounted on a small pedestal. The room was only ten to twelve feet in diameter, with the pedestal against the far wall. Just inside the door, Cross pushed me to the right. "Stay right there. You, old man, stand beside him."

While Cross waited for Fitzpatrick to get in place, Regan entered the chamber and walked straight to the light source. Cross's eyes left us for a moment and followed her to the pedestal. Fitzpatrick's elbow touched my ribs. He lifted a finger, then made an almost imperceptible motion toward the door. I wasn't sure, but it seemed he wanted to make a run for it when the opportunity presented itself. I didn't know how we could possibly get away, but we were going to die anyway.

Cross looked back at us. We hadn't moved a step. He moved slowly toward the pedestal, trying to keep one eye on us and one on the red light. When he'd gotten close, he leaned over to get a better view. Fitzpatrick nudged me. I turned and bolted through the door. Behind me, I heard a slamming sound and the same hydraulic hiss I'd heard before. Suddenly, Cross's gun went off, and I turned to see Fitzpatrick hit the floor as the door closed behind him. I rushed over to the old man. He was hurt badly.

"C'mon, we've got to get out of here and get you to a doctor."

Fitzpatrick looked up at me. "There's no need for a doctor. I'll live long enough to fulfill my destiny."

"What do you mean?"

The old man gasped for breath. He didn't have long. "I'm going to navigate the ship off the planet and destroy it. I have the explosives set. You must get off now, while you can."

"You know how to fly this? How do you know it even works?"

Fitzpatrick smiled weakly. "Trust me, Tex. The power cell you retrieved from Roswell allowed me to regenerate the ship's power. It will work."

"But you're not gonna make it. Tell me what to do."

The dying man gasped. The color was draining quickly from his face. "Find the sun symbol and press it. That will activate the navigational console. Then press V, Red, Left Half-Moon, 11, Triangle, Helix, Green, Right Half-Moon, X, Double Circle."

Each word was more difficult to hear. On the word "Circle," Fitzpatrick shuddered and exhaled loudly. He was dead.

I turned to the console, hoping that the dead man hadn't passed on before completing the instructions. A gunshot rang out, and a bullet ricocheted off the console to my right. Cross had managed to get his gun barrel in the path of the door. It was wedged tightly and, luckily, it wasn't pointed at me. Behind the door, Regan and Cross were yelling at each other. Cross's fingers slipped through the gap above the wedged gun.

I turned back and scanned the console wildly, looking for the sun symbol. In my head, I was repeating over and over: V, Red, Left Half-Moon, 11, Triangle, Helix, Green, Right Half-Moon, X, Double Circle.

V R Moon E T H G Moon X Double Circle.

V R Moon E T H G Moon X Double Circle.

I finally located the sun symbol and touched it. The console burst to life. When I pressed the V symbol, four colored areas appeared. I touched the red spot. My eyes ran over the surface. What was next? I saw two half-moon symbols and pressed the left one. Try to remember. V, R, Moon, E. What was E? Eleven! Close by, I saw a figure of two parallel vertical lines and touched it. A whirring sound ensued. OK. V, R, Moon, E. Now T—triangle, then H—helix. The two symbols were on the same section of the console. All right, so far, so good.

Now G, Moon, X, Double Circle. G for green. I moved back to the four-color display and touched the green spot. The whirring sound stopped. Behind me, I heard a metallic clang and spun around to see that Cross had widened the gap in the door. I moved back to the half-moon symbols and touched the right one. The ship shuddered. What was the next symbol? My eyes ran over the console frantically. No, no, no...X! I pressed the X symbol. Finally, I needed to find the Double Circle. It was placed directly in the center of the console, like a target. I pressed it and heard something mechanical kick in.

The second I touched the Double Circle, I raced to the hatch. A loud, hydraulic hiss hit me in stereo. The hatch was starting to close, and I was fairly sure that Cross had pried the door open at the same instant. With no time to lose, I vaulted through the hatch, down the steps, and away from the spacecraft. A barely detectable humming escalated into a low roar. After several seconds, the ancient ship began to lift off. I watched it shoot straight up toward the sky. Higher and higher it rose, until I could no longer see it. I continued to stare skyward for several minutes. Suddenly, a white flash appeared, brighter than any light I'd ever seen. It filled the sky for several seconds. Then a massive boom echoed from above, shaking the very roots of the stone cavern. It was over.

Chapter
Thirty-Two

Jackson Cross's Black Avatar was hidden a short distance from where the spacecraft had been. I couldn't find a second speeder and, after a quick search of the area, determined that Fitzpatrick must have been dropped off and that no one had stayed with him. My flight home, courtesy of the NSA, spoiled me for life with regard to speeder quality. To my everlasting regret, when I reached the states, I dumped the Avatar and took a commuter flight back to San Francisco. Cross may have had his own agenda and been in Peru on private business, but I certainly didn't want to start an ongoing feud with the NSA. Joyriding in one of their special vehicles would probably fall somewhere between an irritation and an outright breach of decorum.

After I returned, Elijah Witt paid me a visit. I filled him in on everything that happened in Peru, and we sorted out the rest of the details. Witt told me that Fitzpatrick had been one of the scientists at Roswell who'd figured out how to work the particle accelerator. His story of meeting Malloy in China was just a little fiction to disguise his Roswell connection. After the military had used his work to make the world a more toxic place, Fitzpatrick had felt solely responsible.

Apparently, Fitzpatrick had taken off for Peru last night, immediately after I left the Savoy. Witt had discouraged him from going alone, but the old man insisted. Fitzpatrick's death wasn't something to be mourned, Witt told me. He had died at peace with himself, having atoned for his self-perceived misdeeds.

Witt also helped me clear up the unanswered question of who had gotten the five boxes. My problem was that I'd been counting the box given to me by Regan and the box stolen from Ellis as two separate boxes, when they were actually one and the same. Malloy had never intended for Regan to receive a box. That meant that Ellis, Witt, Edsen, and Emily made up four of the five recipients. Witt informed me that Fitzpatrick had received the fifth box, which had contained the instructions for operating the Pandora Device and the set of symbols needed to activate the spacecraft. In the box, Malloy had also included a request that Fitzpatrick tell no one about the fifth box—not even the other four recipients— until after the Pandora Device had been assembled, since without the fifth box, the others were practically worthless. Witt said that Fitzpatrick had planned on telling me about the box when we were all together at the Savoy, but had changed his mind when Regan showed up. Fitzpatrick knew there were five boxes and six people claiming to have received one. He suspected Regan, but couldn't be sure. He also wasn't sure how involved I was with her.

I was still curious about one other aspect of the case. Who was the mysterious caller who'd contacted me at the Twilight Lounge? I wondered whether it could have been Jackson Cross, posing as an anonymous friend to help me do his dirty work. Then I reconsidered. The first call had come very early on, before I ever met up with the NSA. To my surprise, when I asked Witt what he thought, he confessed to being the anonymous caller. He went on to say that he'd been in contact with Fitzpatrick ever since they received their respective boxes. Apparently, Witt had connections high-up in just about every government agency, including the NSA. For no apparent reason, Witt said, Fitzpatrick was sure that I was the man they needed to find Malloy and track down the other boxes. Fitzpatrick asked Witt to help out. It had been Witt's connections that had gotten me into Autotech and Roswell.

I asked Witt if he had allowed me to take the box from his mansion. Witt laughed and shook his head. He said that he didn't know who I was until Fitzpatrick called while I was in the cellar. I apologized for violating his place and punching out his handyman, but he waved it off, saying that everything had worked out for the best. I also suggested that Witt try to let his niece get out a little bit more.

Witt was kind enough to write me a check to cover my expenses. After he left, I finally had time to consider all that had happened. Regan had played me for a sap, but I couldn't help but feel pity for her. The promise of money had been too much. Maybe she was better off. If she'd survived, she'd have nothing to live for.

My thoughts turned to Chelsee. Louie told me that she was back in town, and I arranged to meet her at the Brew & Stew for a drink. The experience with Regan had taught me a few things. I was eager to tell Chelsee everything, including the fact that I'd decided the world was too ugly a place to live in alone. Maybe now I was ready to try the love thing with her...if she was up to it.

"It's sure good to have you back, Chelsee. Looks like your trip did you a world of good."

She appeared radiant. Looking at her over my glass of bourbon, I felt a wave of depravity wash over me. Chelsee looked back at me serenely and smiled without an ounce of coyness. I wasn't altogether certain that was a good thing. "Yeah, I just needed a little time to renew myself."

Her tone of voice was strange. I've never been particularly perceptive where women are concerned, but I had the distinct impression that I was about to be told something I didn't care to hear.

I decided that the best defense against rejection would be an aggressive offense. "Look, right off the bat, I want to say I've been a real schmuck. You know me, most of the time I wouldn't know a good thing if it walked up and punched me in the face. Which has happened on occasion, incidentally."

Chelsee smiled indulgently. "Tex?"

"Hold on, I've been practicing this speech. I have to tell you, while you were gone, I was tempted by another woman. I know, it's hard to believe. I turned her down, but it got me thinking. And everything that's happened since you left has made me look at things differently. Maybe I'm ready to have a real life and settle down. I hope you're still willing to give me a shot." I'd laid it on the line, and I was god-awful sincere. If my self-deprecating humor and down-home charm didn't do the trick, I was a goner.

Chelsee had apparently gone through some kind of Tex rehab program. "Tex...sweetheart...I had a lot of time to think when I was in Phoenix—and I came to the conclusion that I got a little ahead of myself."

A dull ache appeared behind my navel. Chelsee compounded it by oozing diplomacy. "Turning thirty may have caused me to be a little rash."

Make her laugh, Murphy. "No, Chelsee, it was me who was a little rash. One of those red, itchy ones."

Chelsee smiled, somewhat sadly. "It's not you, Tex. It's just...well, I came to the realization that I'm just too demanding and finicky for any normal man."

I dug down for one last-ditch volley. "You think I'm normal?"

Chelsee disregarded my last gasp. "I'd always be asking too much, like wanting you to be totally reliable. I value our friendship—it's something I don't want to spoil."

Oh, the ugly "F" word. Well, one of them. Just like that, she drove the dagger of rejection deep into my chest.

"I can't bear the pain of being friends, Chelsee. I want to be your whipping boy, not your pal."

"Oh, don't give me that." She slid a business card across the table. "Anyway, that's why I signed up for this Holo-Date Service. No hassles, no commitment."

I had no idea what Chelsee was talking about. I picked up the card and looked it over.

Tired of meat markets, blind dates, and neurotic surprises?
Try our brand-new Holo-Date Service:
For Virtual Companionship and Computer-Generated Romance.
This seemed so unlike Chelsee.

"Holo-dating? Never heard of it."

"It just started up...it's the perfect solution."

A movement outside the window caught Chelsee's attention. A smile flickered on her lips, then she turned back to me. "Speaking of perfect, here's my date."

Oh, this was going to be good. I was going to meet Chelsee's perfect man. Talk about an inferiority booster. The door to the Brew & Stew opened, and I turned nonchalantly. My jawed dropped slightly as Cary Grant looked around. Out of the corner of my eye, I saw Chelsee wave. Cary caught sight of her, pointed, and smiled suavely. Chelsee was beaming.

From behind me, I heard that voice. "Hello, Chelsee. Are you ready, darling? We'd better hurry, the Häagen-Dazs is melting."

Chelsee picked up her things and tossed me a cavalier smile.

I looked back at her, more than a little resentful. "Look, I'll admit he's handsome and seems pretty authentic, but he's just not real."

Chelsee slung her purse over her shoulder and slipped her arm into Cary's. "Tell me, Tex. What is?"

I returned to my office at an all-time low. Not only had I lost Chelsee to a computer projection, but I was out of work again. As my Great-Aunt Rita would have said, at least I had my health. And I was caught up on my rent. With Witt covering my expenses, I'd be all right for awhile. Maybe I needed to take a trip, get over Chelsee. Or maybe I just needed to meet another woman. God! What was I thinking?

I looked down at the business card Chelsee had left with me at the Brew & Stew. Maybe I should just call this Holo-Date place. Nah...only a pathetic loser would go out with a hologram. I thought it over for a minute, then punched in the number. After several rings, God himself appeared on the screen. Bogie.

"Holo-Date Service. Here's looking at you, kid. What's your pleasure?"

I was tongue-tied. I knew it was a hologram, but the authenticity was overwhelming. "Well, I...uh, don't know. I've never called before."

"Tell you what, kid. Let me know who the dame of your dream is, and we'll go from there."

I didn't even have to think about it. "Well, I've always had this thing for Jayne Mansfield. And Brigitte Bardot comes in a close second."

Bogie flashed me his dog-eared grin. "I like your style, kid. And this is your lucky day. Since it's Tuesday, we have the two-for-one special. When should we send 'em over?"

I experienced a sudden twinge of excitement, the likes of which I hadn't felt since ninth grade. "Give me about fifteen seconds to freshen up."

Bogie took all the billing information from me and asked if

I had any questions. "No. I just want to tell you, Bogie, I think this could be the beginning of a—"

"Yeah, yeah. You know how many times a day I hear that line?"

I severed the connection and lit up a Lucky Strike. So, maybe it wasn't a perfect world. But there'd be other cases, maybe even a real flesh-and-blood woman waiting for me somewhere down the road. But until then, there were worse ways to spend time than playing strip Parcheesi with Jayne and Brigitte.

Sure, they wouldn't be real, but hey, what is?

Other Proteus Books Now Available from Prima!

The 7th Guest: A Novel $21.95
    Matthew J. Costello and Craig Shaw Gardner

Hell: A Cyberpunk Thriller—A Novel $5.99
    Chet Williamson

Star Crusader: A Novel $5.99
    Bruce Balfour

Wizardry: The League of the
                Crimson Crescent—A Novel $5.99
    James Reagan

FILL IN AND MAIL TODAY

PRIMA PUBLISHING
P.O. BOX 1260BK
ROCKLIN, CA 95677

USE YOUR VISA/MC AND ORDER BY PHONE:
(916) 632-4400 (M-F 9:00-4:00 PST)

Please send me the following titles:

Quantity	Title	Amount
_____	_____	_____
_____	_____	_____
_____	_____	_____
_____	_____	_____
_____	_____	_____

Subtotal $_____

Postage & Handling
($4.00 for the first book
plus $1.00 each additional book) $ _____

Sales Tax
7.25% Sales Tax (California only)
8.25% Sales Tax (Tennessee only)
5.00% Sales Tax (Maryland only)
7.00% General Service Tax (Canada) $_____

TOTAL *(U.S. funds only)* $_____

❑ Check enclosed for $_____(payable to Prima Publishing)
Charge my   ❑ Master Card   ❑ Visa

Account No. _____Exp. Date _____
Signature _____
Your Name _____
Address _____
City/State/Zip _____
Daytime Telephone _____

Satisfaction is guaranteed—or your money back!
Please allow three to four weeks for delivery.
THANK YOU FOR YOUR ORDER

Aaron Conners is uniquely qualified to write the novel based on the game *The Pandora Directive;* he wrote the script and co-designed the game with Chris Jones. He was also scriptwriter and co-designer of the popular game *Under a Killing Moon.* Conners admits to losing a weekend every year re-reading *The Lord of the Rings* from beginning to end. He lives in Salt Lake City, Utah.